STEAMPUNK'D

edited by Jean Rabe and
Martin H. Greenberg

D1634706

DAW BOOKS, INC.
DONALD A. WOLLHEIM, FOUNDER
375 Hudson Street, New York, NY 10014

ELIZABETH R. WOLLHEIM
SHEILA E. GILBERT
PUBLISHERS
http://www.dawbooks.com

First Printing, November 2010
1 2 3 4 5 6 7 8 9

*Alva Edison knew her life would
never be the same again.*

"It can be done. I know it can," her brother told her
again.

"Thomas, I keep telling you, remember Mr. Franklin? The founding father never signed the Declaration
because he foolishly stood out in a rainstorm, with a
kite of all things. And stringing a key on the end? How
foolhardly. Anyone with common sense knows that you
do not want to be near any metal in a storm. No surprise that he was electrocuted. It was such a tragedy that
could have been averted."

"But his idea was right," Thomas insisted. "The power
of those thunderbolts can be harnessed as a new energy
source."

She snorted at that. "Thomas, dear, next you'll be saying that thunderbolts can do all kinds of things, like that
kooky Dr. Frankenstein and his outlandish, sacrilegious
ideas about life and death. They took him off to the sanitarium and not soon enough, I say. Please stop such talk.
I do not want to lose my only brother to some ridiculous
notion."

—From "Edison Kinetic Light & Steam Power"
by C.A. Verstraete

Also Available from DAW Books:

A Girl's Guide to Guns and Monsters, **edited by Martin H. Greenberg and Kerrie Hughes**
Here are thirteen tales of strong women, armed with weapons they are not afraid to use, as well as fists and feet of fury, from authors such as Tanya Huff, Mickey Zucker Reichert, Jane Lindskold, Kristine Kathryn Rusch, Nina Kiriki Hoffman, P.R. Frost, and others. These are urban and paranormal stories certain to appeal to all readers of this most popular genre. So sit back and enjoy as these empowered women take on all challenges with weapons, wit, and skill—and pity the poor monsters and bad guys who'll need rescuing from them!

Timeshares, **edited by Jean Rabe and Martin H. Greenberg**
Welcome to timesharing like you've never experienced before. This is not your chance to acquire some rental property in the Bahamas. The stories you'll find within these pages are your tickets to *real* timesharing—taking a vacation through time. Afraid of flying? The high cost of gas got you down? Want to *really* get away? Step into your local Timeshares agency office, venture through their time travel device, and you can find yourself in exotic, adventurous locations. Of course, you and your fellow vacationers may also find yourselves caught up in all manner of trouble and mysteries—and definitely in danger. With stories by Kevin J. Anderson, Michael A. Stackpole, Greg Cox, Donald J. Bingle, Chris Pierson and Linda Baker, and others.

Cthulhu's Reign, **edited by Darrell Schweitzer**
Some of the darkest hints in all of H.P. Lovecraft's Cthulhu Mythos relate to what will happen *after* the Old Ones return and take over the Earth. What happens when the Stars Are Right, the sunken city of R'lyeh rises from beneath the waves, and Cthulhu is unleashed upon the world for the last time? What happens when the other Old Ones, long since banished from our universe, break through and descend from the stars? What would the reign of Cthulhu be like, on a totally transformed planet where mankind is no longer the master? It won't be simply the end of everything. It will be a time of new horrors and of utter strangeness. It will be a time when humans with a "taint" of unearthly blood in their ancestry may come into their own. It will be a time foreseen only by authors with the kind of finely honed imaginative visions as Ian Watson, Brian Stableford, Will Murray, Gregory Frost, Richard Lupoff, and the others of *Cthulhu's Reign.*

ACKNOWLEDGMENTS

Introduction copyright © 2010 by Jean Rabe.

"Chance Corrigan and the Tick-tock King of the Nile," copyright © 2010 by Michael A. Stackpole.

"Foggy Goggles," copyright © 2010 by Donald J. Bingle.

"The Battle of Cumberland Gap," copyright © 2010 by William C. Dietz

"Portrait of a Lady in a Monocle," copyright © 2010 by Jody Lynn Nye

"Foretold," copyright © 2010 by Bradley P. Beaulieu

"The Echoer," copyright © 2010 by Dean Leggett

"Of A Feather," copyright © 2010 by Stephen D. Sullivan

"Scourge of the Spoils," copyright © 2010 by Matthew P. Mayo

"Edison Kinetic Light & Steam Power," copyright © 2010 by C.A. Verstraete

"The Nubian Queen," copyright © 2010 by Paul Genesse

"Opals from Sydney," copyright © 2010 by Mary Louise Eklund

"The Whisperer," copyright © 2010 by Marc Tassin

"Imperial Changeling," copyright © 2010 by Skip and Penny Williams

"The Transmogrification Ray," copyright © 2010 by Robert E. Vardeman

Contents

Introduction

Steampunk: It's what the future would look like, I heard someone say, if it had come along earlier . . . say during the Victorian Era.

Me? I say steampunk is just good science fiction.

Or fantasy, alternate history, Western, etc.

Just so it's got some steam power and airships and goggles and the like.

I liked it before they labeled the genre "steampunk," back when I was a kid and picked up Jules Verne's *20,000 Leagues Under the Sea* in my favorite bookstore. I remember stopping there one late afternoon when my final class of the day ended and poking through the shelves at the back. That's where the used paperbacks were . . . and that's what I had the budget for. I was digging through the Westerns (I voraciously read Louis L'Amour at the time), and finding Jules Verne's offering by accident. Someone had mis-shelved it. Cost me a whopping quarter. Good thing it wasn't with the science fiction or I might not have noticed it . . . I was seriously into Westerns at the time.

I liked it. Enough so that I picked up a few more Jules Verne books after that . . . which were correctly shelved.

I enjoy the genre even more now, probably because

1

there's more of it, and because what I've been reading has been so very good. Conventions are dedicated to it, with lavish costume competitions. And this anthology is filled with it.

Because some of these tales are on the long side, I'll keep this introduction short.

Enjoy! I certainly did.

Jean Rabe

Chance Corrigan and the
Tick-tock King of the Nile

Michael A. Stackpole

Michael A. Stackpole is an award-winning writer, screenwriter, podcaster, game and computer game designer and graphic novelist. His most recent novel, *At The Queen's Command*, is the first in his *Crown Colonies* series. He lives in Arizona and, in his spare time, enjoys indoor soccer and dancing. His website is www.stormwolf.com.

It was the first time in a long time that he'd heard his name—his real name—spoken aloud. He hated it. "Never heard of him."

"Come now, Mr. Corrigan." The man had come up on Chance's left side—his blind side—which is what men who thought they were clever tended to do. "I can assure you that my employer has been searching for you for the better part of four years. He was overjoyed to learn you were here in Port Said."

Chance turned to face the center of the bar's floor, where a woman danced to squealing pipes. She weaved and undulated, as supple and dangerous as the cobra that would have been charmed by those pipes. Dark, glossy hair, kohl-rimmed eyes full of fire, enough curves to make that rustling belt of coins hang at the perfect angle and flash with every snap of her hips. Luscious lips glistening, those little come-hither motions with her hands, and the seductive rise of eyebrows.

"Mr. Corrigan!" The man moved around to the right, turning his back to the woman. Tall and skinny, wearing a regimental tie despite never having been in the service, he had the arrogance of a minor noble who found commoners revolting. Didn't mean he was really a blue-blood. Most of the Brits in Egypt acted as if they were the reincarnation of Alexander. More than the attitude, Corrigan hated the straight nose, the fancy clothes, the ridiculous bowler, and the gold pocket-watch the man glanced at.

"Still here?"

"Yes, and I shall remain until you do me the courtesy of listening to me." He snapped the watch shut. "My employer . . ."

Even though it meant he'd be reduced to just listening to her dance, Chance turned back to the bar and his whisky.

"See here, Mr. Corrigan." The man grabbed Chance's right shoulder and pulled.

Chance Corrigan came around fast. He slid from the barstool and grabbed the little man around his throat. The starched collar popped. Muscles bunched as Chance lifted the fancy man from his feet, and tossed him toward a knot of men clustered around a hookah.

Chance growled. "I ain't Corrigan." His eye narrowed, then he picked up his drink and shot it.

The liquor burned like the dancer's eyes. It wasn't really whisky, just some local grain alcohol tinted amber. How they made it, he didn't care. That it would kill brain cells seemed like a plus. Chance glanced at the bartender and nodded. The bottle appeared again.

The fancy man stood up. "I had hoped not to have to resort to violence, Mr. Corrigan." He raised a hand and six men—six very large men with a battalion of scars and a regiment of ugly divided among them—stepped up. "If you insist, Mr. Corrigan, my associates will deal with you."

Chance pressed his thumb to a nostril and snorted. He cleared the other side similarly. "Just remember, fancy man, I'll save the worst for you."

They came for him as a gang, which was just what he wanted. They meant to bury him in angry meat, since killing him wouldn't get them paid. They were coming in to grapple, and all he meant to do was deal damage.

A fist flattened a nose. He felt the bone break and the first hot gush of blood. His left elbow came up and around, catching the guy on his blind side in the mouth. Jaw broke, teeth scattered. A knee crushed dangly bits, then Chance hit the third guy again, in the breastbone. Ribs cracked.

A roundhouse right caught him in the side of the head, pitching him against the bar. Chance kicked out, cracking a guy in the knee. He grabbed an outstretched hand and twisted it so the thumb pointed at the floor, then the ceiling and floor again. That man spun away, one shoulder lower than the other. Another elbow dropped an expat Australian. Chance's barstool finished off a big-nosed Frenchman.

Chance slid his eyepatch back into place. He stepped over the Frenchman, toward the fancy man. "Don't run."

The man held his hands outstretched before him. "Mr. Corrigan, I have come to offer you a job, a lucrative job."

"I ain't Chance Corrigan." Chance cracked his knuckles. "You shoulda listened the first time."

The Brit took a step back, then another man, an Egyptian with remarkably blue skin, stepped between them. His shaved head gleamed in the bar's wan light. He wore a loincloth and bore a lotus-headed staff.

The Egyptian looked straight at Chance. His eyes glowed, then he slammed the heel of his staff against the floor. An electric tingle ran over Chance's flesh. The lotus blossomed, the petals danced, and Chance's world went black.

*   *   *

The throbbing pain on the left side of his face woke Chance. He hadn't been hit hard enough for that pain to be there, all fresh and raw. It didn't hurt as much as it did when he lost the eye, but the difference was a rounding error. He tried to raise his left hand, but he'd been restrained.

They know what they're doing. It wasn't the first time he'd been strapped into a chair and blindfolded, but they were among the best at doing it. Chance pushed off with his feet, but the chair had been bolted to the floor.

"Very good, Chance, just in time. I see you're with us again."

Chance's head came up. *I know that voice.*

Someone whipped the blindfold off his face. From his left side. *Has to be the fancy-man.*

Bright light made his eye water. Chance squinted, more trying to trap the tear than anything else. He failed. As his eye drained and the world focused, a large man loomed before him. Dark, curly hair, dark eyes, neatly trimmed beard, they all seemed familiar; he couldn't connect them with the voice. Not immediately, because the man he should have been looking at should have been much more slender.

Then he plucked a pocket watch from one of a half-dozen watch pockets on his vest and flicked the lid open. He tapped the crystal and smiled. *It's can't be . . .*

Chance's surprise apparently made it onto his face.

The large man smiled, his cheeks widening to nearly eclipse his ears. "Yes, Chance, the irony of it. A decade ago at university, you were the fat one. You have changed, too. Tragedy will do that." He patted his own stomach. "And prosperity will do *this*. Life has been very good to Alexander H. Gavrilis."

Chance glared.

"You have no idea how much time we have spent looking for you." Gavrilis began to pace—a well-remembered and well-hated mannerism which confirmed his identity.

"What they did to you was tragic, of course. It was sad to hear of the men who died in the explosion, but it did prove your theory correct. Then the swindle and breaking your heart, all understandably disappointing. We never bought your later 'suicide,' however, and we were right. Thorough waste of time, trying that."

"How did you find me?"

"No matter how hard you try, Chance, you cannot escape who you truly are." Gavrilis faced him, replacing the one watch, removing another and idly winding it. "We tracked little things, things you could not help but do. A locomotive making the run across Siberia faster than scheduled. Water wells being drilled a little deeper in the Australian outback. A tramp steamer having the power to survive the worst of the Cape storms. The improvement to the wireless range on the airship *Selene* when it went down in the Punjab. Had to have been you.

"But we leave nothing to chance—no pun intended." Gavrilis listened to the watch for a heartbeat. "So the order of machine parts your ship picked up in Britain was an order we placed. Having my associate, Mr. Brinkworth, find you in Port Said and bring you to us was not that difficult."

"Leave me alone."

"You believe, Chance, that the offer we will make is . . . what is that colloquialism from your American south that I so love? Oh, yes, it is 'a dog that won't hunt.' We consider your time too valuable to be spent on frippery. Let us assure you it *will* hunt, and hunt very well. But, let me first show you what we are doing, and what we have done, and then you can make your decision."

Brinkworth, the fancy man, approached Chance, his hands laden with chains. He locked them onto the leather cuffs at his wrists and attached them to wide leather belt around Chance's waist. Bending down, he similarly chained his ankles together. The man then released the cuffs from the chair and Chance stood.

Gavrilis waved him toward a lift. "Please."

Two large, muscular men entered the box with Chance, pinning him in the corner. The lift groaned as Gavrilis added his bulk. The fat man worked the lever as Brinkworth closed the gate from outside. The lift, creaking, ascended slowly through a wooden shaft.

After the first twenty feet, heat filled the box. *Still in Egypt.* The two toughs fidgeted, but Gavrilis seemed curiously unaffected. As the ascent continued a rhythmic clicking built. Gavrilis swayed in time with it, imparting motion to the lift's box. The squeal of wheels wanting grease and the hiss of sand blown against the wooden shaft broke accompanied the sound, then all of them grew faint and distant as the box slowed.

Finally the lift stopped. Gavrilis slid the gate back, and then an oaken door opened onto a huge semi-circular room. They emerged into a foyer, then stepped down into an opulent den finished in dark woods and animal skins from around the world. Crystal sparkled from chandeliers and services, silver and gold glinted from platters and gilt-furnishings, and ivory gleamed from a throne built of enormous tusks. A variety of clocks filled shelves and cabinets. One even perched atop a wireless transmitter over in the corner.

Yet none of the decorations attracted Chance's attention. It had been stolen by the bank of windows, ten feet high, taking up the entire western wall. The room looked out over the desert, and the dark ribbon of the Nile where it began its descent toward the Alexandrian delta. Down below, crews worked on a dam.

But not just any crews. Two giant, clockwork lifting-devices, each with eight legs and a clear glass bubble where their terrestrial counterpart's head would have been, dragged blocks into place. Chance stared at them because, unlike the cranes lifting blocks from the nearby quarries, he saw no smoke or steam from the spiders' engines. It wasn't until he stepped right up to the window that he caught sight of the diversionary spillway, and the large Tesla-coil rising from a building beside it, that he understood what he was looking at.

His heart leaped and the resulting emotion surprised him, both for being recognizable and its strength. It had been so long since he'd felt joy—since he'd allowed himself to feel joy—that it staggered him. What he was seeing was something he'd known, *in theory*, was possible but. . . . *Have I been gone from the world that long?*

Gavrilis' reflection appeared in the glass to his right. "Yes, Chance, this is but one of the things we have wrought. This is a dam on the Nile, deep in the south, near Aswan. We will be able to control the floods which, unacceptably, have destroyed Egypt's cotton crops down through the aeons. We will do for Egypt what never before has been done in four thousand years of recorded history. It is our gift to this land of our forefathers."

Chance bit back a laugh. Gavrilis was Greek, not Egyptian. Chance would have chided him over that remark, but then he remembered that Gavrilis had been a member of one of the secret societies at university. The Pharaonic Brotherhood of Ptolemy. It traced its origins to the last Egyptian dynasty, through fanciful lineages, just like any other Masonic-style order.

"But we are not above bestowing gifts upon those who will be of service." Gavrilis reached around and plucked Chance's eye patch away.

Something clicked in the eye-socket which had been empty for ten years. A round lens in a brass fitting, anchored in a larger fitting shaped to run midway around his cheekbone and brow. Again he tried to raise his hand to touch it, but couldn't. He looked down, his hand straining against the cuff, then with three clicks, his hand grew huge, and the blackened grime beneath his nails appeared as wide as the river below.

"What did you do to me?"

"We have a great deal of money, Chance, surely you remember that. We retain the services of the world's greatest engineers. That station below, a year ago we purchased it from Nicola Tesla, had it dismantled in Colorado and reconstructed here. Likewise, and anticipating our meeting again, we had optical specialists create this teleocular device. It is our gift to you, Chance, in hopes you will consider performing a job for us."

"What job?"

"We want you to make this project run efficiently."

"I'm not an engineer."

"It is not for your engineering skill—at least not your construction skill—that you are needed. The project is behind schedule and running tight on budget. Given the cyclical nature of the weather, it is anticipated that 1902 will produce devastating floods. The only way we can finish in time to prevent that is if we increase the power from that station so our spiders can lift more and do it more quickly. Five percent would help, ten would be more than enough, and fifteen would result in a tidy bonus, the majority of which would be yours."

Chance shook his head. "Money is trouble."

"So true, but not in this case." Gavrilis smiled broadly. "You see, Harrison Hudson has taken a number of futures contracts which are, in essence, a bet against this project. Finish early, and he's ruined."

Chance nodded. "No time to spare. Get me a wrench."

The lift which had carried Chance away to be billeted and sent to work, opened again. Gavrilis glanced back over his shoulder. "So he didn't hit you, Brinkworth?"

"No, sir, but he wanted to." The slender secretary frowned. "Are you certain you can trust him, Mr. Gavrilis?"

"Foolish question. He will see what we wish him to see. If ever he sees what is truly going on, it will be far too late for him to do anything about it. But you are suspicious. Why?"

"I find it too convenient that he found his way to that particular bar—one which has served to entertain you in the past and me rather frequently."

"You believe he was sent? By whom? Hudson? Other of our enemies?" Gavrilis' jowls quivered with laughter. "Be assured of one thing, Mr. Brinkworth. The contempt Corrigan has for us is nothing compared to the loathing he has for them. 'The enemy of my enemy is my friend.' And given that truth, Chance Corrigan is, as of this moment, our very best friend in the world."

During the next three weeks Chance Corrigan slept very little. Men on the crew came to think that he was as much a machine as the spiders. At least, that was in the first week. Over the next two they decided he was a genius, and likely a god, because everything he studied and touched ran more efficiently and safely. His first pass at dealing with the hydro-electric turbines in the spillway generation station increased output by seven percent. Those adjustments had been fairly simple—largely based around increasing the efficiency of the magnets being used. Chance had always found magnetism fascinating, and working on the turbines barely caused him to break a sweat.

The second turbine pass upped efficiency to eleven percent, and he would have kept on there, but the spiders—while not yet working at peak efficiency themselves—still performed so much better that the quarry could not keep up. He turned his attention to the ancient steam engines powering the cranes and cutting saws, enabling the crews to increase their pace.

Though the workers' gratitude provided an open door for him to join them socially, Chance held back. From hilltops above the workers' camps he could watch them around their campfire. His new eye did an admirable job of piercing the darkness. The crew—consisting of Egyptians, Nubians and a handful of Europeans—appeared quite happy, in spite of being worked slowly to death.

He looked from their camp glowing with firelight and back up toward the clock-tower atop which Gavrilis' disk-shaped apartment perched. The lift shaft ran up through the clock's base, right behind where an enormous pendulum swung. The clock's face had replaced numerals with hieroglyphics, though if they had any significance it escaped Chance. An airship mooring mast rose above the apartment, with a small and elegant sky-yacht awaiting Gavrilis' bidding. And there, centrally silhouetted, stood the stout man himself, his domain spread beneath him.

Chance marveled at how much work actually was getting done on the dam. The spiders, which stood twenty feet tall when working, would wade out into the water or scuttle along the top of the dam, to place giant stone blocks. They reminded him vaguely of the Martian tripods from that recent novel *The War of the Worlds* despite their lack of a heat-ray. *Though a heat-ray* would *make cutting stone faster . . .*

Developing a heat-ray was the least of the things Chance had to be doing. Inefficiencies riddled the whole project. Supplies came up the Nile on steamers, then were offloaded onto carts and caravans to make the trek up into the highlands. The larger, bulkier items would get loaded onto a pair of cargo airships, but Gavrilis retained them only when a suitable load had arrived. From what Chance had been told, the last-such shipment had been the grand piano in the large man's apartment.

It struck Chance that laying a single iron track, magnetizing it, and likewise magnetizing the undercarriage of a sledge would use magnetic repulsion to eliminate friction. This would, in turn, allow draft animals to more easily haul supplies from the river to the dam. Magnetic levitation would require extremely strong magnets which operated at high temperatures. *A super magnet.*

He thought about it for a bit, and jotted down a couple of chemical formulations he might use to create one. As he made a note, he laughed. For the first time in a decade he was thinking of an experiment that would expand the envelope of knowledge, not just improve some existing technology.

Chance's laughter, which had been accompanied by a sense of freedom, died as invisible chains wrapped themselves tight around his chest. *The last time I experimented, men died.* He stood, shivering, and wandered off to bed. He hoped to sleep, and hoped not to dream, and got half of what he desired.

A week later as dusk approached, Brinkworth rapped on a spider's cockpit shell. The tempered glass—sufficiently thick to withstand water pressure at the base of the dam—made his rapping into a *tink-tink*. Chance imagined that was what every goldfish heard inside a bowl. He finished tightening down the plate beneath the operators' seat, then stood. He couldn't quite straighten up fully, but easily grasped the hatch's edge and pulled himself through. He sat with his legs dangling into the cockpit.

Brinkworth didn't even attempt to hide his contempt. "Mr. Gavrilis requests the pleasure of your company at dinner."

Chance pulled a rag from his back pocket and wiped grease from his hands. "I really ain't . . ."

The fancy man's eyes narrowed. "Mr. Corrigan, I am well aware of your history. Prep schools, Ivy League education. You may have spent the last decade consorting with the dregs of humanity, but you know better. Mr. Gavrilis deserves better."

He pointed to the tower's base. "You'll find appropriate clothing and a showering facility in there. You will then enter the lift and ascend to join Mr. Gavrilis."

Chance didn't need the extra magnification a couple eye-clicks gave him to spot Brinkworth's displeasure. "You can guide me up."

Pure hatred lit the man's face for an eye-blink. "I was not invited. It seems this is to be a dinner for old school chums."

Chance frowned. "There are others here?"

"No, just the two of you." Brinkworth snorted. "You are expected presently. Do not disappoint."

The fancy man turned and stalked away, keeping his head high and spine straight right up to the point where he realized he had no place else to go. He hesitated. Chance lost interest in him and headed off to the tower. He made a detour to his tent, dropping off rags and wrenches, then showered and dressed.

Clothes had been laid out for him: a white cotton shirt, cotton undergarments, a silken vest of navy blue, along with a matching tie bearing their school crest toward the point; and a light tan linen suit. Brown oxford shoes completed the outfit. Everything fit perfectly, which might have surprised Chance, save he remembered being unconscious for the time it took to transport him down the Nile and implant the new eye. Brinkworth could have measured him in every way possible—probably had—and would find some more malignant way to use that information.

Gavrilis smiled, welcoming Chance with open arms—but never letting things get even close to a hug between them. "We had you measured as a precaution. . . ."

"Fitting me for a coffin?"

"Were the unfortunate to happen, perhaps." The large man turned and waved Chance toward a table set for two by the window. "But everything that has happened so far has been most fortunate. We felt you deserved a reward, hence the clothing. And an opportunity for even more prosperity."

Chance walked toward the table. "Such as?"

"Time to speak of business later, my friend." Gavrilis paused at a sideboard and poured three fingers of a dark amber liquor into a pair of matched snifters. "We've been told you drink whisky. This is a Macallan from a cask filled before your War Between the States. We have two more bottles, one of which you will take with you."

Chance accepted it and let his eye click closer. The Scotch drained on elegant legs down the sides of the snifter. The rising aroma warmed his nose. "To your health."

"And that of our project." Gavrilis smiled as their glasses clinked. "Please, let us enjoy our meal."

The meal consisted of four courses and touched upon all of the dishes Chance had enjoyed at one time or another in the Hudson household. He'd not eaten such rich food in a decade, and the avidity with which Gavrilis tucked himself into the meal answered the question of how a man who had once been an Adonis had grown so corpulent. Gavrilis had gained every pound Chance had lost in that time and more; and while they both might tip the scales at the same weight, a decade of adventuring around the world as a mechanic—or anything else that paid—had left Chance lean, hard and scarred.

Chance did enjoy the food, but he forced himself to eat slowly and not finish everything. Gavrilis had chosen the menu to let Chance know he'd done his homework. He knew everything he needed to know about Chance and probably a bit more. He chose the food as an offering of friendship and even a bit of a seduction. Gavrilis was promising more of the same if Chance accepted whatever offer would be coming his way.

Chance realized one other thing about the meal. It was an illusion. It promised a return to the time before. He'd not forgotten that Gavrilis said he would help Chance destroy Harrison Hudson. That was really all Chance wanted. He didn't need the dream that the opulence once denied him could magically be restored.

But Alexander always tried too hard.

After dinner and after several more whiskies, Gavrilis stood before the window, a cigar all the way from Havana clutched between thick fingers. "We are going to share with you a confidence. No one, save my family and the Pharaonic Brotherhood know it. We do remember that you never joined the Brotherhood, but we feel you to be a brother now. We have watched you, in all you are doing, and feel safe in sharing this because of what you have done."

"What, exactly, have you seen me doing?"

"We have seen you *caring*." Gavrilis turned, punctuating his remark with the stab of a glowing cigar cherry. "Even as just today, when you were maintaining the spider, you did more than attend to the engine. You made certain the machine would be safer for the workers. You care about the people."

Gavrilis again faced the window, weaving slightly as he executed his pirouette. "As do we. You did not believe me when I referred to the people as *our* people, but so they are. My family is Greek, yes, but do you recall the last dynasty in Egypt? The Ptlolemaic Dynasty, founded by Alexander the Great, was purported to end with Rome's conquest of Egypt. But the Emperors did not kill the last of the Pharaohs. Roman respect for antiquity prompted them to keep us alive. We are descended from Alexander Helios, Cleopatra's eldest son by Marc Antony. In our veins flows the blood of the last rulers of this magnificent land."

He puffed on the cigar, the red glow causing his face to reflect an infernal mask on the glass. "So these are *our* people. This project will be mildly profitable, but the prosperity of our people is our true goal here. This dam is but the first of many improvements which can raise Egypt back to its former glory. To do just that is our life mission."

Chance sipped some of the Scotch but said nothing.

Gavrilis smiled in the glass, then turned. "So, to the business we mentioned. Sirius will be rising by the end of the month. That is the traditional start of the floods. The dam will hold back a significant amount of water before we have to open the spillway fully to relieve the pressure. We need as much stone on that dam as possible in the next three weeks.

"Business calls us to Cairo, and we no longer trust Mr. Brinkworth. We cannot have him running the operation. In our absence, we will put you in charge."

Chance's eye narrowed. Brinkworth's fury had come

because Gavrilis had already dismissed him. "I'm not an administrator."

"No, but you *are* a leader. A leader is what this project needs. Time is of the essence. Once the rains begin we will be unable to do anything, so we need as much as possible done before the rains come. Brinkworth will do the clerical work. He will embezzle a great deal while he does it, but that is not your concern."

Gavrilis raised an eyebrow. "Will you do this for us? For the people?"

Chance nodded. "For the people."

Gavrilis swirled the last of his whisky in the glass, then drained it. "Thank you. We are mindful of what we promised you in payment. Complete as much of the dam as you are able, and we guarantee you will have much, much more."

The shadow of Gavrilis' airship momentarily eclipsed the sun. Chance watched it sail away, its steam engine belching black smoke in a long tail. He'd already taken to his duties as project foreman, getting up early to organize the airship's refueling. He stared after it until the sun's heat and the glare of Brinkworth's fury made him turn his attention to business.

Gavrilis had been correct. The men were willing to follow Chance, and not just because the big *sahib* had turned things over to him. Chance did not hesitate to leap in where work needed doing. He took his turn driving one of the spiders, dropping blocks in place, even daring to plunge his spider fully beneath the waters to nudge things into position.

Chance enjoyed working the spider. Though he found the combination of levers, cranks, and pedals cumbersome and clumsy, the device worked remarkably well. The steel-lattice limbs provided great strength, the gearing greater torque, and yet the brass, leather, and wood trim gave the cockpit a suitably elegant feel. A Swede,

two Slavs, a Scotsman, and a Montenegrin constituted
the rest of the drivers. Working the machine was exhaust-
ing, especially because the glass cockpit became a hot-
house beneath the sun, so Chance added domed lights
so they could use the machines at night. That saved the
men from heatstroke and preserved them from Brinkworth's spying from on high.

Work progressed even more quickly than even
Chance had hoped. As Sirius made its first appearance
in the east, he found himself again seated on a hill, half-
way between worker camps and Gavrilis' tower. Gavrilis had not yet returned from Cairo, but was expected
within the week. He would return just in time for storms
to come up from the south.

Chance sat there, a bit achy, feeling the heat drain
out of the stone. He had worked hard, taking over from
Swensen for a seven-hour shift. As much as he wanted
to deride what Gavrilis had said, it felt good to be working on a project that would make life better for ordinary
people.

Then he heard the click of a pistol's hammer being
cocked. He turned to look, expecting to see Brinkworth
holding a gun.

But it wasn't Brinkworth.

It was the girl. The dancer in the Port Said bar. Same
dark hair, same fiery eyes, though lacking the kohl. Her
outfit had changed, too. White blouse, tan jodhpurs and
brown riding boots. And a big pistol—a Webley-Fosbery
Automatic Revolver—with a bore which appeared—
without the benefit of any clicked magnification—large
enough to accommodate a locomotive.

Chance slowly raised his hands. "You're making a
mistake, Miss."

"I don't believe I am, Mr. Corrigan. And it's not Miss.
It's Doctor. Doctor Ariella Moorcroft of the Egyptian
Antiquities Service."

"Shouldn't you be in the Valley of the Kings catching
tomb raiders?"

"And let you and your cohort complete your theft of the Hapy Treasure?"

"The what?"

"Don't pretend you don't know. I was in that bar to attract Mr. Gavrilis' attention—or that of his lackey." Her gun never wavered she frowned. "Given the way you succumbed to drink in the bar, I'd not thought you would be useful here, but you have succeeded in moving their mad scheme ahead."

Succumbed to drink? Chance had no idea what she was referring to because he remembered her, and Brinkworth and the fight, then a blue man. *But a blue man made no sense. Was I seeing things?* Chance concluded quickly he must have been. Had a blue man intervened, she wouldn't have ascribed his collapse to drink. *What in blazes were they serving me?*

"I am afraid I don't know what you are talking about, Doctor Moorcroft." Chance shrugged, lowering his hands. "I'm here building a dam to stop flooding downriver."

"You cannot be that stupid."

"Apparently I am."

"Then he hasn't told you?" Her eyes tightened. "Hapy, the Egyptian god who is the Inundation, has been said since antiquity to dwell in a river cave near Aswan. Mr. Gavrilis has narrowed the search for that cave, which is said to hold a treasure trove of gold and other precious offerings from the Pharaohs to assure a flood. Emperor Seti I is said to have taken the spoils from his conquest of Kadesh—a French ton of gold and gems—and conveyed it to the cave himself. It is believed the location of the cave died with the last of the Ptolemys."

Chance gasped. "And if they didn't die, then he *would* know the location."

"Who?"

Brinkworth's pinched nasal voice answered her question. "Alexander Helios Gavrilis." He emerged from the shadows with two large men bearing rifles. "He is the man who will become the new Ptolemy. Put your pistol down, please, Doctor Moorcroft. The both of you will come along without incident. His Highness left explicit orders as to how to handle a situation such as this."

The instructions consisted of handcuffing the two of them and locking them into the tower's dungeon. It really didn't deserve that name, since it remained clean and dry, with a single electric light that burned constantly. Twelve-foot lengths of chain connected their handcuffs to an eye-bolt sunk into the concrete floor beneath that bulb. The chain allowed them access to the two iron cots with straw-stuffed mattresses on the walls and the single small, barred window facing the dam. Brinkworth, flanked by his ruffians, brought them meals of bread and water twice a day. He checked their heavy, bronze handcuffs morning and night, then departed with the air of a man who had outsmarted unruly children.

That first night of their incarceration, Ariella apologized. "I am sorry I got you into this."

Chance, stretched out on one of the cots, clicked the eye up to study the lightbulb. "Brinkworth was looking for an excuse to discredit me. Had it not been this, it would have been something else. In fact, you've saved my life. He would have killed me, fed me to crocodiles, and told Gavrilis I'd embezzled money which he, himself, has stolen. You complicated things by bringing the Egyptian Antiquities Service into it. Assuming the Service knows you're out here."

She winced. "I am afraid not. Gavrilis is friendly with the Director. I was given orders not to interfere. The Director believes I am on a ship bound for England, on holiday. I guess it's a crocodile's belly for the both of us."

Chance laughed. "You'll end up in an Ottoman harem. I always liked Istanbul. The Hagia Sophia . . ."

"Mister Corrigan!"

"Yes?"

"Aren't you going to do something?"

"Sure."

She looked at him expectantly. "Well."

Chance rolled over to face the wall. "I'm going to sleep."

Occasional lightning flashes lit the nights, but rain falling never actually reached the ground. It evaporated well before—the ancient Egyptian gods teasing the mortals below. At least, that's the way Ariella described it. Chance thought of it in terms of air currents and convection, making a few calculations based on windspeed, direction, and the proximity of the storms themselves.

On the fourth night, rains began steadily, accompanied by more lightning and thunder. The storm alone would have been enough to break the boredom of their captivity, but then the door to their prison opened. Gavrilis squeezed his way into the room. The two toughs flanked him. Brinkworth, with Ariella's Webley-Fosbery tucked into his waistband, hovered in Gavrilis' shadow.

The large man sighed when he saw Dr. Moorcroft. "We had hoped, my dear, you would have taken the director's command to heart. You have no one to blame for your current condition but yourself. And you, our dear friend, we had genuine hopes that you would not become entangled in the peripheral aspects of your employment."

Chance sat on the cot, measuring the distance to Gavrilis. The large man stood just far enough away that even if Chance hurled himself feet first at his host, the last Ptolemy would never be hit. Chance shrugged. "Do you mean the treasure? Or the other thing?"

Ariella blinked. "Other thing?"

Gavrilis' smile froze. "I have no idea . . ."

Chance laughed. "I'm not the young kid you and the Brotherhood fooled at school. You told me that Harrison Hudson had taken Egyptian futures contracts out on the 1902 harvest. He was expecting a bumper crop since Egyptian cotton production has been increasing each year for the past fifteen."

Gavrilis looked hard at him. "How could you know that?"

"I crew steamers, remember? Who do you think ships the stuff?" Chance clicked a close-up of Gavrilis' astonishment. "This dam, you've engineered it to fill and fail. Should be around the second week in October, which means the 1902 cotton crop will be wiped out. And you, with your heavy interest in the American cotton crop, will benefit greatly. I believe, this idea is a dog that will hunt."

Gavrilis raised his face, so his double-chin wobbled freely with his chuckle. He clasped his hands behind his back and smiled. "Very clever, Chance. I always thought the others underestimated you."

Brinkworth gasped. "There is no treasure? No dynasty?"

"Fool. There is only money. And Chance is correct. This should please you, Chance, since Hudson will be ruined."

"Not since you warned him of your plan." Chance glanced skyward. "He was in the back room when we had dinner. He wasn't alone. Probably four or five of them. They had fun listening to you confide in me and make a fool of me, much as Hudson did himself years ago. You had to humiliate me to prove you were their equal. They were with you on the airship going to Cairo."

"You couldn't have known . . ." Gavrilis' eyes became slits. "You saw to the fueling of my airship. You measured the speed and realized we were carrying extra weight."

"I realized a lot more." Chance slowly shook his head. "You had no reason to bring me here, except to humiliate me, and I doubted even that would be enough of a motive. Then it occurred to me, you needed a scapegoat. You had Brinkworth all set up, but the opportunity to finish off the life that Hudson had crushed, that was what made my part critical. Putting me in charge of the project gets you clear. After all, all you tried to do was help out an old school chum down on his luck."

"Had you been this clever in school, Chance, you'd be standing where I am now." Gavrilis chuckled. "And for your information, Hudson sold his contracts in Cairo, at a slight loss, to agents of his enemies. They will be as broken as the dam."

"You'll come to realize that leaving me in charge of this project has caused you all sorts of problems." Chance smiled as lightning flashed silver beyond the dungeon's tiny window. "In the last three weeks I've laid enough stone to fix the flaw you engineered into the dam. It won't fail and, in a week's time, the spiders won't be able to dive deep enough to make it fail."

Thunder boomed. "In fact, given how the rain is coming down now, I'd say your plan dies at dawn!"

"What? No!" Gavrilis looked from the window to Chance, then snapped at Brinkworth. "Go, rouse the men. We have to fix things!"

Chance's laughter filled the room. "If you think the spider pilots will destroy the dam . . ."

"I will do it myself and then, Chance Corrigan, I will return to finish you off!"

The quartet fled from the room, leaving the door open. Ariella made for it, but her chain pulled her up short. She tugged on it sharply. "You can't let them go. Help me."

"I have no intention of letting him succeed." Chance dragged his iron cot over toward the center of the room, then stood and grabbed the light fixture. He got his fingernails beneath the edge and began working it back and forth to loosen the screws. The fixture came away in his hands, trailing a two foot length of wire. Chance then slammed the heel of his palm against the plaster and lath ceiling, cracking it along the line of a stud. He yanked the cord, pulling it down, all the way across the ceiling and down along the wall, producing thirty feet of wire.

He hopped off the cot and flipped it over so all the legs pointed upward. He began tightly coiling the wire around one of the legs.

"What are you doing?"

"Getting us out of these cuffs." Chance smacked his cuffs against the top of the bed leg. They slid open as if they'd never been locked at all.

Ariella stared, her face open with disbelief. "How did you . . ."

He smiled. "I've just created an electro-magnet. Brass is not magnetic, but the little steel springs holding the locking mechanism closed are. A quick rap compresses the spring, the magnet holds it open. Come over here. Do what I did."

She complied. "How did you know . . ."

"This ain't the first time I've needed to shuck cuffs."

"Then you could have gotten us out of here any time."

Chance nodded. "No point until Gavrilis got here. He's the one who's got to be stopped."

A couple of gunshots sounded outside. Chance ran to the window. Brinkworth and the toughs were trying to force workers onto the dam. Looked like Swensen was down. Gavrilis was squeezing himself through the cockpit hatch on one spider.

He turned from the window. "Can you work a wireless? Morse Code?"

"Yes."

"Take the lift up to Gavrilis' apartment. Alert Cairo and any place else that the flood is coming."

"What are you going to do?"

He jerked his head toward the window. "I'm going to make sure that Gavrilis doesn't make it worse."

Rain slashed at Chance as he ran down the hill. Thunder boomed and lighting reduced the landscape to a nightmare chiaroscuro through which silhouettes ran. One of the spiders had started out onto the dam. The toughs used their rifles to herd Egyptians toward the construction. The other pilots were nowhere to be seen.

Brinkworth heard Chance's approach. He turned, the pistol coming up, but not quickly enough. Chance leveled him with a roundhouse right to the jaw, and plucked the pistol from Brinkworth's hand with his left. Spinning, Chance brought the pistol up. His eye clicked in tight and he fired.

The gunshots could barely compete with the thunder, but the bullets did their work well. The self-cocking revolver fired a .455 caliber bullet. It wasn't quite the size of a freight-train, but hit as if it were. The toughs went down one after the other, and if they weren't dead when they hit the ground, they soon were after the men swarmed them.

Chance ran to the remaining spider and slid nimbly into the cockpit. Closing switches, he engaged the electric motor. It hummed to life, and the mechanical spider lurched upright. Strapping himself into the control chair, Chance headed out onto the dam after Gavrilis.

The fat man had reached the center of the dam. He'd begun to nudge one of the large stone blocks out of the way. That feat of mechanical strength would have been impossible before Chance had increased the generator's power.

If the dam goes, it is my fault.

Chance charged out onto the dam, his spider's forelegs jutting forward, twin lances of steel. He flicked on the external loudspeaker. "You won't succeed, Gavrilis!"

"But I shall!" Within his spider's shell, Gavrilis pulled out one of his watches. He tugged on the stem, pulling out a wiry radio antenna. He flipped open the lid. A small light glowed, then fat fingers cranked watch hands around. "I shall not be stopped!"

Immediately Chance's left eye clicked out of focus, then back in. Images swam, never matching that of his right eye. Pain jetted through his skull. Lightning flashes all but blinded him. His spider drifted to the left, toward the reservoir side of the dam.

Then Gavrilis' spider pounced. One forearm smashed

Chance's spider-forelegs to the ground. The other fore-limb came around, crashing into Chance's cockpit. Glass shattered, splinters stinging him. The spider tottered and then, in an incredibly lethargic ballet, it slipped to the side and plunged into the reservoir.

Chance reached out and one limb caught the dam's lip. He looked up. Gavrilis' spider reared up, forelimbs raised and pressed together, a dagger waiting to plunge straight through the cockpit.

"Goodbye, Chance!"

Then the unthinkable happened.

A lightning bolt hit the hydro-plant's tower. It exploded in a brilliant shower of sparks. Chance's motor, deprived of the energy to run it, failed, locking his spider up.

And likewise freezing Gavrilis' metal arachnid atop the dam.

Which is when the Inundation came.

The rains that had hit Aswan had been nothing compared to those which had pounded the Ethiopian highlands days before. Water had sheeted off the hillsides, filling streams, swelling gullies, and finally pouring into the Nile. A wall of water surged down the river, raising the water level five feet in a matter of seconds.

The Inundation crashed into the dam and sheered off the top row of blocks. It scattered them and the metal spider as if they were a child's toys. The last Chance saw of Gavrilis was the large man trying, in vain, to haul himself out of the cockpit. One of his watches had caught on the edge, sticking him fast.

The cresting wave carried Gavrilis away. Being tumbled down through the cataracts either destroyed the radio device controlling Chance's eye, or moved it out of range. The explanation did not matter. The eye clicked back into focus.

Just in time so I can watch myself die.

The same water that swept Gavrilis away battered Chance's spider against the dam. It broke the machine's tenuous grip. The spider sank like a stone. Water gushed through the broken canopy, filling the cockpit with silty death while life-giving air bubbled up and away.

Chance held his breath until his lungs burned, his artificial eye letting him see everything with amazing clarity. And then, just before he involuntarily opened his mouth to suck in water, he again saw the blue man, and realized this was the end.

Chance awoke on the side of the river with Ariella's lips pressed to his. "Breathe, damn you!"

He coughed, then rolled to his side. He vomited the Nile back into the channel. He coughed heavily and tried to get up, but she held on and he was too weak to fight her. He lay back.

"Where is he?"

"Who?"

"The blue man." Chance scrubbed a hand over his face. "He was at the bar. He's the reason I passed out. And then, down there, I saw him. He must have pulled me out of the cockpit and gotten me on the shore."

She shook her head. "I didn't see anyone. I sent the wireless message and then came down here. You were alone on the bank. If there were any footprints, they were washed away."

"He was here. A blue man. In a loincloth. In the bar he had a lotus staff."

Ariella looked toward the river. "It's not possible."

"What?"

She hugged her arms around herself. "Remember the treasure in Hapy's cave?"

"Yes."

"Hapy is the god of the Inundation. He's represented as a blue man bearing a lotus." She pointed to the river. "Could it be that he exists? That he knew of the danger the dam presented and selected you to fix things?"

Chance started to deny it, but the river's roar sounded hauntingly like laughter for a moment. "He probably just didn't like having to fit his flood into the last Ptolemy's schedule."

Chance stood and pulled Ariella to her feet. Then he reached up and unscrewed Gavrilis' artificial eye. He stared at it for a moment, then dropped it and crushed it under foot.

She smiled. "You didn't want anything of his anymore?"

Chance shook his head. "Nope. Not while I can make something better."

Foggy Goggles

Donald J. Bingle

Random true facts about Donald J. Bingle: he was the Keeper of the World's Largest Kazoo. He made up the science of Neo-Psycho-Physics for a time travel roleplaying game. He is a member of The International Thriller Writers. He once successfully limboed under a pole only nineteen inches off the ground. He is the author of the novel *Greensword*, a darkly comedic eco-thriller about global warming. He has written short stories about killer bunnies, Civil War soldiers, detectives, Renaissance Faire orcs, giant battling robots, demons, cats, time travelers, ghosts, time-traveling ghosts, a husband accused of murdering his wife, dogs, horses, gamers, soldiers, Neanderthals, commuters, little kids, kender, and serial killers. Of those subjects, he has occasional contact in real life only with dogs, cats, gamers, and commuters (unless some of those are, unknown to him, really time travelers, ghosts, demons, serial killers, or murder suspects). He prefers gamers to commuters. He prefers dogs to cats. He is a member of the Science Fiction and Fantasy Writers of America. He was once hit by lightning. He was the world's top-ranked tournament player of classic roleplaying games like Dungeons & Dragons for more than fifteen years. He is the author of the near future military sci-fi novel, *Forced Conversion*. He was an Eagle Scout. He is currently putting the finishing touches on a spy thriller. He is a corporate and securities attorney. He is a member of the International Association of Media Tie-In Writers. He has a fascinating website at www.donaldjbingle.com. He is a member of the Gen Con Writer's Symposium. He used to write movie reviews for a comic book. He rarely gets steamed, but his work colleagues find him rather punky.

Gavin Ulysses Densmore hardly knew where to look, whether at the engineering marvel above or at the astonishing vista spread out below. As the travel and science reporter for *The New York Times*, both wonders were within his assigned purview and both stories would include information which the NYT's small, but enthusiastic, readership would find fascinating. And while the NYT was just another of a dozen or so journalistic rags competing for attention in New York City, he had a feeling that with the right story it could rise above the rest and take over the loyalties of the best educated and most discerning readers. Certainly, he was fortunate indeed to be given this assignment so as to find himself being propelled through the air at good speed toward his interview destination in the southwestern realms of these United States of America.

He adjusted his goggles for comfort, flipping down the sun-shielding darkened glass feature, as he gazed up into the bright sky at the massive device conveying him with alacrity south and west, currently near the border of the Texas panhandle and Oklahoma. It was, perhaps, too simple to call the transport a balloon. Such huge up-ended bags were typically filled either with hydrogen gas (a substance lighter than air, but dangerously explosive) or with simple hot air, and had been experimented with by many, particularly the French, but without great success. Ordinary balloons floated hither and yon at the whims of the wind, which varied quite unpredictably as to speed and direction at different heights.

While others had attempted to control balloon flight with propellers and wings, these efforts were disappointing, primarily because the altitude of ordinary balloons was also quite difficult to control. Only two means were available for achieving ascension: more lift and less weight. Neither was practical for longer flights. Adding volatile hydrogen to the balloon in flight was a fool's errand and, while producing even a large volume of additional hot air while in flight to achieve more lift was possible, the altitude shift was slow and imprecise. True, a sudden altitude boost could be achieved quickly when needed by dropping ballast, but carrying sufficient sand to maneuver adroitly over long flights was simply not practical.

And even if one could ascend when desired, there was still, of course, the issue of descent on command, an even more important concern given the brisk temperatures that held sway at altitudes approaching those of alpine peaks. While the ambient temperature caused hot air to cool over time, decreasing lift, there was no way to add ballast while in flight so as to be able to maneuver downward with any speed or efficiency whatsoever. Dumping hot air through an opening atop the balloon was an option, albeit often one with disastrous consequences.

Doctor Pendleton Ambrose Merganser's invention of the steam-powered sky-carriage had, of course, solved these difficulties. Two small modified steam engines—of the type typically used for small, narrow gauge mining railways, rather than the behemoths used for transcontinental freight and passenger travel—not only provided power for propeller propulsion and an air rudder, but they also supplied copious amounts of steam, as op-

posed to dry hot air, for lift. The release of steam from
the engines provided a relatively quick burst of lighter-
than-air hot gas at a moment's notice. Dual engines gave
a safety-conscious redundancy to the lift system. Furthermore, the selective use of one engine or the other,
combined with the placement of the dual engines far
fore and aft beneath the elongated ovoid balloon above,
allowed the balloon to tilt downward or upward as it
traveled ahead (at least until the fresh gas fully inter-
mixed), increasing the maneuverability of the balloon in
ascending and descending at will.

All of that was interesting enough, Gavin knew, and
worthy of a four-inch column in the NYT science section. But the real genius, the thing that stepped up the
story from a sidebar to a Sunday supplement feature,
was using steam, rather than simple hot air, to provide
the large balloon's lift. The brochure for the maiden voyage of the "Self-Regulating Steam-Powered Airborne
Gasbag and Associated Sky-Carriage for Extended and
Directed Flight Featuring Maneuverability Accoutrements" included a direct quote from Doctor Merganser,
himself, explaining the theoretical and practical aspects
of his design: "By utilizing steam, which is, after all, simply hot air with a large component of water vapor, we
can easily produce sufficient quantities of lift to carry
the largest and heaviest loads without difficulty as high
as needed to locate winds conducive to efficient travel.
The key to steam, however, is that steam carries its own
ballast. As the steam cools, the water vapor, which ini-
tially was lighter than air and contributed to the lift of
the device, condenses back into water, which cannot
only be recycled into the steam-producing process, but
which when it becomes water essentially provides its
own ballast to counteract the lift of the lighter-than-air
steam remaining uncondensed."

Two accoutrements were, the brochure explained,
important to augmenting and controlling this natural
steam/water dichotomy. The first was that the elongated

ovoid balloon was, in fact, a ring torus, rather than a sphere—meaning that it was in essence an elongated ovoid tube with a central void. The shape allowed more surface area of the balloon to be in contact with the air, facilitating the exchange of heat at the balloon's surface. The cool air of the upper atmosphere descending through this central void accelerated the cooling of the steam within the torus, causing water to condense, increasing ballast as lift decreased, permitting rapid descent.

The second accoutrement was key to taking advantage of the first in a controlled fashion. This second device was an articulated panel of black canvas that could be opened up to cover the entire top of the ovoid shape of the balloon, blocking the top of the central void—in essence a giant, black canvas umbrella, albeit one that opened flat in the fashion of a geisha's fan. This canvas impeded downflow of cold air through the middle of the balloon, slowing cooling and condensation when desired. In addition, the black canvas, when unfurled, soaked up the radiant heat of the sunlight, providing additional warmth to the balloon when employed, reversing (or at least slowing) the cooling of the hot gas in the balloon. By deploying the covering in whole or in part, the lift and ballast of the balloon could, in conjunction with steam engines, be modulated with considerable delicacy.

Doctor Merganser's patented invention was why Gavin was now enjoying the exhilarating experience of transcontinental flight. While the science reporter in him thrilled at the science and engineering of the airborne gasbag, the travel reporter in him was simply agog at the pleasures of air travel aboard the associated sky-carriage. Gone were the bumps and noisy vibrations of riding on the railroad all the live-long day. Gone were the monotonous and irritating clackety-clack of the rails, the dirty, dusty air at ground level, and the dreary views of weeds alongside the tracks. Up here there was fresh air, relative quiet, a soothing sway, and an unparalleled view of nature's bounteous beauty from God's own perspective. Not only that, but the sky-carriage was not limited by train schedules and sidings, nor by rails and stations—it could go anywhere at any time, which is how Gavin was able to arrange a brief stop at a supply depot near the Nevada-Arizona border on the sky-carriage's maiden voyage from New York to Los Angeles. From there he would travel but a few hours by ground transport to interview the inventor himself, Doctor Pendleton Ambrose Merganser. The Doctor was squirreled away in a small town by the name of Las Vegas—meaning simply "The Meadows" in Spanish—no doubt so as to be able to work on his inventions without the constant interruption of admiring throngs.

His stop only a few hours away, Gavin wiped the fog off of his goggles—they tended to mist up when the cool, humid air hit the glass warmed by the heat of his body—to take in the view. He had been told by his better-traveled colleagues to expect hot, arid expanses empty of life or beauty in the southwest, but they had been wrong. Everywhere he looked was lush and green and teeming with life. Perhaps he was not south enough or west enough. Perhaps they had been wrong.

Certainly, there was heat aplenty. As the sky-carriage made its gradual, controlled descent toward his drop-off point, the temperature climbed and then climbed some more. Both steam engines cut off to allow the air keeping them aloft to cool faster and the central canvas was completely open, helping to hasten their descent by assisting in the cooling of the hot air and the condensation of additional ballast.

When colleagues had described the southwest to Gavin, they had been quite clear that it was a hot place. The temperatures they asserted had been documented by actual, scientifically certified mercury thermometers were astonishing. Moreover, their tales of frying eggs on granite boulders were equally astounding, though more lacking in credibility. Still, each one had softened the tale with a wry comment: "But at least it's a dry heat."

Clearly, the joke was on him, because the heat was anything but dry. A steamy haze seemed to envelop the lush ground beneath as they descended, the sort of condition he associated with the swamp of Okeefenokee, back when his journeys for a travel piece on the wonders of Northern Florida as a vacation and retirement destination had been interrupted by a most unpleasant hurricane. Certainly the vegetation reminded him of the tropics, if not the Okeefenokee Swamp. Ferns and palms competed for space amidst thick, flowering bushes, and trailing vines.

He had thought for a bit that, perhaps, he had simply managed to find a swampy niche in the furnace of hell his colleagues had described, a jungle oasis of sorts amidst the silent sands of desolation, but his high vantage point revealed just the opposite. Vegetation had been on the upswing for hundreds of miles and extended north and south as far as he could see. Even the large, canyon-like fissure he had seen in the distance as they approached was covered with plant growth. The area was quite literally a jungle, not the desert he had been told to expect.

A damp mugginess assaulted Gavin's nostrils and a swarm of mosquitoes assaulted his exposed flesh as he disembarked from his transportation and stowed his luggage in the steam-powered land-carriage he had rented for the remainder of his journey. He adjusted his goggles, flipping the dark glass attachment up—no need for sun protection in the midst of the filtered daylight of a jungle—and set off for Doctor Merganser's workshop in the little town of Las Vegas, in the southeastern corner of Nevada.

If anything, it seemed to get hotter as he made his way slowly along the rutted roadway north. He told himself it was the lack of the cool breeze he had experienced during his flight or that, perhaps, the bone jarring rattles occasioned by the rough road made him uncom-

fortable and cranky and therefore more likely to notice
the heat. But psychosomatics did not cause his sweat-
soaked clothing to cling to his body like a jilted lover.
His imagination did not generate the first-degree burn
he received whenever he touched a piece of metal on his
steam-powered land-carriage with bare skin. And most
importantly and most scientifically, grumpiness did not
move the mercury incrementally up and yet up again on
his genuine, lab-calibrated thermometer, which he had
placed on the seat next to him.

It was hot and it was getting hotter.

Just as he was sure he would swoon like an over-
dramatic debutante at her lover's sweet whisperings,
he arrived at his destination: the home and workshop
of Doctor Merganser. He wiped the sweat from his upper lip and brow with an already soaked handkerchief
and rang the bell. Besides broadcasting a deafening
'hoo-haw,' the bell triggered a pneumatic tube device,
delivering with an audible whoosh a small cylinder containing a note. "State your name and your business on
the enclosed pad. Put in cylinder. Return to tube and
ring bell twice."

Marveling yet again at the Doctor's resourcefulness
in all sorts of labor-saving gadgetry, he did as instructed
and his missive was whisked away with pneumatic efficiency at the instant of the second "hoo-haw." He waited
only a few moments before a reply was delivered to his
nervous hands.

"Let yourself in," it read.

Gavin opened the massive wooden door and a
cold, icy blast flowed from the dim confines within and
poured over his body. His goggles fogged over immediately, leaving him temporarily blind as the frigid air
chilled his damp, sweaty clothing, causing his skin to
turn to gooseflesh and his muscles to tense and shiver
uncontrollably. If he had thought to bring in his genuine
mercury thermometer with him from the land-carriage
and had he not been blinded by the condensation which

had formed now on both sides of his goggles, he was sure that it would show that the ambient temperature within Doctor Merganser's workshop was at least thirty, perhaps forty, degrees Fahrenheit below that of the outside air.

He heard a vague shuffling sound and then a voice: "You'll see better if you remove your goggles."

Gavin immediately used his right hand to pull his goggles away from his face and raise them to forehead height, then let them rest there, where they might at least keep his forehead warm. In front of him he saw an unkempt old man wearing a stained gray apron over a plaid flannel shirt and heavy denim jeans, with thick black shoes beneath. The man, of course, wore goggles, as most everyone did these days, though Gavin suspected the scientist wore his more for eye protection from his experiments than from protection from the soot and particulates that so assaulted everyone in today's steam-engine powered world when they traveled out-of-doors.

"Haven't solved the condensate problem when transitioning between temperature gradients," the old man grumped. "Tried wipers, but the mechanism was too heavy and had to be manually activated. No net benefit there. Cleaning them with spit helps a mite—the saliva resists the forming of condensate, though I can't say why."

"Er, n-n-no doubt an intriguing s-s-scientific question," stammered Gavin, whether from cold or nervousness at meeting the great Doctor, he was not sure.

"Not really," murmured the scientist as he turned away, motioning for Gavin to follow him into the confines of his workshop. "I'll leave that one for some Harvard student's thesis research paper. Got more important things to work on."

"Gavin Ulysses Densmore, N-n-new York Times," Gavin replied, establishing his credentials right up front so there could be no complaint that anything said was off the record. "I scheduled an interview." As he waited for a response, Gavin's eyes scanned the room for massive blocks of ice. He'd been in an ice house in Boston for his piece on the New England fishing business— "From Ocean to Plate"—but he couldn't imagine anyone wanting to live in one, though with the heat outside, he could see the need for some respite. "I came here by sky-carriage—at least most of the way. It was quite a delight."

Merganser's right hand fluttered dismissively. "Old news. Maiden flight already underway. Got all the publicity I need for that one already. You're here to get me some press for my latest and greatest, now that it is fully perfected."

Gavin frowned, then shivered as a cold drip of water slid down his back. This was not going as expected. One tended to be treated as a shill for merchant interests when one worked as a travel reporter—free transport, free lodging, all expenses paid to fairs, traveling rodeos, circus adventures, and tours of places of historical significance, but not generally so when interviewing a source as a scientific reporter. It's not that the scientists couldn't use the huskerism, it's just that they were a bit too intellectually caught up in their research to understand that inventions needed a market to be valuable or, frankly, interesting. Maybe Merganser's understanding of this interplay is what made him more successful than most of his peers.

Gavin suddenly realized that his brief reverie had led to an awkward silence. "And what's that?" he asked. "What is your latest and greatest?"

Merganser looked at him as if he had just passed gas and failed to excuse himself. "You're shivering. I'd have thought you noticed."

"The cold?" He never had found any blocks of ice. "You can produce cold?"

"With my invention, everyone will be able to produce cold. I call it my 'Indoor Comfort Enhancement and Temperature Modulation Device', or ICE TMD for short—steam-powered of course."

"But how?"

"Compression, expansion, evaporative cooling. The technical details are not for publication. Some of my fellow inventors are, shall we say . . ."

"Less than scrupulous?" Gavin volunteered.

". . . assholes would be more accurate," grumbled the old inventor.

"Can you tell me how efficient the process is, at least?" queried Gavin. He was a scientific reporter. He had to have some sort of scientific detail to report.

"An astute question from such a young man. I am overjoyed to tell you that although early prototypes were only three to five percent efficient, I have improved the condensate compression ratios, achieved greater coherence from the ring valve seals, boosted fan rotor speeds to facilitate airflow rates over the evaporative cooling plates, and created miniature steam boilers with higher tensile strength capable of greater pressure containment without rupture so that the efficiency ratio is almost eight point two percent. In another six weeks, I hope to be closing in on eight point six percent efficiency."

Gavin tried to do the math in his head, but he was still shivering from the cool damp of his wet clothing. "Given the basic laws of energy conservation and thermodynamics, that . . . that means that the cooling effect utilizes . . . well, a tremendous amount of energy . . . a truly massive amount of energy."

Merganser bristled. "So what?"

Gavin gulped. He hadn't come all this way to insult his interviewee and blow the story. "It's just that . . . it's an impressive amount, I mean. S-s-superlatives sell newspapers." He wanted to ask where all the energy would come from, but he softened the question. "Where do you get your energy from?"

"Bah," said the old man. "There's nothing interesting

in that. There's always more energy out there. I started with coal, but there are plenty of alternatives. There's a natural mineral hereabouts that when gathered together produces heat spontaneously—not a lot, although that can be augmented if you grind it up and concentrate it. And, of course, as you can see, there is plenty of wood hereabouts. Just scythe down the trees—it's even easier to feed them into the boilers before they're full grown and require chopping and sawing."

"What about waste ... er ... by-products?"

"By-products?"

"At the efficiency rating you describe, you're putting ten, twelve times as much energy—in the form of heat—into the outside air as you're taking from the inside air."

"But outside is much more than ten or twelve times as big. Besides, the hotter it is outside, the more people want air modulation—that's what I call what the ICE TMD does, 'air modulation.' That's a self-enforcing marketing scheme, like selling addictive drugs to addicts."

"You're also producing massive amounts of carbon dioxide ..."

Merganser guffawed. "The plants love it. Have you seen the outside hereabouts? The plants will soak up as much carbon dioxide as you can pump out."

"Although it may be a bit off our main topic, I've been meaning to ask about that. My colleagues and all of the scholarly and historical texts I consulted before commencing my journey told me to expect a barren, arid desert, yet all I see about me is tropical, jungle growth. Can you explain why?"

"Plants do love carbon dioxide."

"Yes, I understand," replied Gavin, "but they need more than that to survive. They need water, lots and lots of water."

Merganser gave him another one of those looks reserved for idiots and in-laws. "Didn't I mention it was steam-powered? Let me say it slowly: S-t-e-a-m-p-o-we-r-e-d. You do know that steam is made out of water, don't you, son? Sure, it's contained in the boiler for work purposes, mostly, but still lot's of steam is released into the surrounding atmosphere. That means lots of moisture in the air."

Gavin wasn't an idiot and, if he had his way, he would never be or have an in-law, but despite Doctor Merganser's withering looks, he could not let the question go. "Your workshop here can hardly affect the geographic scope that I witnessed from the sky-carriage, Doctor Merganser."

"What makes you think I'm the only one who has one? Of course, mine is more efficient than the others, given that I'm constantly tinkering with improvements."

"You mean this is in commercial production?"

"Of course. Who in hell would live in Arizona or Nevada without air modulation? You'd have to be stupid crazy! Even with air modulation, you've got to be kind of peculiar. Las Vegas here is the air modulation capital of the world."

"B-but, sir, no one back east has ever h-h-heard of air modulation."

The doctor wrinkled his nose and smiled. "Confidentiality agreements. There's a whole lot of things people back east don't know about me or my inventions."

Gavin was aghast. The State Department didn't have this kind of secrecy. "And no one has ever talked?"

"If anyone talked before I was ready to go public and market nationally, I would have turned off their air modulation and pocketed a key part or six. They can't fix it on their own."

"But it's a desert, or at least it used to be. Where does all the water come from to fill the steam engines?"

"Colorado River. Goes through a big ol' canyon north and east of here a bit. Dammed it up, diverted what I needed. Young surveyor fellow from California, straight out of school—Stanford educated—located the best spot to do it and engineered the dam. Local labor.

Took a few years out of his life, so I named it after him: Hoover Dam."

The epic scale on which the illustrious Doctor Merganser was impacting the environment boggled Gavin's young mind. It was awe-inspiring, yet part of him instinctively rebelled against the thought of so much manipulation. He decided to continue to push. "But as this expands, the water can't last forever, can it?"

"Don't you understand, son, it's a feedback loop. I take dammed river water, I heat it up, release it as steam and it travels east and north. It condenses and falls and nourishes the plants and flows into rivers like the Colorado, where it gets picked up and re-used. I didn't invent air modulation just so folks stupid enough to live in the desert don't die of heat prostration. Mind you, I'm glad they don't and I'm glad for folks to be comfortable, but I'm terra-forming—just like the Martians did with their canals—and I aim to make the southwest a nicer, wetter, more habitable place, not just for people in their houses, but for people, plants, and animals to live and thrive in a jungle, instead of in an arid, God-forsaken wasteland."

That's when Gavin realized that the only thing bigger than Doctor Pendleton Ambrose Merganser's inventions—from the airborne gasbag to air modulation—was the impact that his inventions were having on the world. And the only thing bigger than that was the great Doctor's ego.

"B-b-but, Doctor, who gave you the right to change the world?"

The Doctor laughed out loud at Gavin's challenge. "Son, everyone changes the world with everything they do. I just have a specific outcome in mind and work my changes on a larger scale than most and toward a considered goal. You can see the future, if you look ahead."

"Not if you have foggy goggles."

"Even then, if you have enough sense to take them off and look real close."

"But what happens if you're wrong? What if you

bollix things up? What if there are unintended consequences? What if what you do can never be undone?"

"You're young, son. Earth, she's more resilient than
you think."

Gavin started to interrupt, but the Doctor cut him
off with an abrupt wave of his right hand. "But if I ever
do mess up the entire planet with my energy consump-
tion and my carbon dioxide and my 'unintended consequences,' well then, son, I reckon The New York Times
will have one helluva story and they'll never let it go."

The Battle of Cumberland Gap

William C. Dietz

William C. Dietz is the best-selling author of more than thirty novels, some of which have been translated into German, Russian, and Japanese. He grew up in the Seattle area, served as a medic with the Navy and Marine Corps, graduated from the University of Washington, and has been employed as a surgical technician, college instructor, and television news writer, director, and producer. Before becoming a full-time writer Dietz was director of public relations and marketing for an international telephone company. He and his wife live near Gig Harbor, Washington.

Cincinnati, Ohio
June 16, 1830

British artillery shells rumbled ominously as they passed over the Ohio River, exploded along the length of Cincinnati's chaotic waterfront, and sent columns of soil and splintered wood high into the air. Tiny stick figures could be seen, their arms and legs wind milling, before they were dropped into conflagration below.

From his position on the north side of the river, and just out of range of the British siege guns, French Admiral Philippe Gaudet lifted his brass telescope a fraction of an inch to look at the British forces arrayed on the far side of the river. He shook his head sadly. They were brave. Very brave. But for nothing.

Napoleon Bonaparte and his *Grande Armee* had already conquered most of Europe and pushed the British back onto their island. Now the ailing sixty-one-year-old ruler planned to bring all of the coal producing regions of Kentucky, Virginia, and Tennessee under his control. And for good reason since coal was the substance that fueled his steam-powered war machine.

The voice came from the right and slightly to the rear. "The *Indomptable* is ready for battle, sir. As are our escorts." The voice belonged to Captain Bernard Dubois, who was the land ship's commanding officer.

The admiral could *feel* the power of the *Indomptable's* engines through the soles of his highly polished boots as another salvo of shells exploded along the waterfront. He savored the heady mix of cordite and coal smoke, the weight of the brass telescope in his hands, and the power resident in the weapons ranked below him. The three-inch guns occupied the forward portion of deck two. But it was the battery of two breech-loading five-inch cannons on the *Indomptable's* main deck that were the ship's pride and joy.

Gaudet turned to Dubois. The other officer had the grave demeanor of a Jesuit priest. He was dressed in a bicorn hat and a long blue coat that was decorated with gold epaulettes, matching trim, and two rows of gleaming buttons. A pair of white breeches and knee high black boots completed the uniform. "Thank you, Captain Dubois. Please send the following signal to our escorts: 'Attack.' "

The south bank of the river had been built up, the gun emplacements were only fifty feet apart, and thousands of brightly clad troops were packed into the trenches behind them.

As rounds fired by the heavy guns located well back of the river whistled over his head, Battalion Commander Lieutenant Colonel Trevor Fitzhugh stood on top of the fortified embankment and eyed the French to the north. The Royal Marine officer's tall black shako and blood red uniform were immaculate. Just as the shamefully indolent George IV would expect them to be.

Amphibious vessels were already waddling into the water, and Fitzhugh watched a forty-ton gunboat take a direct hit, as the French battle cruiser *Indomptable* belched black smoke and jerked into motion. The men in the trenches cheered as the gunboat exploded, but Fitzhugh took scant comfort from the momentary victory.

He had seen action throughout Europe and in the colonies. That meant he had been frightened on many occasions. But never more so than on that fateful morning as the French land cruiser approached the river.

And for good reason.

Reading about the *Indomptable* in a two-month-old copy of the *London Times* was one thing. But seeing the monstrosity coming straight at him was another. The hull rose seventy-five feet above a pair of thick axles to which enormous drive wheels were attached.

The *Indomptable's* three-tiered superstructure boasted an equal number of smoke stacks, plus a multitude of secondary weapons platforms. And that was to say nothing of the cruiser's main armament, which was pointed at *him*.

But British officers led from the front.

That was what Fitzhugh had been taught, and that was what he expected of his subordinates. That meant he felt an obligation to remain where his marines could see him until the last possible moment.

At that point it would be permissible to stroll over to one of the wooden ladders where Fitzhugh planned to turn and give the French the finger before retiring to the walkway below. A gesture calculated to evoke a cheer from the lads and give them heart.

Fitzhugh watched as the *Indomptable* crushed a riverside warehouse and splashed into the Ohio River. It was only thirty feet deep at that time of year. So the water barely came up to the top of the churning wheels, as hot steam shot out of the warship's relief valves, and her whistle shrieked like a banshee. But the French ship was within range by that time, and a reedy cheer went up as shells struck the *Indomptable's* superstructure. A flash of yellow-orange light marked each hit.

But the French ship had been designed to take such punishment. So when the puffs of black smoke blew away, and the cruiser fired her guns, it was as if the gates of hell had opened to take the British in. Fitzhugh disappeared in a gout of flame as a five-inch shell landed on his position. Whatever remained of his body was buried by the half ton of dirt that fell out of the sky.

Admiral Gaudet stood with his feet planted wide apart and took pride in his ability to remain upright without taking hold of the rail in front of him as the British soldiers fortunate enough to survive the *Indomptable's* initial salvos poured up out of their hiding places with flags waving. Bugles sounded, and their Scottish pipers played *Bonnie Dundee* as they marched forward to meet the French.

And it was then, as the *Indomptable* lurched up out of the river and her guns were pointed at the sky, that Gaudet felt an emptiness at the pit of his stomach. Because mighty though the land cruiser was in every other regard, only a thin layer of steel protected the bottom of her hull. A compromise necessitated by the need to armor the rest of the ship, carry more than a hundred tons of coal, and still make good time over often difficult terrain.

But the moment of uncertainty was soon over as the bow dipped, a British destroyer appeared up ahead, and the *Indomptable's* main battery fired. There was a bright flash of light as the enemy land ship exploded and jagged pieces of metal were hurled in all directions.

The recoil produced by the *Indomptable's* five-inch gun turret sent it back along its rails to a pair of stops. At that point a steam-powered thruster pushed the battery forward again. Seconds later, having ejected the hot casings from the breech loaders, the battery was ready to fire again.

Except that there weren't very many targets worthy of the cruiser's mighty guns, since with the exception of a few elderly ships like the one that had just been destroyed, most of the British land navy was hundreds of miles to the west responding to an attack on the city of Louisville—a feint conceived by Napoleon himself as a way to draw the British fleet away from the *real* objective. And that was the coal-rich colonies to the south.

Enemy sharpshooters had spotted the admiral's uniform by then. Bullets pinged the metal all around Gaudet as an aide suggested that he leave the bridge. But, with the exception of his daughter's birth, this was the finest day of the officer's life. And he wasn't about to miss the horrible beauty of the moment as thousands of British soldiers swarmed up out of their trenches and rushed forward. The swivels mounted to port and starboard cut them down, as did the multi-barreled Picard guns, which were generally credited for Napoleon's victory at Waterloo.

But the battle wasn't entirely one-sided. The land cruiser continued to take hit after hit from enemy artillery pieces and the three-inch guns eventually fell silent. But there was no stopping the cruiser as its wheels turned red clad troops into mush, the *Indomptable's* steam whistle shrieked defiance, and Gaudet savored the taste of victory. He could see the future from the bridge on which he stood, and it was undeniably French.

Fort Cumberland, Kentucky

The so-called "gap" in the Cumberland Mountains was twelve miles wide. But the only way vehicles could pass through it was via the narrow dirt road that led into the colonies of Tennessee and Virginia. Fort Cumberland had been constructed to prevent rebellious colonists from making use of the pass during the uprising of 1776.

Later, after General Washington and his coconspirators had been caught and hanged, the fort was used as a base for two companies of his majesty's Frontier Guards. Their mission, when not taking part in endless drills, was to chase Shawnee Indians and collect taxes on the freight that passed through the gap.

As Lieutenant Nathan Landry left the bachelor officer's quarters and made his way toward the more substantial headquarters building, there was a tremendous amount of activity and noise all around him. Steampowered tractors puffed furiously as drivers maneuvered the machines into position, chains rattled as trailers were hooked on, and orders flew as the process of loading began. It was all part of the last minute preparations for a journey that would take the 17th Light Dragoons and most of their battalion north and west to Louisville where a great battle was about to be fought.

Landry, who had already been detailed to remain behind, would have gladly traded places with any of the Dragoons. Unfortunately, it was his lot to stay and work on the fortifications along both sides of the road that wound through the Cumberland Gap. The problem being that he was supposed to remove twelve functional, if somewhat elderly nine-pound guns, and replace them with sixteen of the new Lawson steam cannons.

And Landry suspected that it was his objections to the newly arrived weapons that explained why a lowly Engineering Lieutenant had been ordered to report to Lieutenant Colonel Weyth Wilson. A prospect sufficient to cause even the most experienced junior officer a certain amount of concern . . . never mind one fresh from England.

There was one bright spot along the way, however.

And that came as Landry passed the neat two-story structure in which Lieutenant Colonel Wilson and his family lived. Because there, hanging a quilt out to dry, was Sarah Wilson, the battalion commander's daughter.

She had long brown hair, a heart-shaped face, and green eyes that seemed to dance with merriment every time the two of them came into contact, as if she could see to the very heart of him, and found his boyish infatuation to be vastly amusing.

So when Sarah saw Landry, and waved to him as he passed by, the resulting flush of pleasure was so intense he was still in the grips of it as he entered the low-ceilinged headquarters building. Once inside, Landry removed his bicorn hat and presented himself to the fortress-like desk where a Staff Sergeant named Hopkins represented the last line of defense between the Colonel and any fool who sought to see him without an appointment.

But Landry was expected. So after consulting an enormous pocketwatch, Hopkins rose and made his way over to the metal-strapped oak door. It was partway open. Three sharp raps produced the expected response. "Yes?"

"Lieutenant Landry, sir."

"Show him in. And Hopkins . . ."

"Sir?"

"Have one of the men collect my field chest. And tell him to make sure it gets loaded on the first wagon. The bugger will be sorry if he doesn't."

"Sir!" And with that Hopkins left Landry to find his own way into the lion's den.

With his hat held in the crook of his left arm, Landry took three paces forward and came to attention. "Lieutenant Landry, reporting as ordered, sir."

Thanks to his family's wealth, Wilson had been able to purchase a lieutenant's commission. Since then he had risen to the ranks of Captain, Major, and Lieutenant Colonel largely on the basis of competency. Although the fact that his father was a general had been helpful as well.

In keeping with Wilson's background, Landry knew that he looked down on graduates of the Royal Military Academy at Woolrich as "not quite gentlemen." Which meant that any fantasies that Landry might harbor regarding Sarah Wilson were just that. Fantasies.

As if to reinforce that perception, Landry wasn't invited to sit down in spite of the fact that two guest chairs were available. Wilson cleared his throat. His eyes were like chips of Kentucky coal. They stared out from under a pair of heavy brows. "The 17th will depart in two hours," he began. "So I'll keep this brief."

Having separated a sheet of paper out from all the others on his desktop, Wilson held it up for Landry to see. "Please explain why, having taken delivery on sixteen of the new Lawford steam cannons, you saw fit to send me *this* report? Which, if I'm not mistaken, recommends that we continue to use the nine pounders already in place. Weapons which you, a member of the Royal Engineers, know to be twenty years old."

Landry swallowed nervously. "We tested three of the Lawfords, sir. And the new guns fell well short of the performance parameters we had been told to expect. Even under optimal conditions the Lawfords weren't able to propel standard shells beyond a distance of five hundred feet. A range which I think you'll agree is inadequate. The problem may be in vaporizing water quickly enough to achieve the desired result. Whatever the reason, it's my opinion that they are unreliable."

Landry watched with a growing sense of alarm as Wilson's already choleric face took on the color of the bright red jacket he wore. "First *you*, a mere Lieutenant, have the temerity to tell me that all of the experts at the Lawford Arms factory are wrong.

"Then, using your supernatural ability to read minds, you presume to know what I think! Well, here's what I *really* think Lieutenant . . . I think your tests are flawed.

And more than that, I think that when Captain Morris arrives to take command of the engineering company he will figure out where you went wrong and put it right. In the meantime, you will install the steam cannons and do so in a timely manner. Do I make myself clear?"

Landry felt a nearly overwhelming mix of resentment, shame, and embarrassment. He knew his face was flushed, and it was all he could do to keep his hands from shaking. "Sir, yes sir."

"Good. Dismissed."

Near Fort Cumberland, Kentucky

It was a fine evening and Lieutenant Landry was in a good mood as his horse carried him down the dirt road toward the town of Middlesboro. Major Monfort's birthday party had been planned months earlier, long before Lieutenant Colonel Wilson and the 17th had left for Louisville, and Mrs. Monfort was determined to see it through, even if the guest list was a bit thin without the usual military contingent.

But her husband's militia officers would be present, as would the local gentry, all of whom were looking forward to the annual event. Because even though Monfort was the local magistrate, and therefore "the King's man," he was very popular and being invited to his birthday party was a sure sign of one's social standing. Except for junior officers like Landry that is, who were invited as a matter of courtesy.

But Landry was glad to be included regardless of the reason, because Sarah Wilson was almost certain to be there, and since her father was gone he might even have an opportunity to speak with her. Or, if he could muster the nerve to dance with her, although his skills in that arena were somewhat limited and he feared making a fool of himself.

The Monfort house was a large two story structure, with a pleasantly curved drive and white columns out front. Every window was ablaze with light, and Landry could hear the faint strains of a waltz, and an occasional burst of laughter, as he brought his horse to a halt just behind a handsome looking carriage.

A groom was there to take the reins, and Landry thanked him before following a well dressed couple up a wide set of stairs to the point where Mrs. Monfort was waiting to greet her guests. Her hair was piled high on her head, and she had a pretty if somewhat full face. Her beautiful high-waisted gown was from New York, if not all the way from London, and glittered in the lamplight.

Warm greetings were exchanged with the couple, Mrs. Monfort laughed in response to some sort of joke, and then it was Landry's turn. He removed his hat, took a step forward, and bowed. "It's a pleasure to meet you Madam Monfort. My name is Lieutenant Landry. Thank you for inviting me to your husband's birthday party."

"You are most welcome, Lieutenant," Mrs. Monfort replied. "It's nice to know that at least one of the King's officers was left behind to protect us."

"I shall do my best," Landry replied solemnly. "Although I believe it might be advisable for Major Monfort to guard his wife at all times."

Mrs. Monfort's unrestrained laugh was a full throated affair reminiscent of her rural upbringing. "You are an impudent and thoroughly amusing young man. Fortunately, I have no daughter or I would fear for her safety. Henry will show you the way."

Landry bowed and followed a brightly liveried servant into the large, already crowded ballroom. It was painted white and at least a dozen well framed mirrors were being used to amplify the light from dozens of candles. As the Monfort's richly clad major domo announced his name and rank Landry caught a glimpse of his own reflection.

He had brown hair, what his mother referred to as "a serious face," and a rail thin body. *Too* thin in his opinion, which was why he'd never been known for feats of strength as a boy, or been able to distinguish himself at sports within the highly competitive ranks of the military academy.

Then he was in the crowd where he was greeted by the few people he knew, and introduced to dozens more, while he scanned the room for Sarah. Then he spotted her. She and a couple of other young women were standing in a corner talking to a young man who, judging by his clothing and languid demeanor, was something of a dandy.

Landry felt an unreasonable flush of jealousy as a florid-faced farmer lectured him on the finer points of hog breeding. But then, as the young man was called away by a well dressed woman who might have been his mother, Landry saw his chance. "Excuse me, sir," he said to the farmer. "But I have a message for Miss Wilson and it's somewhat urgent. Perhaps we can continue this conversation at a later time."

It was a lie of course, but the farmer was willing to accept it, as Landry made his way over to where Sarah stood and bowed formally. "Miss Wilson. . . . This *is* a pleasure."

Sarah smiled as their eyes met. "*Really,* Lieutenant Landry? And why is that?"

The young women to either side of her tittered. Landry felt the blood rush to his face as he struggled to find a suitable response, and might have been forced to retreat in disarray, had it not been for the voice that called his name. "Lieutenant Landry? I have an urgent message for you, sir."

Landry turned to find that the Monfort's portly major domo was waiting for him. "There's a soldier outside, sir," the servant said. "A Corporal Lewis. He has a message for you."

Landry nodded. "Thank you. Please tell the corporal that I'll be there in a moment."

Then, turning back to Sarah, he nodded formally. "It is always a pleasure to encounter a young woman who is both intelligent and charming. And, if you will permit me to say so, very beautiful. Please convey my best wishes to your mother. Good evening."

Eyes grew wider as the young women around Sarah looked at each other. But there was no laughter as the young man with the serious face left the muggy ballroom for the cooler air outside.

Corporal Lewis was one of Landry's men and came to attention as the officer appeared. He had the leathery face of a professional soldier. "Sorry to bother you, sir. Especially what with the party and all. But Sarn't Major Crowley said to come fetch you. It seems a French land cruiser broke through our lines up north and is headed this way."

Landry frowned. "That's bad news. Has the Captain been notified?"

A middle-aged supply officer named Timothy Samms had been left in command of Fort Cumberland—which meant the situation was his responsibility. Lewis was clearly uncomfortable. His voice dropped an octave. "Captain Samms is indisposed at the moment, sir. If you take my meaning."

Landry knew what Lewis was referring to. Everybody did. Samms was an alcoholic. Or something very close to one. And apparently on a binge. If he was incapacitated, that put Landry in charge.

"Right then," he responded. "See if you can round up my horse. In the meantime I'll have a quick word with Major Monfort. If the land cruiser makes it this far south we'll need help from the militia."

Lewis said, "Yes, sir," and disappeared into the gloom. Landry reentered the house, went in search of Monfort, and having found the Major spent the better part of ten minutes with him. Landry came away with assurances that the local militia would be activated at first light, a process that would take at least a day since the company's men were spread all over the surrounding countryside.

There was some comfort in having Monfort's support. But as Landry's horse carried him back to the fort and the unaccustomed responsibilities that awaited him there, his thoughts were focused on the Lawford steam cannons, and how inadequate they would be against a French land cruiser. But to leave the existing nine pounders in place would be to ignore a direct order with predictably dire consequences.

Landry found himself wishing that Colonel Wilson had never left, that Captain Samms was sober, or that he had taken his mother's advice and entered the clergy. But as the lights of the fort appeared, and a dimly seen sentry offered a hoarse challenge, Landry was forced to face the truth—he was on his own.

The meeting in Colonel Wilson's office was a sober affair as Company Sergeant Major Crowley handed the recently received telegraph slip to Landry, who read the message aloud. "To all British forces: The French heavy cruiser *Indomptable* and her escorts crossed Ohio River sixteen June and are headed south. Repeated attempts to block the raiders have failed. Stop at all costs. Signed, General Benedict Arnold."

Landry looked up at the faces around him, all of which belonged to senior non-commissioned officers. The prospect of a southbound battle group was bad enough. But the *Indomptable?* That was an unmitigated disaster. Landry, like every other officer who had read about the behemoth in the *Military Gazette*, knew her to be the most powerful ship in North America. It was said that the British government had been working to produce three vessels of comparable size when Boston had been overrun and all of the partially completed cruisers had fallen into French hands.

So the simple fact was that if the *Indomptable* was on the way to take and secure the Cumberland Gap, then there was nothing to stop them barring the miraculous appearance of Admiral Haines and his land fleet, which Landry knew was extremely unlikely to say the least. But an attempt had to be made, so like it or not he would install the steam cannons to either side of the gap and attempt to slow the Frenchies down. Work would begin right then—and continue day and night until completed.

Such were Landry's thoughts when the door banged open and a disheveled Captain Samms lurched into the room. He was a big man with ginger colored hair, a spray of freckles across his nose, and pouty lips. "Landry?" the officer demanded, and he waved a bottle. "There you are! Pretending to be a colonel. Damn your presumption, sir. I am in command here and you will answer to me."

So saying, Samms slammed the bottle down onto the desk with such force that the cork shot two feet into the air before falling to the floor. As Landry watched the stopper a wild idea entered his mind, took root, and immediately began to grow.

Meanwhile Samms, who mistook the moment of silence as an act of insubordination, frowned sternly. "Speak, damn you! Or be arrested."

Company Sergeant Major Crowley was six-two and weighed two-hundred and fifty pounds. So when his pistol butt struck the back of Samms' head, the blow packed plenty of authority. The supply officer went down as if pole axed. "Sorry, sir," Crowley said with a straight face. "It appears that the Captain tripped and fell."

Landry smiled grimly. "So it would seem. Please detail a couple of men to carry Mr. Samms to his quarters. And have the medical orderly look at him. Once that effort is complete rouse every man we have. Engineers, clerks, and cooks. In short anyone who can swing a pick or handle a shovel. We have defenses to construct and damned little time in which to get the job done."

Crowley and the other noncoms came to attention. The word "Sir!" was said in unison. And with that the work began. The *Indomptable* might come. And she might win. But if the French wanted to pass through the Cumberland Gap they would pay a price.

North of the Cumberland Gap

It was nighttime, and despite of the fact that the *Indomptable* and her sole surviving escort were at rest, Admiral Gaudet felt as if the land cruiser was still in motion. He was standing in front of the brightly lit plot table located just aft of the command bridge staring at a map of Kentucky as a plate of untouched food cooled on top of New England. He, the ship, and the ship's company had been underway for six days, and during that time they had survived a half dozen encounters with British forces. That included an attack by three steam powered dirigibles which disabled all but one of the *Indomptable's* escorts and inflicted damage on the cruiser as well.

. Now the French force was still fifteen miles short of its goal. And truth be told, they would be lucky to reach the Cumberland Gap, since the *Indomptable* was nearly out of coal. *But,* Gaudet told himself, *if we can reach the gap and hold it for a week all will be well. The area is rich in coal and the supply train is already on its way south from Ohio.* "All I have to do is take Fort Cumberland and hold it."

The last was said out loud and caused the navigation officer to look up from his log book. "Sir?"

"Nothing," Gaudet replied, as he lifted the plate of cold food off the table. "Nothing at all."

Landry was asleep when the French arrived. For days he, his men, and a small army of civilians had labored around the clock to strengthen the gap's defenses. And now, as Company Sergeant Major Crowley shook Landry awake, the officer discovered that he was laying on the ground with a quilt over him—not a wool army blanket but a beautiful coverlet made from scraps of cloth all sewn together to make a beautiful pattern. "Where did this come from?" Landry wondered as he sat up.

Crowley had an enormous mustache. It twitched as if a smile might be hidden beneath it somewhere. "Miss Wilson, sir."

The morning air was cool, but Landry felt unexpectedly warm as Crowley took charge of the quilt, and began to fold it. While Landry lay sprawled in the dirt Sarah had come to visit the troops. Presumably with her mother as part of the effort to keep everyone fed.

But any further thoughts in that direction were forestalled as Crowley placed the neatly folded quilt on top of a crate. "The French are coming, sir." The words were said without inflection, as if such attacks were a routine part of each day.

Landry stood. He was in need of a shave, his uniform was filthy, and his boots were muddy. Hardly the way an officer was supposed to look. But there was nothing he could do about it. "How long?"

"Half an hour, sir. Forty-five minutes at most."

"I will make the rounds and return here," Landry announced. "And Sergeant . . ."

"Sir?"

"Please pass the word. No matter what happens, our troops have done a remarkable job. I want them to know that."

Crowley watched the engineering officer walk away. *He'll do*, the noncom thought to himself. *Yes, he will. If he survives.*

The new defenses were layered on old, which meant that while Landry had obeyed Colonel Wilson's order to install the steam cannons, the nine pounders remained right where they had been, positioned to fire on the road where it passed between two rocky hillsides. It was a passageway that the French land cruiser would be forced to negotiate since it was far too large to circumvent the pass as cavalry or foot soldiers might.

An early morning mist cloaked the hillsides as Landry went from gun to gun. He paused every now and then to have a word with an anxious militiaman or to ensure that the stops that would prevent opposing batteries from firing on each other were firmly in place. Then it was on to visit the concealed boilers from which steam would flow to the steam cannons via a carefully laid system of pipes.

Finally, satisfied that all of his forces were ready, Landry returned to the rocky ledge where a venerable nine pounder and its crew of nervous farm boys waited to do battle with the land cruiser *Indomptable*. One of them mouthed a prayer as a whistle shrieked.

Landry knew that the device wasn't mounted on a destroyer but on the massive warship herself. Because if one of the *Indomptable's* escorts were to be destroyed in the narrow passageway, the larger ship wouldn't be able to pass through.

There was a momentary wink of light as the *Indomptable's* five-inch guns spoke, followed by twin explosions as the opposite embankment took two hits. "Hold your fire!" Landry bellowed through his speaking trumpet.

It was impossible to know how much information French spies had been able to gather regarding the gap's defenses. But if they knew about the muzzle loading nine pounders, then they knew roughly how long it would take to reload them, and would attempt to time their passage accordingly. So one of the things Landry feared most was the possibility that his most reliable weapons would be empty when he needed them.

Metal clanked, steam hissed, and there was another loud boom as the *Indomptable's* guns fired again. The French drew blood as a gun on the west side of the road took a direct hit and vanished in a flash of light.

At least half a dozen British lives had been lost without a single shot being fired in return. Landry gritted his teeth as the land cruiser pushed deeper into what he hoped would be the kill zone. And as the colossal vessel drew closer, Landry was astounded to discover that her stacks towered above him. But there was no time to give the matter additional thought as he shouted, "Fire!"

Rolling broadsides were fired from opposite hillsides and the results were devastating. The nine pounders might be old, but they were lethal, especially at such close quarters. The *Indomptable* shook like a thing possessed as pieces of the superstructure flew off, the navigation bridge was wiped away, and a secondary weapons platform was reduced to a mass of twisted metal.

Landry was exultant at first, but that was before the *Indomptable's* guns fired again, and two neighboring gun batteries were destroyed. The surviving guns were being reloaded, but the militiamen were slow. And Landry knew he wouldn't be able to rely on them for more than a ragged volley or two. Like it or not the time had come to employ the Lawford steam cannons.

Major Monfort appeared at that point. He was a genial man with a moonlike face, a bloody bandage wrapped around his head, and a belly that hung out over a wide leather belt. Though senior to Landry in terms of rank, Monfort had chosen to play a supportive role, which he had done to perfection. Since without him and his militiamen, it would have been impossible to mount any defense whatsoever. Monfort had to shout to make himself heard over the relentless rhythm of the *Indomptable's* running gear, the snake-like hiss of steam, and the persistent rattle of gunfire. "So lad, I came to see the grand finale. You won't disappoint me will you?"

Then Monfort was gone as bullets from a Picard gun tore him apart and Landry was forced to dive for the ground. Banked earth protected him from the incoming hail of bullets, but steam sprayed the air as the control for the steam cannons was destroyed and half of the nine pounder's crew was killed.

Landry swore as he rolled over, stood, and began to

scuttle south along the trail that led to the next gun battery. There was a back-up control there, but because the *Indomptable* was still in motion it would be only a matter of seconds before she cleared the point where the Lawfords could fire on her, and she would be free to attack the fort.

Landry stumbled, fell, and made it back to his feet again. Bullets pinged, whined, and buzzed all around him as he struggled forward. "Fire the Lawfords!" he shouted. "Fire them now!"

Landry felt a momentary sense of hope as he saw a militiaman step over to the row of levers and prepare to pull them. Doing so would release steam to the cannons, enabling them to fire. And even though they were worthless beyond five-hundred feet it was the engineer's hope that they could cause a significant amount of damage close in.

But as he staggered forward a bullet hit the militiaman's chest and threw him back into the embankment. Then Landry was in the gun emplacement, his hands on the levers, as the *Indomptable* caught up with him. The front half of the warship had cleared the kill zone by that time, and it was only a matter of moments before the entire vessel would be safe.

Time seemed to slow as a French officer turned to look at Landry from no more than fifty-feet away. He was standing on a bridge not far from the steel enclosed wheelhouse. An admiral? Yes, judging from all of the gold lace. And it was then, as their eyes made contact, that Landry began to pull the levers.

Steam surged through the network of buried pipes, entered firing chambers, and sent explosive shells straight up out of holes hidden *under* the surface of the road. They went straight up. Half the shells shot into the air, but the rest penetrated the hull, where they went off and triggered secondary explosions.

Landry saw the admiral stumble and reach out to steady himself as the main magazine went up. The resulting shock wave knocked Landry off his feet, destroyed a British gun position on the other side of the road, and sent a column of black smoke roiling into the sky. That was followed by a rockslide that buried part of the wreckage, thereby ensuring that nothing would pass through the gap for weeks to come. The price had been high. *Very* high. But a battle had been won.

Colonel Wilson and the 17th Dragoons returned two days after what was already being called the Battle of Cumberland Gap. They were dusty, tired, and frustrated, having been ordered to return to the fort without seeing a French soldier much less firing at one. Because shortly after the *Indomptable's* widely heralded defeat, the French army's diversionary force had fled north. And making the situation that much worse was the fact that the *real* battle had been fought in their absence.

So having been summoned to Wilson's office, Landry felt a sense of trepidation as an unsmiling Sergeant Hopkins rose to greet him. "The Colonel is in his office, sir. He is expecting you."

Landry entered, came to attention, and announced himself.

Wilson was on his feet, looking out through the window adjacent to his desk. He was silent for a moment before turning to face his visitor. The expression on his face was grim. "I read your report. We'll come back to that in a moment. First there is the matter of Captain Samms to discuss. He claims that one of your men attacked him. Furthermore, he claims that you were present and did nothing to stop the assault. Is that true?"

Landry felt a sudden emptiness at the pit of his stomach. Should he come clean? That would be the right thing to do. But the penalty for striking an officer was very severe. And if Landry confessed, Crowley would not only be broken back to private but sent to prison. All for doing the right thing. Landry kept his face professionally blank. "No, sir. Captain Samms was inebriated, fell down, and hit his head in the process."

Wilson was silent for a moment. Then he nodded soberly. "That matches what Sergeant Major Crowley said. I don't believe a word of it of course—but I'm glad to see that you have your stories straight. But only because Samms is a disgrace to the uniform. I trust you won't make a habit out of attacking superior officers. I won't stand for it.

"Now, as for your report. Using the Lawfords to fire upward into the *Indomptable's* belly was quite unorthodox. How did you know her armor would be thinner there?"

Landry swallowed. "I didn't, sir. Not for sure. But it made sense from an engineering perspective."

Wilson's eyes narrowed. "Perhaps. But you took a great deal upon yourself, Lieutenant Landry. Still, a victory is a victory, and we could use one right about now. General Arnold will join us tomorrow, and I daresay he will take advantage of the opportunity to hang a medal on you. Try not to get a swelled head."

Landry kept his eyes straight ahead. "Yes, sir. I mean no, sir."

"And that brings us to the road," Wilson said. "Leave things exactly as they are until the general and his men have had a chance to inspect the wreckage. Then clear it away and get the job done quickly. Traffic is starting to back up in both directions."

"Sir, yes sir."

"Good. That will be all."

Landry did an about face and was nearly to the door when Wilson stopped him. "And Lieutenant . . ."

Landry turned. "Sir?"

"I was ordered to invite you to dinner this evening. Try not to make a fool of yourself."

Landry felt a surge of joy. *Ordered?* By Sarah perhaps? Yes, he thought so. "Thank you, sir. I would be honored."

"Yes," Wilson agreed as the slightest of smiles appeared on his face. "I should think so."

Portrait of a Lady in a Monocle

Jody Lynn Nye

Jody Lynn Nye lists her main career activity as "spoiling cats." She lives northwest of Chicago with two of the above and her husband, author and packager Bill Fawcett. She has published more than thirty-five books, including six contemporary fantasies, four SF novels, four novels in collaboration with Anne McCaffrey, including *The Ship Who Won*; edited a humorous anthology about mothers, *Don't Forget Your Spacesuit, Dear!*; and written more than a hundred short stories. Her latest books are *A Forthcoming Wizard*, and *Myth-Fortunes*, co-written with Robert Asprin.

The portly man in the charcoal-gray pinstriped suit settled back in the heavy maroon leather armchair in the corner of the library and smiled at the tall, almost gangly young woman in the straight, ladder-backed chair opposite him. He took the pipe—unlit out of courtesy—from his mouth and gestured at her with the carved bowl. "You are so easy to confide in, Miss Galferd. Especially in light of your own most recent . . . misfortune."

Penelope tried not to crumple the plum-colored leather gloves she clutched in her lap. Everyone there in the Chicago Academy of Science, possibly the whole city, had heard about the end of her engagement to Albin Beauregard. To cover her discomfort, she fixed her gaze upon the stout gentleman, making certain to focus the elaborate bronze and steel contraption in her eye on his face. "It doesn't give me any pleasure to speak of it, Professor Finbury. I'd rather hear about your work."

"It's all highly confidential, of course," Finbury said, sitting bolt upright in indignation. Penelope was undeterred. She held his gaze, knowing the spinning crystal lens was doing its work. As she knew he would, he began to relax. He resumed his slouch, casually tucking a thumb into his watch pocket. "Well, a lady like you wouldn't tell a soul, would you?"

Penelope lifted her long, capable hands in the air in a delicate pose, then let them fall as if they were too weak and helpless to keep aloft. It was a pretense, of course, but one that the gentlemen of the club were more prone to accept than her competence. "Whom would I tell?"

Finbury regarded her with paternal approval. "Quite right, I guess, ma'am. Well, I've been working on a design for a portable icebox. I got quite a scare after that Columbian Exhibition a couple years ago. Everything I looked at seemed to be derived from my own work! I began to suspect even my own lab assistants of stealing my designs. Then I started talking to my fellow scientists . . ."

". . . *Our* fellow scientists," Penelope said. Finbury smiled indulgently at her. Since she was on probation from the club of which he was president, her contact with the rest of the members was limited, and few outside would understand the details.

"Sure, my dear, if you like, *our* fellows—and found that every single one of them felt the same way I did. Seems a lot of us have been working on parallel tracks this whole time, and never knew it. Well, we had some good conversations after that, I can tell you! It's the synergy we have together as scientists that is going to create the modern age, my dear, synergy and cooperation."

"Do you really believe that, professor?" Penelope asked, her heart fluttering with agreement.

He chuckled. "Oh, sure, I do, so long as I get my piece first. You see, once I figured out that nobody had an inkling as to the tack I was taking regarding refrigeration, I set to work like I was on fire. I started out with nitrogen derivatives. . . ." He expanded on his theory and the many trials he had made before finding the solution to the problem.

Though Penelope kept nodding and smiling, she had ceased listening closely. Her thoughts were elsewhere. She would not lose his ideas, though. Thanks to a series of inventions of her own—for all Finbury's dismissal of her ambition and skill—his voice was traveling through the air by means of a wireless device in her elaborate brooch, to the nearest electrical outlet, and thence through the new copper cables strung over the city of Chicago to her home not three miles from that spot, to a miniature gramophone with a wax cylinder that her maid had set going at an appointed hour. The brooch was powered by friction generated by the slightly elasticated strings of her corset beneath her shirtwaist that drove an equally miniaturized dynamo hidden in her floor-length corduroy skirt just above her knee. She could feel the small engine thrumming as her breathing increased its tempo. Finbury's confidences to her would be stored securely, until she saw fit to deal with them.

"But Beauregard is the one we're all envying this week." The mention of Albin's name brought Penelope out of her reverie. "You know of your former beloved's success of one of his inventions, Miss Galferd," Finbury said. "It's the talk of the town how the Pinkertons have just taken it to their bosom."

"Yes, I do," Penelope said, grimly. "But it was my invention, Professor, not his, that has made for all the noise. He stole it. I told him about it in confidence, and he copied it."

Finbury chuckled a little uncomfortably. "Yes, we've

all heard you say so before, my dear. But Beauregard is a talented scientist. Couldn't it be a case just like my fellow heating-and-cooling investigators? I'm sure it was just a simple mistake. You can't blame the boy for taking a parallel tack and making a success of it."

Penelope fumed. He had come as close as anyone in the club had to calling her a liar to her face. It was bad enough that her complaint had caused her membership to be called into question for accusations of plagiarism, but the truth was the truth! She could not restrain herself.

"It was not parallel, it was exact! It is a twin-pronged graduated electrostatic probe that separates elements within a solution into fine layers. Even small amounts of a substance can be detected by its atomic weight!"

"Aren't you a clever girl to know all those details," Finbury said, admiringly.

Penelope did her best not to shriek. "I discovered them! I made a prototype, and I made the mistake of telling him about it. He stole my notes and my prototype. I foolishly had not signed the device anywhere, or sent in a patent application, trusting that my own laboratory was sacrosanct. Obviously it was not, to one I thought of as my nearest and dearest."

Finbury regarded her wisely. "Well, true entrepreneurs don't give away the store, my dear, like I told you. We patent our inventions long before we ever reveal them to anyone who doesn't work for us. Otherwise, well, that kind of accusation leads to slander." It was a warning. Another warning.

"I am not slandering him, professor," Penelope said, wearily. The wax cylinder would, thank God, have run out by now. Finbury was the last of the interviews she had sought. She could go home. "I am telling God's honest truth."

"Maybe there's more than one kind of truth," Finbury said, not unkindly. "I'd better get home before one of those truths is that Mrs. Finbury skins me alive because

I'm late for supper. I'm curious, of course, if I may ask without intruding, about your monocle. What's it do?"

Penelope touched the jeweled prosthetic. "It strengthens my weak eye, at the same time giving me a different perspective of the people I observe. My own invention."

Finbury's eyebrows went up. "Interesting. Might I try it?"

"It would be my pleasure," Penelope said, rising. "Come to my laboratory tomorrow, if you like, perhaps about eleven? I have to uninstall it from my own eye socket, but I am sure we can effect the transfer without . . . too much pain or loss of vision."

Finbury gulped. Penelope was amused to see his rubicund complexion pale a little. "Er, no, thank you, then. I'll take a pass. Will we see you at the reception tonight, then?"

"Try and keep me away," Penelope promised. In spite of all the trouble, her invitation had not been rescinded. She was grateful to have him acknowledge it.

Finbury took his top hat off the peg beside the door of the library. "Er, Miss Galferd, you did not ask me what I thought you would."

Penelope gave him a bright smile and set the crystal in her eyepiece twirling. "And what is that, professor?"

"Well, for my vote, Miss Galferd. To reinstate you as a member in this society. Seeing as how you didn't have an invention to submit to the committee this year by May the first. Apart from the one you claim Mr. Beauregard, er . . ." He found himself without a polite verb that would not offend her. She smiled placidly.

"I want you to make the judgment on your own as to whether or not I have done work worthy of this society, professor," she said. She turned up the intensity of her eyepiece and focused upon him deeply. After a moment, she offered her hand to him. "Thank you for a most enlightening conversation. I got more out of it than you can ever believe."

He shook it and bowed over her hand with a puzzled expression. "What conversation, Miss Galferd?"

Penelope went out to find a streetcar going west along Grand Avenue. The streets of Chicago were better lit than they had been before the grand Exposition, but no less crowded. The steam-powered car noted the additional weight on an overhead abacus as she and two other passengers stepped on board, engaged a stronger gear to its engine, and shot an ear-piercing blast of white smoke from its pumpkin-shaped smokestack as it trundled toward the setting sun. Penelope wedged herself into a tight corner of a wooden bench beside two elderly women returning from shopping. The nearer woman's reticule kept poking against the dynamo on her leg. She would be bruised later, but that was purely a physical sensation.

What really hurt her was the assumptions made by the senior members of the Chicago Academy was that she had no workable scientific ideas of her own, and that her complaint that she had been robbed by her former fiancé was a discredit to her more than to him. She was seen as jealous and petty, not to mention delusional. How could a girl of twenty-two, though she had a college degree, have conquered a complex electrical-chemical device when a gentleman of twenty-six had not? Society was changing so fast, what with the new technology coming along with advances every day, every hour it seemed, but some things were resistant to change, such as the attitudes of men. They were far more likely to believe Albin than her. He had slandered her openly, and they accepted his statements.

Justice, indeed! Penelope thought indignantly. Wasn't this the United States of America? Still, science clubs sprang up all over town during Penelope's youth, to rejoice in the new knowledge, not so different from the days of the Renaissance, but over time almost all the girls dropped out. They had good ideas, but lacked the male drive to bring them to fruition, if not to market. Ironically, it had been her former beloved who had pushed Penelope to take her first invention to manufacturer after manufacturer until someone got past the fact it was a person in a shirtwaist and not a vest presenting it. It had done well enough for her to buy Papa that handsome carriage he had so coveted, plus furnishing her laboratory with the latest gizmos. But since then, things had not gone so well. In two years, Albin had sold few of his own inventions. Those had brought in good money, but he craved the headlines, like Mr. Edison and Mr. Tesla were obtaining. So, when her detection device was ready, she had gone to the patent office with it, only to find he had beaten her there by two days with his own rendered drawings of her work. Naturally, the engagement was over, but the humiliation had not ended there. He had gotten his headlines, all right, when he sold the rights to the Pinkertons. They used it to solve a major murder by proving a man's wife had poisoned him with antimony. It was extracted from his digestive juices in such small quantities that the doctor had overlooked it, but a similar investigation of his longer-lived tissues such as hair and nails had proved it was not consumed over years as his wife had claimed, but in a recent high concentration. The widow was in prison, and Albin was in clover. To add further humiliation, Albin was to receive a medal from the governor.

Everyone believed Albin, not her. She was going, though. No one could say she was a coward. Her reputation was at stake. She wanted justice, and she would have it.

The next evening she was met just inside the door of the club by a mechanical porter, which resembled a mobile coat rack that sprouted small trays, hooks, and shelves at intervals down its five-foot length. Its designation, No. 31, was etched upon a small plaque. This was one of the original robot servers that had been designed for the club, and one of its most reliable. Upon approaching her, a lens not unlike the device in her eye scanned down her person. A small gramophone about chest height began to spin, and a needle in a stout round cartridge dropped down upon the disk.

"Good evening—click!—Miss Galferd," said the tinny voice that issued from the round speaker at the top of the brass pole. "I will be your attendant for the evening. Click! May I take your hat (click) . . . and cloak (click) . . . and train case (click) . . . and reticule (click) . . . and fan?"

The manner of its speech was labored, but Penelope was accustomed to it. She surrendered her feather-covered bonnet, her plum-colored wool cloak, the small black morocco case and silk wrist bag, revealing her low-cut but not immodest evening dress of pale blue silk. The silver bangles on her wrists went well with the spinning crystal in her eye. "I will keep the fan, if you please." No. 31 hung the outer garments in a cupboard adjacent to the door, but placed the other two objects upon its frame.

"As you please. Click!" A small black lacquer tray extended itself toward her on a jointed bronze arm. It bore two graceful crystal goblets. "Lemonade or champagne?"

Penelope wished for the fortification of the champagne, but decided she needed a clear head. She took the lemonade and entered the anteroom of the lecture hall, No. 31 close behind.

An orchestra of clockwork musicians with bronze skin and riveted tuxedos nodded along to the beat as they blew or strummed or struck their gleaming instruments. The violinist, his brass eyelids formed as if they were shut in ecstasy, stood at the head of the string section, sawing away at his instrument. Members, men in black suits and women in colorful gowns, chatted around it in small groups. By the movement of their hands, Penelope guessed that they were discussing the contents of the glass case in the center of the room. Penelope identified the contents at a glance.

Floating around the room just above the heads of the crowd were miniature airships from which depended trays of canapés. They lowered themselves upon command to allow the attendees to partake. Penelope glanced at the nearest tray. Salmon croquettes. Those would make her feel queasy. Perhaps not.

She looked up. Her eyes were caught by a pair of brilliant blue eyes of a man on the opposite side of the room. Albin. He nodded to her politely, but his lips smirked. Smirked! What an insufferable clod! She cut him dead, turning her head sharply to the right and breaking off her gaze. Out of the corner of her eye, she saw him look disappointed. Did he think that she would rejoice in his success? Far from it. Penelope felt her heart pound. Albin was the handsomest man in the room, with his shining black hair, waxed mustache, and strong jaw. How could such a rotten snake still make her feel giddy?

"No. 31, will you secure for me one of the small receiving rooms?" Penelope asked.

"Of course—click!—Miss Galferd. I believe—click!— meeting room No. 2 is available."

"Go there and make certain. I shall be there directly." Penelope went in search of her first subject.

"Won't you sit down, Professor Finbury?" she asked, as the president of the club entered. In the distance she could hear laughter and music.

Finbury blinked into the darkness. Penelope had arranged the dome-shaded electric lamps so they were shining full on her face. On the round table before her she had arranged a small tableau of equipment. From her dynamo, a rectangular blued-steel box, black cloth-covered leads draped off the table and disappeared underneath the waistband of her gown. Penelope straightened her back firmly. Her cheeks pinked as the dynamo whirred.

"What gives, Miss Galferd?"

"I needed to speak to you about something very important. I would like to put before you two theories."

Finbury glanced at his pocket watch. "Is now the best time? The governor has just arrived, and the presentation will start shortly."

Penelope nodded. "Now is the only time that is appropriate, sir. It won't take long."

"Very well," he sighed, settling into one of the creaky, rolling armchairs. "What are they?"

"The first postulatum is that I am not the inventive idiot that Albin Beauregard has sworn me to be to you and most of the membership. I claim my inventions, sir. The patent officer has met me many times. The second is that an intelligent being can be so overcome by feelings of trust that one says imprudent or rash things, with a subset of this theory that the person receiving the outpouring may or may not be worthy of them."

"Miss Galferd," Finbury began impatiently, "bringing up this old grievance on the very eve of Mr. Beauregard's triumph before his peers is small and petty, not to mention unladylike!" He rose to his feet. "I have to get back."

"In the name of science, then, in the search of truth," Penelope said, feeling desperate. "I would like to demonstrate something for you. Please."

She gestured Finbury to a seat. It took a while for him, but he settled in the chair. Relieved but wary, Penelope wound up the miniature gramophone and set it running.

"... Nobody had an inkling as to the tack I was taking regarding refrigeration, I set to work like I was on fire. I started out with nitrogen. ..."

The voice was thin and distant, but it was unmistakably that of Professor Finbury. He recognized himself at once. He seemed to wake up from a dream or, by the fiery expression in his eyes, a nightmare. He let the small cylinder play out, then confronted Penelope in a rage.

"When did I say all this?"

"This afternoon, to me, in the library of this club."

"I never did! I would never speak so openly of my research! It is top secret!"

"You did, sir. Your voice went into a radio receiver in miniature concealed in my corsage that traveled through the electrical grid of this city to my home and this gramophone. I had put you in a state of calm receptiveness in which you would confide in me."

"Ridiculous! How?"

She touched her eyepiece. "This also is one of my inventions. After the work of Herr Franz Anton Mesmer, I designed it to bestow a state of openness upon the subject, so that he or she would trust me as if I was a person they dearly loved and wished to please."

"Well, it's not working now!" Finbury said. "I am appalled at you! No. 18, will you ask Mr. Deed of the Pinkertons to join us?"

"Of course—click!—sir." The robot server glided toward the door.

"Just one moment, please," Penelope said. "Don't let it go." Finbury frowned at her, but waved a hand.

"Hold up a moment, No. 18."

"Of course, sir."

"Well?" he demanded.

Penelope steeled herself with resolution. "Professor, I asked you for time to prove my theories. The first is that I *have* scientific abilities. I will show you the patent applications I made out regarding the eyepiece and radio receiver, plus the power source that drives them. The second is that one can be appallingly and catastrophically indiscreet in the face of someone whom one loved or trusted. I *made* you trust me. The device is not operational now. I beg you, in the name of science, to be just and fair. I was robbed of my work and my reputation. I need your help."

Finbury pointed at her face. "Take that thing off, if you mean it."

It took some time, a little pain and tears, but Penelope managed to disgorge from her eye the twinkling monocle. He held it on the palm of his hand, regarding it in wonder. He removed a strong lens on a black ribbon from his watch pocket and went over it, turning it in his fingers.

"This is . . . this is marvelous work, my dear," Finbury murmured, tweaking open the small side hatch that housed the crystal. He played with the minute spindle in the casing that allowed it to spin. "And you say it has a mild Mesmeric effect?

"Mild to strong, depending upon the setting. I thought it could be useful to treat patients with mental disorders. I never dreamed that I would have to use it on . . . people of sound minds. But it does work. As you have seen."

"And the power source?"

Blushing, she described the corset and the elasticated strings. "It runs on alternating current, of course, as dear Mr. Tesla suggested."

Finbury looked up at her sideways. "I . . . er, well . . . and so you are suggesting to me that Albin really did steal your device that the Pinkertons used to solve that murder?

Penelope put her hands on his arm in supplication. "More than suggesting, sir! I need your help to prove it. Justice needs to be done, in more than one way."

Finbury tapped the lens to his lips. He fell silent for a long time. "Don't see that honor leaves me any choice. Very well. It's not just me that has to take you at your say so. But I will back you in your suit to regain your reputation. You deserve that, at least."

Penelope felt as if she might burst into tears with relief, but that would not be the act of a scientist, a vindicated scientist—well, almost vindicated. "Thank you."

"You're going to do all the work, not me." He pointed nervously at the gramophone. "But what are you going to do about that?"

Penelope smiled. She slid the oxblood-red cylinder

of his voice from under the miniature needle and held it up. "This is the only proof that exists in all the world of what you said during our interview. I am in your hands." She gave him the cylinder.

"Well, well." He closed his hand on the fragile tube of wax, crushing it into fragments. He gave her a fatherly smile as he dusted his hands together. "We don't need further proof, not between us. No. 18, will you clean that up?"

"Of course, sir!" A black-bristled brush flipped out from the side of the mechanical attendant's frame.

"I have ... recordings of other members of the board," Penelope ventured. "Do you want to destroy them now?"

"Save them. We might need them later." Finbury smiled as he extended a hand to help Penelope to her feet. "Bring all these contraptions," he said. "We're going to go earn that trust you put in me."

Eyes turned curiously toward Penelope and the professor as they appeared in the hall again, followed by their two attendants. Except for her monocle, Penelope's devices were tucked safely away in her train case on the base of No. 31's frame. She shook with nerves at having to confront the entire membership, but to regain her reputation, she would do worse. In fact, she already had. Professor Finbury clearly thought she was there to blackmail him. It just proved what terrible things happened when one combined emotion with pure science. She never would again.

She made her way down into the raked auditorium and slipped in beside Emmaline Armor, of the meat-packing family, who was a keen chemist, and a firm supporter of Penelope's. When many of the members turned their backs on her, Emmaline stood firm. They squeezed one another's hands affectionately. Finbury strode down to the dais and took his place at the podium. Mr. Deed of the Pinkertons sat at his right hand, his federal badge shining on the breast pocket of his nondescript gray suit. At his left hand, Albin sat with his palms on his knees, delighted to be the center of attention. When he met her eyes, he grinned. Penelope blushed with fury. The display cases from the anteroom rolled themselves down the side ramps of the chamber and arrayed themselves at the sides of the stage.

Finbury opened the meeting. He introduced the eight men and women who comprised the rest of the board, sitting in a row behind him with their arms crossed, the governor, and Mr. Deed.

"All of you read the papers," Finbury said, speaking into the amplifier. His voice emerged from six horn-shaped speakers around the large chamber. "So I don't need to tell you the details of the great case that has brought attention to our fine society. Just let me introduce Mr. Reginald Deed of the Pinkerton Agency of Washington, D.C., and he'll tell you all about what he's here for. Mr. Deed!" Finbury sat beside the governor.

The gray-suited man stood up to enthusiastic applause. Penelope joined in, for he was not the author of her woes. He cleared his throat and leaned into the audio receiver.

"Ladies and gentlemen, members of the club, governor, we of the Pinkerton Agency are here tonight to honor Mr. Albin Beauregard for service to this nation. You are all a lot of noted inventors, but it was his device," he gestured to the case at the far right of the stage, which came forward as if to take a bow, "that enabled us to find evidence to convict a heinous murderess. I am so pleased that a citizen scientist of his mind-power and skill. . ."

"Ahem," Finbury said, raising a finger. "Point of order?"

"What?" Deed asked. "What point of order?"

"Well, sir," Finbury said, hooking his thumbs into his pockets and leaning back easily. "I want to make certain that what you believe is true. It never was asked and answered whether this was solely his device, not to the absolute satisfaction of the entire membership. Or was it?"

Miss Armor stood up. "No, it wasn't!"

Albin, his face scarlet, sprang to his feet. "What is this, sir? What call have you to humiliate me in front of the entire membership of this club, not to mention the governor?"

"Well, sir," Finbury said. "I find myself a trifle humiliated. It has come to my attention that there is some question whether you are the full and sole inventor of this chemical separator. Miss Penelope Galferd also makes a claim to it, and I am inclined to credit her claim. She's been surprisingly reserved about it. In her place, I'd be calling you out."

Mr. Deed looked appalled. "Is this true, Mr. Beauregard?"

Albin glared. "Of . . . of course not! Miss Galferd is a fine and charming lady, but as most of you know, she has little skill at the sciences . . ."

"Well, I disagree with you, sir," Finbury interrupted. "In the past hour she has demonstrated to me her inventive genius, and the detector would be lower on the scale than the devices that I just saw. They are enough to support her accusation. I call on you as a scientist and a gentleman to at least share credit."

Albin was furious. "Nonsense. The chemical separator is mine."

Finbury beckoned to her. "Miss Galferd, will you speak up in your own defense?"

Penelope steeled herself. This is not the way that she thought Finbury would defend her. It drew attention to her, and she deplored the spotlight. She had no choice but to rise and throw her shoulders back.

"Yes, Mr. President. I created that device. In fact, Mr. Beauregard did not aid in its discovery at all."

"I am so sorry to disabuse the lady," Albin said smoothly, "but Miss Galferd, for all that she is an enthusiastic member of this society, is just not smart enough to have designed it." Penelope gasped. "I apologize if I insult her, but it is no more than the truth. After all, what have we seen of her presentations to the club in the past? Trifles, built upon the shoulders of giants." He shrugged, as if to suggest two of those shoulders were his own.

Penelope could not contain herself. "You rotten prevaricator! I am every bit your equal."

"Language, Miss Galferd!" exclaimed Mrs. Shanahan, the vice-president. Boos broke out among the crowd. A few men shook her fists at her.

"Prove it!" Albin said, with an infuriating smile on his lips. She knew she could not. His notes were identical to hers, copied word for word. All she had was her statement against his. The faces of the membership as well as the executive committee were stony.

She would have to defend herself before all of these people. How she wished she had not even started out to challenge Albin. She felt tears start to her eyes. She dashed a hand against them. Her knuckles barked against the hunk of steel and bronze in her eye socket.

Her word—against his!

She had proof, if she could get it. It lay buried within the mind of the perpetrator who had betrayed her. Penelope smiled.

"Sir, I will take that challenge. I will prove to you that what I say is true, from the very mouth of the cad on that stage."

"And how can you possibly do that?" Albin demanded. But he looked worried.

Finbury smiled, catching her notion at once. "In the fashion of Herr Mesmer. The device in her eye causes one to fall into a mild trance so she can reach into the mind and exact unwitting truths. She has given me a demonstration. It was most effective."

Albin sprang up, horrified. "I will not participate in such a charade!"

"And why not, Mr. Beauregard?"

He stammered. His mustache seemed to lose some of its crispness. "Well, well, well ... she's just not that good. Those crystals sitting around her lab—they were just toys."

Finbury tilted his head. "Then you have nothing to fear. If you say she is just not capable of that level of invention, then you can prove it by submitting to the device. If you refuse, we may doubt everything that you have claimed against her. If you are sure it doesn't work, then there is also no reason not to submit. If she tries and fails, your reputation stands; it closes debate for now and all time. It's a foolproof chance to keep your name clear. Will you allow the attempt in the name of science and justice?"

"She has hypnotized you!"

"No, sir, she has *unhypnotized* me. I didn't listen to her before, but I have reason to know that she can treat secrets like secrets. What do the rest of you say?"

"Hear, hear," cried Mr. Tennison, the treasurer. "Show her up. What have you got to lose? Chances are all you'll do is waste a few minutes. I've done advanced work in mesmerism and I couldn't get that to work. I doubt a mere girl could."

"*A mere girl*," Mrs. Shanahan said, clearly stung. She shot an encouraging glance at Penelope. "Go to it, Miss Galferd. Sit down, Mr. Beauregard. If you have nothing to fear, that is."

Albin glowered, but he sat. Penelope trembled as she approached the stage and set the monocle running. She understood now that she was fighting not only for her own honor, but that of every woman in the club. The eyes of the executive committee, Mr. Deed and the governor were on her like concentrated light beams.

She and Albin had played at hypnosis. He was not a good subject. He rarely could relax enough to be in a receptive state. His hostility could prevent him now. She approached him. He turned to face her with an insouciant expression.

"Please just sit back, Mr. Beauregard," she said, nervously.

"I have loved you, Penelope," he said, looking into her eyes with all appearance of sincerity. "Why do you seek to embarrass me now?"

"You have forced me to this," Penelope said tightly.

"I thought we parted on good terms," Albin said plaintively.

A few sighs issued from the female contingent of the audience at his doe eyes. Penelope was furious. She could well understand why the woman who poisoned her husband had done it. She turned the rotation of the crystal in the monocle all the way up.

"Please just relax, Albin."

He beamed. "Aren't you the brave little Daniel for bearding the lion in his den? This is my day. These fine people are all here to honor me."

"For your invention?" she demanded.

He hesitated. His pupils contracted, then dilated. Penelope did her best not to react. It was working. Oh, please, in the names of Euclid, Archimedes, and Sir Isaac Newton, let it be so!

"Do you trust me, Albin?"

"Well . . . yes."

Penelope felt her heart soar. "Why did you claim the invention?" she pressed.

He giggled. "It was too good," he said. "It had to be brought to the public as soon as possible."

"But who originated it?"

He paused.

She leaned forward. "Who? Who made that device?"

He looked over her shoulder at the display. "I did. My name is on the bottom."

"You see?" Tennison demanded. "Her whining has wasted our time!"

Penelope could have fainted with frustration, but she realized her mistake. "Not the one in the case, Albin, but the one you took to the patent office. The original."

"Well, you know," Albin said. "It was you."

A moment's silence, and pandemonium broke out in the hall. Everyone shouted at Penelope and each other. Albin sat regarding them as though they were part of a stage show. Penelope tried to be heard, but the yelling went on.

"Quiet, all of you!" Finbury shouted, deafening them with the loudspeakers. "Miss Galferd?"

Penelope turned back to Beauregard.

"So it was not your own brainchild?" she asked gently.

"It could have been," Albin said.

Penelope beckoned to the side aisle. "No. 31, will you come here, please?"

"Of course—click!—Miss Galferd." The attendant glided up to her and presented her with her train case. With just a modicum of embarrassment, she connected the small gramophone to the lead under her waistband, inserted a cylinder and turned it on.

"Albin," she said. "Tell me again who invented the elemental chemical separator. The original."

"You did," he said.

In the chaos that followed, Miss Armor rushed up to the stage and embraced her. Mrs. Shanahan rose regally from her seat and came to pat her on the back. Even Mr. Tennison shook her hand. Over their heads, Professor Finbury smiled at Penelope. She beamed back.

In the midst of it all, Albin suddenly looked up in puzzlement at the crush of bodies around him. "What is going on?" he asked.

"Well, you're being expelled from the club, my boy," Professor Finbury said. "It is my opinion that you are a lying, low-down skunk who doesn't belong here."

It was clearly not what Albin Beauregard expected to hear. "What? Why?"

"Because science is honest," Penelope said, "and you are not."

*   *   *

It was too much to expect that the medal that the Pinkertons had designed for Albin would be presented to her, but Penelope was asked to demonstrate the inventions at her disposal. In a delightful round of acclaim, her membership was restored by a vote of fifty-six to one against, that one being Albin himself, shortly before he was escorted from the premises by No. 18 and No. 47.

"As long as you get rid of that gizmo of yours," Professor Finbury said, with a laugh. "I'm afraid of our confessions ending up in your collection."

"I promise," Penelope said.

She was toasted afterwards with lemonade and champagne, a glass of the latter she permitted herself in celebration.

"To Miss Galferd," Professor Finbury proclaimed.

"No, friends," Penelope said, modestly. "To the professor."

"No!" Finbury corrected himself. "To science!"

Everyone laughed and downed their drinks. Penelope was glad to remove the heavy eyepiece at last.

"Miss Galferd?" A quiet voice murmured close to her ear. She turned to find Mr. Deed of the Pinkertons at her elbow. "Miss Galferd, as long as you are retiring your Mesmeric eyepiece, might I suggest a use for it? It is such a gentle persuader that it could be of enormous service in difficult situations. Your government would be most grateful and generous."

She placed it gladly in his palm. "It would be my pleasure, Mr. Deed," she said. "It is always important to have the truth come out."

Foretold

Bradley P. Beaulieu

Bradley P. Beaulieu is a SpecFic writer who figured he'd better get serious about writing before
he found himself on the wrong side of a lifelong
career in software. His story, "In the Eyes of the
Empress's Cat," was voted a Notable Story of
2006 by the Million Writers Award. Other stories
have appeared in *Realms of Fantasy*, *Writers of the
Future*, *OSC's Intergalactic Medicine Show*, and
several DAW anthologies. He lives in Racine,
Wisconsin, where he enjoys cooking spicy dishes
and hiding out on the weekends with his family.
For more, please visit *www.quillings.com*.

Behind him, over the hiss of releasing steam, Maks
heard the faint sound of snowshoes trudging
through the drifts on the hill.

The night was growing long. Clearly impatience had
won out over Maks's pleas to be left in peace, and now
the Kapitan was approaching to learn the results of the
augury.

It had been twelve days since they'd left Syktyvkar,
and they had days lying ahead before they would reach
the edge of the striking grounds. This was the first augury of the season and by far the most important to the

Braga and her crew, so of course the Kapitan would be anxious to hear the findings—pleas for solitude or not.

Maks was sitting on a wide woolen blanket with his apprentice, Yevgeniy, close at hand. He had time before the Kapitan crested the hill, so he quickly sighted through the telescope of his sextant, fixing it upon Uranus above the peaks of the Urals to the east. After completing his measurement, he passed the sextant to Yevgeniy and by the light of his whale oil lantern wrote down 13° 22' in his journal. At the top of the page was the date—the 14th of December, 1889—followed by the measurements of the other bodies to which he had visibility: the moon, due south, waxing gibbous; Mars, seventeen degrees above the southeastern horizon; Saturn at thirty-eight.

He turned to a leatherbound case sitting at the exact center of the blanket. After closing his eyes, he set back the lid to expose the brass face of his orrery. With practiced hands he adjusted the nine ivory dials along the top to account for the position of each of the primary heavenly bodies. Then he turned his attention to the six dials made of ebony. These were not turned based on precise locations, but on the small indications of fate that lay all around him—things unexpected, things lost, moods altered. It was an art, what he was about to do, and it was something he had, for whatever reason, been unable to pass down to Yevgeniy. It was also the very thing with which he'd had the most trouble since taking Yevgeniy on as his apprentice.

But he couldn't think about that now.

He cleared his mind and adjusted the dials to account for the state of their journey, the number of men aboard, the pace at which the *Braga* had traveled that day. He took dozens of things into account, touching the dials just so, until at last he was satisfied. And then he turned his attention to the door at the lower-right corner. He lifted it to reveal the three Daimones—the minor deities that ruled the fate of this expedition.

A smile came over him.

Epiphron, Plutus, and Bia ...

Epiphron meant prudence, and the Kapitan and his handpicked crew were nothing if not prudent. The presence of Plutus—or wealth—clearly meant that they would have a good season. He couldn't quite reconcile Bia, which meant force. He would have to think on that more, but he did know one thing: the Kapitan could be nothing but pleased.

Maks's joy frayed just a little when he realized that Yevgeniy was still taking his first measurement. He shook his head, telling himself that at least his augury was complete, and there was nothing Yevgeniy could do to change it. His impatience heightened, however, when he noted that Yevgeniy was training the sextant too far to the north of Uranus.

"Enough," he said, "give me the sextant."

"Master, there is a comet."

Maks's face burned at these words. The sound of footfalls in the snow behind him grew suddenly louder, though he knew the phenomenon was due more to his own embarrassment than anything else. He turned and found Kapitan Shimon, a bear of a man bundled as heavily as one, hiking through the snow toward them. His wide, scruffy face was lit in amber momentarily as he puffed on his cigar. Farther down the slope, the pale yellow lanterns of the walker shined as the crew shoveled snow into the sluice for the walker's reservoir.

"How soon?" the Kapitan called.

"Soon." Maks grabbed the sextant from Yevgeniy and scanned the eastern sky north of Uranus to find the dim tail of Menippe, a comet he hadn't seen in nearly eight years. How could he have forgotten about its arrival, this night of all nights?

"Is there a problem?" the Kapitan asked.

"None at all," Maks lied. "Now leave me to my work, or we'll never be done."

He could hear the Kapitan's heavy breathing, but

Shimon had never been one for the cold, and in moments his heavy footsteps could be heard trudging back toward the walker.

Stomach clenching, Maks turned to the orrery. He closed the door showing the Daimones and then carefully readjusted the six ebony dials to account not only for the presence of the comet but this sharp change in mood. Then he held out his shaking hand, ready to hinge the door open. Even with all of his years in augury, it was rare for him to be so certain of the outcome, but this night he was.

He lifted the door.

And stared.

"You're shaking, master."

Nemesis, Dysnomia, and Moros.

Indignation, lawlessness, and doom.

Maks snapped the door shut and immediately secured the orrery's leather case. It was the height of rudeness to refuse one's apprentice a chance to view the results of an augury, but this was not something he could share with Yevgeniy.

The confusion in Yevgeniy's bright blue eyes was followed by cold understanding. He couldn't possibly know what the orrery had revealed, but just then the possibility seemed so real that Maks stood and pushed him away.

Yevgeniy stumbled back and fell into the deeper snow. "Master?"

"Return to the walker," Maks said, trying and failing to hide the shiver that ran down his frame.

"Can I help with the—"

"Go!"

Yevgeniy bowed and complied. As the plodding sound of his snowshoes faded into the night, Maks turned and considered the silhouetted peaks of the Urals and the heavens beyond. He understood this reading like none other in his life. There would be tragedy on this journey, and betrayal, and the source could be none other than his young apprentice. He was tempted—as he had been many times on receipt of ill tidings—to urge the Kapitan to head for the southern range instead of the northern, to return to Syktyvkar and seek guidance from the oracle, or even to simply wait a few weeks before continuing on, but he knew that such a thing was foolish. As far as the gods were concerned, this bit of history he and the crew were about to experience was already written, and running from it would only serve to anger them.

Five days later the *Braga* stood upon a narrow ridge dividing two slender valleys from one another. The sky was dark, but the eastern horizon was beginning to brighten. Kapitan Shimon, a telescope pressed against his eye, was standing on deck directly over the ore chute hatch, while Maks sat at the base of the aft watchtower to the rear of the main deck, reading his journal by the light of a small lantern. Yevgeniy sat nearby with a lantern of his own, scribbling in his journal.

Ever since the augury, a sinking feeling had settled into the pit of Maks's stomach when he considered the role Yevgeniy would play in their coming misfortune. The meteorite strike Maks had predicted was late, and the feeling was stronger than ever, but Maks ignored it as best he could and used his sextant to sight Uranus to the west. There was always the chance he had missed a number here or there, but the three falling stars they'd spotted on their way here had confirmed his initial prediction. So what had gone wrong?

The entire crew had waited up through the night. They were hoping that with a large strike—and a heavy amount of ore—they could disprove Maks's initial reading. But this was not to be. By the time the sun was fully up, the heavens had remained closed and Shimon was furious.

"You said before dawn."

"Kapitan, you know these things—"

"Are never accurate, but I expect *some* accuracy,

Maksim." Maks knew that this was as much a show for the crew as it was for him. "What of Yevgeniy?" Shimon continued. "What does he have to say?"

Yevgeniy, the wind tugging at his short blond hair, sat silently on the deck with his nose in his journal. He was either ignoring Shimon in deference to Maks or so absorbed in his scribblings that he truly didn't comprehend what was happening around him. Maks was surprised to realize he didn't know which it was.

Refusing to let Shimon bully him, Maks stood and faced Shimon squarely. "Yevgeniy is an apprentice."

"And has been for nearly three years. You hold him back, Maks. Let him stand and say what he thinks."

Maks placed himself between Shimon and Yevgeniy. "He will do no such thing. He has not been properly trained."

The Kapitan scoffed. "He is gifted, Maksim. When are you going to realize it?"

"Gifted or not, I will be the one to decide when his time has come, not you, and not our circumstances."

"Circumstances you should have foreseen."

"I did!"

Shimon's eyes narrowed and he pulled his bearskin cloak around his frame. "So you did."

Maks felt himself tighten. Shimon was implying that the augury had been Maks's fault. Shimon was smart enough to know that such a thing wasn't true, but the crew *would* believe his words. It was a blatant attempt at applying pressure, but Maks would have none of it. He was about to order Yevgeniy belowdecks when Leonid cried above him, "Strike!"

All eyes turned upward. Streaking through the pale sky was a trail of white. It flew overhead, less than a mile above them, and bit into the far side of the valley. Moments later, a boom shook the forest around them. Maks felt it not only on his scalp and on the hairs along the back of his neck, he felt it in his bones.

The crew raised their arms to the sky, shouting their

elation. But the Kapitan did not. He stared at Maks, and Yevgeniy behind him. "We have work to do, and I'm thankful for that"—he nodded in Yevgeniy's direction—"but from now on I'll hear what your apprentice has to say."

Maks stood, his face burning, knowing it would be foolish to question the Kapitan openly. He would wait instead and approach him when he was alone. Shimon was always more reasonable when alone.

As the Kapitan began bellowing orders, Maks turned to Yevgeniy. His apprentice did not look cowed, as Maks thought he might, or embarrassed. Instead there was a measure of sadness in his eyes—sadness, as if Maks were the one deserving pity.

Maks snatched the journal and threw it to the deck at Yevgeniy's feet. "Prepare yourself."

Upon a rise above the strike site, Maks hunkered within the closeness of a dense thicket. He used his telescope to study the valley wall opposite him for any signs of pirates. Old mining trails could easily be seen, but it was not these that Max watched most closely. He looked for any sign of new trails, especially those that might lead to a copse of larch or pine that might be large enough to hide a walker.

From the base of the valley, sounds from the *Braga's* rock mill cracked and whined as the men continued to break down the meteorite. At times like this Maks was struck by how much of the world now revolved around meteorites that struck in only a bare handful of places around the world. The coarse powder now filling their holds would be refined in Saint Petersburg and sold to the Brits for their war over opium with China, or to the French for their never-ending war with Teotihuacan, or even to the Boers and their Dutch allies as they struggled to wrest South Africa back from the Zulu. The Empire didn't much care where the ore went as long as it expanded their coffers.

A lucrative trade such as mining, however, always attracted scavengers. Pirates, with no equipment of their own, would wait for a walker to finish a mining run and then strike, taking what ore they could to sell in the black markets of Syktyvkar or Arkhangelsk or Chelyabinsk. It was rare for pirates to attack so early in the season, but some would risk it for that very reason—caution would be at its lowest, leaving some walkers easy prey. Shimon, however, always stationed four lookouts—expensive but necessary in his eyes, not just for the preservation of the haul, but for morale.

Maks was too old for the laborious work going on down below—he could not fell trees for the furnaces or haul water for the boiler, nor could he handle the mill, so he was left to this, sitting and watching as the crew did their work. Which was fine with him. He had always loved the chill air of the northern climes, the silence when the walker was still, the balance he felt being so close to the heavens. He found it difficult, however, to attain any sense of balance after the exchange he'd had with Shimon. It was something he'd been thinking much about of late: the suitability, or lack thereof, of Yevgeniy. The young man had never been one to use the sextant or armillary with any great attention to detail, and too often he was unable to concentrate on the demanding requirements of the orrery. He was always sneaking time to write in his journal, to whisper to himself, to watch the nighttime sky as if it were the first time he had ever seen it. Despite Maks's orders forbidding the practice, he sometimes spoke of the future as if he understood it. No doubt the crew had overheard some of his ramblings, and maybe one or two of these prophecies had come true. It was easy for simple men like Shimon and the crew to become absorbed in such things, and perhaps this was the root of the warning couched within the augury—lawlessness in the eyes of the gods for disobeying their strictures, indignation over Maks's inability to reign Yevgeniy in. Doom in judgment.

He had no doubt that without Yevgeniy's clouding presence he could return to his past success. Perhaps he should release the boy, concentrate on his own studies and return to Shimon the level of success he'd had in years past. He could do so as soon as they reached Narodnaya. He would not be working against the augury. Their fates had already sealed by the Moirae—he knew this—but in the understanding of one's fate, one might blunt the impact. Surely the gods would not begrudge him that.

Even as these thoughts were settling in his mind, footsteps approached from behind. Maks knew without turning who it was. Yevgeniy had a gait as tentative as his craft.

"Return to your watch, Yevgeniy."

"Forgive me, Master, but we must speak."

Maks turned and found him standing outside the thicket, wrapped in his dark red robes. His hands were hidden inside his sleeves, no doubt wringing around one another like snakes.

"Nyet, Yevgeniy. Return to your post."

Yevgeniy seemed rigid, both in stance and expression. "Master, the mining is still hours from completion, and we are so rarely alone. I would speak with you of a formation I've found."

"In the stars?"

"In the snow. The rocks, to be more precise. They're just over—"

"How many times have I told you that such things are nonsense?"

"But the oracle—"

"You are no oracle, Yevgeniy."

Yevgeniy ducked his head. "Of course, Master. I only meant—"

"Go," Maks said as he turned around and resumed his watch of the far slope. "Keep your watch or return to Shimon and have yourself replaced."

"I've used the orrery . . ."

The words hung in the chill air, as brittle as the surface of the snow. The hair along Maks's forearms rose as he turned and regarded Yevgeniy as coolly as he could manage. "You what?"

"Several times since leaving Syktyvkar." He glanced to one side, as if he wanted nothing more than to survey the land behind him, perhaps to look upon the stones in which he'd read his future.

Maks crouched out of the thicket and marched forward. Yevgeniy, to his credit, did not wilt. "You were never to do such a thing."

Yevgeniy bowed his head. "I know, Master, but . . ."

Maks grabbed his robes and shook him. "Explain yourself!"

A crack sounded above them on the slope. Maks recognized it immediately as the sound of a stout leg of wood giving way to some greater force. It was followed by a cacophony of lesser snaps and splinters and the screech of metal against stone. The tops of the young trees above them swayed as if the arms of Heracles himself were spreading them apart.

Then Maks saw it: a walker, obscured by the trees, sliding with ever greater speed. It came closer, more and more of it coming into focus.

It had eight legs, all of which were pulled as high and as tight as possible against the rounded hull, allowing it to slide down the snow-covered slope on its thick underbelly, a maneuver common among the pirates.

With Yevgeniy close behind, Maks ran as the nearest of the trees split wide. The walker continued as Maks and Yevgeniy dove to the ground. The crack of a musket, then two more, sounded behind them. Snow puffed into the air near Maks's face, spraying him with biting chips of ice and snow. The walker continued on, sliding directly over the thicket in which Maks had been hiding only moments ago.

"Hoy!" Maks yelled, following the trail he had forged through the thick blanket of snow on his way here. He waved his arms over his head, keeping as many trees between him and the pirates as possible while still remaining in view of the *Braga*.

The walker slid into the valley, coming to a rest near the bank of a river. Three men held tight to the gun emplacement at the rear, but as soon as the walker ceased rocking, they swung the cannon around and trained it on the *Braga*.

"Hoy!" Maks continued to yell. He reached the open grassland just as the pirate's cannon barked and belched black smoke.

A scream of metal and sparks centered on the foremost of the *Braga's* starboard legs. It caught the first joint squarely, sending the entire armature forward with a spray of sparks and an explosion of sound that echoed along the valley walls. The leg crashed against the hull—ruined—but thank the gods the hull and the other five legs had been left intact.

More musket shots rained in, one whizzing over Maks's head, but the pirates had the crew of the *Braga* to worry about now. Three of Shimon's men had regrouped behind the hull and were returning fire while the Kapitan and Vitaliy hoisted themselves up to the primed and loaded cannon. The Kapitan took a moment to sight down the barrel before bringing a waiting brand to the touch hole.

The cannon thundered. The shot struck the pirates' walker, but too far forward. It glanced off the forward hull and exploded into the stony earth along the bank of the river.

The crack of musket fire filled the air. The pirates were focused solely on the men surrounding the *Braga* now. One of them crumpled as he was struck, but their cannon was ready to fire once more. It shot, this time striking the *Braga* dead center, causing the entire ship to shake and rattle. The *Braga* was stout, but still a hole the size of a powder keg was left in the hull. Maks prayed that the boiler hadn't been struck.

Maks and Yevgeniy finally reached the *Braga*. They ran behind the hull for cover, their breath coming in great ragged gasps. More than a dozen pirates had poured out from the belly of the walker and were moving forward with muskets at the ready. They stayed in a spread formation, disciplined, firing and reloading as others moved forward and did the same to cover them.

The crew of the *Braga* was small—only ten men in all. They couldn't hope to stave off so many, and even if they managed to, what shape would the *Braga* be in by the time they did?

Danila, standing behind the prow, stepped out and brought his musket up quickly, but before he could pull the trigger, a shot tore into his shoulder with a meaty thump and spun him around. He fell to the ground, the snow breaking his fall.

Maks grabbed for Danila's trouser leg. Another musket shot came in, striking near his feet. "Help me!" he shouted, but Yevgeniy was already there, grabbing Leonid's other leg, and together they pulled him to safety.

Most of the pirates were flanking wide to the left; another four had broken away and were crossing the river to the right.

Another cannon shot came in with a deafening roar right above Maks. Vitaliy screamed. A moment later, Kapitan Shimon was beside them, rolling away and then to his feet. In that one instant, he gave Maks a vicious look, as if he were to blame.

Vitaliy dropped behind Shimon. He screamed, gripping his left hand tightly. Blood poured from his ruined hand, staining the trampled snow beneath his feet.

"What shall we do?" Leonid said. He was gripping his musket fiercely. His entire body was shaking.

Shimon, breathing heavily, looked up to the ship and out toward the grassland where the pirates would soon be. He was clearly debating whether he should surrender, but what choice was there?

The boom of another cannon came from behind

them. Maks thought it might have been an echo from the pirate ship, but Iosef shouted and pointed to the valley's northern slope. At the crest, already making good headway as it slid down a shallow slope toward the river, was another walker—a miner, not a pirate. And it was big—one cannon at the front, another at the rear, and nearly twenty men at the gunwales, muskets at the ready. Maks recognized it immediately as the *Drozhnost*, the ship his brother, Savil, had been serving on for the past eight years.

Three strikes of a bell cut through the cold air, a signal from the pirate Kapitan to his men. Maks dared a glance beyond the prow and saw them beating a hasty retreat back to their ship.

Another cannon shot from the *Drozhnost* narrowly missed the pirate ship, and soon after their walker was steaming away, crawling beyond the river and into the nearby trees. By the time the *Drozhnost* had launched one last warning shot, the pirates were lost from view, a column of steam rising high into the air, marking its passage as it crawled up slope and away from danger.

For long moments all Maks could do was breathe. The men raised their hands in the air and cheered. Yevgeniy, however, ran to Vitaliy's side and dropped to his knees.

For a moment—a moment only—he stopped. He became still, and there came a look on his face that made Maks's breath catch. It was a look of regret, as if he felt responsible for what had happened to the man lying before him.

The moment passed, and Yevgeniy moved quickly, unwinding Vitaliy's scarf and wrapping it tightly around his bloody hand. The other crewmen swarmed in to carry Vitaliy up to the ship, to get him warm, and as soon as they had moved to the far side of the *Braga*, Maks grabbed Yevgeniy by his coat. "You knew!"

Yevgeniy's cheeks were red with shame. "Knew what?"

"You knew they were coming! How?"

"I didn't know exactly."

Maks worked it out in his head, realizing that this went much farther than Yevgeniy was letting on. "They knew we would be here. They knew where our first strike would land." Maks worked backward through time. They hadn't known until after leaving Syktyvkar the region they would be heading toward, but they had stopped at Narodnaya, a small mining village, two days into the mountain passes. "You sold my findings, didn't you?"

Yevegeniy shook his head violently. "Nyet, Maksim, I would never!"

"You did! And the word from the oracle as well."

"Maksim, I told you, when you were sleeping I looked at the orrery."

Shimon's steps came from around the front of the walker and bore down on them. "What is this?"

"It's my fault, Kapitan," Maks said. "I should never have agreed to take him on. He is from a poor family, and his father is sick. He's sold the only thing of worth that he has."

"What do you mean?" Shimon asked.

"The list of sightings from the oracle, and the ones we've collected since."

Shimon stared down at Yevgeniy, his unshaven jaw working back and forth. "You have proof?"

"I need no proof, Shimon. He is guilty."

Shimon turned his stare on Maks, his breath white on the wind. This was a man that years ago would have trusted Maks implicitly, but now there was doubt in his eyes—skepticism for a man who had failed him more often than not in the past few seasons. He looked up to the woods, where the pirate walker could still be heard. Then he looked to the meteorite, black and glimmering in its blasted hole. "Come, Yevgeniy, we have work to do."

Maks raised his hands. "Kapitan—"

"You have work to do as well, Maksim. Speak to your brother. Get the sightings you need."

Shimon left to continue work on the meteorite. Yevgeniy paused, looking to Maks as if he regretted what had just happened, but then he followed in the Kapitan's footsteps, leaving Maks alone with only the gentle wind and the sound of the nearby river to comfort him.

Maks sat beneath the boughs of a tall larch as a healthy fire spat and sparked a few feet away. Maks tipped his head back and allowed a healthy swallow of vodka from Savil's pewter flask to burn down his throat. Across from him Savil was just finishing his task of copying Maks's most recent sightings into his thick, leatherbound journal. The sun had long gone down. The stars and moon were bright, and Maks could see the silhouettes of the *Braga* and the *Drozhnost* against the white field of snow as the crew of both walkers fed the last of the meteorite into the mills. The sound of stone being crushed rose high into the valley air, making Maks nervous that the pirates would hear it and return to catch them off guard, but the ore was simply too lucrative to abandon, even splitting it with the *Drozhnost*.

Savil continued to scritch and scratch at his journal, taking detailed notes on Maks's observations and how they squared with his own. It was something seers did for one another, this trading of information. It was essential; without reliable updates as to the patterns of starfalls one could not predict the future. For anyone else Maks would have copied his sightings down—perhaps four of every five sightings—and given them over, but this was Savil; he was family, and even though the two of them worked for competing mining outfits, neither owner would grumble. It was understood that family warranted special consideration.

The years had not been kind to Savil since Maks had last seen him. His face was ragged, his eyes worn and defeated. Savil was fifty-four, three years Maks's senior. Maks remembered him as a stout old oak, but here he looked bent and broken, like a tree that had finally given in to the storm.

Footsteps approached, crunching over the snow. Kapitan Shimon stepped into the firelight, his face grim. "You wished to speak?"

Maks stood, preferring to stare Shimon in the eye. "It's Yevgeniy. He confessed—"

"That he stole a look at your orrery? What of it?"

Maks stared, unable to collect himself for a moment. "Kapitan, the orrery is a delicate instrument. Yevgeniy may very well have fouled its calibration."

"And he may very well have seen something that you did not."

"That's just it, Shimon. I don't think he saw it at all. I think he's in league with them."

"In *league*?"

"He's selling information to the pirates. My sightings." Maks tipped his head toward Savil. "Those of others."

"And if he had, why would they have attacked the very ship that was supplying them with information?"

"He would have sold it to middle-men, men who could easily have resold it to the pirates who attacked us."

Shimon pulled his heavy fur coat tighter over his frame. The night was growing cold. "This sounds desperate, Maksim."

"I—" He was referring to Maks's own difficulties over the past few seasons. "I would never blame another for my own—"

"Inabilities? The truth of the matter, Maks, is that you're readings have become more and more erratic. We barely saw profit last year. With the repairs the *Braga* needs now, if this season goes the same way, we'll lose money. I can't have it, Maks. I can't."

"It has been difficult, but now that I have Savil's sightings, I can correct."

"I would prefer that there was nothing to correct."

Maks shook his head. "Kapitan, I'm sure that Yevgeniy—"

"Yevgeniy may be your apprentice, but he's helped the crew more than you ever have. He stays." He turned to leave, taking several long strides back toward the ship, but then he stopped and turned around. "And Maks?"

"Kapitan?"

"You had better find us meteorites, and more than this cartload we found today."

When the Kapitan's tall form had long since melded into the darkness, Savil pulled the spectacles from around his ears and closed his journal. He stared deeply into Maks's eyes. "What has happened to you, Maksim?"

Maks sat, feeling sick. "Yevgeniy—"

"Yevgeniy or not, you are master of your orrery, are you not? You are a seer trained by the oracle Vadrim, himself, are you not?"

"It is a run of bad luck, Savil. Nothing more."

"There's no such thing as luck."

"I need no reminding of that." He motioned to the *Braga*, where the men were beginning to stow the equipment. "It's nothing I can't handle."

Savil stood and stared, a confused look playing over his face among the shadows of the nearby fire. "We'll see each other again, da? After the season? We have some things to talk about."

Maks stood and embraced him. "Such as?"

"After the season, Maks." Savil hugged him and slapped his back. "I'm glad we came upon you in time." His words were strangely spoken, as if Savil felt them more deeply than he had a right to.

Maks pulled away and stared into his brother's eyes. "You saw it, did you not?"

"Still"—he winked—"a bit of luck never hurts, da?"

Maks laughed and embraced him one last time.

Within the hour, the *Braga* and the *Drozhnost* had gone their separate ways.

By the edge of a tranquil mountain lake, Maks sat before his orrery, confused. The stars and the delicate gauze of the universe that lay beyond them were bright, casting a perfect reflection over the placid surface of the lake. By the light of a bulls-eye lantern, he studied the detailed notes he'd taken of his own sightings and those of Savil. The dials had been set and reset, but the location it was giving for the next meteorite strike was over a thousand miles to the southwest, placing it somewhere along the northern coast of the Black Sea. The orrery had been built in Delphi by women handpicked by the Pythia herself. It could not be the fault of the machine. And yet Maks was doing nothing different than he had for years. He had gauged the amount of sunlight, he had measured the wind, he had taken the mood of each and every crew member. Even Yevgeniy and the angst and uncertainty he brought had been taken into account. His use of the sextant was impeccable despite his aging eyes.

Menippe still burned in the northern sky, but its tail was growing dim. He had struggled with her presence ever since Yevgeniy had spotted her. She and her sister, Metioche, had sacrificed themselves when Aonia was visited by a plague. They had invoked the names of the infernal gods, and Persephone and Hades had responded, turning them into comets. Maks knew that his fate was tied closely to Menippe, the younger of the two sisters, and he was more than conscious that her light was fading, which could not be good unless he could unravel her mystery before she faded entirely. The only trouble was that there were so many aspects to consider that he was driving himself mad. Sacrifice, plague, rising to a higher station. The shuttle, back and forth, the weaving of fate.

The reading he'd drawn on the hills leading up to the Urals had been Nemesis, Dysnomia, and Moros. Indignation, lawlessness, and doom. His fate was clearly wrapped within that first augury. But how?

Somewhere in the distance, a wolf howled. The stars were beginning to fade, and the eastern sky was brightening—golden light over an indigo field.

The Kapitan approached. Behind him were Yevgeniy and Leonid.

"Where do we go, Maks?"

Maks, his heart sinking, shook his head slowly. "I'll know soon, Kapitan."

"You've had two nights."

"These things take time."

"More time than we have." Shimon paused, perhaps debating on whether to act upon his instincts. "Why have you not allowed Yevgeniy to perform an augury?"

"I told you, his presence now will only interfere."

Shimon, shivering, pulled his heavy fur cloak tighter about his frame. "Perhaps you're afraid he'll succeed where you have failed."

Maks stood, facing Shimon squarely. "Whether or not he had anything to do with the pirates is irrelevant. He will foul my readings, Shimon, and he is unprepared to make his own."

"And if I say different?"

"It is not your place to say."

"It is," Shimon said, his face ruddy in the growing light of dawn. "He will perform a reading, Maks, with or without your consent."

"He will not."

Shimon stood stock still, his breath coming quickly. His gaze darted to the orrery, and then something inside him seemed to break, and he motioned to Leonid.

Leonid stalked forward, his eyes intent on the orrery— or, more accurately, *not* intent on Maks.

Maks placed himself in Leonid's way, but the stout crewman merely shoved him to one side. Then he snapped the lid of the orrery shut and hefted it up from the blanket.

"That orrery is mine! You have no right!"

"We have a contract, Maks. If you're no longer able to uphold your end of it, we must find someone who can."

"He will fail."

"We'll take our chances."

Leonid moved behind Shimon, continuing to avoid Maks's gaze.

"You may come with us to Unladansk," Shimon said. "But from there you'll be on your own."

"The oracle will hear of this."

"I'm no thief. You'll have your orrery back. But don't think that the oracle won't hear of your treatment of Yevgeniy as well. It's shameful, what you've done"— Maks opened his mouth to object, but Shimon spoke over him—"holding him back when his gifts are plain to see . . ."

Shimon waited, daring Maks to reply, but when Maks did not, he turned and headed for the *Braga*. "We leave on the hour."

Maks didn't follow. He couldn't remain with these men, certainly not with Yevgeniy.

Shimon stopped and turned. "You'll freeze, Maks."

Maks breathed in the cold morning air, feeling small, as light began to fill the valley.

"Suit yourself," Shimon said, and off they went.

Yevgeniy watched for a time, but then he too turned and followed.

Maks, his mind swimming in a haze of vodka and bitters, lifted his head as the door to the tea house opened and five men filed in. The patrons spread among the tables in the warm, smoky room looked up but quickly returned to their conversations. Maks recognized the Kapitan of the *Drozhnost* and thought surely Savil would be right behind him, but his brother was not to be seen. Had he been sober, he would have asked what had become of him, but he was not, and he was content to sit and wait.

Over an hour later, Savil finally came. When he entered the inn, Maks felt a mixture of shame and relief. Savil was headed for the table his crew mates were sharing in the corner, but when he spotted Maks, he stopped—a look of mild surprise on his face—and changed course. "I didn't think you'd be here for a month."

"Neither did I." His words were slurred, but he didn't care.

"What happened?" Savil asked as he sat down at Maks's table.

"Can you not guess?" Maks answered.

After Shimon left him near the mountain lake, it had taken Maks well into the following day to reach the trail leading up to Narodnaya. He had accepted a ride on another walker. The Kapitan had been a superstitious man, unwilling to take on a seer both lost and alone, but in the end he had agreed to take Maks on, for they were heading back to Syktyvkar with a haul the size of a mountain. Maks had debated continuing on with them, but something wouldn't allow him. His business in the Urals was unfinished.

Savil waved a serving girl for a drink. "I never thought Shimon would do it."

"Well, he has, Savil, and I'm finished."

"You're drunk, Maksim. Don't be so glum."

"It's true!" Maks roared. "What walker will have me when word gets out?"

"Lower your voice. The world isn't ending."

"It is for me." Maks downed the last of his drink and slammed the heavy glass snifter back down onto the table. "I'm ruined, supplanted by a boy who two years ago couldn't tell his ass from the belt of Orion."

Savil glanced sidelong toward his Kapitan. "I wanted to wait Maks, but since you're . . . no longer employed, I might as well tell you now."

"Tell me what?"

"As it happens, I'll soon be in need of a seer."

Maks stared, his eyes suddenly refusing to focus.

"For my first walker," Savil continued.

"You can't afford such a thing."

"I've been saving."

Maks was shaking his head before Savil had even finished speaking. "Two years ago you barely had two kopeks to rub together."

"Things change."

Maks felt the blood drain from his face. His fingers

began to tingle, and though his mind was fogged with drink, he heard Savil's words from their talk beneath the larch ringing in his head: *I'm glad we came upon you in time.*

"What have you done, Savil?"

Savil paused, running the tips of his fingers around the rim of his glass. "Nothing dozens haven't done before me. Nothing that won't be done as long as men live and meteorites fall among the Urals."

"You *sold* them?"

Savil looked up, his jaw set grimly. "Why shouldn't I? Why shouldn't I have some money to put away before I die? Why shouldn't I have money to leave for my grandson?"

"But pirates, Savil?" The words came out in a whisper. Maks could hardly believe them.

"Brother, don't be like this. They would have found out anyway. Why shouldn't I profit from the sightings I've collected?"

Maks stood unsteadily, staring down at Savil's bald head and wiry white hair. He had been wrong about Yevgeniy—so wrong—and it had taken all this for the truth to come clear. How could he have been so blind? How could he have failed to piece together the clues that had settled around him like flakes of gentle snow?

A cold realization washed over Maks. He stared into Savil's eyes, knowing the answer before he'd even uttered the question.

"Did you sell them my sightings?"

"What does it matter?"

Maks could hear the Moirae laughing as they tugged at the threads of fate, leaving him to struggle with all that had happened and all that lay before him.

"Come with me, Maks. Come with me to Syktyvkar. I know a man with a walker. We'll buy it cheap, and by the time next season ends, we'll be living like kings."

Maks spat on the table, spraying both Savil and his drink.

With Savil staring, confused, Maks left the tavern and headed for the stables. His mind was awhirl, his memories of Yevgeniy reordering themselves into a new understanding of who and what he was. Yevgeniy's flighty nature, his inability to perform auguries, Maks's growing difficulties with his craft from the day Yevgeniy had entered his life—all of it was adding up to one inescapable truth. And now it was important—more than ever—that he reach Yevgeniy, that he save him from his fate.

Riding the stout mountain pony he'd purchased from the stable master, Maks headed up a steep rise. He reigned his pony to a stop and listened for the hiss of a steam release, or the clang of an articulated leg cycling, or the crack of a tree as it succumbed to the passage of a man-made beast.

He had spent the last three nights studying the stars carefully. Menippe could barely be seen, but the fact that it was there at all was a positive sign. It meant that Yevgeniy was still alive, and that there was time to save him. He had marked more than a dozen shooting stars. By careful observation of how they crossed certain constellations—as well as his constantly changing mood— he was able to see with some accuracy where he would find the *Braga*.

And it was here. In this valley. He was sure of it.

A boom somewhere ahead made him sit up in his saddle. The faint crack of musket fire came soon after. He kicked his pony into a trot, but the snow was deep, the going rough. Several more cannon shots sounded, and the battle reached a fever pitch—musket fire going crack-crack-crack, men shouting and screaming. A massive boom rent the cold mountain air, but then, just as he was cresting the ridge, it all stopped.

Far ahead, deep within a dense forest, a column of black smoke trailed up into the clear blue sky. Maks descended the slope and entered the forest, hoping he would make it in time. He lost his way among the landscape that was at times impassable and at others dense and confusing. Finally, though, hours after entering, he came to a clearing where the *Braga* lay fallen.

Maks swallowed, suddenly unable to clear his throat.

The walker was a blackened shell. The rear magazine had clearly been struck, causing the entire back half to be shorn free in the explosion. The rest was little more than a broken husk. He approached, jaw clenched, eyes watering. The crew lay all around. Aleksei. Danila. Leonid. Vitaliy. Andreyu. All of them dead from gunshot wounds.

Maks approached the hull and found Shimon hanging over the gunwale, his throat cut.

But of Yevgeniy there was no sign.

Maks looked up to the sky, praising the Moirae for their kindness. He dismounted and climbed into the hold through the gaping maw at the rear. All of the ore had been taken, but he cared nothing about this. He searched the entire ship, including Shimon's cabin, praying he wouldn't find Yevgeniy dead. He came at last to the small cabin he had shared with his apprentice. He opened the door slowly, but when he found it empty he brought his fist to his lips and kissed it three times, for again the Moirae had been kind.

There was one last thing. The ornate blanket hanging on the wall looked untouched. He pulled it down and maneuvered the wooden panel behind it. In the small space hidden there he found the orrery, still in its leather case. He had always kept it here, just in case, and—he kissed his fist again—apparently so had Yevgeniy.

He took it and moved from the ship as quickly as he could. After placing a coin under each crewman's tongue, he mounted his pony and rode for all he was worth.

The pirate's walker was not difficult to find. It had crashed through the forest, making a line for the western passes, perhaps heading for Syktyvkar to sell the ore that now filled its belly. Most likely they were planning to sell Yevgeniy as well—a seer, even an apprentice, would fetch a handsome price in the Egyptian slave markets.

As the sun was going down he found their ship at a thin mountain stream refilling its water reservoirs. He approached openly, knowing how foolish it would be to hide his presence. When the pirates saw him, he waved his hands high over his head, making it clear he was unarmed.

Several of them—men wearing long threadbare cherkesskas and bright scarves around their heads—trained their muskets on him.

"I would speak with your Kapitan." It was difficult granting the leader of the pirates the same title as Shimon, but he would not risk offending them.

"You were with them, were you not?" This came from a man standing on the walker's deck. He was nearly as old as Maks, and he had a long face and a graying beard. He was pointing a cocked flintlock pistol at Maks's chest. Maks could feel where it was aimed from the tickle just below his breastbone. It took all his courage not to cringe, not to look away from this man who had murdered the men of the *Braga*.

"You have one of my own," Maks said as boldly as he could manage.

The Kapitan smiled. "Yours no longer."

"He is a seer of Syktyvkar, a man trained in the arts of fate, a man anointed by Vadrim Khemiliov himself."

They knew who Yevgeniy was—it was why they had taken him instead of shooting him like a dog—and clearly they were not the sort of men inclined toward repentance, but to be faced with what they had done, to have their sacrilege spoken aloud, was quite another thing.

"You would sell him?" Maks continued. "You would treat him like a prized goat when the gods themselves watch his every step?"

"You could join him if you wish." The Kapitan's face was bold, but his words were hollow.

"Then you know who I am . . ." Maks could see in his eyes that he was not willing to speak sacrilege a second time. After allowing those words to sink in, Maks continued, "I propose a trade."

The Kapitan's hold on his pistol wavered. "Speak on."

Maks swung the leather case that held his orrery around until it rested in his lap. "You had hoped to find this, had you not?" The Kapitan remained silent, but his gaze drifted down to the case more than once. "You may have it. It is mine to give. In return you will give me Yevgeniy."

There was a long pause as the Kapitan considered his offer. The wind was blowing among the nearby trees, a soft sigh among the bleak winter landscape. The Kapitan raised his pistol, and Maks thought surely this had all been for naught, but the pirate merely held it steady while staring intently at Maks, as though he could see into his soul—or wished that he could.

"Why were there two?" he asked.

"Two what?"

"Two seers."

"I was the only seer."

The Kapitan shook his head. "Then what of the other? What is he?"

"Do you not know? Can you not feel it?" Maks paused, suddenly afraid to speak, but after a moment the feeling passed, and he knew that by speaking it aloud, he would declare it to the world. And it felt right.

"He is an oracle."

In the heart of Syktyvkar, within the Temple of Apollo, a line of supplicants waited to speak with the oracle. Maks had brought Savil in his wheelchair and had waited his turn like any other. After five hours he was next in line to step onto the dais and speak with His Eminence. Gripping the handles of Savil's wheelchair, he studied this oracle who not so long ago had been a young, unburnished man navigating his way through life in the wilds of the Urals. He was speaking with a prim young woman, an aristocrat. The woman was stunning—

she commanded attention—but she was nothing next to Yevgeniy, who had grown into a proper man these past four years. He was confident, now—Maks could see it in the way he spoke, the way he drew the eye of each and every one of his supplicants.

The woman grew silent, her question complete. Yevgeniy reached up and pulled the thick rope hanging next to him. The bell at the top of the temple, exposed to the frigid elements outside, rang slow and long. Yevgeniy closed his eyes and listened carefully.

When the last traces of sound had fallen away, Yevgeniy opened his eyes and spoke to the woman. She nodded pleasantly, but then heard something—perhaps unpleasant, perhaps devastating—and she stiffened. She swallowed and then bowed her head. She was shaken, and she swept from the room as though each and every person in it had offended her.

Yevgeniy smiled and beckoned to Maks. Maks turned Savil's wheelchair around and heaved him up the two steps to reach the dais proper. Then he spun around and wheeled Savil forward. Yevgeniy had clearly not recognized Maks up until this point, for as he stared, his eyes widened, and a curious smile played across his lips.

"Maksim," was all he said as Maks approached.

That one simple utterance sent a chill running down Maks's spine. "It is I," Maks replied.

Yevgeniy's eyes narrowed, and though there was no enmity there, there was confusion, and curiosity. "Dear Maks, what happened to your brother?"

"He slipped on some ice three years ago," Maks said simply. "Struck his head on the stones only a block from here. He's been like this ever since."

"I am sorry."

"Thank you, Oracle."

The silence between them lengthened, and Maks had the distinct impression that this was the first time Yevgeniy had been caught off-guard in months, perhaps years.

"You never answered my invitations," he finally said.

Maks nodded. "Please forgive me. It was boorish, I know. But I was busy in those early days . . . And then I had Savil to deal with."

Yevgeniy shook his head. "I would have taken care of everything."

"I know, and I thank you for it, but I could never have accepted."

Yevgeniy paused. He seemed saddened. "Of course. Though why have you come? Why now?"

Maks shrugged. "I leave tomorrow for Constantinople. I merely hoped . . ."

Yevgeniy nodded. "Speak on, Maksim."

"I had hoped that you would read Savil's fortune."

"And not your own?"

Maks's chest tightened. He had known Yevgeniy would ask, but he hadn't known until this very moment what his answer would be. "Please," he said.

Yevgeniy smiled. He reached to one side and pulled the rope hanging next to him. The bell pealed long and loud, trailing away as the wind played among the belfry high above. Yevgeniy waited, his eyes closed, his arms spread wide.

At last, when the sound had fallen away, he opened his eyes and regarded Maks with an expression that hid all. Or *nearly* all. For a moment there was concern, but it vanished and the placid expression Yevgeniy had shown to all the other supplicants returned.

"You will do well in Constantinople, Maks. You and Savil, both. You will live out your life in peace, though in little prosperity. Savil will be by your side until the black sea burns red. And you . . . You will find in that city what you have ever searched for."

Maks listened to these words and let them settle over him like a blanket of soft, worsted wool. They filled him with hope, and it was a welcome change from a life that had been filled with so much misery these past years.

He also knew that Yevgeniy was lying.

But he didn't care.

He stepped forward and kissed Yevgeniy's cheeks—a horrible breach of protocol—and then pulled him into a deep embrace.

"Go well, Yevgeniy Udmanoslov."

"Go well, Maksim Vadimov."

That done, his heart lifted, Maks left the temple.

The Echoer

Dean Leggett

Dean Alan Leggett lives near the train tracks running through his current home in Sussex, Wisconsin. He enjoys riding his bike on the trails through the woods and marsh nearby. He is known to stop at the old wooden bridge that crosses the tracks. In the winter months he enjoys seemingly endless snow shoveling and spending quiet days with his wonderful wife, Annette. While this is his first story set in the genre, he has found the steampunk world rich with all types of artistic talent. When he isn't working in the bizarre world of information technology he can be found writing about worlds yet to be or worlds that should have been.

I never thought the dim lights of Beaumont would feel so welcoming. Even as an experienced rider, extended travel on horseback had taken its toll. Our journey started in the burning heat and dust of Amarillo. It isn't the typical dust that clings to the brim of your hat. It is unique. It finds its way into every crease of your body and dries you to the bone. No amount of water can remove the empty taste it leaves in your mouth.

But things changed as the weeks and miles ticked by.

The heat dissipated, and a cold rain came that tamped down the dust. I didn't feel that I was in the same country, though even after three weeks of travel I was still in the same state. The vastness of Texas is now imprinted on my soul.

The wind gusted, causing cold water to pelt me in the face. I let off yet another string of curses as Kendo rode close. "Brandon, how many days ago did you cry to the heavens for even a few drops of rain?" he asked.

Why did my crew always take such pleasure in my discomfort? Even Kendo taunted me. I guess I should have expected it. Kendo was Texas. Take a cactus, add some twigs for arms, some old cowhide for skin and hair as black as oil and you have my guide. Kendo Crowfeather of the Kiowa Clan is also my good friend. He knows Texas, and more importantly the sign language, of the various tribes . . . the ones that are still left that is, most are scattered like tumbleweeds in a twister.

I am a half breed Indian myself, even though I don't look it. My father's Irish blood provided me fair skin that took three years in the desert to harden. And while skin will darken, no amount of sun could take away my red hair. It was too red for Texas or any place west of Vermont for that matter.

For this journey Kendo brought along his squaw. Shelia has long blonde hair, a tiny waist, and a thick German accent. She needed boots to stand above five feet. The three of us made quite a sight; we were the talk of Fort Worth, and I am sure will be the talk here in Beaumont.

Shelia rode ahead to the inn, giving me some time to get a feel for the town. Sheila holds our makeshift crew together. I consider her insight invaluable. When she isn't reminding us to pick up taters for dinner, she's bartering for new wheels for one of the supply wagons. I call her our little logistics goddess. This particular project wouldn't be where it is today without her. She found the parts we needed and the parts we didn't yet know we needed.

Our goal—to build the greatest airship of all times—the *Echoer*, the ship I once drew in the school yard sand. The ship I promised Allison I would take her away in.

I was smitten with amber-haired Allison from the first day I saw her at Endrich Catholic Boarding School. I was scared witless and barely ten winters when I was taken from my home and placed in Endrich. They tied my hands to the rail of the open wagon to keep me from jumping off and running away. I tore most of the skin off my wrists trying to work free. I didn't know where we were going and I was surrounded by strangers that spoke in sounds I didn't understand.

I don't remember the day I arrived at Endrich. But what I do remember is Allison's eyes and smile as she held my hands and applied cool salve to my wrists. She wasn't much older than I, but this was her world. She took me under her wing and sat as near as she could during classes. Every time I knew the answer she would smile, so I fought to learn everything I could. Education became my obsession. Within a few years I was at the head of the class. Allison and I made a great team. She was my whole world, and I promised I would take her away. We would fly high in the sky and visit amazing places together . . . all on our very own magical aeronave called the *Echoer*.

Now all I needed was her. Literally, I needed her. After Endrich we both were both selected to a math program and sent to the East Coast. Later, with Allison's family connections, we were admitted to Durham University in England. If you ever have doubts about airship travel, try being tossed around at sea for endless weeks. Even on calm days I couldn't be near the railing. Come to think of it, horseback isn't recommended either, but I digress.

My time in England wasn't the best. I thought eight years in Catholic school would have prepared me for anything, but I was wrong. The rules were absurd. The main thing I learned was that the English didn't like being told what pompous asses they really were. Allison tried to keep me focused, but the harder she tried to make things right, the farther I seemed to push her away. My grades fell.

I kissed Allison goodbye and told her I would wait for her back in the United States. Did you know that no matter how angry you get, or how much you plead, they will not turn those blasted ships around?

Waiting for her to finish school was awful. And in my boredom I started to look for like-minded inventing folks . . . folks with the skills I needed to realize my airship. I knew that with the right crew the *Echoer* would be possible. My crew officers—currently Kendo and Sheila—became my friends and we worked on my design.

I tried to stay in touch with Allison, writing her about my crew and project. I wanted her to know where she could find me. When I learned she'd returned to the United States, I tried to get her to join us. But she said she wanted nothing to do with my childhood fantasy.

My last contact with her was a few years ago.

Today that childhood dream is real. The *Echoer* is almost completed.

There were times along the way where I almost gave up. So did Kendo and Sheila. But when one of us would give up, the other two would supply the needed encouragement. As far as I was concerned, we were missing only one person to complete our family . . . Allison. After years of listening to me, Kendo and Sheila knew all about Allison.

We had a solid understanding of what we needed to make the *Echoer* fly. What we truly lacked was Allison's intuition of metals. She had an innate skill with gear assemblies. She may have inherited some of that from her watch-making father, but she honed her skills with insatiable drive for perfection.

So we needed Allison's divine connection to metal to remedy our current perplexity. I didn't dare unmoor the *Echoer* until I was sure this divine connection was made.

Allison, however, was still refusing my requests for help. It seemed she was roped into a very prestigious position with the Catholic Church. She said she needed the stability of that job and that she was not about to give up a lucrative future by ... as she put it ... "running away with me." I might have been a little hot-headed in some of my letters. I might have said some unkind words. I wrote the requests in anger, and I didn't mean some of the things I said. I tried to take them back. But did you know postal riders are fast?

Ah, I digress again.

Kendo, Sheila, and I first took our project to Amarillo, the helium capital of the world. It is amazing how helium can leak out of the best air bladders after a just a few weeks. Helium is hard to transport and not at all cheap.

Kendo didn't like our hanger idea for storing the *Echoer*, said it would attract too much attention in Amarillo. He suggested looking for a dry river bed, one that cut deep so we could set up at the bottom. We could run rigging lines across the top and canvas to shelter us from the summer sun. I doubted we could ever find one large enough to hide a fifty-foot tall airship. But once again I was proven wrong. The rancher actually liked having our crew on her property. She said as long as we helped keep trouble off her land we were welcome to use a chunk of it for our project.

Then I caught word that Allison was going to be in Texas.

I was elated. How far from Amarillo could Beaumont be? It was the same state, after all, and so I made plans to travel there. I had no idea just how ... big ... Texas was.

I hope Sheila finds us a proper inn to pass our time here while I find Allison.

Shelia said she was here a few years ago, and that since Spindletop blew, Beaumont had become the place everyone wanted to be. Hence, the inns were full, and I figured that finding even an old barn to sleep in would be next to impossible. But Sheila said she has connections. Actually, she has a friend who knows a friend who knows the proprietor of one of Beaumont's finest inns— the Beaumont House. Shelia crafted a beautiful silver maple music box to give him (I helped her with the mechanics), and said it should net us rooms and hot baths.

Looking at the finished work, I thought a long, hot bath was indeed in my near future.

The Beaumont House was an impressive sight. The aroma coming from its eatery made my mouth water and my stomach growl in anticipation. We waited well more than a handful of minutes ... to give Sheila time to meet with the proprietor ... before we stopped our horses at the rail. Kendo helped me through the front door; I wondered if I would even be able to walk fully upright again.

The drinking hall was shoulder-to-shoulder. The cigar smoke made my eyes water. We made our way to the bar and found Shelia. She stood at the counter chatting it up with the proprietor, Frank, who had a winning smile and served us food unlike any I have ever had.

Later on, Kendo and Shelia didn't need to help me waddle up the stairs to our rooms; the railing was sturdy enough for me to lean on.

The inn workers were already bringing up buckets of steaming water for the bath. If only I could cut the soreness from the ride with a nice bottle of whiskey. But I needed a clear head for tomorrow; the hot bath would need to do.

I eased myself into the tub after learning our horses were being tended to. Sheila was Shelia, seated at a small table, her back to us, quilling a list of supplies we would pick up in the morning.

Later, Kendo and Shelia left me to rest while they said the night was still too young to waste. I could still hear them whoopin' it up downstairs as I drifted off. Longhorns crashing down the hall wouldn't have woken me.

In the morning, however, a repeated rapping at the door jostled me. It took me a few ticks to get my wits about me. I wrapped a sheet around my waist and opened the door. A well dressed boy brought in a hot pitcher and a bowl. He spoke with a slight European accent: "I was to tell you 'she' is in town, sir. She can be found at Saint Anthony's five blocks directly south of here. You can't miss the tall, round tower."

I thanked him with a silver piece and dressed for the day.

I was excited. I could hear my heart beat as I headed down the stairs. The main room was still crowded, but thankfully less smoky. Folks of all nationalities were bustling about. It reminded me of a sea port, only sea ports didn't smell like fresh bacon.

Kendo and Shelia were easy to spot. Shelia placed her hand on my arm as I sat to join them for breakfast. "It will be fine, Brandon," Sheila told me. "Allison will join us. I can feel it."

Kendo pushed a mug toward me. I took a sip and held it high, "If not, we can tie her to the extra horse we brought and work things out on the way back."

Shelia let out a loud giggle and was elbowed by Kendo. I ate quickly and waved my last strip of bacon at them. "What's going on here, you two? Something's up. Don't keep secrets from your boss. I can see it in your faces."

Shelia tried to mask her smirk with her mug but broke out laughing. "We are going to sell the horses and take the rails back. We wouldn't dream of having Allison ride through the length of Texas on horseback. That would be downright cruel."

My eyes grew wide as it sunk in. "Then why didn't you talk me into taking the train to get here? I still can't walk straight."

Sheila drew herself up. "Because on horseback we didn't have to listen to your prattle, you had to put all your energy into riding. I could just imagine you pacing the length of the train cars telling everyone about Allison . . . not to mention about our little project."

I was caught between full anger and pride at her genius. Shelia pulled her chair closer for more privacy. "Brandon, now go get Allison while we arrange rail travel back to Amarillo."

It was raining outside. It felt refreshing.

I stowed the plans for the *Echoer* inside my leather long coat and headed toward Saint Anthony's. I could honestly say I had never looked forward to going to a church before. I could see the front towers of Saint Anthony's clearly, even from the steps of the inn. Then I caught a glimpse of a figure in black dance across the puddle-dotted road a few blocks ahead. The pounding in my chest told me the woman with the parasol was my Allison. Who else but Allison owned a black parasol?

I hurried along.

The magnificence of Saint Anthony's could be felt in the air. The solid brick building looked plucked right off the street of Venice. Then it clicked and I stopped dead in my boots. Saint Anthony . . . the saint of finding things you lost, the saint of the traveler.

Was God taunting me with his signs?

Or was he guiding me across the vast expanse of Texas to find my lost Allison?

Either way he didn't spare any expense. The two massive towers framing the entry doors must have reached at least sixty feet in the air, making the front pillars look small in comparison. It also made the building look closer than it actually was. I could see the woman in black present her parasol to a worker before pulling a cloth over her head. She wasn't looking my way and slipped inside the doors . . . pulled away from me yet again. That had to be my Allison.

I took a deep breath crossing the last street and headed up the front stairs.

The church looked complete in its construction except for a few makeshift tables near the entrance. I stepped inside and allowed my eyes to adjust to the darkness. The only light came through stained glass windows, and the cloudy sky cut most of that. Still, I could tell that the windows were amazing. They gave a deep blue hue to the interior and made me feel like I had just stepped into another world.

The scent of Allison's perfume still lingered in the vestibule.

I could not think of a more beautiful place to repair my heart and rest my soul than this magnificent church.

The central archways opened the worship area toward the sky. The side walls were braced with marble pillars. The design drew my eyes toward a solid marble altar. From there, a series of domes supported by ever larger pillars reached up toward an even larger copper dome. I was certain that even the most traveled bishop would be in awe walking toward the solid white marble altar. I took my hat off and gave a heartfelt 'thank you' to anyone that may be listening.

My trance was broken by a Spanish accented "Sister Allison, I think someone is here to see you."

Sister?

My heart leaped into my throat. I turned quickly toward the voice. Out of the shadows Allison strode toward me.

She was wearing a deep purple layered dress, so dark that no wonder when I spotted her out on the street I'd thought it was black. Her head was fully covered in a black lace cloth. My heart restarted when I saw her waist. I let out an audible sigh. Nuns don't wear corsets or elaborate passementerie dresses.

Through the lace I saw her eyes grow wide. I gave a deep bow, holding my hat tight to my chest. "Milady Allison Marie Emmery, I beg an audience with you." I held my breath.

"Brandon Peter Lynch . . . is that you hiding under that mop of red hair? Still wearing that ole leather duster?"

I held my bow until she lifted my chin toward her.

"You almost shaved, how sweet." Allison was as tall as I in her boots. I stood straight as she inspected me. "What happened to you? Your skin is so dark." Her eyes grew wet and her smile lit up the very air around her.

"Milady, I may have weathered on the outside, but my heart is still strong and beats only for you." Even after these years I could still make her blush. I could feel tears tease the edges of my eyes. I had much to say and didn't wish to become all choked up. I pulled my eyes from hers and motioned around me with my hat. "Alice, your adventures have seemed to take you to wonderland. I feel like I am being watched here." I turned back and again locked my eyes on hers.

Allison pulled the lace cloth from her face, but kept her head covered. "Welcome to Saint Anthony's. Let me give you a tour." She put her hand on my arm and motioned me forward, pointing out key design features.

I could feel the love the workers had put in their work, guided by Allison's designs.

"The bishop arrived last week. The dedication will be this Sunday." She turned quickly in front of me and grasped my hands. "Will you attend with me? You will need to get a shave, and I know a tailor that owes me a favor."

I said 'yes' before I realized what I was getting myself into. I hoped Sheila hadn't purchased train tickets for tomorrow.

Allison continued to point out her handiwork as the church continued to brighten. The rain had stopped and the sun sent shafts of colored light into the worship area. We stopped near the large stained glass image of Saint Cecilia. This time it was I grasping her hands in mine. "Allison, your work here is wonderful. It also sounds like your work here is complete. Will you please join me and help make . . ."

"I told you 'no' last time, and my answer hasn't changed. You need to find your own path." She pulled away leaning against the nearby pew.

I stepped closer as she crossed her arms in defiance.

"Allison, I didn't come here to tussle. I came because I need you. I need your skills, your eye for detail. The *Echoer* is having issues with the main gearing. We all checked the math, so that isn't the issue. The problem must be with the combination of metals. You know each metal has its own personality better than anyone. You always had a magical way with knowing the right metal to use where." I gently placed my hand on her shoulder. "Look around you. You can make any metal you touch sing. I dare not take the aeronave into the sky without being sure everything is right as rain. I need you. The *Echoer* needs you. We all need you. Please."

She squinted as she stared at me, "You actually built your airship? Did you finally take the Union offer or did you sign on with Blue Skies Corporation?"

"Neither! They don't appreciate beauty. They only lust for pure function. I found a few financial backers and it took three years for us to build her. Only one main problem remains. She needs your talent." I motioned toward the makeshift tables set up in the vestibule. Pulling out a large leather envelope from my interior coat pocket I headed over and prayed she would follow.

Gently unfolding the stiff linen design sheets, I set one on top of the other. The last one unfolded was our girl, inked in color, the *Echoer*. Not the common single oval air bladder design, but a right angle boomerang shape. The gondola descended from the center with each wing pulled back like a bird diving toward its prey. The wingspan was listed at the bottom: 150 feet. I let her page through the sheets in silence, biting my tongue to keep quiet. She always said knowing when to keep my mouth shut was not my strong suit.

"Brandon this isn't just an airship, it's a clockwork!" Somewhat stunned, she glared at me. "This isn't one of your shenanigans is it? You really built this?"

I gave a confident smile for my answer.

She pulled back the first few sheets and tapped her finger on the left mainspring. "This is not possible! You can't make a mainspring of that size. Even if you did it would be dangerous!"

It was time for me to seal the deal. "Well, my dear Allison, some folks like danger. Some folks live to prove that nothing is impossible. All you need is faith and friends. Isn't that what you always told me?"

She spent less than five minutes reviewing the designs and found the flaw we'd spent a year trying to pin down.

"And this problem . . ." I turned to the next sheet. "This is your impossibility to solve. No matter how we reinforce the gear train, it keeps slipping out of place. Allison, we need you." I need you.

Allison scowled and pulled the page out of the stack to get a closer look. "The gear train should be fine. You really don't even need it. It would only slip out of place if you planned on reversing the motion." She tilted her head and glanced at me with those amazing eyes. "Why would it go in reverse?"

Finally, after ten years of school together I stumped her! I wanted to let out a loud, 'whoop,' but that wouldn't have helped at this moment. I just gave her my broad smile. "We decided we needed a method to wind her up while it is still in the air." I pulled the bottom page and set it on top. "We use this piece as an anchor hard point. We anchor the ship in the air. We let the wind rotate the ship. Once the ship is pointed into the wind we reverse the main propeller shaft drives here and here. Then we let the air turn the propellers the opposite direction and wind ourselves back up."

When it fully sank in, she stepped back and sat on a nearby pew. "You did it. You actually built your dream ship." She shook her head and smiled.

"No, Allison Emmery, I built *our* dream ship." I dropped to one knee in front of her and took her hand in mine. "Allison, will you come fly away with me?"

I looked into her eyes and time stopped. Memories of our past and visions of our future flooded through my mind. As tears streamed from her eyes she smiled. Time restarted as my heart filled with joy. She wrapped her arms around me and whispered in my ear "yes."

Nine months have passed and it's been clear sailing ever since. We are currently anchored in Nepal. Never let your dreams slip away, I say. Just believe in yourself—and those around you, and most of all never give up.

Of A Feather

Stephen D. Sullivan

Stephen D. Sullivan first encountered steampunk as a child, when he got swept up in the original run of the TV show *The Wild Wild West*. That's also around the time he got swept up in sci-fi adventure, lost worlds, and monsters—all of which make an appearance in this tale. When asked to contribute a story for this anthology, a very strong picture of an airship, an adventurer, and a flying monster appeared in Steve's head. And though the Amazon is an unusual place to set a steampunk story, he went with it; when an image comes in that strong, it's folly to ignore it. Steve hopes his readers will enjoy the incongruous blend. You can find out more about the author and his work, and sign up for his mailing list, at: www.stephendsullivan.com.

O'Brien grabs his Remington from the map table and swings it toward the incoming ranodon. "Miss Kit! Miss Tesla! Duck!" he hollers. The prehistoric beast—jaws open, talons extended—dives directly toward me and Zoe as we stand together, amidships.

"No!" I shout. "No guns! Use the cannon!" While I admire O'Brien's devotion to keeping us safe, I'm not about to lose months of careful scientific work because of his superstitious nature.

But the captain of the *Louisa* isn't listening. He draws a bead on the center of the ranodon's forehead. Fortunately, Armstrong grabs O'Brien's arm, spoiling the captain's aim. The shot goes wide, merely clipping a hairy feather from the trailing edge of the pterosaur's left wingtip.

The ranodon's eyes blaze with reptilian hate as it swoops in. At the last instant, I throw my arms around Zoe, carrying us both to the deck. The beast's talons flash harmlessly over our exposed backs.

The creature wheels for another pass, but as it does, I spring to my feet and run for the cannon mounted in the bow of our shallow-draft steamer. Armstrong continues wrestling with O'Brien, struggling to keep the captain from shooting our prize before I can carry out my plan. Zoe—often the wisest among us—lies flat on the bottom of the boat. Miz Tesla isn't on this trip because of her bravery; she's here because there isn't a piece of equipment in the world that she can't fix.

I swing the cannon around as the ranodon comes for me, murder in its yellow eyes. I tick off the range in my head, waiting for the optimal distance. *Thirty meters. Twenty. Fifteen. Ten . . .*

I pull the trigger, and the specially manufactured shell bursts from the end of the big gun. A weighted net billows out, surrounding the reptilian monster. The ranodon squawks, entangled, and crashes into the side of the boat before plunging into the murky Greenwater.

"Quick!" I call. "Help me pull her out before she drowns!"

Immediately, Armstrong appears at my side with a pair of boat hooks. My cousin has his faults, but superstitious fear of monsters is not among them. Together, we quickly snag the net and pull the raging, sopping-wet beast aboard the steamer. The ranodon snaps ineffectually at us as we pin the netting to the deck. O'Brien inches forward, his gun leveled; Zoe follows a few steps behind, her eyes wide with wonder—and more than a little fear.

The ranodon is all flailing wings, snapping teeth, and sharp talons. Even its brilliant plumage doesn't make it appear any less threatening. I can hardly blame Zoe and O'Brien for being frightened of it. If I hadn't devoted so much time to studying this creature and its ilk, I might be afraid myself. As it is, all I can see is the monster's immense archeobiological value: the last known ranodon, east of the Antes! Most scientists in my field would give their lives to see something like this—and more than a few have.

"Take it easy, big guy," Armstrong says, pushing the barrel of O'Brien's Remington toward the deck. "No sense shooting it now. Kitty and I have everything under control—and, besides, you wouldn't want to hit one of us by mistake." Reluctantly, O'Brien lowers the gun.

Armstrong smiles at me, and, for a moment, I see what every other woman in the world sees in Ray Armstrong; my cousin is one handsome piece of work. Fortunately, being a blood relative, I am immune to his legendary charms. "Nice shot, Kitty," he says, beaming. "Everything went just like clockwork."

I smile back, ignoring his use of a nickname I abandoned as a child; being family does have its privileges, after all, and Ray is the only kin I have left. I shrug. "Months of planning ... a dash of research ... and enough money to choke an anaconda ... anyone could have done it."

"Anyone with the last name of Chapman-Challenger," Armstrong says, apparently trying to give me a swelled head.

"Or Armstrong," Zoe adds. Armstrong blows her a kiss, and my mechanic blushes.

I take a deep breath, more relieved at the capture than I had first realized. I needed a big score on this expedition—we all did.

"Fetch the Rolleiflex, will you?" I tell Armstrong. "We're not getting paid for shots of the landscape, and my trust fund is looking awfully skinny lately."

"At least you still *have* a trust fund," Armstrong replies, eyes twinkling.

"Lucky for you that I do," I shoot back good naturedly. Money runs through my cousin's hands like water. "Otherwise, who would hire an old sot like you?"

Armstrong gazes up, thoughtfully. "Some rich widow, I'm sure. You know, come to think of it, that might be a good career move for me. . . ."

I laugh. "Zoe, bring me some of that bait, will you?"

Zoe's bespectacled eyes, both wary and fascinated, remain fixed on the prehistoric creature thrashing in our net. If the ranodon were free, it could easily carry her ninety-pound frame into the wild blue yonder. "Do you want the f-fish or the meat?" Zoe asks.

"Antean ranodons are flesh eaters," I say, "so we'll try the meat first." Zoe nods and goes to get the bait from the steamer's storage locker.

"This beauty's a long ways from the Antean Mountains," Armstrong observes as he comes back with the camera.

"Not as the ranodon flies," I note. My cousin focuses and takes pictures as I examine the hissing, snapping beast.

"A female, just as I expected," I say, pleased.

"Do you really think there's a nest nearby?" Zoe asks. Gingerly, she hands me a strip of meat. I flip it to the ranodon, careful not to lose my fingers to the pterosaur's sharp teeth.

"She's mating age," I reply. "And it's the right season, and the locals did bring down that male six weeks back."

"So the time is about right for hatchlings," Armstrong agrees.

"Just what we need," O'Brien grumbles, "more of these blasted gooney birds! I give you three-to-one that they get one of us—or all of us—killed before this is over."

"If they get all of us killed, how are you going to collect?" Armstrong asks.

"Well, we could turn back," the captain suggests.

"When we've already got a mother ranodon in our nets?" I ask. "When we're so close to a nest I can almost touch it? Not on your life."

As one, all of us turn and gaze at the tepui rising from the Amazonian jungle a short distance upriver. The plateau rises precipitously from the river's edge. Its sides are sheer rock, wrapped with tenacious, clinging greenery. Bushy thickets cover the top of the escarpment.

"Like something out of the family album," Armstrong notes.

I nod. We have Amazon explorers on both sides of the family—extending back into the seventeenth century. One ventured even further into the jungle than we have, in search of the legendary Maplewhite Land; another freed some local Indians from a slave mine run by a psychopath with a trained ranodon as his "guard dog." Those triumphs were ages ago, though, and, at the moment, I wish we had our ancestors' elaborate equipment—and funding.

"An autogyro would really come in handy about now," Armstrong observes.

Zoe sighs; there's one back home—from grandfather's day—but not enough cash for the parts she needs to repair it. "Or one of those new Russian helioships," she adds.

Armstrong grins at her, sharing my mechanic's fantasy. "Yeah ... Even one of those small twin-rotor jobs with the overhead gas cells would do. 'Course, if we're dreaming, we might as well dream of a new helioliner, with all the trimmings."

"I'd settle for a small, heavily armored gunship," O'Brien puts in. "If we're going after more of these crazy birds."

"Pterosaurs," I remind him. "More like feathered reptiles."

"Whatever they are, I don't like 'em," the captain says, "not even when they're netted and pinned to my deck. That devil would just as soon take off your fingers as look at you." He glares at the ranodon and clutches his gun tighter.

"Why don't you check the boiler," Armstrong says. "I think it might be low on pressure." It's more of a command than a suggestion. O'Brien grumbles, but turns to check on the boat's aging engineworks.

My cousin shades his eyes and gazes toward the tepui's summit. "You going up?" he asks.

"That's crazy, Miss Kit!" O'Brien calls from near the wheel. "We already got one specimen. We should head back downriver to Elturu. Your monster will fetch a pretty penny there. I heard they cut up the male and sold it as an aphrodisiac for 100 Golden Re-als an ounce! And someone told me about some Russians what might give you even more!"

For just a moment, I consider setting the ranodon free so it can claw O'Brien's eyes out. I don't know what infuriates me more, superstitious locals or Russian weapon prospectors.

"This expedition is about science, not profit!" Zoe scolds, glaring at him. She's taken over feeding the beast from me, though her hands still shake as she proffers the strips of fresh meat.

O'Brien folds his arms across his beefy chest and sulks.

"You'll have to keep mama ranodon here while I look for her nest," I tell my cousin.

"How long?" Armstrong asks, glancing toward O'Brien. Clearly, he can't trust the captain to help with the job.

"From the observations we've made over the past few days, I think I have a pretty good idea of the nest's location," I reply. "With luck—and a little help from Zoe's clockworks—I'll be back before nightfall."

"And if you're *not* lucky?"

"Then I'll be staying the night on the plateau."

O'Brien shivers, and Zoe looks worried, but Armstrong merely nods.

"Ranodons don't survive long in captivity," he reminds me. "At least, they never have before."

I prickle. "Some archeobiologist I'd be if I didn't know that!" I reply. Sometimes it seems like Ray forgets who the sober and well-organized one is in this family.

"All right. Obvious," he says. "Sorry, Kitten."

I take a deep breath, knowing he means well. "Neither one of us wants to kill her—either on purpose or by accident. She's probably the last of her kind in these parts."

"Not too many left in the Antes, either," Armstrong adds. He kneels beside Zoe and reaches out as if to stroke the ranodon's head. It snaps at him. Unflappable, my cousin pulls his hand back just far enough that it can't reach. "Easy, girl!"

"Antean government protects what's left of them," Zoe says. "Or tries to. Lost a couple of adventurous tourists last week—a scientist trying to study the roosts a month before that."

"Damn fools! Both them tourists, and the Antean government!" O'Brien interjects. "These brutes should have gone extinct long ago. No room in this day for prehistoric monsters!"

"But plenty of room for prehistoric superstition, it appears," Armstrong jibes.

O'Brien glares at him.

"Lucky for you the ranodons haven't gone extinct, either here or in the Antes," I tell him. "Or the magazine and I wouldn't be funding this little expedition."

"*Underfunding* is more like it," O'Brien grumbles.

"Shooting a ranodon, like the villagers did here—or like you tried to do—is a capital offense in the Antes," Zoe says. "Either the government gets you, or . . ."

"Which is why we're not even *trying* to study that

nesting cluster," I say, attempting to calm the rising tensions among my crew. "I can handle a little government trouble, but I don't want Quetziqa Indians dipping their fingertips in my blood to paint their faces."

O'Brien makes the sign of the cross. Even though we're far from the Antean Mountains, the Quetziqa Indians are still greatly feared. The Antean government gives them wide berth—and wide latitude in the rule of traditional Quetziqa lands. Even the Russians don't mess with the red-fingered tribesfolk.

Zoe hands the feeding of our feathered guest over to Armstrong and fetches some equipment from her locker. "Don't worry, CC," she tells me. "I'll have her tagged and ready to track by the time you get back. Assuming that Ray can keep her quiet enough."

"Hey," Armstrong shoots back, "She's no trickier than most women I've dealt with. See? I've already got her eating out of my hands."

Zoe's climbing rigs make ascending the tepui easier, but it's still tricky going. The clockwork ascender fastened to my equipment harness makes me nearly weightless as I climb, but most of the pitons still have to be placed the old fashioned way: via hammer. The sheer cliffs are slick, both from the local humidity and from the soggy vines and mosses clinging to the rock face. When a gap appears in the escarpment, I fire a piton-anchored line across it using my miniature crossbow, and then slide over with a simple pulley rig. The crossbow fires grapnels as well, making ascent quicker when I can find a solid ledge above me to anchor the hooks.

Even with the assist from my Master Inventor's gadgets, I still sweat buckets. So I take frequent breaks on the way up, both to catch my breath and to rehydrate. When I rest, I plan the safest route to where I *hope* to find the nest: a narrow ledge three-quarters of the way to the top. It takes me most of the afternoon to reach it. Vegetation hangs thick on either side of the ledge. It's too dense to drive a piton through, but not solid enough to hold my weight. Even the crossbow is no help here. I can see the nest on the ledge though—a bushy thatch of dry vegetation amid the rocks. It beckons to me, like King Solomon's Mines, but I can't tell if there are any eggs, and—from here—I can't reach it to find out.

Rappelling down from above seems my only option, but the cliff juts out at a right angle above me—a great lip of rock nearly four meters wide. Even with my years of mountaineering experience, it will take me hours to safely navigate that slick surface, if I can manage it at all. Fortunately, Zoe has provided a solution to this problem, too: the *spider grapnel*. I take the metal arachnid from my pack, wind it up—remembering to prime its anchor charge—and set it to work.

As nimble as a real spider, the mechanism's carbon-steel legs scuttle across the underside of the ledge and over the top. I hear the tick-tick-ticking as it probes for a solid spot on the upper surface, then the sharp "crack" of the black powder as the spider sinks its anchor deep into the rock. I test the line gingerly, despite my faith in Zoe's inventions, making sure the anchor will hold my weight. It does. Just in case, I deploy some of Zoe's elastic anti-fall netting. Then, trusting to luck and experience, I hoist myself up the spider-line.

It takes me another half hour to make my way above the nesting ledge, find a safe anchor, and then rappel down to my goal. A thrill shoots up my spine as my boots touch solid ground and I get a clear look at my prize. Inside the nest is a dozen eggs, each the color of speckled sand and half the size of a football.

For long moments, I can only stare; this is a site few humans have ever seen and fewer still lived to talk about. Only traditional Quetziqa initiates—and two recorded scientists—have ever observed an unplundered ranodon nest, and no nests have ever been observed east of the Antes. Do the ancient beasts migrate from here all the way to that distant range? With luck, the tracking tag Zoe's putting on the mother will help us find out. We will be the first: the first people to know the secrets of ranodon migration, just as I am the first person east of the Antes to ever glimpse this sight.

I feel immensely honored and proud of the work my team has done to get me here. Zoe ... Armstrong ... even grouchy O'Brien. Everyone has performed their jobs above and beyond the call. We've gotten here on a wing and a prayer, without any Russian technology or backing. That's a rarity nowadays.

Before I start measuring the nest and taking notes, something else catches my attention: the vista. Though sheltered by the surrounding vegetation, the ledge has a clear view of the silver ribbon of the Greenwater as it winds east toward mother Amazon. Far below, O'Brien's flat-bottom steamer bobs gently on the placid waters. I can see the tiny figures of my crew moving about the *Louisa's* deck: Armstrong and Zoe working with the netted mother; O'Brien pacing amidships like a nervous tiger.

Further downstream, storks, fish, and caimans prowl the shallows. Upstream, the canopy closes in around the tributary, forming a living green tunnel around the river. Packs of monkeys—capuchins, probably, though I can't tell from this distance—cavort in the foliage, leaping from tree to tree. All of the creatures I see, except for the largest caimans, would be fine prey for a hungry ranodon and her brood.

A sudden stab of worry flashes through my mind: Has Mother Ranodon been away from the nest too long? Existing information on ranodon brooding habits is sketchy. Does she need to sit on her eggs to keep them warm? By holding the mother captive, is my expedition hastening the extinction of this magnificent species?

I reach for one of the twin pistols holstered at my hip. The plan was to fire a off a single shot after finishing my research. Upon hearing the shot, Armstrong will set the mother ranodon free. Of course, by that time, I'm supposed to be well out of the nest—and out of the reach of mother ranodon's talons. But is it too early to fire that shot, or is it already too late?

I watch the sunshine glinting off the speckled shells. The daylight should be enough to keep them warm for a while longer, I reckon, but I'll have to hurry to complete my work.

Quickly I unpack the Rolleiflex and begin taking pictures. When I've got what seems like a full set, I start measuring the eggs, being careful not to touch any. I wouldn't want them contaminated by my scent, and I've gotten too close to the nest as it is. Hopefully, my furtive presence won't make the mother angry enough to abandon her unborn chicks.

The sun's nearing the Amazonian treetops by the time I finish, and the air is rapidly cooling. Again, my fear for the eggs' warmth rises in my mind. I decide to cut some vegetation and cover them—to try and hold in a little of the heat until their mother can return.

My machete makes short work of the greenery hanging nearby, and I carry a thick blanket of leaves back—in gloved hands—toward the nest. I hope it will be enough. And I hope the scent from my sweaty clothing won't contaminate the foliage and spook the mother away.

I pause, just a few feet from the eggs, unsure of whether to continue, when a loud "Crack!" fills the air. I look toward the top of the tepui; the sound is like pebbles rattling down a cliff face. Another "Crack!" and another, but I see no rocks falling. Then I realize the source of the sound: the eggs!

I drop the thatch of vegetation from my arms and fish out the Rolleiflex again. The baby ranodons are hatching before my eyes! I am definitely the first scientist to ever observe this! I'm so excited that, for a moment, I forget that this could be a very bad thing. Ranodons and humans do *not* mix. They might be hostile to me from the instant they hatch. Will they be able to fly the minute they're out of the shell?

No one knows, and—for a few seconds—I wish I were *not* the first scientist ever to witness a ranodon hatching.

Then the first shell splits open, and a feathered, reptilian head pokes out. It stares at me with big, golden eyes. I stare back, as its brothers and sisters hatch, each emerging from their eggs only seconds apart. And as the eldest ranodon and I stare at each other, entranced, I know that this brood will not attack me. I am safe—at least until I fire the shot to set their mother free. But by the time she arrives, I will be long gone.

Zoe checks her home-built directional radiographer. "They're heading toward the Antes all right," she announces, "just as you predicted, Kit. Tracking signal remains strong."

"That's my Kitty," Armstrong boasts, slurring his words. "Always knows what she's up to."

I smile at my cousin, but I wish I could say the same of him. Armstrong is a good man, but this morning his eyes are cloudy and he smells of drink. Though I trust him with my life, I don't trust him around booze or unescorted women. In the nine weeks we've waited for the ranodon brood to begin their migration, he and O'Brien have spent more time on "errands" in Elturu than they've spent at base camp. O'Brien usually returns in better shape than Cousin Ray, though that's not saying much.

Fortunately, we're back on the river and Armstrong is away from the drink and the dames—except for Zoe. Occasionally, I catch him eyeing her when he thinks I'm not looking. I realize that's the aftereffects of the booze; sober, he's like an older brother to her. When tipsy, though, anything with a bosom—short of a blood relation—starts looking good to my cousin.

"Man the Rolleiflex, would you?" I ask, hoping to keep his mind on our job.

The pictures we've sent by courier so far have been

a sensation with the editors. Once they're on the stands, they'll take the world by storm—and maybe even help to restore some of my family's lost fortune. But the editors want the whole story before they publish, and that story includes the ranodon migration.

Twice this week we've had false starts: the mother taking her flock out for long flights, heading west—toward the far distant mountains—only to turn back at midday. Why they're doing this, we can only guess: building up their strength, perhaps? Scouting the territory ahead for food . . . or predators?

Each time we've followed, only to do an abrupt about-face and chase them back downstream. Captain O'Brien's had a few choice words about that. I think he's annoyed at having to keep the *Louisa* running in top shape for so long. We need his best, though, and the ship's best, too. We'll need everyone's best, if we're to seize the prize at the end of this expedition.

"I'll give you two-to-one that they don't even migrate this week!" O'Brien announces.

But despite the captain's prediction, today's flight seems to be the real thing. Migration at last! Midday comes and goes and afternoon fades toward evening, and, still, the flock of ranodons shows no signs of turning back. We follow upriver, *Louisa* giving us all the steam O'Brien can muster. As the orange orb of the sun kisses the treetops, mama and her brood settle down, roosting in niches high up the verdant sides of a crumbling riverside tepui.

"Maybe we can get some good shots when they take to the air again in the morning," Zoe suggests.

"Which means being ready at sunrise," I conclude.

Armstrong groans at the thought, but he's up before the ranodons—along with the rest of us—the next morning, and completely sobered up as well; thankfully, my cousin seldom drinks while adventuring.

Zoe mans the Roleiflex with the telescopic lens, which she manufactured specially for it. I'm no judge of editorial whims, but by late morning I think she's garnered enough shots to pay for this leg of the trip—and maybe even the false starts we had the last few days. O'Brien builds up enough pressure in the *Louisa's* boiler to keep the ranodons in sight, despite the twists and turns of the Greenwater. As we steam upriver, the Amazonian canopy opens and closes above our heads, making the world a kaleidoscope of green tunnels and sweltering sunlight.

We branch onto the Naconda shortly before midday, when the Greenwater twists south, deeper into the jungle, and from the Naconda into an unnamed tributary heading almost directly west. Fortunately, the ranodons seem to be following the waterways; I wonder if it's because of some ancient homing instinct, or if we've just gotten lucky.

At nightfall, they roost on another tepui, this one little more than a finger of rock jutting up out of the surrounding rainforest.

"Like frogs hopping from lily pad to lily pad," Armstrong observes as we bed down for the night.

"Bloody ugly frogs," O'Brien adds. "I'm surprised I ain't got nightmares yet."

"If you're going to dream of something green," Armstrong suggests, "make it all the lovely money we'll get for the pictures of this expedition."

O'Brien sighs contentedly. "Ah, now there's something to sleep on!"

"I wonder . . ." Zoe muses as she stands in the *Louisa's* bow during the afternoon of the next day's pursuit. She has her goggles put up on her forehead and a pencil tucked, as usual, behind her right ear.

"Wonder what?" I ask.

"I wonder how many eons ranodonkind has been following this very route. What do you think, CC?"

"Perhaps after we discover exactly where they're going, we can come back and dig for evidence," I suggest.

"Good luck finding anything in all this tangled greenery," Armstrong replies. "Maybe you could make a dent with steam shovels."

Zoe rolls her eyes. "And ruin whatever Kit hoped to find in the process!"

"We'll worry about that when, and *if*, the time comes," I say. "Let's finish *this* expedition and pay some bills first."

"Amen to that," O'Brien adds.

Armstrong jerks a thumb toward the captain. "Our friend ran up quite a debt on Elturu's game tables while waiting for the migration."

"*Me?*" O'Brien shoots back. "That's nothing compared to the tab that you ran up at Miss Juanita's bordel—"

"I've never paid for any such thing!" Armstrong contends hotly.

"Pipe down, everyone!" I shout. "I hear something!" I hold my hands up for quiet and look around. "Can anyone else hear that?"

Everyone stops and listens, but the sound remains a dim whine; I can barely pick it out over the boat's sputtering engine.

"Idle her, will you?" Armstrong tells O'Brien. The captain throttles back the *Louisa's* engines; the boat slows, and the puttering subsides into an occasional low hiss.

Now everyone can hear what I hear—a constant pulsing thrum, the distant engines of a helioship.

"I see her!" O'Brien says, pointing.

The sleek craft glitters in the late afternoon sunlight, like a tiny bronze bird skimming the horizon. Its powerful twin rotors and single gas cell hold it effortlessly above the jungle. It's not large as helioships go, just four or five meters long—but that's big enough to hold plenty of trouble. The craft is far away but moving upriver swiftly, coming toward us . . . or perhaps toward something else.

Zoe swings the telescopic lens of the Rolleiflex in the direction of the distant craft. "Russian, I think, CC."

"I'd guessed that from the sound," I reply, knowing my mechanic probably had, too, even before she focused the camera on the intruder.

"You don't think it could be...?" Zoe says, arching her eyebrows in worry.

"Ivanova," I agree. "Who else?"

"Like a bad hangover, she returns to haunt us once more," Armstrong says.

"You think she's here for those blasted birds?" O'Brien asks.

"Of course she is," I say, almost spitting the words. Pavlina Ivanova used to be one of Russia's leading military psychics; now she's one of their top procurement agents. "If it can be used as a weapon, she—and her government—want it. Ranodons would be perfect for their cryptobiologic breeding programs."

"But how could she find out about *our* ranodons?" Zoe asks.

"She could have read the same newspaper accounts that brought us here in the first place," Armstrong suggests.

O'Brien shakes his head. "The locals shot that male a long time ago, now. It's ancient news."

"Maybe news travels slowly in Russia," Armstrong replies. "I hear they're pretty stingy with information."

"Maybe," Zoe agrees. "But how is that witch able to home in on our flock?"

"Easy," I reply. "She's following your homing signal."

Behind her lenses, Zoe's eyes go wide. "How could she even know about that? Unless somebody told her." Her stare turn cold and she fixes it on O'Brien. I turn an accusing gaze toward the captain as well.

"The flock would be a whole lot more valuable than pictures," Zoe says icily.

"Don't look at me!" O'Brien protests. "You know I'd never sell you out to the Russians! We've worked together for years! Off-and-on, I'll admit, but you're practically like family to me! Family's got to stick together."

Zoe and I glance at each other, both of us thinking about the long hours O'Brien spent in Elturu—drinking and gambling—while we were waiting for the ranodons to migrate.

"What about those gambling debts you ran up?" I ask.

"Sure, I like cards," he says, "but ain't a card game in the world worth losing friends . . . I mean, *family* over!" He looks Zoe right in the eye, and she softens.

"Maybe you wouldn't betray us deliberately," she admits, "but I've seen you do some pretty stupid things when you're drunk."

He starts to say something, but she's run out of sympathy, so he turns to me. "Honest, Miss Kit," he says, "I didn't."

I say nothing, trying to read the truth behind his words—wishing, just for a moment, that I had Pavlina Ivanova's psychic gifts.

Finally, O'Brien rubs his head and adds sheepishly, "At least, I don't *think* I did."

"It doesn't matter how she found us," Armstrong interjects. "What matters is what we're going to do about it."

"It's like the Pyrenees all over again," Zoe moans.

"Ivanova's not going to do to the ranodons what she did to the Neanderthals," I vow.

Armstrong looks at me, hopeful. "Do you have a plan?"

"Not yet," I reply. "But the ranodons will be bedding down for the night, soon, and there's only one tepui along this course—and it's only about a klik ahead. Ivanova's at least an hour away. If we can reach it before she does, get to the ranodons first, maybe we can do something."

"I ain't messin' with that Russian witch," O'Brien says. "Sorry, Miss Kit, but—even though you're practically family—you can't pay me enough for that."

"Kitten," Armstrong says, "he's right. Lina's too dangerous. Maybe we should let this go."

"No," I say. "You didn't see this flock up close . . ."

"I saw *one* of them up close," Armstrong puts in. "And that was enough. They're vicious beasts. The Russians and the ranodons deserve each other."

"You can't mean that. You know what kind of weapons they'd be in Russian hands. They don't deserve that. No creature does."

"Whatever you decide, CC, I'm with you," Zoe says.

"Me, too," Armstrong adds. "I just don't want to charge in without a plan."

"By the time we reach the top of that tepui," I say, "we'll have a plan."

When we anchor at the base of the tepui, O'Brien, true to his word, stays with the boat. I don't blame him; I've seen what kind of damage Ivanova can do to people's bodies . . . and to their minds. Her days in Russia's secret services served her, and the state, well. I doubt the MGB wanted to let her go, but—as I've discovered firsthand on several occasions—she can be very persuasive with both man and beast.

True to form, the ranodons roost on the nearby tepui. Zoe, Armstrong, and I don our packs and gear hastily, and begin to climb. We can hear the helioship clearly as we ascend, even over the scrabble of our feet and the pounding of our pitons. The Russians are almost on us now. We're probably in range of their binoculars, and we can only hope they're not looking for us—at least, not yet.

The tepui is tall, though not so tall as the one I ascended to the original nest. Fortunately, it's not as slippery, either; we make good progress, even though we don't have time to deploy Zoe's elaborate clockwork climbing gear. As near as I can tell, the ranodons have picked a ledge near the very top for their roosting place. We've got a lot of climbing to do if we're to beat Pavlina Ivanova to the roost.

The sun's nearly kissing the jungle by the time we're three-quarters of the way to the plateau top. The helioship is very close now, angling for the best approach. Looking through my binoculars, I can clearly see the hovercraft's occupants. Ivanova is leading them, all right; I'd know her trim, fashionable silhouette anywhere. She's brought three of her Neanderthal goons with her, but I'm glad she didn't round up more. Nachtu, the head Neanderthal, is among them. I silently curse our deteriorating luck.

Our bad fortune doesn't stop there, either. Zoe is already exhausted from the climb. My mechanic is always game for an adventure but seldom gets out of the shop. She pulls herself onto a narrow ledge and leans back against the sheer rock, sweat pouring down her thin frame. "Go on!" she insists, gasping. "I'm just slowing you down. I'll try to catch up."

Armstrong and I nod and continue climbing. There's no sense in arguing; she doesn't have the strength, and we don't have the time.

A sudden blast shakes the cliff face. Armstrong's boot slips, but I grab his hand, saving him a fall back to Zoe's ledge. My cousin looks suitably abashed.

"What in hell was that?" he asks.

We look down and see the *Louisa* burning. Thick black smoke rises from the wreckage of the boat, and debris lies scattered on the quaking surface of the river.

"Pavlina Ivanova does not like competition," I reply.

"That bitch!" Armstrong snarls. "I hope O'Brien got out before the bomb hit."

"Me, too." It's ironic that O'Brien's loose lips might have gotten him killed. He'd have been better off selling us out for money. For a moment, I'm more angry at the captain than worried about his survival. I chide myself for the uncharitable thought.

Armstrong starts climbing again, more quickly now. I follow. "Think she meant to kill us, or just slow us down?" he asks.

"She certainly didn't do O'Brien any good." Unbidden, I remember the captain saying we were *like family* to him. "I don't know," I continue. "She could have seen we weren't there, or maybe her psychic powers told her who was on the boat—and who wasn't."

"I don't think she's got that kind of range," he replies. "At least, she didn't last time we met. You know, this may sound crazy, but I always thought she liked—or at least respected you."

"Not enough to avoid hijacking my research," I reply. "Or blowing up my friends, apparently."

The helioship makes two passes over the ruins of the *Louisa*, maybe looking for survivors. Either they don't find O'Brien—if he's still alive—or they do him the favor of not turning the helioship's Gatling gun on him. Satisfied with the destruction, they start scanning the tepui, homing in on the ranodon's roost. Fortunately, by then, Armstrong and I have already reached the last ledge before the top.

We pause, catching our breaths and unlimbering our guns before the final push. No spider-grapnels or antifall netting needed this time, just three meters up and over the top into a Russian hornet's nest.

I check the handheld radiograph that Zoe whipped up. "The signal's coming from the top of the plateau," I whisper to my cousin.

"Unfortunately, it's led the Russians right to the ranodons, too," he says.

"Damn O'Brien and his drinking!" I cast my eyes back to the boat's smoking remains, torn between worry for the man and frustration at his lack of discretion.

Armstrong leans back against the rock, looking up at the sky. "Look, about that, Kitty . . ." he says. "I don't think it was O'Brien who tipped off Ivanova."

"What?" I say, confused. "Who else could it have been? You're not suggesting Zoe . . ."

He shakes his head. "I can't let you go on thinking O'Brien might have done it, not with him maybe dead and all."

"Ray, what are you saying?"

"I . . . I might have let something slip to one of the girls in town. I didn't mean to . . . Just boasting, the way I do sometimes when I—"

"When you get drunk and sleep around," I whisper.

"Look, Kitten, I'm sorry."

Despite the anger boiling in my gut, I know he means it. He's family, after all—*real* family, the kind that means to do right by you, even if they don't; the kind you always have to take back, no matter what they've done. Rationally, I know all that. But just at the moment, I really hate my cousin.

"How was I to know that the Russians'd get wind of it? But . . . I should have used better judgment. As usual."

I don't want to snap at him, not when the two of us are about to climb into death's open jaws, so I don't say anything.

"I guess you're probably wishing I was on the boat right now—instead of O'Brien." Again, his eyes flash toward the smoke and flames.

"No," I say, putting my hand on his arm and taking a deep breath. "I'm glad you're here with me. There's no one I'd rather have at my side."

"Except maybe Zoe."

"Well," I admit, "at least she doesn't sleep around and blabber our trade secrets to the first Russian spy she takes a fancy to."

"Tight as a banker's purse, that one," he says, some of the Armstrong gleam returning to his eyes. "She should loosen up a bit. At least once."

"Maybe you can work on that . . . assuming Ivanova doesn't kill us."

He nods, grim and determined once more. "What's your plan once we top the escarpment?"

"Try to scare the ranodons off before the Russians capture them."

"How?"

"Shots in the air, maybe?"

"When we shot at momma bird, she kept coming," he notes.

"That was before she had chicks. Let's hope that, with the flock to protect, she'll prefer flying to fighting."

"How are we gonna handle Lina? Shoot her?"

"Disabling her ship would be a good start," I reply. "And then shoot her if we have to."

"And her apelike friends?"

"We hold her hostage against their good behavior. All of them are completely devoted to their mistress, especially Nachtu."

Armstrong shakes his head. "Poor saps. *Homo sapiens* should know better."

"Ivanova has a bad effect on some people," I say, and both of us remember a certain incident in St. Petersburg.

My cousin almost blushes. "Holding Lina hostage won't work if we shoot her."

"Then we improvise."

Armstrong grins. "As usual."

"As usual. Just make sure you don't look into her eyes."

"I don't think her psi-powers are sight based."

"No, but your libido is," I reply. "She's got enough advantages without you admiring her figure."

"The ship's throttling down," he says, listening. "They must have found the roost." He chambers a round in his carbine.

I switch the safeties off my 45s, keeping the weapons loose in their holsters. "Time to go." I quickly hoist myself up to the lip of the escarpment; my cousin follows right behind.

The top of the plateau is a flat, rocky expanse one hundred meters wide. The only cover is a few dozen boulders and a smattering of twisted scrub. Ivanova's ship hangs in the air on the far side, about four meters above the surface—its buoyancy envelope slackened for hovering, its steam engines whirring quietly on low power.

Colonel Pavlina Ivanova clings to the last rung of a chain ladder dangling from the side of the helioship. She's staring at something in a thicket nearby, concentrating her entire attention on a single point: the ranodons, which have bedded down for the night amid the greenery.

The flock, eleven plus the mother, are giving Ivanova their undivided attention. Their feathered reptilian bodies are tense, and murder lurks behind their yellow eyes, but each beast remains fixated on the Russian, rapt in her psychic power. Damn! In another moment, they'll be hers. My mind flashes back to the Pyrenees, and how close I came to saving that band of Neanderthals, all of whom are now in the Russian's thrall.

She's brought all three of the ape-men with her. Each is dressed in a black Special Services uniform. They stand on the plateau in a rough triangle, guarding their boss. Two, including Nachtu, have their Thompson submachine guns trained on the pterosaurs—in case Ivanova's hypnotic powers don't work—but one is watching the colonel's back. He spots us immediately and doesn't wait for her order to open fire.

Armstrong dives right and I dive left, avoiding the deadly spray of bullets. Both of us take shelter behind boulders near the plateau's edge. Armstrong returns fire, felling the first of the ape-men. A twinge of guilt rushes up my spine, and I hope—just for a moment—that my cousin hasn't killed him. But before the thought can fully form, the other two turn and begin strafing the area.

"*Nyet!*" Ivanova commands. "Stop!" But, with her psi-powers focused on the ranodons, the Neanderthals aren't listening. And the moment her attention wavers, the ranodons snap at her hungrily.

Overcoming my guilt, I fire back at the ape-men, along with my cousin. Nachtu keeps Armstrong pinned down with an erratic volley of shells. The other, perhaps having heard Ivanova after all, rushes toward my hiding place. I manage to wing him, and he drops his Thompson as he comes in. Like a charging rhino, he slams his considerable bulk into the shoulder-high boulder I'm crouching behind.

The rock shudders and skids, ramming into my body as the Neanderthal pushes both me and the boulder toward the edge of the cliff. I try to shoot him, but the moving rock totters between us, spoiling my aim. The Neanderthal's powerful muscles force me back, and my feet can't find the purchase to stop his advance.

I drop my 45s and grab for the cliff as he forces me over the edge. Pain shoots up my arms as the rocky ledge scrapes the skin from my fingers, but I catch hold. The brute smiles a crooked smile and keeps pushing, looking to drop the boulder on top of me.

I try to sidle sideways, feet dangling in thin air, but I know I'm not going to make it. The rock will either crush my fingers or carry me to the jungle floor below, or both.

"CC!" someone shouts from below, and I realize that Zoe is still making her way to the top—but she's too far away to do me any good. I glance over my shoulder, thinking that maybe I can drop down to safety, but the ledge Armstrong and I ascended is too far to my right. The only thing that will stop my fall is the jungle floor—hundreds of feet below.

Desperately, I heave myself up onto the edge of the boulder as the Neanderthal pushes. Spiderlike, I cling to the rock as it protrudes over the cliff face, knowing that I've bought myself only few scant seconds of life.

The Neanderthal laughs and reels back for a final shove. But as he does, a shot echoes through the humid air. The brute staggers, blood gushing from his mouth, and falls heavily against the rock. It shudders, but does not go over the edge. Then the wounded Neanderthal is slipping past me, making one final grab for my leg as he pitches over the cliff.

I scramble atop the boulder and out of his reach; he doesn't even scream as he falls to his death—one more lost member of his dying race. The boulder finally overbalances, and as it falls, I spring, crashing down atop the plateau.

I land in direct sight of the remaining Neanderthal—Nachtu. Unlike the one who just fell, he's blocked from Armstrong's fire by another boulder. Unfortunately, I'm right in the head ape-man's line of fire. A look of delight crosses Nachtu's brutish face as he swings his Thompson submachine gun toward me.

"Hey!" Armstrong calls, stepping from concealment and into the line of fire. Now *he's* in peril, too, and he still doesn't have a shot at Nachtu. For a moment, I fear my cousin has doomed us both. Then I notice that he's not aiming at Nachtu; he's actually drawing a bead on Ivanova, who's still staring down the ranodons.

The blindly loyal ape-man throws himself into the line of fire just as Armstrong pulls the trigger. Nachtu falls, saving his evil mistress, as I scramble to my cousin's side.

"Lina!" Ray calls to the Russian. "Get back on your ship and fly out of here, before I'm forced to do something we'll both regret."

Colonel Pavlina Ivanova turns her steely gaze towards us and smiles. "I do not think you will do that, Mr. Armstrong," she says.

"Why not?" Armstrong replies, his finger tightening on the carbine's trigger.

"For one, because my new friends would not like it," she replies. As she speaks, the ranodons squawk and flap agitatedly. "And for another . . ."

Ivanova's blue-gray eyes seem to blaze with the light of the setting sun, and—for some reason I can't fathom—I begin to feel dizzy. Beside me, Armstrong sways as well.

". . . I do not believe that you actually want to shoot me." Ivanova finishes with a smile. "I believe you would rather shoot . . . someone else."

"I—" Armstrong begins. His aim remains fixed on Ivanova, but his eyes flash toward me, and in them there is murder.

"Ray!" I blurt, unable to move. "Don't look at her! Remember what I said!"

"I—" he begins again, but he can't seem to break Ivanova's hold on his mind. Slowly, he starts to swing the gun from her, toward me.

"Ray, no!" I scream. The Russian's spell over me breaks, and I lunge for him. At the last instant, he swings his gun away from me and fires.

Ivanova winces, but—luckily for her—my cousin hasn't completely escaped her thrall. Instead, his bullet rips into the helioship's gas bag. Unbalanced and with no one at the helm to right her, the ship veers to port and lurches toward the ground.

Anger flashes in Ivanova's eyes; Armstrong relaxes as the Russian loses her psychic grip on him.

Before he can turn the carbine on her, though, she screams, "Get him!"

Instantly, the ranodons take flight, the air filling with teeth, talons, and feathery bat-like wings.

"Sorry, Cuz," Armstrong says. And before I can react, he shoves me away from him, deep into a thicket. The ranodons swarm toward my cousin like a school of hungry piranha.

"Ray!" I scream, trying to disentangle myself from the bracken.

He fires two shots, killing one of the beasts, and then they're on him, biting and clawing, buffeting him with their wings. They back him toward the edge of the cliff . . . and over!

Ivanova laughs.

"You *bitch*!" I cry. I rip my hunting knife from the holster on my right calf and sprint across the plateau toward the Russian.

She turns, drawing a Luger from the holster at her waist. Before she can bring it to bear, though, I'm on her. I thrust for her gut, but she blocks the blow with her pistol.

I twist my wrist, wrenching the gun from her hand. It skids across the ground and over the edge of the tepui. But even unarmed, Ivanova's no pushover. She grabs the wrist of my knife hand before I can recover and, with her other fist, aims a haymaker at my jaw.

I intercept the blow with my free hand, and now we're grappling together, face to face, our hands knotted in a battle of strength and willpower.

"Too bad it has to end like this, Katya," she says, fixing her steely eyes on mine. I feel her psychic power boring into my brain, trying to loosen my grip, but I resist.

"It's not over . . . yet!" I drop to one knee and twist, sending her over my shoulder in a text-book judo throw.

Ivanova skids across the ground and crashes into an upright boulder, but she scrambles to her feet before I can spring on her.

"Give up!" I command. The advantage is mine, now. I have my knife, and I've steeled myself against her mind tricks. She's still unarmed, and her goons' submachine guns lie five meters away. Before she can reach them, I will gut her. If she doesn't give up, I'll do it with pleasure— for my cousin, and O'Brien, and the dead Neanderthals, and all the other victims she's left in her wake.

Yet, somehow, Ivanova keeps smiling. "You've forgotten about my friends," she says.

I wheel as the ranodon flock reappears over the edge of the cliff. "Get her," Ivanova commands with a sneer.

I am totally screwed. The pterosaurs are between me and Ivanova; they will intercept a thrown blade or tear me to pieces before I can reach her. My knife will be sparse protection against the flock, and I can't reach the discarded Thompsons in time, either. I brace myself, staring death in the face—not for the first time, but for what I feel certain will be the last. The ranodons swarm toward me as Ivanova laughs.

I lock eyes with my reptilian adversaries, inwardly vowing to go down fighting. Then, suddenly, they break off, backing wings and veering away from me. In moments, they've parted around me as though I were Moses amid the Red Sea—all but one.

Mother Ranodon keeps coming, claws extended, jaws wide, yellowish saliva dripping from her crooked teeth. I duck, slashing with my knife. Her jaws snap shut inches from my face, and my blade deflects her talons as they rake for my guts. She twists, seizes my backpack, and lifts me into the air.

I cut the straps and fall two meters to the ground, landing lightly on my feet. She drops the pack and banks, coming in for another attack. Then, unexpectedly, I'm surrounded by feathery, bat-like wings once more, as the rest of the flock returns.

The mother ranodon turns away as the fledglings, each only half her size, interpose their bodies between me and the adult's flashing jaws. For a moment, a chaos of talons and teeth swirls all around me. Then the mother arcs away, up into the sky, as the fledgling ranodons settle around my feet, chirping and looking at me expectantly.

It takes me a moment to figure out what's happened. Then I smile. "Sorry, Lina," I call to the Russian, "but it looks like family ties are stronger than your psychic powers. I was there when these chicks hatched—and I guess they're bonded to me for life. Am I lucky, or what?"

"Not lucky enough," the Russian says, and I realize that while I've been fighting, she's recovered one of the submachine guns. She swings it in my direction, but before she can pull the trigger, my flock takes to the air once more.

In an instant, they're on her, all beating wings, snapping jaws, and raking talons. Ivanova screams as the gun is slashed from her hands. She tries to run for her crippled helioship—now resting atop the plateau—but the flock surrounds her like seagulls on garbage. She stumbles, flails wildly, and, topples over the edge of the escarpment.

For a moment, the flock follows her down, only to rise above the cliff top en masse a moment later. I expect to see shreds of Russian flesh dangling from their jaws, but no gore stains their toothy beaks. Apparently, Ivanova has fallen to her death in one piece.

I go to the edge to make sure, while the young ranodons flutter to rest around my feet once more. What I see enrages me.

Two figures rise from the verdant abyss. Ivanova, her fine uniform shredded and bloody, clings to the talons of the mother ranodon. The adult pterosaur—still under Ivanova's power—carries the Russian east, back toward civilization.

I grab up a discarded Thompson and fire at them, trying to keep Ivanova from escaping with her prize.

"Don't bother," says a deep voice from behind me. "They're already out of range."

I spin, my heart pounding in my chest. "Ray!" I cry.

My cousin and Zoe are standing near the far edge of the plateau. Armstrong looks like hell; he's bleeding from numerous wounds and his clothes have been torn to shreds—but he's *alive*.

I have never been so glad to see anyone in my life. I sprint across the top of the plateau and throw my arms around him.

"Ouch! Take it easy!" he says. "You want to finish the job those crazy birds started?" He and Zoe eye the flock of juveniles warily; the ranodons edge toward us, walking like bats on their wing joints and hind legs.

"Don't worry about them," I say. "They're with me."

"B-but . . . how?" Zoe asks, keeping her pistol trained on the flock.

"They must have bonded with me when they hatched," I explain. "When Ivanova forced them to attack me, their primal instincts kicked in and they turned on her instead. All except the mother."

"Too bad," Armstrong says wearily. "Looks like the Russian got her prize after all."

"For all the good it will do her," I reply. "Even with ranodons, it takes two to reproduce."

Zoe frowns. "With Russian technology, I wouldn't be so sure."

"Speaking of which, do you think you can get this airship going again?" Armstrong asks, looking at the grounded vessel.

"Absolutely," Zoe says.

Armstrong nods approvingly. "Good. With the *Louisa* out of action, we're going to need some way to get back home. I just hope O'Brien didn't go down with the ship."

"I'm pretty sure he's okay," Zoe says. "I used a mirror to flash some Morse code toward the wreckage while I was resting, and I got a couple of flashes back. He's pretty upset, though."

I shake my head in disbelief. "Then he's as lucky as you are, cousin."

"Luck had nothing to do with it," Armstrong replies. "Zoe saved my bacon."

"After I saw that Neanderthal go off the escarpment, I got some anti-fall netting out of my pack and reeled it across the cliff face, just in case. I know you didn't want any of them killed if we could help it."

"So her natural reverence for all life saved my worthless hide as well," Armstrong puts in. Zoe blushes. A low moan comes from nearby.

"Hey, one of these guys is alive!" Armstrong says, moving over to one of the two Neanderthal bodies lying on the cliff top.

"Which one?"

"Three guesses," he replies.

"Nachtu," I say. But it seems like good news anyway. "What about the other?"

Zoe checks his pulse and shakes her head. "Sorry."

I sigh, sad at the loss. Even though they're on the

wrong side, there are too few Neanderthals left in the world. "Well, maybe once Nachtu has recovered, we can break Ivanova's hold on him."

"How do you plan on doing that?" Armstrong asks.

"We'll figure something out," I reply. "In the meantime, I'll go down and check on O'Brien. You can patch the ape-man up while Zoe works on the helioship."

"Then what?" Zoe asks.

"We find a hospital for those who need it," I say.

"Good luck on that, out here!" Armstrong quips. "I think I'd rather tend myself."

"You may have to," I reply, "because we have one last thing to do before we go home."

Armstrong looks puzzled. "What's that?"

"We need to help our ranodon flock complete their migration," I say. "After all, they're family."

Scourge of the Spoils

Matthew P. Mayo

Matthew P. Mayo's novels include the Westerns *Winters' War*, *Wrong Town*, and *Hot Lead, Cold Heart*. His non-fiction books include *Cowboys, Mountain Men & Grizzly Bears: Fifty of the Grittiest Moments in the History of the Wild West*, and the forthcoming *Bootleggers, Lobstermen & Lumberjacks: Fifty of the Grittiest Moments in the History of Hardscrabble New England*. Matthew's short stories have appeared in a variety of anthologies, including DAW's *Timeshares*. He and his wife, photographer Jennifer Smith-Mayo, travel all over the world in search of lost treasure . . . and tasty coffee. Visit him at: www.matthewmayo.com.

Tico squatted in riverbank mud the color of an old miner's skin. His coarse brown hair hung from under his hat like ends of frayed rope, and the water he scooped in the bowl of his hands leaked slowly through his thick fingers. He cut his eyes upstream, then back to the girl. Finally he drank, swallowed, made the noise that men the world over make after they've finished a needed drink, like pressure released from a worn valve.

"Shall we continue, then?" asked the girl from a horse behind him.

Tico remained squatting in the mud, his suede boots darkening as the water leached upward. "No."

The young woman said nothing, but straightened in the saddle and gritted her teeth.

Tico drank more, filled his canteen, and then squelched back through the mud to where his horse, Colonel Saunderston the Third, had finished drinking. Tico checked the four glass tubes that served as reservoir level indicators, one in each of the horse's legs, the graduated numbers long since worn away. Satisfied with the water levels, he gathered the sopping reins from where they hung in the water, sluicing the excess through his fingers, then he mounted.

The young woman forced a smile and nodded toward Colonel. "I've been meaning to ask—is that a special model? I don't recall seeing any quite—"

"Modified mount, same as that one." He nodded toward her horse.

Under the grime and welted ropes of brazing from years of repairs, Constance Gatterling saw something of the beast it once was. "The original creature must have been a beauty."

Tico stared at her as if she were speaking a foreign language. "Been a long time since it was a real horse."

"Surely you're curious."

"Gets me from here to there and back." More of the stare, then he said, "You talk too much. Let the bay drink full, then catch up with me." He heeled Colonel into a lope.

"Catch up? What? Hey!" Constance looked at the receding back of the stained buckskin shirt, an ancient holstered pistol bouncing on the man's hip with each clanking gallop. "Hey, Tico! I'm paying you to get me to the West Edge, not leave me here!" But the horse decided for her and plunged into the river up to its knees, the cool grey water sizzling and becoming steam vapor where it touched the hot metal of its legs and sipping muzzle.

"Damn you, horse, no! Tico is getting farther away with each second you waste in this disgusting runnel of stinking liquid!" The flurry of words, which would have impressed her friends back home in East City, sounded childish out here in the Spoils.

The reins, looped in her hands, slipped free and slid into the water. She grabbed after them, bending low, the saddle leather creaking with her weight, her stirruped left boot inches from the river surface. As she reached out, her fingertips trembling, clawing at the dangling rein, she noted with despair that the frilled edge of her tailored shirt's cuff, jutting from beneath the blue crushed velvet sleeve, was now grimed from constant wear. Still she strained a little further . . . then slipped from the saddle, a quick cry and her splash the only sounds until she rose spluttering and gasping from the rank, swirling river.

It was the clanking, and more than that, an overriding grinding screech of steel on steel that pulled Constance from her bankside nap—her pounding heart seemed to fill her throat. The sounds, from the east, grew louder, but still she saw no sign of anything interrupting the flat, stark land.

She had not intended to fall asleep, but figured Tico would ride back, at least for his other mount, if not for her. She'd stripped off her smelly, wet garments and arranged them on the twisted branches of the stunted trees lining the river. Perhaps Tico was only scouting ahead, and left her here because he knew this spot was relatively safe from the people of the Spoils. Constance chose to believe this, and so had waited for her hired guide's return. After all, she reasoned, she was his employer.

The grinding noise increased by the second. And then she noticed something else was wrong—the horse, what Tico had called "the bay," was gone. How could that happen? Horses, even modified mounts, didn't just vanish, did they? But it was full of water, so it could well walk off for miles, perhaps days, in any direction. She saw no tracks, even though on both sides of the river, the solid-seeming earth gave way to softer sandy soil as the land stretched away from the river. Constance held up a hand against the dimming light and stared southward, then west, toward the far bank.

The clanking grew louder from behind her, now joined with a grinding screech as though sand were being pressed between spinning metals.

Constance turned in time to see emerging from the sand the nose of what looked like a pre-war steam-power locomotivator drive upward from beneath the ground, churning and chewing raw earth—rocks, clods of dried, powdery dirt bigger than a man's head collapsed into clouds of powder, boulders cracked like rifle shots.

It dragged itself free from its earthen tunnel, a collapsing ridge of sand, its forward set of great steel mandibles gnashing the last rocks, bouncing in its maw like unpopped corn kernels in a cast-iron pan. She was surprised to see the rest of the machine was not black steel, but instead an old-time elixir wagon, wood, from the looks of it, like she'd seen pulled behind horses in pictorials in history tomes. She knew such transports still existed, but back east they long ago had been replaced with soft-tracked conveyances topped with polished chrome travel compartments.

The grinding, squealing sounds lessened, and great jets of steam drove at the ground from between the spoked wheels, raising swirling clouds of dust. A smell like melting metal curled its way into her nose and she fought down a sneeze.

A third of the way back, where steel met wood, a thick plank door with black strapping squawked outward and a stout little man in a long, plaid coat with once-sculpted tails, a style the likes of which Constance hadn't seen except in books, nearly fell out, surrounded by belching clouds of smoke.

He swung on the door, the hinges screaming for lubrication, and coughed as if soon he would be overcome. He stopped abruptly, pulled in a deep breath, and then spat a great quantity of something that splattered in the dust, before hopping down and slapping his coat sleeves. He strode forward from out of the last of the steam, and stood still, smoke rising from a dented black bowler hat.

The little man reached up and pulled at massive goggles that came free from his face with audible pops. He lowered them to his neck, but his eyes were still covered with what looked like smaller goggles in thick brass frames. The lenses, of a dark hue, perhaps black, were surrounded with dials that looked to be for focusing. He reached up with practiced, albeit greasy, fingertips and adjusted one.

Then he just stood there smiling, his doughy, sweat-pocked face bubbling through a sparse beard, ginger eyebrows, and thick side whiskers. His coat continued to smoke, as if he himself were a source of heat.

"Good day to you, sir." She pointed at him. "You appear to be on fire."

His eyes never left her, though he slapped at himself a few times more. In a voice that rattled like gravel in a cup, he said, "It gets a bit . . . hot . . . in there." He spat again, then slowly stepped closer. Everything about him seemed of another time, as if he'd been apart somehow from normal society and fashion. He stared at her.

"Is there a problem?" she said, a hand still visoring her eyes.

"Oh, no, no, ma'am. That is to say, I'm not put out in the least by your state of . . . undress, as it were."

Constance barked an oath she reserved for more private affairs and felt her face heat even as she turned away, groping for the stiff garments draped on the shrubs. "I'm . . . I'm so sorry to . . . ."

She pulled on her clothes fast, noting the sad, wrinkled state her expensive fashions were now in. Blue velvet, silk luxlace, and camphor cotton had perhaps not been the best choices for traveling across the Spoils. At least they were drier than she expected. She continued picking and plucking her clothes from the brittle arms of the bushes, all the while keeping her brocade satchel close by, nudging it from bush to bush as she dressed.

"Why, sir, surely you must have a sense of decorum, propriety? Avert your eyes."

"I think not."

She heard the smile in his voice.

"It's been far too long since I've seen such an exquisite female form and I'll not look away. No indeed, I shan't do it."

She half-turned toward him as she finished buttoning her second blouse. "Then you, sir, are a rogue."

"Mm-hmm. Among many other things, I can assure you."

"Who are you?" she finally said when she had covered enough of herself to feel bold again.

"Who am I?" The portly man spluttered, stepped aside as if to let a lady pass him on a crowded streetside, and waved an arm at his wagon. "Can you not read, my dear?"

Constance leaned to her right as she continued to button and smooth her shirt. She saw faded writing on the side of the caravan through the dissipating steam and smoke. She shook her head as if disagreeing. "I can't make it out yet."

The man sighed, let his arms drop. He looked at his belly. "Ocularius." He looked up at her. "My name. It's Doctor Ocularius." His ample eyebrows seemed to rise higher with each syllable. "And you are . . . ?"

Constance froze in the act of primping the once-stiff collar of her inner coat. "I am Constance Gatterling. But wait . . . you said you are Doctor Ocularius?"

The man smiled and pulled the massive goggles away from his neck, stretching his chin. "Why, yes. Are you unimpressed?"

"No, it's just that . . . well, I didn't expect you to use your own name."

"Ah, so you have heard of me. Why should I not use

my name? I know I'm here, they know I'm here. What good would it do to try to deceive anyone?"

"Pardon me, Doctor, but isn't that what you're best at?"

"Deceit? No, dear lady, that's but a sideline. An admittedly practical, and occasionally profitable one, but nonetheless a sideline to my primary distraction."

"Which is . . . ?"

"Ha—I like you already. Come, let's resume this conversation over a blue flame and a decanter of refined mint wine."

She raised her eyebrows.

"Yes, dear lady, you don't think Doctor Ocularius travels the wastelands of the Spoils without the refinements of clean fire and fine libation, do you?" He smiled and disappeared inside the wagon.

In faded yellow paint arched across the side of the wagon, she read his name and the words, 'Traveling Tinctures, Tonics, and Bifurcated, Multi-Purpose Nostrums for the Betterment of the Eyes, Ears, Nose, Throat, and Sundry Other Parts. . . .'

"So, Doctor, what do you call this contraption?"

"Contraption!" He peeked out the door. "You cut me to the core, dear girl! Why, this 'contraption,' as you call it, is more than a mere conveyance. It is more than a converted burrowing miner, more than a superior collection of hydraulic, steam, and forever-gear technology." He hopped down, green bottle in hand. "It is more than a home, it is more than a workshop, it is, indeed, to a man once said to have promise—considering the limitations forced on me due to my unfortunate and unearned yet imposed exile—this beautiful brute," he patted the cooled black steel of the silent mandible, "is the incubator of my brilliance."

"Well your incubator sounded to me like it's on its last legs."

He pursed his lips, his brow puckering as he dragged an ancient gasbox from its rack underneath the wagon and rummaged in a vest pocket until he produced a small box of scratchers. Within seconds a warm, blue-flame fire hissed on the ground at their feet.

He stared at the flame. "Well, it is true she isn't suited to much more than sand travel these days—this river-valley rock nearly killed her, but this is where I found you."

"Why, Doctor, I am flattered. . . ."

"Think nothing of it, dear girl. Thoughtful is my middle name."

They were quiet a moment, dark rose around them, and Constance pulled her satchel close. She thought she saw the doctor watch her, though with his eyewear, it was difficult to tell just where he was looking. "Tell me about those peculiar spectacles, Doctor."

"Ah, you have a gift for stroking the peacock's feathers, my dear!" He smiled, sipped his wine, smacked his lips, and added, "In a nutshell, these odd eyepieces enable me to not be seen better."

She snorted, covered her mouth with a hand, and said, "Please, continue."

He sighed. "The technology is something I've spent my life developing. It's far more advanced than anything those dolts back East have come up with, I can assure you."

She regarded the pudgy man for a moment, and then shook her head, smiling. "I think you're a tale-spinner, is what I think."

"Believe what you need to," said the Doc, finishing his wine. "I do." He winked and slapped his knee. "So, just what brought you out here?"

"Simple. I am a spirited young woman with a certain proclivity for the hard sciences who has just spent her formative years in the clutches of well-intentioned but fusty instructors, and I am desperate to do something tremendous with my life. Before I become one of those fusty instructors myself."

"And so. . . ." prompted Doc, pouring more wine into their goblets.

"And so," said Constance, crossing her boots "I aim to become the first person—a woman, no less—to cross from east to west. At least since the Long War ended, that is."

"But no one's—"

"That's why I'm doing it. If someone had, then I wouldn't be here."

"No, I suppose not. But that still doesn't explain how you came to be alone at this spot." The blue flames of the gasbox reflected in the small, dark lenses of his glasses.

"I hired a tracker who came recommended ... in a roundabout way. And then he abandoned me here, at the river."

Doctor snorted. "Let me guess. His name was Tico?"

She sat up straight. "How did you know?"

"And you paid him half up front?"

She nodded. "How do you know... ?"

"Everybody knows of Tico. He's no guide. He's more like ... a sort of an anti-bounty hunter."

"How's that?"

"He loses people."

Constance nodded but couldn't think of a reply. She felt an urge to stretch her legs. It had been a long day. She stood—and a strange dizziness pulled at her from all sides. Then she fell prone by the gasbox. She tried to rise and could not figure out how to do it. Doctor Ocularius stared at her, not quite smiling, not moving to help her.

"What's wrong, my dear?"

"The wine—what did you do?"

He spread his arms wide. "The wine, the night air, the gas, the Spoils, me—something isn't agreeing with you." He laughed then, an abrasive chuckle built into a head-thrown-back guffaw that rocked his slab of a belly.

He rose from his seat and with a grunt, snatched the loop handles of her satchel and dragged it back to where he was sitting.

"Why?"

As he untwisted the clasp and parted the bag like the

mouth of a fish, he said, "I know Tico. And I know he always gets half up front for taking people across. I figure the other half has to be here somewhere. I didn't see it on your person earlier." He winked at her over the hissing gasbox.

Another short laugh erupted from him and trailed into the darkening, still night. The last thing Constance saw before her eyes closed was Doc rummaging in her satchel, smiling and humming as he held up various articles and marveled at them in the blue light.

"Hey."

Constance opened her eyes, shut them. She felt like mud. Aching mud. Her neck was as stiff as wood and it throbbed.

"Hey."

Something nudged her leg. "What?" She squinted her eyes open. The sun was up. A dark shape hovered over her and she raised a hand to visor her eyes. Someone in a wide-brimmed hat. The hat turned, looked up toward the sky, then back down. In that moment, something had glinted beneath the brim—glasses? The shape shifted, blocked out the sun, and she didn't have to squint so hard. A faint image of Doctor Ocularius filled her mind for a moment.

"Who—" She coughed. Her voice was dry, full of holes. She tried it again as she sat up. "Who are you?"

"Nope, that's my question."

"What?"

He sighed, and said, "I'm Rollicker, Sheriff of the Spoils." He sent a rope of thick brown liquid to the ground, dragged the back of one hand across his mouth, then smoothed his ample moustaches. He squinted at her through finely wrought spectacles, small lavender lenses set in brass frames.

"Are you sickly?" she said, standing and stretching her back.

"What? No, not that I'm aware of. . . ."

"That . . . stuff you just spit up. . . ."

"Chaw, missy. That's all."

"That was intentional?"

His jaws chewed slowly, then he pursed his lips and sluiced another stream just a few inches from her boots. "Yep."

She looked at him fully for the first time. He was a tall, thin man and wore a sweat-stained shirt of rough cloth the color of sand. His trousers were of a darker, stronger material, tucked into tall boots. His hat was a stained affair, massive in height and width, and a dull brown leather vest ended just above a holstered pistol that seemed crude and of old-time construction, certainly older than the one Tico had worn.

She wondered if these men carried their ancient guns as an affectation, in the way the wives of Societeers back home carried their clockwork pets, yipping, purring, growling knots of gears wrapped in fur and feathers, as a way to show they'd not lost touch with their urban forebears, what they liked to call their "instinctual selves."

"You must be parched," he said as he untied thongs that held a leather-wrapped bottle to a saddle horn. He handed it to her.

"Is that a real horse?" She nodded toward the beast behind him, the same deep brown color as his spittle.

Rollicker snorted a laugh, "As opposed to what? One of those modified steam-powered contraptions you're used to? By god, if those dandified clothes didn't give you away, your reaction to seeing a live, kickin' horse surely does."

She uncorked the top of the bottle, sniffed it, and did her best to keep from gagging as she swigged. "It's just that in the civilized part of the country we have modern conveyances of all manner that are far tidier and less cruel."

He shook his head, half smiling, then said, "Tell me, missy, if it's so grand in the East, what are you doing out here alone into the Spoils?"

She turned her back on him. "Constance Gatterling. That's my name."

He gave her a nod.

"Thank you for finding me."

"Dumb luck on my part—and yours. I'm headed back to town anyway. So, what are you doing out here?"

She said nothing. Despite the morning's dry heat, a shiver worked up her back. "It's so bleak."

"Didn't used to be—used to be beautiful prairies, rich with wildlife, birds, grasses taller than a man's head."

"What happened?"

"Long story." He mounted the horse and gathered the reins, then offered a hand down to her.

She backed up and said, "Hmm, that vile doctor told me to be wary of you people of the Spoils. . . ."

So fast she had no time to react, the sheriff leaned and snatched her shirtfront, balling her four layers in a grimy, calloused fist. "You saw Doc?" He shook her once. Her head wobbled in a nod. "Doc Ocularius?"

She nodded again.

Rollicker released her and said, "Take me to him and I won't leave you out here." They stared at each other a moment. His jaw muscles working hard, his eyes glinting behind the lavender lenses. Then he freed his left boot from the stirrup and extended his arm again. After a moment, she mounted up behind him and he guided the horse north.

Most of an hour passed, and she found that if she turned her head to one side and breathed, she could lessen the blended stink of horse, unwashed man, and raw Spoils air. Finally she said, "What do you hate Doctor Ocularius for?"

He answered quickly, as if he were waiting for Constance to ask. "You name it—theft, murder, trickery. Years ago, when the damnable Long War was still on, the dust from the blue stone you all so desperately need back East was making everyone who mined it go blind. Some genius decided that would be bad for business, so they sent Doc Ocularius out here to help us all keep our sight, since he seemed to be the greatest thing since wind-up lightning. But they didn't figure on him bein' a greedy little weasel. He's been playing the middle against both ends ever since, keeps everybody blind, so to speak—us and the powers that be back East, while he drains off profits for himself."

"So you're out to get him."

"Pure and straight. All I need is one clear shot at his mangy hide. . . ."

"But why? Didn't he save everyone's sight? And that in turn kept the mineworks open, correct?"

"You know, for a little bit of a thing, you sure talk a lot."

"You're not the first to tell me that."

"Might be you wanna listen to others once in a while instead of flapping your gums."

"For better or worse, it's my curiosity that got me here."

"Yeah, smack dab in the Spoils. If this is the plan you had for yourself, I'm not so sure your gears are lining up quite right." He tapped his forehead and grinned.

"Well, aren't you going to tell me?"

He sighed. "Tell you what?"

"Why you haven't eradicated the Doctor."

He was silent for a few paces, then in a lowered voice said, "I can't find him."

Behind him, she smiled. "Well, that doesn't seem so difficult. I found him in short order."

To her surprise, he nodded and kept riding. After a few minutes of silence, he spit again and said, "He fixed me up, same as the rest. Only he did a little something different with my eyes. I suppose you noticed these here spectacles."

She nodded. "They're not the most masculine look-ing things, I'll grant you. But at least you can see."

"Yep, I can see. But not everything."

She waited for more, but he grew silent again. After a few quiet minutes, Constance said, "What is that stench?"

The sheriff sat up straight, tilted his head back, and pulled in a deep draught of air. "Aaahh." He half-turned to her and said, "That, little missy, is the smell of fashion, and music, and theatres, and cinematographs, and cyclerigibles and all manner of modern advance that you so enjoy in the East." He turned fully toward her, his leather saddle creaking. "That, little missy, is the smell of Rankton."

"I should say. . . ."

He laughed wide-mouthed then, and she saw for the first time the blackened nubs of his teeth. "Capitol city of Abandonia. . . ."

"How very wistful. Tell me, is it as forlorn as it smells?"

"No, Lord no . . . it's worse."

"If it's so bad, then why don't you leave, Sheriff Rollicker?"

"You know, for a smarty-type, you're none too bright. There ain't no leaving the Spoils, girl. Once you're in, you're in. The only folks ever end up here are those born into it, those sent here because they have no choice," he spit, looked her right in the eye, and said, "and fools."

As the horse walked slowly into the little town, the whole of which seemed backed up to a blunted rise of blue-grey rock, everywhere she looked Constance saw remnants of what seemed a thriving mining past. Great steel-and-wood conveyors, their canvas belts tattered and hanging, jutted at the base of a sprawling mass of shale that leaked between buildings and dissipated in the street. Brass tubes and mammoth rusted gears poked between leaning planks of wind-chewed boards the color of thick smoke. Valves and smokestacks atop steel skeletons on steel wheels, shot through with rust and holes, lay dragged and forgotten in the middle of the street, the rotted carcasses of the machinery of promise.

Signs on some of the collapsed, gaunt buildings told of once-lively trade: Abandonia General Mercantile; Flo's Pleasure Palace; The Blue Dream Bar, and at the end of the street, faded black letters on a leaning sign close by a gaping hole in the rock mound read: J.S. Kalibrator's Blue Stone and Gasworks. To her surprise, Constance saw smoke lifting up and out the top of the entrance rough-cut into the rock, and several men straggled in and out, carrying arc rods and flatpicks.

"We'll get you cleaned up at the jail house, then set to work finding Doc. Strikes me he's never too far off."

"No need."

"Now see here, missy...."

She sighed. "Keep your big hat on, Sheriff Rollicker. He's here."

"What ... in town? How do you know?" He looked left and right, his glasses glinting.

"Sheriff—he's right over there." She jutted her chin toward The Hard Shine Saloon. "See, there's his wagon."

Rollicker followed her pointing hand, looked right at the wagon, then to the left and right of it, shaking his head.

She opened her eyes wide and stared at him as if he were a dumb child. "You know, the one that reads: 'Doctor Ocularius and his Traveling Tinctures, Tonics, and Bifurcated Nostrums for the Betterment of the Eyes, Ears, Nose, Throat, and—"

"Girl, I don't see a damn thing but Horace Gorton's broke-down mule and a drunk floozie sleepin' off a toot by that post out front. What are you playin' at?"

She stared at Rollicker. "You're not kidding me, are you, Sheriff?"

With his little finger he pushed the glasses up the bridge of his nose and smoothed his moustaches. She guessed he was fighting the urge to shout at her again.

Then she understood and her mouth dropped open as she stared at him. He looked away. "So that's what you meant when you said you can't see everything. Of course! Last night I laughed at the Doctor when he said his glasses helped him to not be seen. It must have been the wine that made me so very ignorant. Those spectacles of his would make—"

"Girl, you're doin' it again. Chattering away like old Judge Bulger when he gets a few snorts in him—"

"Sorry. . . ."

But the sheriff was squinting harder now at the mule. "Doc Ocularius, huh? Right here under my very nose! Hell, I'm callin' him out right now."

"What? Wait, what does that mean?"

"Means I'm aiming to get the Doc out here, settle his hash once and for all, right here in the street."

"But how will you see him?"

"I won't," he smiled and spat at their feet. "But you will."

"What?"

"Yep, just muckle onto him when he tries to climb aboard his wagon there. I'll see you and I'll pepper whatever it is you're grabbin' onto."

"I'll not do it."

"You will . . . and I'll tell you why." He smiled wide. "I'm the only one here who knows how to get you back East to your fine, cushy life. All this here could be but a bad memory and a hell of a story to tell your little friends when you sit around a fancy dining table some night back in East City."

She smiled. "I'll just find Tico. He'd take me back to the border." She looked around as if expecting to see him waiting for her.

"Sure, just wave a coin in the air. He'll find you."

Her smiled faded as the sheriff forced his moustache into a big frown. "What? No money? Oh that's right, Doc Ocularius took your traveling cash. And if I'm not mistaken, he's in the Hard Shine right now, transforming it into little glasses full of libation for him and all his new friends." As if on cue, a round of laughter bubbled out the batwing doors.

She bit the inside of her mouth. Of course she wanted out of the Spoils, but she also wanted the Doctor's glasses.

If she could get those, her future would be set—no dry academic career for her. She could travel, see Europaia, the Far Orient. The world would be hers. . . .

"Alright. I'll do it. But first I need a sip of that foul water."

"Attagirl." He handed her the leather-covered bottle. "Now here's what we'll do. . . ."

In her mind Constance replayed her plan, meager though it was, as she crossed the street to the wagon, swinging the leather-bottle canteen by its strap handle. Up close and even in such grey light as Rankton received, the doctor's old burrowing mine machine was nothing more than a bent, haggard relic—wood and steel, grimy, worn out, and faded. Like everything in this place.

If this withered, bled-corpse of a country had a face, she thought, then it was certainly this toothless crone of a town. What had the sign at the end of Main Street said? "Rankton, Jewel of Abandonia?" Jewel indeed. Get me those glasses and a ride out of here and I'll not so much as give it a second thought for the rest of my days.

"Well, little lady! Imagine my surprise at seeing you here."

Constance froze, then turned and looked up, and there stood Doctor Ocularius on the boardwalk, leaning against a faded wood post. The drunk floozy continued to snore, propped at the base of the next post, wearing nothing but one holey brown sock, a tattered under-dress, and two black eyes beneath small brass spectacles with green lenses.

Doc's head wobbled enough to tell Constance he was inebriated. He held her satchel by the handles, almost bouncing it against his knees. A short, thin man and an even smaller woman, both wearing clothing so begrimed she didn't know where skin ended and fabric began, walked right by the doctor, close enough that they nearly brushed his arm—and they paid him no heed. And both wore green-lens eyewear in brass frames.

She waited for them to pass, then Constance strode to him and swung the glass-and-leather water vessel hard by the thong handle and caught the doctor just above his left ear. His dented black hat pinwheeled upward, then dropped to the street. He grunted and sagged to a sitting position on the edge of the boardwalk, his back to the post.

She rummaged in the satchel. "My, but you made a mess of my things, Doctor. Shame on you."

Doctor Ocularius sat weaving and shaking his head.

She pulled a white shirt from the bag, held it up, sighed, and tore at a hem with her teeth, ripping it in two. With one half she tied his hands together behind the post.

His struggles were weak. "What are you doing? Oh, my head...."

She lashed his feet together with the other half-shirt. "It occurred to me, Doctor, that the bounty on you I would imagine is rather substantial. Not to mention what I can do with those glasses of yours." She smiled and depressed a small button on a polished copper device she'd retrieved from her bag. It was palm-sized and when the click sounded, it split in two, and she pulled the halves apart. Between them stretched a thin, limp thread. "Why go all the way to the West Edge—if it's even possible—when you represent all I've been searching for."

The doctor swallowed. "What ... what is that, my dear?"

"I believe I hinted that I was a recent graduate of the Academy? I fear I may have neglected to mention some of the Chancellor's last words to us all: 'Bring me the head of Doctor Ocularius and your future is secure!' Funny thing at the time. We all laughed. But now I know exactly what he meant."

She pulled tight the device in her hands and the thin wire glowed a vivid blue. "Yes, this little notion heats water, helps with manicures, oh, and did I mention that it's also useful in . . . slicing? You see, it cauterizes as it cuts. Makes rather a neat job of it, really."

The doctor swallowed audibly, straightened against the post. "You think you're the only one to come after me? Every time a new class graduates, it seems at least one fresh face intends to make a quick name for himself by capturing me."

She raised the wire up and held it at neck level. "Now, I'll need my money . . . and those glasses."

She lowered the device and with the back of one hand patted the worn black fabric of his vest. Then, still watching his dark lenses, she reached in a pocket and pulled out a wad of wrinkled circular paper bills. Coins, green with tarnish, spilled to the dirt at his feet.

"And the glasses," she said.

"N-no, no, I can't! They are part of me, you see. Attached directly to me, to my skull, in my eye sockets. They can't be removed. . . ."

"Masterful, Doctor. But I will have them, one way or another—" She pushed the wire closer to his neck, so close that the hairs of his shaggy whiskers smoked and curled. A sound like steam hissing from a touchy valve rose from his mouth.

"I can't let you do that, missy!"

Behind her she heard the sheriff's voice, ragged like wind through shredded metal.

She turned her head. "Why ever not, sheriff? You're going to do the same thing. . . ."

He didn't respond, but lurched into the street, his pistol drawn and aimed at her, though it wagged in time with his unsteady gait. His hat was gone and she was shocked to see the split purple welt and spatter of blood that covered the side of Rollicker's face, an unfortunate by-product of hitting him with the water bottle. He'd dropped as if shot, but she hadn't thought to take his pistol.

"Yes, but I'm a lawman, and you're doing it for the wrong reasons."

She snorted. "Sheriff, my reasons are as valid as yours. Perhaps more so, considering I have a future—a brilliant career ahead of me as potentially one of the greater minds of my generation. While you are, well, here. A comparison can hardly be drawn, Sheriff."

"Badmouth me and Rankton all you want, girly." Rollicker's voice was right behind her now. "I've heard it all before. I got to go through you to get to him, fine by me. You're both burrs under my saddle anyway. One shot, two burrs gone." She heard the throaty click of the ancient gun's mechanism, felt the barrel of his pistol grazing her ruined blue velvet coat.

Constance's lips drew tight across her straight, white teeth. She stared at the doctor's unblinking lenses, the fine, beautiful precision work of the thick brass mechanisms surrounding them. And she also smelled the foul, bitter stink of his boozy breath. She wanted nothing more than a long bath in clean water—and she knew there was only one way to get back to that life. With a slight grunt and a strained smile, she pushed the wire forward.

From the sagging balcony of the Hotel Abandonia across the street, Tico saw the sheriff's knuckle whiten, and he knew that trigger was but a baby's breath away from opening the ball.

"In for a penny," Tico mumbled. He took one step sideways, eyeing the scene in the street below, his boot heel clunking soft on the rotting wood, his spur singing like the whisper of a far-off breeze. Then he shot the sheriff in the back.

It all played out as he expected: the sheriff lurched forward, squeezed his pistol's trigger, the girl's pretty blue jacket burst apart, she pitched forward with her hotwire tool straight into Doc's throat . . . ssup! Clean as you please, the old goat's head burned free from his body, teetered for a second on the stump, like a coin dropped on a bartop, then it flopped to the ground.

Tico led his horse from the shadows across the street and stood looking down at the unfortunate trio. Doc, he was sagged against the post, belly-blasted and headless, and the other two, their last blood was bubbling up, soaking into the dust. The sheriff's trigger finger kept curling into the dirt, reaching for the thing that was no longer there.

The girl whimpered something, her mouth moving like a clockwork toy nearly wound down.

"You talk too much, girl," said Tico, looking at her.

He rolled a quirley, patted his vest for a scratcher. "Aw hell." Then he saw the girl's gadget still gripped in her hands, the blue wire arcing small sparks against the dirt. He stepped on her hand and lifted it free, fiddled with it a moment, and worked it back up to a full glow, hot enough to light his cigarette.

Tico heard a scuffing sound, looked up at the dozen or so drawn faces of the diggers trying not to look at him, the dark green lenses of their spectacles not quite hiding their fear. They advanced, hoping, he knew, for a chance at something of value. He stared until they turned and dragged themselves back inside the Hard Shine to whimper about this day for years to come. From her post, the drunk floozy snorted in her sleep.

Tico snatched up Doc's head by its greasy knot of hair, stared into its taught, shocked face, and worked a grimy couple of fingers on one of the dials surrounding a lens.

"Well, that's one way to get ahead." He blew smoke in the dead man's face, then dropped the head into the satchel. He plucked the wad of cash from the girl's hand and stuffed it into his vest pocket.

Then Tico looped the handles of the satchel over his saddle horn, climbed atop the waiting Colonel Saunderston the Third, and spurred the clanking horse east, toward the sunrise.

Edison Kinetic Light & Steam Power

C.A. Verstraete

Christine Verstraete is a Wisconsin author who's written children's books, short fiction and non-fiction. Her latest story, "A Night to Forget," appeared in *Timeshares*, also from DAW. She says she'd love to go back in time to Tudor England, provided she could avoid the fleas. Visit her website at www.cverstraete.com.

Alva Edison realized her life would never be the same once she acknowledged her brother Thomas' foolhardy idea.

"It can be done. I know it can," he told her again.

"Thomas, I keep telling you, remember Mr. Franklin? The founding father never signed the Declaration because he foolishly stood out in a rainstorm, with a kite of all things. And stringing a key on the end? How foolhardy. Anyone with common sense knows that you do not want to be near any metal in a storm. No surprise that he was electrocuted. It was such a tragedy that could have been averted."

"But his idea was right," Thomas insisted. "The power of those thunderbolts can be harnessed as a new energy source."

She snorted at that. "Thomas, dear, next you'll be saying that thunderbolts can do all kinds of things, like that kooky Dr. Frankenstein and his outlandish, sacrilegious ideas about life and death. They took him off to the sanitarium and not soon enough, I say. Please stop such talk. I do not want to lose my only brother to some ridiculous notion."

The tears that she squeezed out did their trick, just as she'd hoped. She admired her brother's talents and his amazing imagination, but her job was to keep him safe, especially now. Things had become more dangerous for inventive types like him since The Puritans came to power in the recent election. She tried to keep Thomas focused on small, low-key projects that were unlikely to cause much interest outside his little circle of friends. Some of them, like his Kinetic Clock-Winder, were useful, too. The little cog-driven instrument reset the clocks at the touch of a button. Ingenious.

He had been working on an interesting device using wax cylinders that supposedly would capture music and voices. He described it well enough, but she heard the note of discontent in his voice.

"I'm sorry to be such a killjoy, brother. I really am. I know you feel stifled, but you must be careful."

"I know, Alva. The Puritan Party's win has sent all the inventors underground. But we haven't given up. We're biding our time. We feel that things will change the next time around."

She sighed and went from lamp to lamp, dusting the glass, emptying the drippers, and inserting fresh wicks and cotton before lighting them with the taper she kept for just that use. It was a tedious, laborious process that was usually best done by a servant, but given the times, she thought it best they kept visits from outsiders to a minimum. Except for the weekly visit from the laundress and the cook who brought in their meals, she thought the fewer ears to hear, the better.

Luckily, Thomas disassembled and cleaned the lamps every few days, a job she didn't care to tackle. She hated the smelly oil and the soot they left, sometimes wishing her brother's ridiculous, blasphemous ideas were true. Harnessing God's power, right in their own home? Oh, the hours of toil it could save! Such thoughts she kept to herself, of course.

Alva massaged her sore fingers, the knuckles starting to swell. She'd have to rub some camphor or maybe some of that interesting new product called Bag Balm on her hands and take an aspirin. She might even have one more brandy than usual in the hope something, anything, would help ease the pain. If only . . . No, best not let her thoughts wander. What would her brother say if he knew his arguments were beginning to win her over?

With most of the lamps done downstairs, she decided to finish the job later. She ran the hot water and ducked her aching hands under the warmth, if only for a moment of relief.

Her brother came in and caressed her shoulder, the container of camphor in his hands.

"Alva, here let me. Is it getting worse?"

"It's fine. Muggy days like today make my fingers ache more. I'll manage."

Directing her to a chair, he rubbed in the balm and massaged her fingers, then offered her a warm compress. "This should help."

The stuffed bag provided a steady stream of warmth. She smiled at him. "It is helping already. But what is this? A new invention?"

He shrugged. "I thought of it watching you make rice for dinner last night. I put some of the uncooked grains in a cloth bag and I found that if I put it on the stove to heat for a few minutes, it offers a portable source of heat that lasts for at least an hour. And it can be used again and again."

"How clever, thank you."

"Sister, don't you see how my other idea could make your life so much easier? Instead of the repeated light-

ing, cleaning, and relighting, you could flick a lever and
have a source of light, ready for your use."

"Thomas, hush! You can't let anyone hear this. If you
want to help, get up and clean the rest of the lamps for
me."

"I'll do that, but you know there has to be something
to the idea if the Puritans are so against it. One of the
leaders, Master Dogood, denounced inventing totally,
calling it 'a tool of the devil.' Hogwash! Why would God
give us an imagination except for it to be used?"

Alva paused and held a hand over her pounding
heart. "Thomas! Be careful; the walls may have ears."

"Don't worry, I am being careful. But you know that
I cannot stop inventing, just like I cannot stop breathing.
It's impossible."

"I know, dear, I know, but take care."

Not long after, Alva struggled to her feet and tried to
grasp the cane in her crippled hand. She winced at the
pain that shot like daggers through her swollen knuckles
and gnarled fingers. Her condition's aching progression
made contacting the apothecary for an increased mor-
phine dosage more of a possibility. She'd ignored the
doctor's instructions for fear of becoming too depen-
dent on the elixir, but the steady throbbing prompted a
change of heart.

The noise that drifted from the cellar did nothing to
improve her mood. She muttered under her breath and
banged on the floor with her cane. Her eyes filled with
tears as the action made her nerve endings sing an unwanted tune.

"Thomas! Keep it quiet down there!"

"Sorry, Alva," he called. "I'm almost done. Soon, I'll
have something to show you. It'll make all this work and
me hiding in the cellar worthwhile."

"Yes, yes, I'm sure it will. As long as it's quiet."

Shaking her head, she sat and slipped on the gloves
attached to her brother's recently created hand-warmer.

She spun the dial and listened to the steady click of the cogs falling in place. It was a bulky, ugly contraption, but she couldn't criticize the outcome. Steady warmth flowed over her fingers. She sighed in relief.

The hours Thomas spent working in secret (on what?) still worried her, especially when the walls shook and puffs of dark, evil smoke billowed upstairs, filling the house with a horrible sulfurous smell.

"Thomas!" She gasped and held a scented handkerchief over her nose. "What are you doing?"

He bounded into the room, gave her a quick hug, and opened the windows in an attempt to clear the air. "Sorry, Alva, sorry, but oh, I am so close! The answer is finally near!" With that, he fled back down the stairs. She uttered a most unlady-like curse and vowed to one day make her way to the cellar. She had to see what monstrosity he'd concocted.

Her brother's secret project took a backseat to more exciting developments as the next election neared. Like everyone else, Alva devoured the news accounts in the paper, and waited anxiously for her brother to bring home the latest reports and gossip. She thrilled at casting her vote, reveling in the chance to not only mark a ballot for the first time, but to choose candidates who valued freedom of expression and artistic vision.

They toasted the new government with glasses of red wine. The future held promise as the Puritans lost to members of the Inventor's Party who favored a new direction for the country and renewed societal freedoms.

"Just think what I can accomplish without all those silly restrictions," Thomas said in celebration of their victory. "Think of the possibilities!"

"More noise and smoke?" she asked with a chuckle.

Thomas invited members of the party and other like-minded thinkers home. As they gathered with their cigars and brandy in the parlor, Alva retired to the kitchen to sit by the fireplace and warm her crippled hands. Sometimes she listened in and marveled at the unbelievable topics these men of science discussed: flying machines, home-contained power, and old favorites like Thomas' wickless lights. It amazed, and at the same time, frightened her. Where would such thoughts lead?

It was after one such late-night meeting that Thomas, fired up from goodwill and a few too many glasses of good wine, went back downstairs to, as he put it, "fiddle some more."

The jolt an hour later shook Alva from under the covers and threw her half out of bed. She hurriedly slipped into a quilted wrapper, shoved her feet into slippers, and rushed downstairs, for once paying no mind to the shooting pains in her fingers.

Dark clouds billowed from behind the open cellar door. "Thomas? Are you all right?"

Fear gnawed at her like an undiscovered cancer. She grabbed the rail and pushed through the dark plumes of smoke, carefully going down each step like it were made of glass. "Thomas?"

She screamed at the chaos before her. Dark blotches, looking like those newfangled Rorschach blots, she thought, covered the walls. The air stunk of spilled chemicals and sulfur. She sniffled, pulled herself to her feet, and approached the ragged remains of the giant wood worktable.

A moan at the other end of the room grabbed her attention. She found her brother wedged against the wall, his body twisted, an arm bent and bloody. He breathed in heavy, loud wheezes. She grabbed his unhurt hand and held it.

"Thomas, I'm here. Hold on. Help will be here soon. Someone had to have heard the ruckus."

His voice came out in a raspy croak. "No time," he muttered. "B-b-b . . ."

"Shh, rest. Don't tax yourself."

His agitation grew as he tried to make his wants known. "G-get boo . . ."

"You want me to get something for you? By the table?"

He gave a slight nod. She hated to leave his side, but didn't want him to push himself further. Seeing no other choice, she hurried to the table, or at least what remained of it.

What in the world does he want? What could be so important?

Broken bottles and jars, the spilled contents thick and gooey, littered the floor. She shuffled through piles of stained newspapers and tried to regain her balance as her feet slid on the papery mush. The pile shifted, revealing a worn, leather journal. *That must be it.* She wiped the cover and rushed back to her brother, concerned at his gray color and shallow breathing.

Despite his fading condition, he tried to give her directions. "K-keep f-from D-d-d . . ." He stopped and gasped several times.

Alva grabbed his hand. "Daniel? Keep it from him?"

His voice came out in a throaty whisper "You . . ."

"Me?"

"Yesssss, finish," he whispered and fell silent.

Alva held his hand, worried at the weak pulse and ragged breathing. Hearing someone call her name, she quickly shoved the book under her favorite quilt on the shelf.

"Miss Alva?" The man pounded down the stairs. "Are you all right? I saw the smoke. The doctor and fire briga-diers are right behind me. How is Thomas?"

She recognized the suave, over-confident demeanor of the handsome Daniel Defore, her brother's rival and the man he apparently didn't want knowing his secrets.

Her attention remained fixed on the doctor and oth-ers who rushed in. They began to treat her brother and transferred him to a stretcher. She said a silent prayer as they carried him to the medical wagon waiting outside.

"Miss Alva, is there anything I can do?"

She started as Defore grasped her hand. "Oh, no, thank you, Mr. De—"

"Please, Daniel is fine. Don't worry. Thomas is a strong man. They've made such great advances in medicine. He's in good hands."

She nodded, grateful for his support as her foot slid on a piece of paper. He helped her to a chair, away from the shelf, away from the homely quilt that held her brother's secrets.

"It appears that Thomas was working on something important?" he asked.

She chose not to answer. Let him get his information elsewhere; he wouldn't hear a thing from her. "Thank you, Daniel, for your assistance. If you don't mind, this has been quite a shock. I'd like to be alone now."

"Very well." He took one last look around. "I'll go check on Thomas and see myself out."

Feigning tiredness, she shooed out the rest of Thomas' friends who had wandered in to share their good wishes and the latest on his expected recovery. The news cheered her, but she needed time to adjust and recover over her near loss.

The door locked, the shades drawn, and a pot of strong black tea at her side sweetened with sugar (and a good dash of whiskey), she pulled over the quilt and carefully opened it. A sob escaped as she caressed the cover of the worn journal inside.

She sipped her tea and read the neatly written script, the pages accented with small, detailed sketches and numbered schematics.

Alva didn't have her brother's mechanical aptitude, yet as she studied the drawings and read his detailed instructions, everything became clear. Amazing! She finally understood what Thomas felt with each new discovery.

She marveled at how the mathematic and scientific

equations read like passages from a Jane Austen novel. Now she knew what kept him toiling in secret until the wee hours of the morning. She was invigorated and ready to work. With Defore sniffing about, it was doubly important that she and Thomas be the first to complete the experiments, but it would have to wait. The giant grandfather clock in the hall struck two. The book closed, she hugged it close to her heart, anxious for Thomas to return home, impatient for him to hear her ideas.

Two days later, Alva smiled at her brother, happy to see him seated in his favorite worn chair by the fireplace, an afghan over his wounded leg, a glass of brandy beside him. It seemed impossible that the worst of his injuries amounted to a broken arm, bruised ribs, and a few gashes on his head.

"It's so good to see you seated there," she said again. "You looked so awful, I feared the worst."

He nodded. "I know, I know. I truly wish I hadn't worried you. I'm sorry."

"While you recovered, I did what you wanted. I read your journal."

He leaned forward, his eyes lit with excitement. "And?"

"It's like poetry! I always thought what you did was far beyond what I could comprehend, but it was so clear and easy to understand!"

"Alva, no medicine could be better for me than your words."

"Good, then let me help. I can be your hands and do the things you can't do yourself right now. And if you don't mind, I know what went wrong with your little experiment."

That brought him to his feet. "Alva! You know? Tell me!"

"From what I saw, you had some wires crossed wrong and others touching when they shouldn't. And the cogs were out of alignment."

He limped to her side and kissed her cheek. "Alva, you don't know how happy I am to hear that. I guessed later what might have been faulty, but hearing you say it so soon after reading my journal puts me in awe of your thinking process. Just think what the two of us can accomplish together!"

She went to the cellar door and opened it. "Shall we?"

"By all means! Ladies, first."

They went down the stairs slowly, she careful not to grasp the rail too tight with her swollen hand, he as careful not to bump his wrapped arm.

He laughed. "We're quite the pair, aren't we?"

"I guess we are. But let's see what we can do," she said. "If you don't mind, I'd like to finish this first project on my own. You can check if anything is wrong before we test it, all right?"

He nodded and settled into an armchair to watch. He'd already done the preliminary work, soldering copper and zinc sheets around a box filled with water instead of the dangerous acid used in earlier charging cells. His cell ran on kinetic energy and steam power using a complex grid of interconnecting cogs and other components.

Alva searched the cabinets for what she needed: lamp, check; wicks, check; wires, check; wire cutters, check.

The book open, she pulled over the lamp and followed her brother's detailed sketches. She attached the raw wires to the bolts according to the diagrams. A couple of twists, a few more adjustments, and voila! Thomas' joyous expression told her she was on track.

He checked and double-checked each attachment. "We don't want a repeat of my earlier performance," he joked. "It looks good. Wind it up. Oh, better put these on." He stared at her from behind frog-like goggles.

She adjusted a pair over her own eyes, pulled the knob, and let it go. The gleaming cogs began to turn with a steady *tick-tick-tick*. Such a marvel!

Thomas pulled her back a few feet. "Just in case," he said.

The ticks gave way to a low hum. The box's vibrations made Alva uneasy. "Thomas . . ."

"Wait, look!"

The box rattled and shook like a mini earthquake. She stared and bit her lip, worried that the bolts and connections would shake loose. Suddenly, she yelped and held out her hands as a snap, crackle, and pop filled the air. She reached out to Thomas and regretted it the instant her hand touched his with a sharp jolt of static. "Oww!" she yelled. "Thomas, your hair!"

His hair stood straight on end. "You, too," he yelled as the crackling became louder. His crazed laughter didn't make her feel any better. The humming increased.

"Thomas, we have to go!" she screamed.

"No, Alva, look!"

The wires inside the small glass bulb inserted in the center of the lamp started to glow. The brightness resembled a firefly and then a sunny day.

"Thomas, it worked!"

She hugged him and stared, still in awe of what they had accomplished. The buzz softened; the brightness faded. The bulb dimmed and went out. She eyed the blackened surface and poked the bulb, pulling back at the hotness of the glass.

"Now what? It's dangerously hot and the light doesn't last very long."

"It's a start," he said. "We'll perfect it. First, we have to file the patent. I'll call it Alva's light."

"I appreciate it, but how about the light-bulb? Makes more sense." She watched him unhook wires and disassemble parts. "Thomas?"

"Mmm?"

"While you were in the hospital, I did something else."

"Oh?"

She held out a pile of papers. "I found your other

notes. You know, what you wrote about your discussions with Mr. Wells."

"You mean H.G.? He has some interesting ideas, but they're not ready yet. Those notes were just scribbles. You know, scientific doodles."

"Can I show you something?"

His tinkering done, he followed her upstairs and out to the storage barn behind the house. He laughed as she pulled the door open.

"So you found my other secret. The dirigible went together well, but H.G.'s directions were far too complicated. It'll take me a while to simplify them."

"No, it won't." She took a lamp down from the wall and lit it with a candle.

"For land's sake!" he yelled. "Alva, what did you do?"

The gleaming silver bullet had been streamlined: the outer panels stripped away, the inside but a shell of itself. All that remained were the two seats set on a small base, a skeletal frame, a control board with an array of different size dials and a giant lever.

The look of amazement on his face was worth all her effort, she thought, as he ran around the contraption. "But . . . what? Alva, how did you do this?"

"I couldn't sleep while you were ill, so I worked out here. You were right about Mr. Wells' ideas. I simplified the wiring and stripped off all the extra metal to make the machine lighter. Everything's connected now."

"Did you try it?"

"No." She shook her head and laughed. "I wanted to wait for you. All it needs is a source of power like your charging cell."

He pondered the idea, a hand on his chin. "Yes, but that may not be able to power it for a long enough period of time."

"The larger cogs I installed should overcome that. Should we try it?"

"But what if the charge fails?" he asked.

She shrugged and rubbed her hands. "Now you sound like I used to. I've decided it is worth every risk. Just think . . . if it works we can go into the future. You will be rich from your inventions and can create other wonderful things. And maybe there will be a cure for my condition."

He looked thoughtful, but still hedged. "That would be grand. But what if we're wrong? We could be stranded in an unknown dimension. We could be stuck in some alternative space, or we could simply disappear."

"Do you really believe that?"

"Well, no. All my studies on matter seem to point otherwise. Time is never-ending. But it's also yet unexplained."

"Isn't that what you do when you invent, explore the unknown?" she asked. "All your inventions require someone, namely you, trying them for the first time. So why not this?"

"You may be right," he said.

"Good, let me get my cloak and we'll be off."

That made him laugh. "Your cloak? Do you think we're taking a turn in the buggy? My dear, if something goes wrong, being cold will be the least of our worries."

She rolled her eyes. "Leave it to a man. All the same, a woman never goes anywhere unprepared and underdressed. Give me a moment."

Several minutes later, she returned wearing a saucy gray hat decorated with gray and blue feathers, the wide bow tied under her chin. She wrapped the matching wool cloak around her shoulders, sat, and buckled herself into the machine. "All right, shall we go?"

"So impatient!" He sat next to her, tightened the belt around his waist, and turned the key. The machine roared to life with a purr and a puff of steam. He studied the glass dials and smiled. "Might I say you look pretty? So where to?"

Her smile matched his. "Since we're taking a chance no matter what we do, why not set it for one hundred years ahead? The nineteen hundred and sixties sound interesting."

"So they do, sister, so they do. Hold on tight!"

The humming increased in volume as he pulled the lever. The machine shook, rattled, and disappeared in a burst of gray smoke. As the clouds cleared, a lonely blue feather floated to the ground.

The Nubian Queen

Paul Genesse

Paul Genesse is a registered nurse on a cardiac unit in Salt Lake City, Utah, where he works the night shift keeping the forces of darkness away from his patients. He lives with his incredibly supportive wife, Tammy, and their collection of well-behaved frogs and moderately scary dragons. He is the author of several short stories featured in *Fellowship Fantastic, The Dimension Next Door, Furry Fantastic, Imaginary Friends, Catopolis, Terribly Twisted Tales, Pirates of the Blue Kingdoms* and more. His first novel, *The Golden Cord, Book One of the Iron Dragon Series* was published in 2008. Book two, *The Dragon Hunters*, came out in May of 2009 and more novels are in the works. Download the first ten chapters of *The Golden Cord* for free, listen to podcasts, or watch videos about the *Iron Dragon Series* at www.paulgenesse.com.

Lower Nubia, 1854 A.D.

Queen Sahdi gave the command to destroy the tracks ahead of the armored train as it steamed through the savannah beside Lake Nubia. She stood behind the thick ramparts of Gebel Adda, an ancient fortress situated in the hills that marked the border, wondering how many of her brave soldiers, and how many of the Egyptian emperor's, were about to die.

Through the telescopic sight on her rifle, Sahdi inspected the canon barrels and machine gun turrets that bristled from every car on the train. The emperor's generals would use the railcars to spearhead their attack for as long as they could. Her artillery hidden in the hills and the big guns at Gebel Adda would kill everyone who remained in the flatlands and leave the train a burning wreck.

A puff of white smoke, then a thunderous boom echoed from the bottleneck canyon that led to the train yard at the base of Nubia's largest fortress. Boulders tumbled and covered the iron rails and the handful of unfortunate Libyan scouts inspecting the tracks for sabotage or explosives. The war train screeched to a halt a hundred yards away from the rock fall as dust filled the air.

Queen Sahdi lowered her rifle as General Kemani waited for her signal to open fire on the invading army now that the first part of their trap had been sprung. Five thousand Egyptian infantrymen in green tunics and tan trousers marching in columns behind the train formed firing lines, and some took cover beside the elevated train bed. The two dozen rhino mortar and machine gun trucks stopped rolling forward on their spiked metal wheels, smoke from their flash-boilers mixing with the dust, as they took aim at the hills on either side of the canyon.

A flag-bearer exited the train.

"A white flag?" Sahdi quickly looked through her scope as a group of men exited the second car and walked ahead of the locomotive carrying what appeared to be a folded up shade tent and poles—in addition to the unexpected truce flag.

"Your Majesty, shall I send our terms?" General Kemani asked, his weathered face bearing little emotion.

Sahdi sucked in her breath as far as the ivory corset in her dress would allow and got a mouthful of chalky dust as she beheld the face of the man standing beside the flag-bearer. It was General Nahktebbi himself. Seeing the man who had humiliated her when she was a girl stoked the kind of rage in Sahdi reserved for the cruelest criminals. The vile man had harmed her in a way no one else could. It had been so many years, but she could neither forget nor forgive. She rested the gun on her shooting tripod on the rampart wall, trying to calm herself and slow her pounding heart. She applied a subtle amount of pressure to the trigger. It was a far shot, but with the scope and her years hunting on the Nubian savannah, Nahktebbi would be a dead man shortly after she pulled the trigger.

"Your Majesty," General Kemani said. A note of alarm had crept into his voice. "They're under the white flag and I've noticed you've released the safety on your rifle."

Sahdi let our her breath, taking very careful aim at the general's broad chest and noting the slight westerly wind. "Yes, but it is Nahktebbi." She corrected her aim. "When he falls, send the signal for the artillery to open fire. Then contact the Meroë Cavalry Division and have them cut off any escape. Our spies must cut the telegraph lines at Abu Simbel immediately. I want the first message the emperor gets in Luxor to be Nahktebbi's head in a reed basket."

The general cleared his throat. "Your Majesty, please ask yourself why the emperor sent General Nahktebbi to fight this battle. He knew you would be here. He knew how you would react." Kemani stepped closer, his boot heels scraping on the stone. "Word of this breach of protocol will reach every court in the empire. What chance will we have then against the emperor?"

Sahdi pulled away from her rifle, slowly regaining control. She was the ruler of Nubia, not some barbarian queen like Victoria from the British Isles who executed enemies with her own hands. Sahdi had studied for nine years at the Library of Alexandria with the greatest philosophers, historians, and scientists in the world, then spent a dozen years ruling her own country. The blood of Cleopatra the Great flowed through her veins. Despite all of this, Sahdi had almost taken the bait. Emperor Demetrius had known how to make her blood boil. In a fit of blind rage she had almost pulled the trigger, dishonorably killing an enemy general under a truce flag and guaranteeing a long and bloody war with her portrayed as a criminal. Her reputation would be smeared like Cleopatra's had been by Octavian and the Roman senate.

Sahdi turned around, her long tan dress fringed with a lion's mane swirling about her. She stood tall, a full head above most of the men behind her. Nubia's brightest generals, ministers, soldiers, and servants would spring into action once the words of command fell from her lips. She was so proud of what they had all accomplished during her reign. These women and men had helped guide her sweeping social reforms, built up Nubia's massive industries along the Nile, and established Meroë as the dominant center of trade in the entire Sahel. These few could accomplish anything, and Sahdi's fierce dark eyes, full of pride, passed over all of them. Their skin was dark brown like hers, but she could see into their souls like they were wearing the sheerest linen. Not a coward or incompetent fool was among her inner circle.

How could she have allowed herself to come so close to destroying what they had accomplished together? Sahdi would speak to the leaders of the Holy Coptic Emperor's army and give them one final chance to leave her country in peace. Words could be more powerful than bullets. Sahdi rested the butt of her rifle on the ground. She would give it up for something much more intimidating. Queen Sahdi gave her order with the confidence only someone in her esteemed bloodline could muster. "Bring me my crown."

* * *

Sahdi strode into the shade tent near the Egyptians' armored train wearing her double uraeus crown, the two golden cobras poised to strike. Accompanying her were General Kemani, First Minister Akar, and Sahdi's most fearsome personal bodyguard, Shahkto—a scarified warrior from the Kush tribal lands.

General Nahktebbi, the former Marshal of the Nubian Legions, stood alone with a deferential expression on his face. He wore a tan uniform with brass buttons, epaulets, and a leopard skin belt that Sahdi remembered from her childhood when Nahktebbi had been an officer in her father's guard at the palace in Meroë. Someone must have dusted his shiny black boots while he'd been waiting in the tent—probably one of the other three men in his party who waited several steps behind him. Two appeared to be Egyptian officers, but the third was a tall and handsome man of mixed African descent. He was in his mid-thirties and wore a bright white tunic with ornate bronze buttons and tan trousers. His skin was not as dark as most Africans, and had a golden brown glow, showing his mixed ancestry.

"Your Highness." Nahktebbi spoke formal court Latin, and bowed at the waist.

"You will address Queen Sahdi as, 'Your Majesty'." General Kemani shot a withering glance at his former best friend who was obviously following the emperor's orders and referring to her with a lesser title.

Nahktebbi bowed lower, and Sahdi could see white hairs on the back of his shaved scalp. He was nearly forty when he . . . *knew her* in the palace . . . and now they were both twenty years older. How many other little girls had he defiled in the past two decades?

Nahktebbi stood up and she realized she was taller than him, though not by much. He had been a giant when she was a girl, but as a grown woman she was over six feet tall, even without her uraeus crown and black mamba-skin boots.

The unknown nobleman bowed low to Sahdi and nodded to Kemani.

"General, who is this gentleman who accompanies you?" Kemani asked.

"May I present Duke Zander of Attica, the official envoy of King Antyllus Alexandros Constantius IV of Athens, Ruler of Greece and all the Coptic Greco-Russian people."

Sahdi raised an eyebrow, intrigued, and very suspicious of the handsome foreigner. The envoy came forward and Sahdi noticed his amber eyes, the color somewhere between green and gold, so exotic. He was a hundred times more handsome than King Antyllus. The emperor had sent her a portrait of the king some years ago and the old king had a pig's face that only his half-Russian mother could love.

"Your Majesty." Duke Zander bowed deeply at the waist again. "I wish to convey the goodwill of King Antyllus. His Majesty bears no ill wishes toward Your Majesty, and is very understanding of your reluctance to leave Nubia and marry a man you have not met."

The Duke had a charming northern accent and Sahdi regarded the foreigner with suspicion, wondering if he was a spy of the emperor, or if he truly did serve the Greek king.

"Your Highness—" Nahktebbi began again, as meekly as she had ever heard a general speak, "—in regards to your title, the emperor requested that I inform you that you have never been anointed as the queen of Nubia by His Imperial Majesty, nor the Pope of the Holy Coptic Church, and thus, the emperor ordered me to refer to you as, Your Highness, and most definitely not, Your Majesty. My deepest apologies."

"General, did you come to insult me or invade my country?" Sahdi asked.

Nahktebbi's eyes filled with pain. "His Imperial Majesty has sent me and this *honor guard* to remind you that your presence is required in Alexandria. Upon your arrival in the capital you will be married to King Antyllus of Athens at the earliest possible convenience acceptable to His Majesty in Greece."

Sahdi pressed her lips together, not bothering to hide the revulsion she felt at the prospect of marrying the venerable king of Greece. For seven years the emperor had been sending the same messages via ambassadors, delegations, personal appeals letters, and even a talented poet who told tales about the beauty of Greece and the frozen mountains of Macedonia from whence Sahdi's ancestor Ptolemy I originally came. It was no secret that the emperor wanted to use his status as her imperial cousin to exile Sahdi as far away as possible from the vast wheat fields, iron works, trade routes, and gold mines of Nubia. In the north, she would be kept busy fighting the starving barbarian hordes that were trying to escape the snow and glaciers that had migrated south across Europe for the past five hundred years. From northern France to the Alps and all the way east to the Black Sea the snow and ice had destroyed everything. Famine, plagues, wars, and the destruction of all the once-great peoples of Europe had ushered in the African Age. The Sahel had become a water rich paradise and the Sahara a verdant savannah of thriving herds and productive farmers. Nubia itself was as close to the Garden of Eden as the Coptic bible described, and Sahdi would never leave her homeland for a king with Russian blood and some frozen palace perched on the acropolis of Athens. If she ever married, the man would move to her home in Nubia.

Sahdi stared harshly at the vile man. "General, the emperor should find King Antyllus another wife, as I will never leave Africa."

"Your Highness," Nahktebbi said, "if you do not consent to accompany me back to Alexandria, I have been instructed to invade Nubia and capture you as rapidly as I am able."

Sahdi and her advisors scoffed. "You propose to invade my country with five thousand men and capture *me?*"

"I propose nothing of the sort." Nahktebbi shifted his feet.

"Then what are you doing here?" Sahdi asked.

The general took a step closer to Sahdi, his wrinkled hands open in front of him. He got down on both knees, apparently not caring about his own pride or time-honored protocol. "*Ehu Kandake—*" he whispered "My Queen" in old Bantin, an amalgam of Bantu and Latin—a trade language few of the aristocracy outside of Nubia spoke. The three men behind Nahktebbi would not understand, and that had to be why he used the old tongue. "—I have been sent to start a war. The emperor knows you will never consent to come with me. He knows that my presence here will only infuriate you and cause a terrible battle. My army, and me specifically, are all to be sacrificed. We are to enter Nubia and wait for you to fire the first shot. The emperor hopes that you will kill me and most of my soldiers."

"It would be a massacre," Sahdi promised.

"Undoubtedly, but then the emperor will send his vast army from Luxor with the support of his allies in Africa and the Middle East."

"The emperor's ego has grown larger if he thinks all of the African kings will oppose me."

"My Queen, few will stand against the emperor's forces once he describes how your army ambushed and slaughtered the honor guard sent to retrieve you. You will be disgraced, outside the protection of all laws. The emperor will invade Nubia, take over the cities, seize all the raw materials and goods you've withheld this past year from Egypt, and spend as long as it takes to find, capture, and execute you as a traitor to the Crown."

"I will never be taken alive."

"The emperor counts on that," Nahktebbi whispered, then glanced back at the Duke. "He does not want you alive. He needs you gone forever, and this battle will be an excuse to start the war."

It was the same challenge her ancestors had faced time and time again. The Egyptian Pharaohs had always hated an independent and strong Nubia. Why would Demetrius XII be any different?

"My Queen, in the end, you will be dead," Nahktebbi said with more sadness than she would have anticipated, "*our* country will be in ruin, and the king of Athens will still not have a queen—just as the emperor has planned. Contrary to what he or his ambassadors say, he does not want to bring the two bloodlines of Cleopatra the Great back together."

Sahdi shook her head. Was the emperor that devious to arrange a royal marriage between her and the Greek king with the knowledge that it would never come to pass? She had not thought him capable of such diabolical plans. However, Nahktebbi had a point. Keeping the bloodlines of Cleopatra the Great's twin children—Alexander Helios and Cleopatra Selene II—apart did make sense. The blood of Alexander Helios was thin after all the Roman, Nubian, Egyptian, and most recently, Russian blood that had entered into the Grecian royal line; but it was still powerful, and their descendents would have a stronger claim on the throne of Alexandria with Sahdi's more pure blood added to their line.

Sahdi was not sure what to make of Nahktebbi now. Was he lying or was he trying to make amends? "Why would you agree to sacrifice yourself for the emperor?"

"My life means little to me. All of these years I've been exiled from my home, and the woman I loved." He stared at her remorsefully, his love for Sahdi bleeding from his eyes.

Embarrassed and taken aback, Sahdi wished he would be more discreet in front of her advisors. She expected him to be contrite, but lovesick and forlorn, never.

"My feelings for . . . Nubia, have never faded," he said.

Sahdi had no doubt that Tebbi was sincere, and was glad he had said "Nubia" instead of "woman" again.

"I am so sorry for what happened." Nahktebbi's eyes misted over.

Sahdi's infatuation for Nahktebbi as a girl splashed her in the face like icy water. She had been obsessed with the dashing older man, spending every moment she could in his company. Then came the night after her thirteenth birthday feast when she had helped him back to his private chambers when he had become drunk on Judean wine. Why had she not let one of the servants light the way for him in the dark palace? Once in his chamber he had refused to let her leave. Nahktebbi had groped her young breasts before throwing her onto the bed. There was no magical kiss like she had been imagining with the handsome older man. He would not stop his advances despite her tormented pleas.

Later, in the darkness, Sahdi lay paralyzed beside the man she had once loved. He gasped in shock when he saw her anguish. Nahktebbi jumped off the bed and fell to his knees begging her not to tell anyone what had happened. After his tearful apologies he vowed to leave Nubia forever and tell no one of his crime. She had never spoken of it, but Nahktebbi's best friend, Kemani, had seen little Sahdi slinking from Nahktebbi's chambers.

The warm wind blew through the tent as General Nahktebbi knelt in front of Queen Sahdi again, waiting for her to reject or accept his heartfelt apology. Before she answered, she had to know one more thing.

"Did you tell the emperor?" Sahdi asked.

Nahktebbi blinked. He knew what she meant. "A few years ago, before we defeated the Ottomans outside Constantinople, I confessed to a priest."

Sahdi removed her thin gloves and slapped Nahktebbi's cheek as hard as she could with her bare hand.

He picked himself off the ground and bowed, eyes downcast and full of shame. "*Ehu Kandake*, I wish I had had the courage to end my own life so many years ago."

"You will have your chance to redeem yourself. Now, stand up, General."

Nahktebbi stood with his delegation as Sahdi considered her next words. She was angered beyond measure that the emperor had played her as a fool for years pretending he wanted her to marry King Antyllus. Now she would beat the emperor at his own game with a move he would be hard pressed to counter. She would consult with her advisors then set her plans in motion. She would buy her people the time they needed and Nubia's salvation was clear to her now. All she had to do was secure an alliance with the second most powerful man in the Holy Coptic Empire, an old friend of her father's, Pope Cyril of Alexandria. With the Pope's help, she could orchestrate the fall of Emperor Demetrius. "Gentlemen," Sahdi began, "I will not sacrifice the Nubian people for my own interests. There will be no war with Egypt. I will accompany you to Alexandria, where I will marry King Antyllus."

Nahktebbi looked stunned, but Duke Zander, strangely, was smiling.

"Nubia has protected me for my entire life," Sahdi said, "and now I will protect her. Tomorrow, I depart for Alexandria."

And God forgive me, Sahdi thought, *I go to kill the emperor.*

The ironclad Egyptian war-barge *Ibis* carried the Nubian queen and her entourage down the Nile. She felt like she had been captured by one of the ancient pharaohs as they passed the massive statues of Ramses II and his wife Nefertari at Abu Simbel. At least she had Shahkto and a small cadre of armed loyal bodyguards, in addition to Duke Zander, who had requested to be in charge of her guard detail. She had read the secret message he'd passed to General Kemani detailing the danger she would be in if she let the emperor's men assume control of her safety. She also took his advice and had several female attendants accompany her at all times, preparing her food from stores they had brought with them.

After midnight on the first day of the voyage a faint knock, barely audible above the loud boiler under her quarters, sounded on her stateroom door. On her command, Shahkto let the gentleman inside.

"Duke Zander, do you always call on royalty after midnight?" Sahdi asked in Latin from the divan where she reclined, swathed in Sumatran silk.

He bowed low. "To be truthful, Your Majesty"—he spoke in Macedonian Greek—"I do. I have even been known to disturb emperors and their mistresses while engaged in their bedroom sport."

Sahdi laughed, pleased to hear the language she had used during most of her schooling in Alexandria. She had forgotten how much she enjoyed the exaggerated movements her mouth had to make to form the words. She changed to Greek. "In that case, perhaps I should be honored at your visit. Now, please explain why you're here, and worry not about formalities."

"Forgive me then for being direct. As I mentioned in the note, the emperor does not wish for you to survive this voyage."

"What do you suggest?" Sahdi wondered if he knew something she did not, as she found her eyes lingering on his lips, and the contours of the handsome face.

"Get off this ironclad as soon as possible. We'll be in Kôm Ombo in the morning. We can take an airship from there to the Temple of Karnak in Luxor."

"An *airship*?" Sahdi shook her head. Just thinking of the dangerous flying contraptions made her uneasy. "Someone as well-informed as you should know that I shall never ride in an airship even if I *am* outside my homeland."

Zander blanched at her words. "I was very sorry to hear of your father's accident, but that was one of the first models, built many years ago."

"Twelve years is not so long."

"Of course you're right, but still, the airships today are much better. I thought it would be the safest way for you to get to Luxor. The one I flew on from Athens, *Bucephalus*, is ready to carry you to see the emperor and will fly you to Alexandria. It will take only a few hours, rather than the days you will spend in a watercraft."

Sahdi shook her head and thought about her father. Ever since his small airship crashed in the plains while he was hunting lions he had barely been able to speak, let alone understand complex thoughts. She had been forced to return from Alexandria before her studies were complete and assume the throne—without the pope's or the emperor's blessing—while her father spent his days with physicians from as far as India who still said they could heal his damaged brain even after a decade of no progress.

"It's late." Sahdi feigned a yawn. "We shall speak of this at a later time."

"Shall I call on you in the morning?"

"No. I shall call on you at a time of my own choosing."

"As you wish." The Duke bowed, his amber eyes never leaving hers. "Sleep well, *Ehu Kandake*."

Later that night, wrapped in a simple servant's cloak, Sahdi concealed herself in the darkness near the midship starboard railing. A man in soft-soled shoes, trousers, and a waistcoat approached cautiously.

"You're late," Sahdi whispered, letting the cloak fall to her shoulders.

"Forgive me," Duke Zander said. "I could not decide what to wear with my bed slippers."

Sahdi stopped herself from laughing and grinned as he stepped closer. He had put on a touch of cologne and the musky scent teased her senses. What did he think she wanted with him in the middle of the night? She toyed with the scandalous thoughts for a moment, before regaining her focus. "Do you have the time?"

Zander deftly withdrew a pocket watch on a chain, squinted in the darkness. "Three minutes to four."

"I'm afraid we haven't got much time." Sahdi reached for his hand and strongly drew him toward her.

Zander did not seem surprised until she led him to the railing a few steps away and pointed at a rope ladder hanging over the side. "You're climbing down."

"Though I am a gentleman, this is not what I hoped for when I received your summons," Zander said, his hand gently squeezing hers.

Sahdi lost herself in his words, staring at his face and forgetting everything until the Nile splashed against the hull, bringing her back to the present.

"*Majesty, please.*" Shahkto whispered from a shadowy turret overlooking the rope ladder.

"Climb down," Sahdi ordered Zander.

Zander resisted. "You're throwing me off the ship?"

An Egyptian colonel with a pistol drawn—though aimed at the deck—came through a metal door in the wall paralleling the railing. Another imperial officer came from the other direction and stepped in front of the ladder, guarding it with a cocked revolver. "Highness," the captain said, "I must escort you to your stateroom. Now."

Sahdi glanced at the officer just more than an arm's length behind her, blocking her escape, then made eye contact with the colonel. "I need fresh air, and the Duke and I have not finished our conversation." Sahdi stepped closer to Zander and wantonly opened her cloak with both hands, exposing what lay beneath. "You see, I did not know what to wear either." She pushed her hips against him and put his hand on the handle of the saber hanging unsheathed from a cloth belt around her waist. Her eyes met his as she nodded her head. "You know what to do."

Zander grabbed the handle and thrust the sword up and into the throat of the officer as Shahkto killed the surprised colonel with a throwing knife.

"Majesty, climb down!" Shahkto's urgent plea echoed voices at the base of the ladder.

The explosion ripped through the war-barge like an earthquake as the boiler and aft powder magazine exploded at once. Sahdi held onto Zander's hand as they tumbled over the railing and into the crocodile infested Nile below.

Three hours after sunrise a caravan of nine steam-cars and three rhino machine gun trucks rolled north on the road that followed the Nile at the edge of the plains.

"Right on time," Sahdi said, "unlike some." She flashed an upturned eyebrow to Zander, who was now wearing a dry set of plain clothing as they stood in the verdant hills miles away from where the *Ibis* had sunk and where they had left their small rowboats.

"That fool of a colonel must not have known about the bombs, how did you?" Zander asked for the second time.

"I am the Queen of Nubia." The hint of a smile appeared on her lips as a stone faced Shahkto waved to the lead steam car.

"You could have told me when I spoke to you at midnight." Zander was still upset. "I could have disarmed it. Saved the ship, and all those men."

Sahdi faced him. "So could I. Better for the emperor to think we're dead. It was his bomb after all. Let him think his plan worked." Sahdi wrapped a scarf around her face and hair. "Now come. Content yourself that we've changed modes of travel as you suggested."

She got behind the wheel of the lead car and invited Zander to ride in the front with her.

"The paint is fresh." Zander touched the Egyptian flag painted on the door and commented on the Egyptian uniforms worn by the Sahdi's Nubian soldiers.

"Quite fresh." Sahdi put her hands on the wheel, loving the smell and the vibration of the rumbling steam engine.

Shahkto dispersed the royal servants, guards, and luggage into the caravan and then manned the machine gun turret in the rear of Sahdi's armored car while the drivers poured water and shoveled fresh loads of coal into the boilers.

"Wear these." Sahdi handed Zander a pair of brass goggles similar to the ones she adjusted over her eyes. Shahkto handed Zander the tunic and hat of an Egyptian general.

"I am quite a proficient driver," Zander said. "Perhaps I—"

"Ready?"

The Duke nodded as Queen Sahdi released the throttle. He hung on as she accelerated to the steam car's top speed of nearly fifty miles per hour. The bumpy road, frequent stops at water stations, and a handful of surprised soldiers at checkpoints slowed their pace, but at the end of the day they reached the emperor's palace outside the temple of Karnak in Luxor.

Sahdi's spies were correct. At least a hundred and fifty thousand men were camped around the city where Demetrius planned the invasion of Nubia. According to Zander, the emperor felt safe there from his rivals that were gathering in Alexandria as Actium Day approached. Representatives from all over the world were assembling to celebrate the victory of Antony and Cleopatra over Octavian on September 2, 31 B.C., which guaranteed the fall of the Roman Republic and the ascension of the modern Egyptian Empire that had lasted for more than eighteen hundred years. The empire was no longer entirely intact, but most of the Mediterranean world owed allegiance and respected Egypt's vast wealth and power, which was second only to Nubia.

The next morning, Emperor Demetrius Andronicus Marcus Ptolemnus XII met Sahdi in his elevated palace overlooking the ancient temple of Karnak. The gigantic columns, pylons, and obelisks—all painted and replastered to look as they did in the time of the ancient pharaohs—were a stunning monument to the restoration efforts of the Ptolemaic Dynasty.

"Crown Princess Lumasahda Cleopatra Selene I," the herald announced as she entered the lavish throne room filled with courtiers, guards, and various nobles. Considering how many slaves were in Egypt, Sahdi was surprised not to see any snowfaced Europeans.

"Sahdi, my favorite cousin. You are a glorious sight." Demetrius stood from his golden throne as he called out with false cheerfulness.

She wore her ostrich feather gown, white lace gloves, and an ivory corset and bustier that kept her large breasts in their most powerful and uplifted position. She had worn her mound of dark hair inside a tall blue and gold flat-topped crown—a style made famous in antiquity by Queen Nefertiti—to whom Sahdi's beauty had often been compared. In addition, Sahdi hoped to upset her cousin further by wearing the double uraeus circlet crown of Nubia.

"Imperial Majesty." Sahdi bowed half as far as she should, easily keeping her balance despite the high-heeled boots she wore under the hoop dress. She was a giant among the men and women of court with her tall crown, heels, and the tremendous stature she had inherited from her father.

The emperor's four sons and three daughters stood at the edge of the aisle leading to the throne. The oldest boy was in his early twenties and oldest girl perhaps fifteen. Sahdi gave them a withering look as she wondered after Empress Galatia. There was no sign of the famously fertile and fat queen who was thought to be pregnant once again—though no one could really tell for certain.

"It is splendid to see you, dear Sahdi. I'm so relieved that you survived the accident aboard the *Ibis*. How dreadful that must have been." He pretended not to see the Nubian crown, and his eyes roamed over her hips and chest. "How long has it been? Fourteen years since I visited you in the depths of that rotting library?"

The royal guards stopped Sahdi five paces away from the ostentatious throne. She smiled at Demetrius, letting the silence chill the humid air. She had nearly forgotten how boorish he could be, but it was not without purpose. He was baiting her, though she would not take the lure like she almost had at Gebel Adda.

"Cousin." The emperor sat with a grin. "I've been looking forward to this day for some time and am thankful we could put our differences aside. I've already sent a shipment of four thousand Jewish slaves up the Nile to show the world we are trading again, and as a wedding gift I will give Nubia one thousand of them for each barge of the famous Nubian iron sent downriver. Let no one say I am not gracious to the Princess of Nubia with her dowry either. I will contribute six thousand snow-faces to King Antyllus, mostly Franks and Spaniards, some Jews. He can use all the chattel he can get in his coal and silver mines."

"No thank you, cousin Demetry." A scandalous murmur went through the court at the use of his familiar name. "The laws of Nubia and its trade policies have not changed since I've left, nor will they." Slavery hadn't been permitted in Nubia for more than two years and any country that wished to trade with the Nubians without paying excessive tariffs had to abolish the practice as well.

The emperor shook his head. "Well then, it is good to see that you have not lost your spirit. I do not envy the task of King Antyllus." Some nobles in the court chuckled softly. "Your upcoming wedding will take place on Actium Day, thirteen days hence. His Majesty will be in Alexandria for the festivities and I'll send a telegraph to Athens immediately confirming that there will indeed be a marriage. I shall hold a gala the likes of which no one has ever seen. Does that please you, dear cousin?"

Her mouth twisted in a mock smile. "Does it matter if I am pleased?"

Demetrius cleared his throat and looked at his courtiers and family. They all looked away, mortified at her monumental impertinence to the most powerful man in the world.

"Oh Sahdi, I'm certain we'll have much more time to speak after the wedding, and of course before your husband whisks you off to glorious Athens. I'm sure he'll take you in style. He's so fond of his airships, though mine are still the best in the empire. You will take one of them to Alexandria, avoid the mosquitoes along the riverbanks."

"No." Her tone was as cold as the frozen Black Sea, and much more treacherous.

"Ah, yes," Demetrius said. "You are still quite afraid after what happened to your father."

The way he said "happened" made Sahdi want to pull the revolver strapped to her right thigh. She had a secret slit in her gown that would allow her to draw the pistol and shoot it without pulling the weapon from her dress. Though it wasn't part of the master plan, she had considered shooting Demetry since entering the room, and now she had a strong suspicion that her smug cousin had something to do with her father's accident. There had always been suspicions, but never a shred of proof.

"How is my addled uncle?" the emperor asked. "Is he still drooling most of the day?"

Before Sahdi realized it, she had reached into her gown and locked her hand on the pistol. She regained control of her senses as the guards flanking her came closer. "I'll give my father your regards," Sahdi said, releasing her grip on the weapon, "when I return to Meroë."

"Still thinking about being buried in one of those pagan pyramids?" the emperor asked. "What a quaint practice. I should think that the next time you'll be in Meroë will be long after your death. The Athenians will have to mummify your corpse in the old way so it won't putrefy as they transport you across the Mediterranean. I suppose they could pack you in Macedonian ice and fly you over on an airship."

The throne room went silent as the emperor glowered at Sahdi, daring her to respond.

Sahdi made the sign of the cross on her chest. "I shall have a Christian burial, Demetry. Have you considered what kind of funeral you will have?"

The emperor pulled back in his throne.

Sahdi strode out of the chamber without bowing and kept a haughty grin plastered on her face for all to see. She entered the private waiting room where she had prepared for her meeting and locked the door. General Nahktebbi stood stiffly in the back of the room wearing a parade uniform thick with medals and ribbons, probably from the Egyptian campaigns in the New World to conquer the Sioux tribes in Mexico.

"No one knows you are here?" Sahdi whispered in Bantin, noticing he had shut the discreet door that adjoined the waiting room where he had been sequestered.

He shook his head and bowed to her. "Your Majesty, you wished to speak with me?"

Sahdi drew the pistol she had kept under her gown. Nahktebbi's eyes went wide. The assassination attempt on the *Ibis* had changed everything, and she handed him the gun handle first. Sahdi would strike now as the circumstances allowed. "Tebbi, make yourself useful for once and all is forgiven."

Nahktebbi looked stunned as Sahdi opened the adjoining door to his waiting room, and waved for him to go.

She waited for several moments until Nahktebbi was brought into the throne room. She listened for the sound of a gunshot, and the screaming that would follow.

"General Nahktebbi, our Nubian worker of miracles!" the emperor bellowed, preempting the herald. "Name your reward, General. I am a man of my word."

"Imperial Majesty, I wish only to serve at your side," Nahktebbi said.

There was no gunshot, and Sahdi clenched her fists, enraged that Nahktebbi had betrayed her trust yet again. How foolish she was to believe he would help her.

Moments later, she composed herself and exited the waiting room. She walked quickly, unable to listen to the pompous emperor or endure the gazes of his sniveling sycophants scrutinizing her in the hall. She would have her revenge, but not today.

Alexandria was larger than Sahdi remembered, and the harbor smelled much worse. Fisherman from all across the Nile Delta were ordered here with their catches to feed the sudden influx of visitors. The city had grown to almost twice its previous size since she had attended the university, and the streets were packed with tens of thousands of citizens from all over Egypt, plus countless foreigners attending the Actium Day celebrations. Just getting into the capital proved to be challenging, as the roads were thronged with travelers—and according to Duke Zander's contacts and Sahdi's spies—a small army of assassins hired by intermediaries of the emperor bent on ending her life long before she arrived in the capital.

The Duke of Attica was determined to please his king, and deliver Sahdi to the wedding unharmed. Taking an airship from Luxor seemed the best course of action, but Zander never once tried to convince Sahdi to take *Bucephalus,* and instead helped arrange for two separate steamships on the trip from Memphis, then a train conveyed them to Kanopus where they "became separated" from their imperial guards during what was to be a brief horse ride. The horses carried them to the coast where they took a short voyage on a leaky Athenian submarine called *Triton,* which brought them into Alexandria's harbor. Sahdi had doubts about the health, intellect, and age of King Antyllus, but his most trusted servant, the Duke of Attica, was a man as clever as Odysseus.

A day after arriving in the capital, the emperor's informants found Sahdi, Zander, and a very belligerent Shahkto hiding in Alexandria's vast library complex. Much to the disgust of the scholars who had come to study there, a small army of Egyptian soldiers proceeded to clear any floor where the Nubian queen wished to go. To remove any potential witnesses, Shahkto had said. Despite that fear, the guards set up an armed vigil around Sahdi.

The emperor and his family would arrive the next day, just in time for her afternoon wedding at Saint Mark's Cathedral. The emperor would save a lot of coin holding her marriage feast on Actium Day—blending two expenses into one tremendous celebration for all the dignitaries and nobles in the Coptic Empire. Dozens of airships, including *Bucephalus,* and King Antyllus' airship *Achilles Revenge,* had arrived. Several more were anchored around the colossal Lighthouse of Alexandria, which sat on the concrete island at the mouth of the harbor. Cleopatra the Great had rebuilt the lighthouse and each generation had added to or renovated the gigantic structure. The current emperor's father had scrapped the old stone building and constructed the modern lighthouse using the design of an immigrant engineer. Alexandre Gustave Ivvel had been delivered to the Egyptian court, and his masterpiece was the tallest building in the world, a phallic symbol of steel girders topped with a light that had no equal.

Sahdi left her brilliant view of the Ivvel Lighthouse from a balcony of the library and drifted through the stacks of scrolls and books with Zander and Shahkto in front and behind her. She wondered how things would have changed if the fire that started when Julius Caesar came to Alexandria in 48 B.C. had spread beyond one small shelf.

The section where Sahdi eventually found herself after wandering for some time with a well-armed Shahkto and Duke Zander, as well as the emperor's minders, was of course in the specialty stacks dedicated to Cleopatra the Great. In the seventy-four years of her reign, Cleopatra VII wrote many books and three memoirs . . . the first a few years after Antony had destroyed Rome for good; then after Antony's death from an excess of wine when Cleopatra was in her fifties; and lastly in the final years of her life when her power was at its zenith, just before she abdicated all her duties to her son with Julius Caesar, Caesarion.

Sahdi had read the exact copies of the memoirs multiple times—and not the museum versions for the foreign scholars, but the secret ones reserved only for relatives of the famous empress written in the original ancient Greek. That's what Sahdi wanted to read tonight. She would read through a copy of Cleopatra's first memoir, studying how she considered suicide during the battle of Actium when the outcome was in doubt. If the wind had blown the other way and the naphtha sprayers could not have been used, Antony and the fleet would have been lost. Rather than be paraded through the streets of Rome with a golden chain around her neck like her sister Arsinoë had, Cleopatra would commit suicide. Sahdi liked to think her life would never come to a moment of utter hopelessness. Still, one never knew.

Sahdi reached for a copy of Cleopatra's first memoir that had been placed on a reading table. Perhaps she could find some clue to how Cleopatra endured the seduction of Julius Caesar when the man that she truly loved, Mark Antony, was only an arm's reach away. Sahdi began to open the large book when she noticed the guard captain glance at her expectantly, his eyes nervous. She stopped opening the book, sat, and pretended to adjust her dress as she inspected the side of the large tome. Someone had tampered with it. She could tell by the way the pages lay together unevenly. What was inside? An asp? A bomb?

"Captain," Sahdi asked the stern man who watched her every move, "when will you take us to see Pope Cyril?"

"Tomorrow, Your Highness. It has been arranged." The captain's tone and fake smile told her volumes.

"We're going now," Sahdi said. "Form our escort."

"That is not possible," the captain replied. "Please, Highness, entertain yourself a little longer."

"We're going now," Duke Zander said, as he too eyed the book.

"No." The captain gestured and nodded to his seven men. "You're staying here."

The imperial guards suddenly raised their rifles toward Sahdi as the captain drew his pistol.

Shahkto shot two of the soldiers with his revolver and slashed a third across the throat with a dagger before they could fire. Duke Zander ran one man through with his saber and shot another in the side of the head. The final two riflemen and the captain fired at the Nubian Queen's chest.

Shahkto lunged forward and shielded Sahdi as the bullets pierced his back. She held up the tall warrior, hugging him as the captain fired another salvo into the dying bodyguard. The bullets did not strike her, but part of her heart would perish with Shahkto, a Nubian tribesman more noble than any emperor.

"Drop your weapons!" the captain ordered the Duke as Sahdi laid Shahkto's body on the table. The two remaining riflemen held their guns on Zander, each aiming point blank at the sides of his head. The captain pointed his pistol at Sahdi's heart.

Zander let his bloody sword and smoking pistol fall to the wooden floor. No alarm went up and no other guards came running to the scene in the wake of the commotion. They must have all been under orders.

Sahdi picked up the heavy book, holding it against her chest like a shield that would stop the captain's bullets as he stepped toward her. Her pistol, dagger, and even the vial of poison she had hidden in her clothing were out of reach now.

"Put that down." The captain motioned hesitantly to Cleopatra's thick memoir.

Sahdi shook her head. "You soldiers should not be afraid of books." She flipped open the cover aiming the front of it at the captain who dodged too late. Four simultaneous bangs and a puff of smoke exploded from inside as she triggered the trap. A quartet of tiny pocket pistols in a hollowed out cavity hidden behind the first few pages tore into the captain's body.

Zander stepped back, jerking the barrels of the soldiers' rifles causing them to pull the triggers, discharge their weapons, and kill each other instantly. The Duke snatched up his revolver as Sahdi lingered over Shahkto's body.

She kissed her brave bodyguard on the cheek and fought back her tears.

Imperial soldiers closed in around them.

"Please, Your Majesty," Zander said. "Allow me to escort you to Pope Cyril's residence. If there is anywhere in this city where we'll be safe, it's with him."

Sahdi picked up Shahkto's pistol, drew her own, and motioned for Zander to head for a hidden staircase that led into the basement of the library. "There's a secret way out." Sahdi cocked the pistols. "We shoot anyone who gets in our way."

His Holiness Cyril IX, Pope of Alexandria and Patriarch of all Africa of the Holy See of Saint Mark welcomed Sahdi into his private apartment at Saint Mark's Cathedral on the day of Sahdi's wedding. Comfortable chairs in front of a gigantic picture window faced the harbor in the elegant sitting room. The pope wore orthodox black robes with twelve golden crosses stitched into the fabric, and the upside down bowl-shaped *kolonsoa* hat over his head with flaps that covered his ears. Despite his beard being much grayer than Sahdi remembered, he still had the sparkle in his dark eyes that she always loved. After she kissed the ring on his wrinkled hand he blessed her and then sat in a plain padded chair that easily accommodated his small body. A single attendant remained as they spoke of her father and his unfortunate health. The pope held a small bronze cross in his hand as they chatted.

"Your father is always in my nightly prayers."

"Thank you, Your Holiness. That is most comforting."

"You have done well in his place. I know it has not been easy for you, but the Church applauds your efforts to live the principles of the gospels in Nubia and beyond. It's a shame that Emperor Demetrius doesn't share your vision for reform, or care about the poor and the slaves as you do."

"Your Holiness, there is much more that I would like to do, if only I had your blessing to remain in Africa."

"I should imagine your soon-to-be husband will want to live in Athens."

"Your Holiness, perhaps we could speak, alone."

Pope Cyril dismissed his attendant and Sahdi waited for the heavy door to close. She wanted the drapes pulled over the window, but didn't want to prolong this any longer. Confessing to her personal priest was hard enough. Now she planned to conspire with the most holy man on Earth. She took a deep breath and imagined what would happen to Nubia if she failed. "Your Holiness, I must confess my sins."

"Of course."

Sahdi made the sign of the cross on her chest. "In the name of the Father, and of His Son, and of the eternal Holy Spirit. My last confession was four weeks ago." She paused and gave Pope Cyril a chance to recite scripture.

"Bear with each other and forgive whatever grievances you may have against one another. Forgive as the Lord forgave you."

She recognized it, a passage from the Book of Colossians. He must have known that her confession would involve grievances against the emperor. She thought about the words for a moment and realized she could never forgive Demetrius. God would have to do that. "Your Holiness, my sins are many. In the past weeks I have wished death upon my enemies, especially Emperor Demetrius. I ordered his murder in Luxor after he insinuated that he may have had a hand in my father's accident. I have also planned to overthrow the emperor and invade Egypt." She paused, intent on going through with the marriage no matter what. Cleopatra had partnered with Julius Caesar, a man thirty years older than her. She would do the same with Antyllus. The old king had outlived two wives, and she would outlive him. Perhaps Zander would wait.

"Go on, child."

She bit her lip. "I have lusted after a man who has sworn to protect me, and deliver me safe to his king. I think I may have fallen ..."

"Continue, please." The pope was unfazed.

She couldn't tell him any more about Zander. "Your Holiness, I must ask a favor of you that will save the people of Nubia."

He nodded.

"Before you marry us, give me the blessing of the Coptic Church and officially coronate me as the queen of Nubia in front of God and all of the foreign kings and dignitaries."

He squeezed his cross, knowing this would make her queen of Greece and Nubia. The emperor would be enraged. "If I refuse?"

"I will take a weak poison and will blame the emperor. I will live, then I will charge Demetrius—fabricate evidence if I must—and when I recover, I will stand with my husband, rally all of Africa and the Middle East against the emperor. There will be a terrible war. Hundreds of thousands will die, and in the end, he will fall."

"And if I do this for you?" The old man sighed.

"Coronate me, and I will use politics instead of war. To win with words, I must officially be queen of Nubia and Greece."

"This is wrong." Pope Cyril furrowed his brow. "There are other ways. Think of your eternal soul."

"Your Holiness, I have. It's better for me to sacrifice my salvation than to watch as the northerners starve while the ice slowly buries them. They trade their freedom for chains and a belly full of bread for their children. I cannot abide this when there is land enough for all."

Sahdi got on her knees, hands in the prayer position. "Your Holiness, I beg you. Coronate me as queen of Nubia and I shall spare Africa the horrors of machine-driven warfare the scale of which the world has never seen. As an act of contrition for this request, I will build Coptic churches in every town in the Empire. The other religions will fade from memory. Every man, woman, and child will hear the gospels from Coptic missionaries."

The pope closed his eyes and prayed silently. When he opened them at last, he looked at Sahdi with a grave expression. "I will do as you ask. Then you will grant a request to the church once you are empress. You will agree to whatever we demand."

"Yes, Your Holiness. Whatever you ask." Sahdi made the sign of the cross and swore to herself, and to God, that this vow would be kept.

The pope suddenly pointed out the window at a vast airship flying over Alexandria's harbor en route to the imperial palace. "The emperor and his family return from Karnak." The long, gray artillery-shell-shaped balloon glided slowly through the air, four propeller engines steering it. A grand brass-colored gondola hugged the base of the airship as it approached the landing field.

Her wedding was upon her.

She would meet Antyllus at the altar, officially become queen of Nubia, exchange vows with her aged husband, dance with him at their feast, then conspire with him after consummating their marriage. The only thing she looked forward to was seeing the emperor's face when Pope Cyril put the uraeus crown on her head.

A flash of light above the gondola made Sahdi blink. The front of the balloon exploded in fire, and the fabric shell disintegrated as the flames spread to the rear with demonic speed, consuming everything as billowing smoke filled the air. Sahdi and Pope Cyril leaped to their feet and stared out the window.

Deep within her soul, Sahdi knew this was no accident. General Nahktebbi had found redemption.

The door to the pope's chamber burst open and Duke Zander rushed in with a few others as the nose of the airship tipped straight up. The rear of the craft crashed toward the harbor in a ball of flame. In only a brief moment, the airship plunged into the water and the gondola sank into the harbor, dragging the wreckage down. Smoke and pieces of burning airship floated on the surface.

Pope Cyril clutched his cross and fell to his knees gasping in front of the window.

"*Your Holiness*." Duke Zander supported the shaking pontiff as the remains of the airship sank into the bay.

"Your Majesty, thank you," the Pope said.

Sahdi's brows furrowed together. *Your Majesty?* There were no kings in the room and the pope wasn't speaking to her. She turned away from the window and noticed Zander kneeling by the Pope. The old man must have made a mistake. The Duke of Attica carefully helped Pope Cyril stand and led him to a chair.

"Sahdi," the Pope held out his hand to her, "you were not supposed to meet this way, but let me introduce your betrothed, King Antyllus Alexandros Constantius V."

"The fifth?" Sahdi asked, her mind reeling. "Zander?"

The pope nodded. "Unbeknownst to the emperor, King Antyllus IV has transferred the marriage contract to his son, the newly anointed Duke of Attica, who has been traveling in disguise these past weeks. King Antyllus will abdicate the throne upon his son's marriage to you."

"Your Highness." Zander bowed lower than he ever had, his amber eyes never leaving hers as he removed his gloves and tenderly kissed her hand. His broad smile stunned Sahdi. She was speechless as the scope of the deception momentarily paralyzed her vocal cords. "Your Majesty . . . I . . . I don't know what to say."

"Please, this is a difficult moment," Zander said. "We are all in shock, but I should hope that to my proposal of marriage, you will say 'yes.'"

They turned back toward the window as surface ships began steaming toward the wreckage while the last of the hydrogen from the airship, and Sahdi's fear of getting married, completely burned out.

Official word from the First Minister of Egypt arrived a few hours later. He had personally questioned the survivors of the airship disaster. Crewmen confirmed that Emperor Demetrius, Empress Galatia, and all seven of their children were aboard the doomed vessel. They were in the forward observation deck. A day later, all of their bodies were recovered from the submerged gondola. Pope Cyril called for three days of mourning before the mass funeral. It gave time for a temporary tomb to be prepared in the royal cemetery of Alexandria.

Three days after the entombment, the House of Nobles recognized the official line of succession to the throne of Egypt. Pope Cyril crowned Sahdi Empress and Zander Emperor of the Holy Coptic Empire moments after they were married.

On their wedding night, Sahdi poured the poison she was prepared to take into the drain of her bath, and made her blissfully satisfied husband an offer. "We'll hold court in Athens during the summer—if you insist; then fall in Alexandria. Winter and spring, we'll live in Nubia."

"My empress will hold court wherever she desires, and I will be there at her side until the day I die."

Two days after the wedding, Sahdi and Zander finally left their bedchamber. A servant placed an opened package on their breakfast table and explained it had come from the recently deceased General Nahktebbi himself, the newly appointed military advisor to Emperor Demetrius, and also a confirmed casualty of the airship accident. Inside the package, Sahdi found the pistol she had given to Nahktebbi outside the throne room in Luxor. A note was rolled up in the gun barrel.

> *My Queen,*
> *Please forgive the surprising nature of my gift, and my absence at your wedding.*
> *I am sure you will understand. Please know that it matters not how I will be remembered.*
> *However, I have no doubt that when the scholars write their histories, you will be remembered as Sahdi the Great.*
>
> *Your Humble Servant,*
> *General Nahktebbi of Nubia*

Sahdi passed her husband the letter, relieved to have confirmation that Nahktebbi had been the cause of the emperor's airship accident.

"He gave us quite the gift." Zander made certain the servants were not looking, then leaned forward and kissed Sahdi on the cheek. "He was quite right about what they will call you."

"I've been thinking about Pope Cyril's proposal." Sahdi smiled.

"About letting the Jewish refugees live in Palestine and have their own territory?"

"Yes," she said, knowing that the pope's demand could not be refused.

"But what about the Germans who live there now?" Zander asked.

"After a time, they'll learn to live with one another. I'll personally make certain of it."

Zander smiled, his amber eyes sparkling. "My beautiful Nubian wife, I have no doubt that you will."

Opals from Sydney

Mary Louise Eklund

Mary Louise Eklund grew up near Asheville, North Carolina, and frequently went to Biltmore House and Gardens on school field trips. Since then she has made pilgrimages back to see more rooms as they have opened. A special thanks is extended to them for their inspiration of daydreams growing up and for Mr. Johnny's home in *Opals For Sydney*. Mary Louise now lives in Wisconsin where she's working on her own multitomaton to shovel snow once her teenage son leaves for college. However, if that should fail she's attempting to convince her husband on the virtues of a snow blower.

"I think that covers everything Lady Espear. Is there anything else you'd like to address?" Paul Toiter, a tall, angular man who was overtly proud to be a personal secretary, peered over his half-glasses. Across the large desk sat his employer, the head of Espear Imports and Exports.

Lady Sydney Espear swirled her tea in the bone china cup. Her pale robin's egg blue gown matched her eyes, and her ebony hair shown as the silk in her gown as she rolled back her chair. She was a Baltic Beauty and a shrewd business woman.

"Actually, there is. I want to visit this man." She sat down her cup and pulled an envelope from the soft ostrich leather attaché. "I'm interested in pursuing his business proposal."

Toiter frowned, looking at the heraldry on the envelope. It featured automatons holding a crest of airships crowned by an aviator's cap and goggles. "I'm not familiar with the family, but then again we're into seafaring not airshipping." His face darkened as he read the note.

> *"Dear Lord Espear,*
> *I have heard of your interest in the development of a multitomaton. I have manufactured a functioning multitomaton that I call Tom, who now performs as my butler.*
> *The part that allows him to be multi-functional is a sliver of Mation's Opal that you gave to Sir Gregory Cheekbalm. I acquired the item, as Cheeky is horrid at cards.*
> *The sliver's abilities intrigued me, and after some years, I've mastered its unique properties. I desire to make multitomatons to sell, and with your help I could succeed.*
> *I am writing to inquire about purchasing the entire Mation's Opal. If that is out of the question, perhaps we would enter into a business partnership where your opal is used to make additional slivers. As partner you would share in the profits of such an endeavor.*
> *Please let me know your level of interest in my proposal. All is, of course, open to negotiation. I merely wish to open communication.*
>
> *Sincerely,*
> *Jonathon Q. Plebeman"*

Toiter flung down the letter onto the desk with disgust. "YOU can't be serious!" He rolled his eyes. "The man doesn't have the decency to find out that Lord Espear passed three years ago! He writes to a titled position with the familiarity he would use to address a drinking buddy! Then to assert that a parlor trick of temporarily animating things is useful to science . . ." He squared his shoulders and peered down his ample hooked nose at the offending letter. "That proves he's a few sails short of sane wouldn't you say?"

Lady Espear stood. "No, I wouldn't." She gestured at him with a full cup of tea. "Go ahead, take it. I'd dare say after the indignation you just suffered you need it."

Sydney's deceased husband's dream of multitomatons doing unpleasant tasks to free humanity for enlightened pursuits was one she shared. If the odd properties of the Mation's Opal could do that and produce a profit, all the better.

She strolled to the case where the opal sat as a glowing bauble of decoration in the shelf-lined office. Colors radiated from the white orb and were softly reflected in the polished teak paneling.

"You know of David's dream for multitomatons." She opened the case and picked up the large stone with both hands. "I think it's only proper we investigate the possibility this man has succeeded." She smiled at the prickly tingling sensation that radiated from the opal. Its internal fire began to burn more brightly. "If this beautiful trinket can do that, then why not? It'd be a profitable expansion for the company. Airshipping is picking up, and seafaring ships are being used less. It would be good to have another market."

Toiter stood rigid as if at attention with his tea cup daintily held in front of him. He took care in choosing his words. "I don't think a multitomaton is possible, much less with a stone used for parlor tricks. Lord Espear tried to use that opal on something larger than a cigar box but that failed. How could it work in an automaton?"

Sydney shrugged and put the opal against the small statue of Neptune on the guest table. "I know, but if this man has found a way to harness this, it would be worth seeing."

The orb dimmed, and the small Neptune stretched from his pose and began to walk around the table, taking stock of the items stored there.

"I want to see what he's done, what this Tom of his can do. I'll take along Mation's Opal to see if the effect is repeatable. If he's on to something then we may both benefit from a deal."

Toiter sighed as Neptune scratched his nether regions inelegantly and poked open a book with his trident. "Let's hope he's done something that could improve the manners of things such as Neptune here."

Sydney laughed as she picked up the opal and returned it to the case. "I hope he doesn't deanimate in that position. It'll be most upsetting to Mrs. Barkley, who already doesn't like dusting the nude male form no matter how classically tasteful it is."

They both watched the little figure scratch his back with his triton as he attempted to make sense of the color plate in the book he opened. He froze with a quizzical look on his face.

"I leave the arrangements of our trip in your most capable hands." Sydney put on her hat, and Toiter rushed to assist her with her cloak.

Toiter made the arrangements with Mr. Plebeman's people. A personal airship would be provided from the Plebeman Estate near Asheville, North Carolina. Once the trip was scheduled, preparations on the Espear end began.

On the morning of departure, Sydney climbed the metal stairs at the airship docking station. She marveled at the copper and teak gondola of the private ship. The interior was bedecked in plush Asian carpets and highly polished cherry furniture. The colors were green and black and reflected the Plebeman family heraldry prominently displayed over the red glowing heater disguised as an ornately carved fireplace.

"My, what a lovely custom zeppelin." Sydney commented as the airship's Captain shook her hand.

"Why yes ma'am. The Plebeman family has manufactured fine airships for two generations now. However, with Mr. Johnny at the head this doesn't get used the way it did." He looked a bit wistful as he tugged the hem of his green uniform coat. "I'm Captain Aphram Opram. I'll be in charge of your flight today."

"Oh, thank you." Sydney turned to allow Opram to assist with her cloak. "As a matter of curiosity why doesn't the ship get as much use?"

"Well," Opram looked taken aback. "Mr. Johnny. . . doesn't fly as much as his brother and father did." He turned to hang up her coat and latch the closet. "Our flight time will be just under two hours depending on the winds around Mount Pisgah."

Sydney settled herself in her seat and shifted so that her bustle was comfortable on the horsehair chair. The furnishings were designed for male travelers, not women's attire. "I've never been to the Appalachian Mountains. I understand they are lovely."

"Yes, ma'am they are. Nothing like the Alps, mind, you but more forested and gentler." He nodded to Toiter, who was settling in the chair opposite Sydney. Then he smiled at Beatrice, Sydney's Lady's maid, who made herself comfortable on a settee. "If you need anything to make your trip more comfortable, just let Ashley know. She'll be tending to your needs." Captain Opram took his leave and departed toward the front of the cabin.

Sydney looked out the thick purplish glass and watched the distorted view of tarnished automatons loading her luggage into the cargo hold of the gondola.

"Wouldn't it be wonderful if they could do more than one task?"

"Yes, it would. Woulda saved my poor daddy's back in them mines." Beatrice held her ribbon embroidery in her lap as she looked out the window on the other side.

"No, it wouldn't." Toiter glanced out and then back

to the ledgers he was putting on the table. "Then they'd want a wage, I'd suppose, for oil and such. Show up all rusty and do poor work but expect the same pay."

Sydney watched the familiar steeples of Charleston fade away to the rolling land of the Piedmont then finally to the rounded lumbering mountains of the Appalachians. Beatrice sat spellbound, her embroidery unattended in her limp hands. Even Toiter quit grumbling over his ledgers and watched as the gently rolling ridges and valleys of the chain became more dramatic.

A large castle-like home with manicured gardens and vineyards surrounding it came into view. The ship began to descend near the southwest side of the house. Soon automatons dressed as gondoliers were running out to take the guide wires that whirled down from their remotely controlled spools. The landing was gentle with a soft bump as the base of the gondola nudged the immaculately trimmed turf.

Soon Opram entered and bid them welcome to Plebeman Estates. He graciously took Sydney's hand and escorted her to meet Mr. Johnny Plebeman.

Mr. Plebeman was a man of medium build. The most striking thing about him after his black goatee and mustache was a generally rumpled look without being able to point to any article of clothing actually being rumpled. His hair had been combed and pomaded, but a strand fell forward giving him a disheveled look. His glasses had tortoise shell frames of the finest quality, but were perched a bit too far down his nose, as if they'd slid there of their own accord and he was too engrossed in what he was doing to notice. As Sydney approached, he smiled broadly. A flash of two gold teeth on the back left gave the feeling of a lothario, but the sparkle in his eye and the handsomeness of his face softened it with boyish charm.

Sydney was taken with the man. He was interesting and definitely more entertaining than any company she'd kept since David's death.

"Mr. Johnny, I'd like to introduce Lady Sydney Espear." Captain Opram graciously indicated Sydney on his arm. "Madam, this is Mr. Johnny Plebeman head of Plebeman Estates."

"I'm pleased . . ." Sydney was cut off by Johnny.

"Yes, yes thanks. Opie, once all the guests get off that contraption take it away will you?" He extended his hand to Sydney, taking his searching eyes off the airship and putting them on her. "Welcome Lady Espear. It's good to . . ." He raised an eyebrow, as if first noticing her, and then rakishly glanced up and down before smiling again and returning his attention to the airship over her shoulder. ". . . welcome you to my estate."

"Thank you. That is a lovely zeppelin you have there." Sydney took his arm and stood beside him as he strained to look over his airship.

"Airship, rigid airship or dirigible if you please. Zeppelin is a rival German company," he replied in an off-hand manner.

"Oh, I'm sorry."

"Don't be. My father or brother might have been offended, but I'm not." He glanced at her with an indulgent smile. "I hate flying. Hate those contraptions."

Sydney looked perplexed. "Hmmm. Mr. Plebeman . . ."

"Johnny. Call me Johnny, everyone does." He squeezed and patted her hand on his arm as he again leaned from side to side watching his airship.

"Yes. Well then, Johnny, what are you anxiously looking for?"

He stopped and turned to face her ice blue eyes. "Why, the arrival of your husband, Lady Espear."

"My husband?" She looked at Toiter coming off the airship with a chatty Beatrice following him. "Well, that would be shocking considering he passed three years ago. I can see why you are anxious."

Johnny turned to look at her. "I . . . I thought he was coming to see the multitomaton."

"No, that would be me. I now handle all the affairs

of Espear Imports and Exports. You have been corresponding with Mr. Toiter, my personal secretary." Sydney said Toiter's name loudly as he approached and indicated him with a wave of her hand. "I take it he didn't adequately inform you of the situation."

"No, no he did not." Johnny dropped her arm and looked around nervously. Then, gathering himself, he buttoned his long coat. "However, I don't see a problem. A quick retooling of the weekend plans and all should be fine." He turned and proceeded toward the marble staircase that led to the house.

Sydney glared at Toiter, who took her arm.

"If he wasn't going to do his research why I should I do it for him?" Toiter glanced down uneasily then back to their host, who was talking to a servant as he led the way. "Be wary of him. Before his father and brother were killed in an airship accident he was quite the philanderer."

"Now you tell me." She cocked her head. "Likes women but won't do business with one eh? I'd swear you love to stir up trouble and then just watch what happens, don't you?" She glided up the wide steps.

He suppressed a grin. "No ma'am, just doing what you requested—setting up a meeting with the lunatic."

They followed Johnny through two large wooden doors and across a portico of Portuguese tile, entering a large hall. The winter garden to the right included a domed glass ceiling held in frames of mahogany. It featured an indoor jungle of palms and a quietly bubbling fountain. Surrounding the fountain, positioned to catch the sun streaming in the glass dome, were chairs and settees of bamboo. A brandy service had been set up to welcome the guests.

Johnny turned and smiled. Another piece of pomaded hair had fallen downward, framing his face in a parentheses. "Ma'am, it's not that I mind doing business with a lady." He gestured to the brandy service. "It's just I'd planned the weekend to engage a potential *male* busi ness partner." He pushed one of the errant strands behind his ear. "Things may be on the masculine side, but adjustments can be easily made. Would you like a brandy or something else to refresh you after your travels?"

Sydney looked over to the offerings as she removed her gloves. A footman in black and green livery took them and her cloak.

"The Gaston de Casteljac cognac will be excellent." She took a seat on a settee and admired the tropical scene embroidered on the cushions.

Johnny poured the drink and took it to her personally. Turning to Toiter, he nodded. "So what will it be my man?"

Toiter stumbled with his answer. "I'll have... uh ..." He looked to Sydney for guidance. She sipped her cognac and raised an eyebrow as if to tell him to do his own research.

"I'll tell you what. Leave it to me." Johnny turned, letting the uncomfortable man off the hook. "Try this one. It's not as sweet as Lady Espear's choice but not as coarse as those our brothers from Kentucky prefer." He poured a red-gold liquid into a snifter and brought it to Toiter. "Taste it and give me your verdict."

Toiter sampled a rich flavor without the stickiness of excessive sugar. A pleasant warmth followed the swallow down his throat. "It's wonderful, thank you."

"Excellent! It's one of my favorites too." He poured himself a glass.

At Sydney's request Johnny led his guests on a tour of the hall's art.

After inspecting a hippogriff on a table from a medieval monk cloister Sydney asked, "So when do we get to meet this wonderful Tom of yours?"

"Before dinner I'll introduce him. You can then observe as he assists in the service." He handed off their empty glasses to a maid without looking at her.

"I'll bring Mation's Opal at that time." Sydney looked up the grand spiral staircase.

"I'm anxious to see and discuss its properties. We'll take the appetizers in the tapestry room." He turned to her with the roguish smile flashing the gold teeth again. "That's if you don't mind finger foods for appetizers, as I said I'd planned a gentleman's weekend."

"I don't mind at all" Sydney nodded. "Now if *you* don't mind I'll go freshen up. Will this attentive footman show me to my room?" She gestured to the footman who was pleased to be acknowledged directly.

"Yes, he will." Johnny indicated the stairs with a wave of his hand. "I believe your lady's maid should have things in order, but if anything isn't to your liking or you have need of something, just let us know. Call buttons are labeled on the brass plates in your room."

"I'm sure everything will be perfect." Sydney glided up the stairs, quietly engaging the nervous footman in polite conversation.

Sydney was given the south tower room, a large round room decorated in a subdued neoclassical style. The soft pastel colors and dainty floral prints were complimented by ivory trim.

A wide-eyed Beatrice greeted her. "He sure ain't courtin' you fer your money, is he? Just look at this place. I bet this is how royals live!"

"No, money isn't something I believe Johnny needs. He needs my opal." Sydney flopped down on a pale blue silk tufted sofa. "I've yet to see much regular automation, here much less innovation. I can't help but wonder if my expectations were too high."

Beatrice began taking down Sydney's hair and brushing out the curls. "I can tell you that downstairs there's much automation. Stuff I've never see afore. There's a switchboard that don't just do calls but sends moving pictures with them. That's if the other party has one of those devices, too."

She put down the brush and picked up a slim box the length of a cigar box but the thickness of a cigarette case. She opened it to show a round black portal that illuminated, presenting a stylish woman in a headset. "Yes, Lady Espear, may I assist in placing your call?"

Sydney took the wireless box from Beatrice. "No thank you. I was just inspecting this astonishing device. I don't wish to place a call at this time."

"Very well, ma'am. If you do just push the green button to buzz me. I'll be glad to assist." The woman vanished from the portal.

Sydney looked over the numbered ivory buttons, the aforementioned green button made of jade, and a red one of coral just below the portal. "This is amazing. So light and wireless too! Where is the lens that sees me?"

Beatrice shrugged as she watched over Sydney's shoulder. "Dunno ma'am."

Sydney spotted the small lens hidden in the ornate carving of the dark wood. "There it is! You say Johnny created this?"

"Yes, ma'am. That's what Rocco told me. He's the technical assistant here for all the inventions Mr. Johnny has installed. The goal of the estate is to have all the modern conveniences without them intruding on the mountain retreat feel." She recited the last bit as if she'd put it to memory. "Oh, Mr. Johnny invented special goggles to let people see at night. That way the gardeners can tend the grounds without guests seeing such things as fertilizer carts. Rocco said they make everything look green because you look through an emerald!"

The two women continued to chat about the estate and the unique items it contained while they prepared Sydney for evening dinner. They chose the pearl gray dinner dress with a short train and a square neckline that wasn't as plunging as some of her other evening gowns. Sydney thought it best to err on the side of conservatism given her host's reputation.

"Now, go be comfortable with the wonderfully dark Italian Rocco." She smiled leaning forward a bit coquettishly.

"Oh, missus! It ain't like that." Beatrice waved off her

employer. Then pausing, she blushed and smoothed her skirt. "But I'd not be against it if it was done properly."

There was a soft knock on her door. "There's Toiter to take me down to dinner. This should be interesting." Sliding her wrap onto her elbows, she picked up Mation's Opal as Beatrice opened the door. "I wish you luck with your new friendship." She patted Beatrice's arm as she passed to greet Toiter.

The tapestry room was a long room containing two large soapstone fireplaces with flues painted in the Flemish style to accentuate the room's three large silk tapestries. The modern dark green English club furniture gave the room a welcoming feel. In the far corner a quartet softly played chamber music. Luxurious Persian rugs muffled their steps as they entered. Mr. Johnny, in stylish evening attire, stood with hands behind his back as he gazed into the fire.

"What a breathtakingly beautiful home you have." Sydney extended her hand in greeting as she approached.

Johnny stirred from his contemplation. "I have to admit I had nothing to do with it. My mother was a woman of impeccable taste. I only strive to maintain it for my own comfort."

"You have succeeded gallantly." Sydney sat near the fire. The large elegant home was like her host—dressed to party but sadly melancholy.

Toiter placed the case with the opal on the table and opened it. The stone glowed brightly in the firelight. "This is Mation's Opal."

"Ahh, yes, it's lovely." Johnny flipped his coat's tails as he knelt to look at the opal. "I hadn't realized it was so large. I think I've come up with a way to make slivers without damaging the original."

Sydney chuckled. "David would just place smaller opals in the case with it. After a time they would take on the same properties."

Johnny turned. "Exactly as I'd supposed. Does the

whole opal animate objects larger than those it can charge?"

"Oh yes. Go ahead and use it on that statuette there." She motioned to the small black statue of a rhinoceros.

Johnny took the opal out of the case. His eyes widened at the sensations. "Yes, it feels strong."

Toiter put the case under the table out of the way. "Sometimes things can run about."

Johnny touched the opal to the rhinoceros. The stone dimmed as the statuette came to life. The animal charged out onto the polished table. Toiter grabbed the opal as the little beast threw its armored head to and fro. The creature huffed about for the five minutes until it became listless, freezing in a pose with its head hanging down in a manner of defeat.

Johnny rocked back on his heels as he intently watched the display. Sydney, an excellent judge of character, watched Johnny. His reaction had been one of boyish pleasure and amazement. There was no guile or conniving about his manner.

"That was amazing!" Johnny picked up the rhinoceros. "The effect lasted a full five minutes on this heavy specimen. It's all I thought it would be and more." He turned excitedly. "I'm sure you're anxious to meet Tom and see how this can be used."

Pushing the butler call on the brass panel, he continued, "I can see why selling it would be out of the question for you. However, if we go into business I'd like to have time to study the properties of the original opal."

"If we become partners that only seems reasonable." Sydney stopped when she heard the whirling and slight hydraulic hissing of an automaton approaching.

Tom entered the room carrying a tray of champagne glasses. He was brightly polished brass and wearing a dark black jacket with green lapels. The details of his styling reflected elements of a butler's uniform. Above his speaker was a full brass mustache. Above his eyes were full brass eyebrows. His chest was in the fashion of a brass waistcoat complete with buttons.

"Greetings Lady Espear and Mr. Toiter. Would you like some champagne?" Tom approached Sydney, leaning down with the tray.

"Greetings, Tom. It's nice to meet you." Sydney took a glass. "Thank you."

Toiter accepted a glass as he skeptically watched the butler. "What's different from any other automaton that serves drinks?"

"I have many other functions," Tom replied. The butler's voice had a mellow hollowness to it, as if he was speaking into a bucket.

Johnny grinned broadly, showing his gold teeth. "Tom's right. He'll answer questions. He organized our menu tonight and will see to its proper serving, adjusting the flow of the courses to meet our needs."

"Sir, speaking of courses." Tom tucked the tray under his arm after Johnny took the last glass. "May I bring out the appetizer?"

"Yes, by all means do." Johnny sipped his drink.

Tom turned to address both Sydney and Toiter. "Tonight's appetizer is Oysters Katharine on the half shell."

"Can you describe the dish for us?" Toiter continued to inspect the machine skeptically.

"Yes, sir." Tom turned to face his guest. "Chef Weir has created a baked dish of oysters on the half shell. The oyster is topped with a sautéed mixture of onion, garlic, pimento, mushroom, and parsley. This is crusted with a topping of grated parmesan cheese mixed with specially seasoned breadcrumbs. It is then baked on the shell until golden brown. The dish is one of delicately balanced flavors of the savory crust complimenting the firm ocean flavor of the roasted oyster. If you like, I can have the chef alter the recipe to suit your gastric needs."

"No, that won't be necessary." Toiter no longer looked skeptical. "It sounds wonderful."

Just prior to sitting down for dinner, Johnny placed several opal slivers in the case with the Mation's Opal. At Toiter's request, Tom politely opened his chest to show the sliver that animated him in its electrically charged setting. The opal was fiery with flashes of colors. Johnny offered to remove the opal, demonstrating how Tom regressed to a regular automaton. Sydney, horrified at the idea, waved it off.

The trio enjoyed a Chablis as they adjourned to the dining room. There the tooled Spanish leather wall covering glowed from the incandescent lights.

"The nights here can get quite chilly." Johnny held Sydney's chair as she took her seat in front of a roaring fire in the Wedgewood fireplace. "We have central heat, but nothing knocks the chill of the mountain away like a fire."

The meal progressed through six more courses, each announced and described by Tom. The food was impeccable. Sydney complimented each dish. Toiter lost all form of etiquette and cleaned his plate at each course.

"I have already built two other multitomatons that I call Dick and Harry. I intend to have Dick train as chef and Harry as gardener."

"Tom, Dick, and Harry. How original. Like naming cats Puss and Boots." Toiter hefted his claret that had been served with the beef au bordelaise.

"Not really. I did imagine that selling the trio would go something like—no home is complete without Tom, Dick, and Harry." He chuckled to himself. "But they are prototypes. We might decide my humor isn't as good as the concepts of advertising professionals."

"It is amusing, but I'm not sure it's the image we'd want to project. I'm glad you are open to discussion on the matter should it come to production." Toiter took another bite of the beef. "This is marvelous. Why you'd want to replace this chef with a machine is beyond me."

"I don't want to do that." Johnny placed his folded napkin on the table and leaned forward solemnly. "I envision chefs, such as Chef Weir, train the automations in making such fine dinners possible at homes that can afford a multitomaton but not a full staff."

Sydney suggested training a multitomaton to fill multiple staffing positions, thus expanding the market. Her business prowess and insight were invaluable as they made plans. By the time the demitasse was served, all assumed a deal would be done and a project outline had been sketched out.

The trio retired to the tapestry room. The opal sat in its case, dimming and brightening. The slivers placed against it had begun to slowly increase their own illumination.

"Do you know how long it'll take to charge these?" Sydney was intrigued by the process, having never seen it herself.

"I'm guessing only a few more hours." Johnny again knelt to better view the stone. "Did your husband ever have any theories as to how the opal gained this?"

"No, nothing more than it was used in ancient rites." Sydney knelt. "I suppose it's something esoteric or mystic."

"That's my interest, Lady Espear. Understanding and utilizing the esoteric, mystic, and all things paranormal. I think all can eventually be explained scientifically." He turned to face her as he spoke in earnest. "My father thought my collecting such items was a folly." He looked down at his manicured hands. "I have many faults and made many mistakes, but this isn't one. I want to understand how our universe works."

Sydney felt the sincerity of his words. "I believe you, Johnny. It sounds like a most worthwhile endeavor. One I'd be intrigued to investigate myself. What an adventure to be on the cutting edge of new inventions and discoveries!"

He smiled, but his delight faded quickly. "It can be all that, but it's dangerous too. I've dealt with some very contemptible characters to acquire items. I fear it led to the death of my brother and father, who took the flight that day instead of me." He hung his head. "I was quite a profligate in my youth. I was to enter the family business and gain respectability. The day of the flight I was ill from too much of that lifestyle. In such a condition I couldn't travel. My brother and father took on my trip at the last minute." He sat back on his heels he stared into the fire, his face a mask over pure pain. "Their airship crashed due to an explosion that was never explained. I am sure it had to do with the Claw of Destiny, a relic I'd recently gained that the Kismet Cult wanted returned. There was no proof, and no one took me seriously because I'd never acted seriously. Eventually my gambling debts came to light and some assumed that was motivation to kill my family. They didn't take into account that I had money, I made and paid such debts regularly. They just assumed I wanted money more than I wanted family, and had them killed to gain an inheritance." He turned to rub his face and collect himself.

Sydney glanced at Toiter, who was glumly standing by the cheerful fire. His eyes met hers. Both better understood their eccentric host.

Sydney placed her hand on Johnny's arm. "For what it's worth, I believe you. I know the danger of exporting exceptional items. Still, I'd like to assist in the investigation of your family's demise and your exploration of the mystic."

Johnny sighed. "That is kind of you, Lady Espear, but I couldn't allow you to put yourself in danger. I will bring those who killed my family to justice and vindicate my name. However, you could assist my study in two ways-first by informing me when your company locates such fantastical items, and second by performing lab work."

"I'd be pleased to do both." Sydney stood, smoothing the silk of her dress.

"It's getting late. We'll discuss those projects over breakfast in the morning." Johnny took her hand in his. "Thank you for your kind offer. It's been some time since I've had a real friend." The evening complete, they all retired to their rooms.

Later that night Sydney couldn't sleep. She tossed in the oversized. She looked for something to read, but only found an estate guide for guests. It was obvious that at one time the home had been a place alive with visitors. It was now occupied by a melancholy man trying to regain his family honor and prove his innocence.

The guide indicated a discrete stair to the library for guests to retrieve reading material. Deciding to leave her hair down, Sydney pulled on her riding trousers and uncollared shirt. The galleasses caused the shirt to blouse about her waist, but she didn't care, thinking it was sufficient for a quick run to the library.

The staircase came out in the library from behind the flue of the fireplace on a balcony. She felt on the wall for a light switch. Just as she pressed it, she noticed Johnny standing on the main floor. He was staring out the French doors, wearing green goggles, and holding a large gun.

He wheeled around to see her and shouted "GET DOWN!"

Sydney froze for a moment before throwing herself on the floor. The room filled with brilliant white light, and the balcony pitched from the percussion of an explosion. She squeezed her eyes shut and clung to the carpet. Once the light faded she raised up on her elbows.

"Are you all right?" Johnny called from the floor as he staggered over stone rubble that had once been the wall. He shoved the goggles up onto his head. "I can't see yet. Are you all right?"

His voice was faint in her ringing ears. "Yes, yes I'm fine, but you're bleeding from your head!" Scrambling to her feet, the rush made her ill. She assumed Johnny was both temporarily blind and deaf because he kept calling for her despite her answering.

"SYDNEY, ARE YOU ALL RIGHT?" he desperately shouted as he struggled over another stone.

Before she could descend the stairs a group of men wearing clockwork armor and carrying various armaments entered through the hole in the wall. They quickly grabbed the dazed Johnny.

Sydney crouched low, peering through the brass railing of the balcony. Her heart pounded in her throat.

Johnny struggled against his captors, flailing blindly. One placed a device at his neck that emitted a blue arc of electricity. Johnny shrieked, and then went limp. The men dragged him through the blast opening.

Silently, Sydney struggled for control as her reaction dithered between hiding in fear and retrieving Johnny's gun to run out and rescue him. Regaining her focus, she came up with a plan to rescue Johnny without placing more people in danger.

Once she was sure the kidnappers weren't returning, she dashed down the stairs and into the tapestry room. She hit the butler call, and then dropped to her knees at the table where Mation's Opal sat with its charging slivers.

Tom arrived. "May I be of assistance, ma'am?"

"Take me to Dick and Harry." She stood, holding the newly charged slivers. "Your master has been attacked and I need all of you to rescue him."

Tom's head cocked to the right as his eyes opened wide. "Then that noise was not one of his experiments." Tom's eyebrows clicked as they furrowed. "Yes, ma'am, follow me. It appears time is of the essence." He turned on his heels and hastened at a pace. Sydney had to run to keep up with him.

They took the grand staircase down into a tiled hallway. Sound reverberated from the tile, the click of Sydney's heels rang out over the hiss of Tom's hydraulics. Once arriving at a large door with ornate brass hinges and locks, Tom stopped. One of his fingers opened and a key appeared that he used to unlock the door. "My brothers are there."

Sydney rushed in, seeing two automatons similar

to Tom. Large black cords came from the ceiling and plugged into their heads.

"They are fully charged and programmed." Tom opened their chests to reveal the holder for the opals. "They were only waiting for the slivers to awaken them."

Sydney placed an opal in the first one and a shudder ran through the machine.

"I'll activate Dick while you prepare Harry." Tom pulled the large black plug from Dick's head, and the wire retreated like a cobra into the ceiling. He snapped the portal closed and Dick whirred to life. Sydney quickly copied the motions after placing a sliver in Harry.

Once both multitomatons were activated, they settled their gazes on Sydney. "We are here to serve." Their voices were similar to Tom's though slightly lower.

"Mr. Johnny is in danger." Sydney rushed with an explanation of the events. "You must rescue him and capture his kidnappers. Tom will direct you."

"We need to secure weaponry and night vision," Tom said. "Proceed to the armory and wait for me there."

"We will proceed to the armory." Dick replied.

"We will wait for you there." Harry's voice was a pitch different. "Then we shall rescue our master." They departed.

Sydney turned to Tom. "Mr. Johnny's injured. His head is bleeding. I will instruct the housekeeper to prepare to treat his wounds and I must summon the authorities and a doctor."

Tom took two of the wireless picture phones from the work bench and handed one to Sydney. "We can communicate with these. You can also call authorities outside the estate." Tom bowed. "Thank you for your prompt assistance."

"Stay safe, Tom, and bring back Johnny." Sydney whispered the words as she clutched the phone.

"We will endeavor to do just that, Lady Espear." Then he left.

Sydney raced upstairs to the second floor living hall

where she rang for the housekeeper. Closing her eyes for a moment, she gathered her thoughts. She tried hard not to see the blinded and bloody Johnny stumbling over rubble, calling out to her and disregarding his own safety. She was on the phone with the police, who apparently also had one of Mr. Johnny's picture phones, when the housekeeper, Mrs. Potts, arrived.

Mrs. Potts went into action. She sent a maid to fetch medical supplies and set up a ward. She placed a call summoning Dr. Chickering. Another maid roused the men of the estate to protect the home and await the return of Mr. Johnny and the multitomatons.

Beatrice arrived in her dressing gown, face stern and ready to assist. "Toiter's gone with the men, and they gave him a gun. I worry that—"

The rest of her words were drowned out by a loud crash as the front doors were thrown open. Tom entered, carrying an unconscious Johnny. Dick and Harry followed, each dragging two unconscious men in black suits covered with gears obviously intended to strengthen them beyond normal human capacity. Dick and Harry stayed on the main floor, dropping their charges onto the carpet. Tom ascended the stairs with Johnny.

Mrs. Potts directed him to the makeshift ward. Beatrice guessed that Johnny had a slight concussion, nothing serious, but he would require a few stitches once the doctor arrived. Smelling salts brought him round.

Sydney entered in time to hear Tom's report to his master.

"They are members of the Kismet Cult from which the Claw of Destiny was originally obtained before you purchased it. They were seeking to get it back and punish you. We took this from them." He unclipped from his waist the electrical device that had knocked Johnny unconscious. "We used it on them after they admitted their group had sabotaged the airship that killed your father and brother." Tom nodded with a hiss. "You are now proven correct, sir. Everyone will know of your innocence."

Johnny sighed. "Little comfort that. Are all my guests safe?"

"Our guests are unharmed. Everything is under control. Lady Espear has summoned the authorities. The garden staff has taken up arms to protect our home. Dick, Harry, and I saw no indication there were more than the four we apprehended, but we will assist the authorities in verifying that." Tom bowed. "If you will excuse me, sir, I will greet the authorities. I hear them approaching." His gears purred as he turned to take his leave.

Johnny shifted the ice bag on his head and put the intruder's device on the nightstand. "It was your fast thinking and heroic efforts that activated my rescuers and alerted the house and the authorities. I am ever in your debt."

"It's nothing one wouldn't do to help a friend." She stepped over to the bed and sat on the edge, taking his hand.

By the time morning dawned, the authorities had taken the multitomaton's, Sydney's, and Johnny's statements. The doctor stitched Johnny's head. Dick and Harry cleared the debris from the explosion.

"Shall I have a contract for business drawn up?" Toiter hoisted a blunderbuss over his shoulder while looking at Sydney and Johnny. "A full partnership venture?"

"Yes, definitely." Sydney smiled at Johnny's bruised face.

"Hopefully, it will lead to full partnerships in many other ventures." Johnny put his arm around Sydney's waist. "That is ... if you were serious about wanting adventure."

"Oh I was. I am." Sydney rested her head on his shoulder.

The Whisperer

Marc Tassin

Marc Tassin is the author of numerous science fiction and fantasy short stories. He has also written and edited material for the *Shadowrun* roleplaying game and for *Dragon Magazine*. Marc lives just outside of Ann Arbor, Michigan with his wife and two children, although each August he embarks upon a week-long pilgrimage to Indianapolis where he is a panelist at the annual Gen Con Writers' Symposium.

"I don't understand, Mr. Carmichael," Avery whispered. "Why can't I see Lily?"

The well-dressed fat man sitting across the table from Avery leaned back and tucked his thumbs into the pockets of his green silk vest. Before answering, Mr. Carmichael let out an exasperated puff of air that caused his substantial red moustache to flutter.

"We've gone over this already, boy," Mr. Carmichael said. "The girl has the fever. She's in no condition to travel. As soon as she's feeling better we'll have her brought straight down from the hospital to see you."

Avery smelled scotch on Mr. Carmichael's breath. It mixed with the musky aroma of Mr. Carmichael's cologne, and reminded Avery painfully of his father. Avery looked around the cell. *Workshop*, he corrected himself. They didn't like it when he called the room a cell. He glanced at the concrete walls, its solid metal door, and the hissing gas lamp mounted in a cage on the ceiling. For the thousandth time he wished for a workshop upstairs, one with a window.

"Perhaps," Avery whispered, hesitating a moment before continuing. "Perhaps I could go see her?"

Again, Mr. Carmichael puffed.

"Out of the question," he said. "One of those damned recruiters might see you. Healthy young man like you? They'd snatch you up and ship you off to the war before you could say 'tea time.'"

Mr. Carmichael stood, walked around the table, and gave Avery's shoulder a squeeze.

"And you know how people feel about your kind, son. They aren't like Company men. They don't appreciate your gifts like we do. You were committed for your own safety. Heavens knows how people would react if they found out just how much you 'whisperers' can do."

Carmichael turned and walked to the workshop's iron door. He rapped his chubby knuckles on it three times in rapid succession, and then looked back at Avery.

"As soon as Lily is feeling better we'll have her brought down."

With a clunk and the sound of gear teeth clattering against one another, the door slid slowly aside.

"Wait!" Avery whispered, pushing his chair back and getting to his feet.

"What is it, son?"

"How bad is she, sir? Is she really getting better?"

Mr. Carmichael stopped, thumbs tucked into his vest pockets again. He pursed his lips and his moustache stuck out like a hedgehog's spines.

"You young people are resilient. I'm certain she'll recover and be back here in no time."

At this, Mr. Carmichael pulled out his pocket watch and snapped the cover open.

"Fiddlesticks," he said. "I'm running late. Got to go, Avery, but don't you worry about Lily. We've got lots of work for you today. We just received a shipment of ethereals we need you to whisper. We don't want you distracted, now do we? Take care, son."

Mr. Carmichael stomped out, and the door clattered shut behind him. Avery thrust his hand into his pocket and pulled out the little clockwork device he'd hidden there. It whispered to him in its tiny mechanical voice; the voice only a whisperer could hear.

"Yes, no. Yes, no. Yes, no. Yes, no."

They weren't allowed to make things on their own, and they certainly weren't allowed to *whisper* them, but Avery didn't care. His heart ached without Lily. The people at the London Marvel Company's asylum weren't unkind, but Lily was special. After five years in the asylum, Avery had finally met someone who truly cared for him.

It started as a friendship, Lily chatting pleasantly with him whenever she brought his food, but it blossomed into something wonderful. Avery's chest tightened just thinking about her. How badly he wanted to see her. They'd even talked about what they might do if the Company ever allowed Avery to leave, about how they'd move to Somerset and start a farm there, far from the noise and stink of the city.

"Yes, no. Yes, no. Yes, no. Yes, no."

The whispers of the little device pulled him out of his reverie. He could no longer avoid it. Avery raised the device to his mouth and whispered to it.

"You listened to all, just as I asked. You heard him say she would be better soon. Now tell me little friend– truth?"

"No, no. No, no. No, no. No, no."

Avery slumped into the chair. Lily was not well, and she was not getting better. Lily was going to . . . .

Avery covered his face with his hands and wept. A long time later, when the tears subsided, or perhaps when he just had no tears left, a strange calm slipped over him. Nothing mattered any longer. Not the threats the Company made against him or his estranged family. Not his fears about the outside world and how much they despised his kind. Not concern over what might become of him.

Nothing mattered except for Lily.

Clenching his fists, feeling a heat rise within him, Avery made a plan.

Like one of the clockwork devices Avery worked on every day, the serving girl arrived at precisely 7:55 p.m. with his supper. She brought it on a tray and sat it on the table next to the many contraptions the Company had brought him to whisper to. Meanwhile, a uniformed guard, an electro-pistol tucked snugly into his belt, watched steely eyed from the door.

When the girl went to leave, Avery leaped from his seat, grabbed her about the shoulders, and dragged her to the floor. The tray and its contents clattered across the concrete. The poor girl screamed and fought against Avery. It took the guard a full three seconds to even register what was happening.

As Avery wrestled with the girl, he pulled her in close and whispered, "I won't harm you."

At that moment the guard's hands clamped down on Avery and yanked him off her. As the guard pulled him away, Avery saw a look of utter bewilderment on the girl's face.

"Get off her, ya crazy bastard," the guard shouted.

He spun Avery around and cocked back a fist. Rather than pulling away, Avery used the momentum to tumble into the guard. Avery wrapped his arms around the man, put his lips to the guard's ear, and whispered.

The guard released Avery and stared blankly into space. Avery stepped back, shaking with a mix of fear and exhilaration. He'd never tried this. He hadn't known if it would work. As the guard drew his weapon Avery recoiled, fearing that he may have misjudged the extent of his power.

"I will help you," the man said in a voice devoid of normal intonation. With his pistol in hand, the guard walked out of the room.

"You . . . you *whispered* that man," the girl gasped from the floor behind Avery. "You can't do that. It doesn't work that way."

Voices came from the hallway.

"What are you doing, Jenkins? Put that weapon away before I—"

The sharp zap of the electro-pistol discharging echoed in the hall, accompanied by a short scream. The girl covered her mouth and made a squeaking noise.

"Merciful heaven," she gasped.

Shaking, balanced precariously on the edge of panic, Avery hurried out of his cell.

"I'm coming, Lily," he whispered.

Two hours later, Avery stumbled through the streets of central London. He'd left Jenkins back at the asylum with whispers of "Forget" and "Sleep," and he'd been wandering ever since. Once or twice he thought Company men were following him, but each time it was just someone hurrying off on their own agenda.

He had to find St. Mary's Hospital. He tried to remember where it was, but he was just a boy when his parents had sent him away to the asylum. Even if he could remember, the city had changed in those years. Where rows of quaint shops had once stood, great brick and iron towers now rose into the sky. Autonomous carriages clattered down the streets, jockeying for space and careening narrowly past one another. High above, rumbling airships trundled along between the towers, navigating iron canyons.

Avery tried desperately to concentrate, but the noise assailed him. Not just the usual noise one finds in a city like London, but the other noise; the noise of a thousand-thousand whispers. They filled his mind like the piercing hiss of a steam engine's release valve on full, battered his senses, almost blinded him with their ceaseless cacophony.

"Go, go. Go, go. Go, go," whispered a passing autonomous.

"Shine, shine. Shine, shine. Shine, shine," hissed every lamp on the street.

"Sing, sing. Sing, sing. Sing, sing," whispered the speaker on the wall of the café.

And they weren't just whispering. They were whispering *to him*. It was as if they were children, trying to show him how well they were performing their tasks, trying to impress him with the skill and quality with which they accomplished their missions.

And there were so many of them. Far more than he'd whispered into being. How many other young men and women were locked in the Marvel Company's asylum? He cursed himself for not checking the other cells.

And it brought him back to Lily. How they'd kept her from him, how even now she was surely fading, and how desperately he wanted to see her. Avery wondered what a hundred ... two hundred ... a thousand, perhaps, of his kind might do if they were free. And what if he shared what he knew? What if he told them the secret; that whispers worked on more than just machines?

"Go Spin Sing Run Flap Turn Sing Turn Go Play Rattle Push Up Down Go Spin."

Avery covered his ears. It did no good. The whispers went straight into his mind. He slumped against the wall of an alley and slid to the paving-stones, his arms clasped tightly around his head. As he sat there, a smartly dressed young couple passed by. They gave him a glance, but hurried on when Avery let out a whimper.

Gritting his teeth, Avery clambered to his feet. Lily needed him. He had to find her. Stumbling out of the alley he whispered to the couple.

"Wait! Please!"

The woman stopped, despite the protestations of her escort, and turned to Avery. She looked beautiful in her long dress, the hoops making it sway like gentle waves on a lake.

"Are you all right, sir?" she asked, her voice kind but tinged with a hint of fear.

She smelled good. She looked like an angel. Avery thought that someday he would buy a dress like that for Lily. Lily always talked about the dresses in the fancy stores, dresses a serving girl's wages would never afford.

"Sir?" she said, coming closer. "Do you need help?"

Avery whispered, "St. Mary's. I can't find St. Mary's."

The woman held out a gloved hand. Her escort stepped up beside her, frowning.

"Good heavens, Francis," the man said, glowering at Avery. "What if he's sick? And did you hear his voice? What if he's one of those *whisperers?*"

"He wouldn't be out on the street if he were a whisperer. Maybe he was in the war, like my brother," she said. "Here, I won't hurt you."

"Open, open. Open, open. Open, open," whispered an automated door on a nearby shop.

Avery winced against the noise, but the woman did not pull her hand away. She continued to smile at him, her eyes kind, if a bit sad. Reaching out, he took her hand. He could feel the warmth through the soft cotton glove.

"This way," she said, still smiling and leading him down the street.

They reached the corner and she led him around to the other side.

"You see?" she said. "It's just up there, on the hill. You've almost made it."

Avery choked back a sob. Lily was so close. The woman's escort came up beside him. Despite the man's earlier comments, he too looked at Avery with a sad kindness.

"Can you walk it?" he said. "Should I call you a public autonomous?"

Avery shook his head, but never took his eyes off the hospital.

"No," he whispered. "No, thank you."

He pulled his hand away from the woman and started toward the hospital. He began slowly, but with each step he went faster until he found himself racing down the sidewalk at a run.

"Well now, there's a miraculous recovery," he faintly heard the man saying.

Avery arrived, out-of-breath, at the gates to the hospital. The monumental five-story brick building stood across a wide lawn, looking serious and academic, if a trifle rundown. Avery pulled at the bars of the gate and found it locked. From a small hut just inside the compound, a pebble eyed security guard wandered out.

"Can't you read?" he said, and pointed to a sign mounted beside the gate. "Hospital's closed for the night. Come back in the morning."

"Please," whispered Avery. "I have to find my friend."

"Speak up, will you?" the man said.

"I need to see my friend. Her name is Lily," Avery whispered.

The guard spat on the ground and then stalked over to the gate.

"I said, speak up. I can't hear a damned thing you're saying."

"Please," Avery pleaded. "I need to see her. She's very sick."

"Well she wouldn't be in hospital if she weren't, now would she?" the man said, sneering at Avery and stepping right up to the bars. "But that don't change a bloody thing. Closed is closed. So go on. Come back in the morning."

Avery glared at the stupid, selfish man. He felt his anger rise, fueled by the fear that he might already be too late.

"*Open the gate and let me in,*" Avery hissed.

The man blinked, his jaw went slack, and then he reached into his pocket and withdrew a huge ring of keys. He walked over, picked through the keys until he found a particularly large one, and unlocked the gate.

Avery pushed it open and rushed through. He stopped and turned to the man.

"*Go sit in your hut,*" he whispered.

The man wandered back to his guard booth as Avery ran up the hospital drive. When he reached the main building, he headed for the front door, but stopped short. Reconsidering, he went around to the back and located the staff entrance. A small metal box, with a pair of flickering red lamps on it, was mounted beside the door.

"Lock, lock, wait for the card. Lock, lock, wait for the card. Lock, lock, wait for the card," it whispered.

Avery bent down and whispered to the lock, "*Open.*"

There was a click, the lamps flashed green, and the door swung inward. Avery rushed inside and closed the door behind him. He found himself in a room lined with lockers. He rifled through them until he found a long white coat. Pulling it on, he slipped out of the room.

The halls of the hospital were empty, although they were far from silent, at least for Avery. The whispers of a multitude of Marvel-made devices filled Avery's mind. He shook his head to force them back and then continued on.

At each doorway he looked inside. Room after room after room was filled with rows of beds divided by white, hanging curtains. The patients that he could see were all sleeping, the sounds of their breathing mixed with the whispers of the machinery attached to them. There were a few nurses roving between the beds, but they worked silently, never disturbing their charges. Focused as they were, the nurses paid no attention to Avery.

Avery soon realized that he would never find Lily by searching every bed. Spotting a clipboard on the wall by one of the doors, he grabbed it. It had a list of names on it. He scanned the list and did not find her, so he raced to the next clipboard. Nothing.

Door after door. Clipboard after clipboard. No Lily. Despair crept into his mind. He wondered if Mr. Carmichael had lied about where they were keeping her. Avery hadn't thought to confirm that. As he scanned what felt like the hundredth clipboard, a woman's voice interrupted him.

"Excuse me," she said, "but I don't believe I know you."

Avery froze, unsure of what to do. He thought about using a whisper on her, but despite its effectiveness, the ability frightened him. It felt wrong in some way, and he worried that there might be some unintended consequence. Trying to formulate a plan, he turned to face her and found a portly, middle-aged woman with a kind face, her hair up in a loose bun. With no other ideas, Avery did the only thing he could think of. He told the truth.

"I'm looking for Lily Morgan," he whispered.

"Oh, you must be the man Harland was sending over," she said. "Well you should have just asked at the desk. This way."

She turned and marched down the hall, Avery following in her wake. His heart pounded in anticipation. He could picture Lily's handsome face, her bright eyes, her soft lips. The nurse turned a corner and stopped in front of one of the rooms.

"Third bed on the right," she said.

Avery whispered, "Thank you."

He entered the room and headed for the bed. It took all of his willpower to keep from running. As he passed the other beds, he noticed that they were all empty.

"Didn't expect to see you tonight," the woman said, behind him. "Thought he'd send someone over in the morning. Then again, what do I know? I imagine undertakers have to keep peculiar hours."

Avery froze and felt as if his heart had stopped. In a

rush, all the heat left his body, and his head swam. He blinked, trying to refocus the spinning room.

"Are you all right?" the nurse said.

Avery bolted to the third bed. He tore back the curtain, nearly ripping it from the rod.

Lying on pure white sheets in a crisp hospital gown, her blonde hair draped gracefully over her shoulders, was Lily. She looked more beautiful than he'd ever seen her. Her face was placid, every muscle relaxed, although her skin was pale. With a trembling hand, Avery reached out and touched her cheek. It was cool but not cold, a tiny bit of warmth still clinging to the flesh.

Avery threw back his head and mouthed a silent scream. Eyes wild, he looked around and spotted the little table beside the bed. A tray holding a cup, a pitcher, and various medical implements lay on it. With a sweep of his arm he sent them flying. They crashed to the floor, scattering in every direction.

At that same moment, an orderly came dashing in, speaking in a rush, "Ms. Hayes! We just got an ethereal from the police. There's a whisperer on the loose and he's heading this way. They say he's danger—"

Avery watched as it dawned on the orderly what was happening.

"It's him," he gasped.

"Why didn't you save her?" Avery hissed, his hands in fists, every muscle shaking.

The orderly stepped in front of the nurse and held out his hands.

"Just stay back," the orderly said. "The police will be here soon. They'll take you someplace safe."

"No!" Avery half-sobbed and turned back to Lily.

Looking at her still, perfect form, Avery's knees weakened. There were footsteps behind him. He reached into his coat and pulled his one souvenir from the asylum. Spinning around, he pointed the electro-pistol at the charging orderly.

"Stay back," he whispered.

The orderly skidded to a halt. In the distance Avery heard sirens, and his mind raced. What was there for him now? How could he go on? Why go on? Why had God taken her from him? All he had wanted was a life with Lily.

If only he could bring her back.

A dark thought came unbidden into Avery's mind. It caused him to recoil with horror. It was wrong. It broke every law of God and man.

To hell with man, and to hell with God too, he thought. They'd taken Lily from him. They'd stripped him of the one thing connecting him to this miserable world. If he could do this thing, he would. Keeping the gun pointed at the nurse and orderly, he leaned down and put his mouth to Lily's ear. His lips brushing her cool flesh.

"*Live*," he whispered.

Lily's back arched violently, and she gasped. Her body convulsed, and her eyes snapped open. Behind him, Avery heard a cry as the nurse fainted.

"God in heaven," the orderly cried, before running out of the room.

Avery dropped the gun, grasped Lily's shoulders, and whispered, "Lily, it's me. Avery."

Her convulsions ceased and she fell back onto the bed. Slowly, she turned her head to look at him.

"Avery?"

Tears rolled down Avery's cheeks. He grabbed Lily up in an embrace, his body wracked by sobs.

"Yes, Lily," he whispered. "It's me, my sweet Lily."

"What happened?" she said. "I was so sick, but I feel better now."

The sirens were coming closer. Avery looked out the window and saw police cars in front of the hospital gate. Officers were gesturing wildly at the gate keeper who refused to leave his hut.

"We've got to go, Lily," he said, releasing her from his embrace. "Can you walk?"

Lily slipped out of the bed with ease. She was still

pale, but otherwise looked every bit as healthy and strong as when she worked at the asylum.

"Yes," she said. "I'm fine."

Scooping the gun off the floor, Avery grabbed her by the hand

"This way," he said.

They raced through the hospital. A few nurses came out to see what the commotion was about, but at the sight of Avery's gun they screamed and fled.

"I asked to see you, Avery," Lily said as they ran. "I begged them to bring you. They said you didn't want to see me."

"Lies," whispered Avery.

He led her back to the staff room, and they burst out the back door. A dozen police officers armed with electro-rifles stood facing them.

"Drop your weapon," one of the officers shouted.

"*Leave us alone*," Avery whispered as loud as he could muster.

The police did not move.

"It won't work," the officer shouted, tapping his ear. "We know what you can do and we're prepared. Now drop your weapon or we *will* shoot."

Avery gripped Lily's hand tighter. He looked over and saw fear in her eyes.

"I won't let them take you from me again," he whispered. "I won't go back to the asylum."

He saw her gaze drop to the gun in his hand.

"They'll kill you, Avery," she said. "Please."

Avery looked to the police, to Lily, and back to the police. If he shot, they might shoot Lily as well. All the strength in his body drained away as his hope fled. His shoulders slumped. His arm, the one holding the pistol, went limp, and the weapon slipped from his fingers.

In a rush, the officers charged. One of them was holding some sort of gag. They grabbed him and slammed him to the ground, yanking his hand out of Lily's. There was a scream, and he saw that they grabbed Lily as well.

"Lily!" he hissed. "Please! Let her go!"

The officers wrestled him, trying to get him into hand cuffs while simultaneously trying to get the gag on him. One of the officers shoved Avery's face into the dirt. He could hear Lily screaming.

"No!" she cried. "You're hurting me. Please stop!"

A slap and Lily screamed again. Avery bucked and fought. His body shook with a burning fury. An officer shoved Avery's face into the dirt again. Avery had to stop this. The dirt in his mouth gave him the answer.

"*Shake*," he whispered.

From deep beneath the earth came a low rumble. The officers stopped, and a silence fell over them.

"*Shake,*" he whispered, more forcefully this time.

The ground trembled, as if a train were passing. The officers released him, and suddenly everyone was shouting. The rumble grew louder, and the earth began to roll.

"*SHAKE!*" he hissed.

The earth bucked. He heard a crash as one police car was tossed against another. Screams. Running. Avery leaped to his feet and saw Lily on the ground a few feet away, her eyes wide with fear. He ran to her and helped her up.

"Run," he whispered to her.

Hand-in-hand, they ran madly across the lawn. In the distance they heard a crashing noise and more screams. Suddenly, Lily stopped and pulled on his arm.

"Avery!" she shouted. "Look!"

Avery looked back. The entire hospital rocked. People stood in the windows, screaming. Nurses were trying to get patients out. A large crack ran up the middle of the old building.

"Make it stop, Avery," she cried. "Oh, please. Make it stop."

Avery dropped to the ground and whispered into the earth, "*Stop*."

The shaking ceased . . . but the screams didn't.

"What have I become?" he whispered.

Lily said nothing as she pulled him away into the night.

The next day they put together disguises and bought two train tickets at a station on the outskirts of the city. They had to steal clothes and money; Avery refused to whisper anyone into helping them. Lily did not argue.

They stopped in Newbury, and there was a wait while the engine took on water. Avery and Lily walked into town. The sun shone brightly, and to Avery's relief the village had few of the Marvel Company's miraculous devices.

"It's quiet," he whispered.

Lily understood, and she leaned in close.

"Do you think they'll try to follow us?" she asked.

"Yes," he whispered. "They'll want me back, now more than ever."

"If only you could throw it away," she said. "Toss it into the rubbish bin."

Avery stopped in front of one of the shops. A variety of phonographs were on display in the window. As he examined the devices he spotted one of the latest varieties. His breath caught in his chest.

"Wait here," he whispered and rushed inside.

It only took him a minute. He was forced to whisper the shop owner, but it was necessary. He came out a moment later, smiling, and holding a wax cylinder.

Lily stood a few steps away. Two constables were talking to her. One of them held a circular with Avery and Lily's pictures on it.

"What did you say your name was again?" the first officer said, his hand on the butt of his holstered weapon.

"Eleanor. My name is Eleanor."

"Do you have any identification?"

Lily blanched and started fumbling around in her stolen handbag.

"Yes, I have it here somewhere," she said.

Avery rushed over and put his arm around her.

"You there," the constable said, looking at the picture on the circular and then at Avery. "What's your name?"

"My name is Albert Prescott," Avery said in a clear, strong voice. "We're heading for Somerset on holiday."

The two constables looked at one another, glanced at the circulars one last time, then looked at Avery.

"Sorry for the trouble, sir," the first constable said. "We're looking for a whisperer that caused a bit of a commotion in London last night. If you see him, stay away. He's dangerous."

"Of course, constable," Avery said.

The constables left, and Lily turned to Avery, a tear in her eye.

"How?" she asked.

Avery held up the wax cylinder and pointed at the recording phonograph in the window.

"My whispers work on everyone," he said.

The train whistle blew, signaling that it was ready to leave. Lily, eyes shining, stood on tip toe and kissed Avery full on the lips.

"Let's go, love," she said.

Hand in hand, they headed for the station.

Imperial Changeling

Skip and Penny Williams

Skip and Penny Williams have learned a thing or two about castles and old intrigues from poking around in archives, used book stores, and historical sites. The couple lives in a century-old farmhouse on a Wisconsin hillside along with their extensive collection of books and a pride of unruly housecats. Skip keeps a garden and an orchard, but never carries a pocket watch. Penny teaches a variety of subjects, including physics and chemistry. Thus far, none of her students have managed to make anything implode.

The great pond rippled under cool, brilliant light from a waxing moon. Acres of close-cropped turf ringed the water, and clumps of ancient evergreens stood along the shore, leaning out like eager anglers searching for a glimpse of their finny quarry. No breeze wafted the pine boughs' resinous scent through the air, but the waters still lapped at the grassy shore, murmuring like a restless sleeper. The bubbling song of a waterfall, somewhere near at hand, gave quiet testament to what kept the waters astir.

As the moon began to set, a darker shadow stirred under one cluster of trees. Presently, a slim woman draped in peasant garb stepped into moonlight. Turning her gaze across the vast lawn, she noted the lights twinkling from dozens of windows in a sprawling edifice whose walls, roofs, and gables were all but invisible in the dying moonlight. With a half smile, the woman turned to the water, where, perhaps a hundred meters distant, rose the low mound of a tiny island wreathed in vines and wildflowers. Gazing at this small hump of land, she produced one long feather, snowy white, and cast it upon the water. It bobbed and floated for a moment, then silently ballooned into a graceful swan boat, with an arched prow and a padded seat. Once the peasant woman settled in the boat, it glided smoothly to the islet, without any visible means of propulsion. As it grounded on the shore, the woman stepped out and turned once again to gaze at the distant lights, standing as though transfixed. A few minutes later, a pale dove came winging out of the darkness to alight next to her with a flutter of wings.

The dove rose on its toes, as though to take flight once again. But instead, it stretched and filled out, until it had turned into a stately, dark-haired woman wearing a gown of the latest aristocratic fashion and diamond stars in her hair. The moment the dove's transformation was complete, the peasant woman sank before her in a deep curtsey.

"I must know the results of your divinations, Teca," said the noblewoman, laying a protective hand upon her swelling belly.

"Very well, Your Highness. Your daughter will be born vigorous and healthy. Her life. . . ."

The pregnant noblewoman raised a hand and shook her head. "Say no more, Teca." She walked along the shore, the peasant at her side. "I cannot say I am displeased. A healthy daughter—what more could a parent wish for? Still, Franz will be crushed at the birth of a third female child. He will doubtless wish to try again for a male heir. I have mixed emotions about that."

"There are other ways, my lady," replied Teca in a soothing tone.

The noblewoman frowned. "I would not consign my daughter to Ludwig's fate," she stated emphatically.

"But your friends and relations on the other side might help," persisted the peasant woman. "Think of it as the ancient practice of fostering—one child in your court, one in theirs, so to speak."

The noblewoman pondered for a moment. "A change-ling heir to the House of Hapsburg? That could prove troublesome—in a political sense, I mean."

"Or very helpful," Teca pointed out with a sly smile.

Some four months later, in a shuttered chamber in the imperial apartments of Schloss Laxenburg, near Vienna, Empress Elisabeth bore the daughter Teca had foretold. The attending physician handed the child to a wait-ing nurse—a golden-haired girl with a thin frame and jade-green eyes—who quickly bathed and wrapped the child.

"A lovely boy," she remarked to the doctor.

"What?" snapped the doctor in a harsh whisper. "What sort of nurse are you?"

"A very special one, sent from far away," replied the nurse, her green eyes blazing with other-worldly fire. "As I said, a lovely boy."

"A lovely b-b-boy," the physician agreed with a stam-mer, his own eyes taking on a glazed look.

The nurse threw open a shuttered window, and her far-seeing eyes fell upon on a certain moonlit island ris-ing from a pond in the distance. From it arose a snowy swan that rushed to the chamber, swift as an arrow. The bird, several times life-size, halted at the window, hover-ing, with a bundle. An exchange for the newborn was quickly made, and the swan took wing again, soaring high until it was lost among the night stars.

In the next few hours, the citizens of Austria-Hungary

began celebrating the birth of the long-awaited imperial heir, Crown Prince Rudolf Karl Franz Joseph. At last, the people said, the succession is assured.

Empress Elisabeth pulled on a pair of doeskin gloves to complete her traveling ensemble. Critically examining her reflection in the ornate gold mirror, she nodded in satisfaction at the green gown with white trim, the gold mesh shawl, the pert green hat, and the diamond-and-emerald necklace. "Wherever one goes, one should always look one's best," she mused. "After all, having a reputation for being a fashion trendsetter has come in handy more than once."

Turning from the mirror, she crossed to the bed. Withdrawing a stiletto from beneath her pillow, she slipped it into the specially made sheath in her boot. Hesitating for only a moment, she then moved to her armoire and took a hatbox from the top shelf. She slipped her hand into the space where it had been and removed a small pistol. "One can't be too careful in these times," she whispered, dropping the gun into her reticule. "Magic goes only so far, after all."

Stepping out of her boudoir, she nodded to her Hungarian maid. "Have Eduárd bring the carriage around, Ludmilla," she said.

"How long will you be staying with your kinsman, Your Highness?" asked the maid, closing the lid on a trunk full of expensive clothing.

"I'm not sure," replied Elisabeth. "Probably a week or two, at least. Ludwig is certain to have some new toys to show off."

"Will you need all twelve trunks then?" asked the maid.

"Of course, Ludmilla," answered the empress with a smile. "I may wish to go directly to Greece from there."

With a nod to her mistress, the maid departed to supervise the loading.

*   *   *

"Your Highness, are you quite certain that you're well enough to travel?" asked Hans, Franz Joseph's trusted retainer, eyeing his mistress's emaciated face. "You have been so very thin of late—perhaps the fever has left you too weak."

"Nonsense, Hans," snapped the empress. "I am perfectly well. It would behoove the members of my husband's court to embrace my strict diet and exercise regimen as well. The nobility around here is entirely too fat. If double chins were gold, we would never have to worry about taxing the people."

"I was merely concerned about your majesty's health," replied Hans stiffly. "The courtiers complained constantly of how dull life was in Vienna during your recent convalescence—and even the carnival did little to lift their spirits."

"Last night's revel should keep their tongues wagging for quite some time," replied Elisabeth with a smile.

"Indeed it should," said Hans. "Archduke Rudolf is as charming as his mother. None of the ladies can resist him."

"The lad is in love," whispered Elisabeth. "At last he has found his heart's desire in the lovely Baroness Vetsera."

"His wife will not be pleased," remarked the old retainer.

"Princess Stephanie is not pleased with life," snapped the empress, her eyes flashing. "I cannot imagine what Franz was thinking when he married poor Rudolf to that witch."

"He was thinking of the monarchy, as usual," replied Hans.

"Bah! The monarchy that represses the freedom of Hungary? The monarchy that fights endless wars for domination of land that belongs to others? Sometimes I wish I were a peasant."

Hans surveyed the servants as they loaded the last of

the empress's trunks into the wagons in her entourage. "Still, the monarchy does have its good points," he said dryly.

Elisabeth's lips twitched as she saw the direction of his gaze. "My dear Hans—always bringing me up short. I thank you." The empress leaned up to kiss his weathered cheek.

"Your majesty!" he cried, raising a hand to his face and glancing about nervously.

With a giggle entirely unbefitting her rank, Elisabeth climbed into her carriage and ordered the driver to be off. As the royal conveyance jolted forward, she pulled off her gloves and looked thoughtfully at her long, thin hands. *I shall have to order three desserts this evening, to help get my weight up,* she thought ruefully. *People find my natural frame quite disturbing, aerodynamic though it is.*

Two days later, Elisabeth's carriage arrived at Neuschwanstein Castle to the strains of carnival music. The empress looked out upon the garishly painted structures that dotted the grounds. All around, courtiers were taking turns throwing colored balls into small tubs for prizes, watching puppet shows, and awaiting their chances to ride a huge, steam-powered carousel with rank upon rank of fanciful beasts and horses wearing gaudy harnesses. Somewhere deep in the mechanism, at the carousel's heart, a calliope played.

An old man dressed in Bavaria's livery appeared at the door of her carriage to help her out. "His Highness King Ludwig will be pleased to see Your Majesty. Please accompany me to your apartment and refresh yourself after your long journey."

"Thank you, Immanuel," said the empress, taking his arm. "It was a rather grueling train ride. What goes on here?"

"A carnival to celebrate the completion of His Majesty's new rail line," replied the old man. "His Majesty decided that experiencing the entertainments of the common folk might make his courtiers less stuffy—at least for a few days."

Elisabeth chuckled softly. "How very like Ludwig. You'll make sure my trunks are delivered to the apartment?"

"Of course, Your Highness." The aged retainer led the Empress of Austria-Hungary to her chambers.

Once the door had closed, Elisabeth quickly changed from her traveling gown to a light yellow day dress with lace overlay. As she was taking down her hair for combing, the door burst open.

"Sisi, my dove!" cried a girlish voice. "I'm so happy to see you!"

Elisabeth turned to embrace the tall, dark-haired girl. "Ludwina, you haven't aged a bit."

"Neither have you, of course. You must come with me and see my new water-flowers chamber." The girl, tugged at Elisabeth's hand.

"Later," said the empress, slipping an arm around her cousin's waist. "I've come to visit the High Court. And you're coming with me."

"Sisi, not now! I have Richard here!"

"Richard? You brought him here again?" Elisabeth's eyes grew wide. "Aren't you afraid he'll find out?"

Ludwina giggled. "No. He thinks I'm Ludwig's niece, sent here by my family because I'm too wild."

Elisabeth grinned. "And so you are, my darling eagle. But Richard or no, we have work to do."

"Sisi, you're so tiresome sometimes," pouted Ludwina.

"I could say the same about you," pointed out Elisabeth dryly, "lolling in the arms of an aged composer while your kingdom goes to rot."

"He's not so old since I took him to the faerie realm," replied the girl saucily. "We had to fake his death and give him a new name to get him away from that horrid Cosmina, but he's still Richard to me. He says I make him feel young."

Elisabeth snorted.

"And furthermore, my kingdom isn't rotting. My people love me."

"Of course they do," agreed Elisabeth. "Who wouldn't, given your habit of bestowing lavish gifts on random peasants? But your nobles don't love you. They tried to depose and assassinate you three years ago, remember?"

Ludwina giggled. "And a clumsy job they made of it, too. Still, I owe you for saving my life at the time."

"They still complain endlessly of your inattention to affairs of state," Elisabeth pointed out.

"Well, that's half your fault, you know." Ludwina grabbed a diamond clip to pin up her hair. "You had me out of the palace for three months on our last adventure."

"If we hadn't dismantled that madman's doomsday machine, half of Europe would be missing now."

"I know, and it *was* important. But I had to leave orders not to be disturbed and pretend I was absorbed in building a new opera house while we were gone. Besides, I eventually did get an opera house."

"Which you immediately dedicated to that lover of yours," observed Elisabeth, folding her arms.

"He says I inspire him. His new piece, the Flight of the Eagle Maiden . . . he's going to put it in his next opera."

Elisabeth raised an eyebrow. "He saw you fly?"

"Yes," replied the girl sheepishly. "But he thinks he dreamt it."

"Haven't I told you to be more careful?" fretted Elisabeth, turning to the mirror to slip diamond clips into her mass of dark hair. "Now kiss Richard goodbye and get your feathers on. We have work to do."

"So what has you so distressed that you have to seek out the High Court?" asked Ludwina as the two women slipped into the secret passageway behind the ornate harpsichord in the conservatory. "I haven't seen you like this since that incident with the Greeks."

"The island sank last week," replied Elisabeth.

"Sank? How could an island sink?"

"That's what I've come to find out. It was my gate to the faerie realm. I think someone closed that gate—purposely."

"Do you think they know about you—and Rudolf?" Ludwina withdrew a tube from her pocket and turned a small crank. Instantly the corridor was bathed in a green light from the transparent crystal mounted on the end of the tube.

"I'm not sure. But I am certain that they knew about the gate to faerie—and eliminated it. I've heard stories of similar incidents across Hungary and elsewhere. Someone is slowly removing the magic from Europe."

"How can that be?" asked Ludwina. "Magic is magic—it's energy."

"And so is the steam that powers the engines that are taking over civilization," replied Elisabeth, stopping abruptly to touch a hidden switch on a panel to her left. It slid open without a sound, revealing a round chamber lit from the ceiling with what looked like sunlight. Within the room grew a fantastic garden, filled with fruit trees, rosebushes in hues of red, yellow, white, blue, and violet, and evergreens both tall and small. Through the room flowed a stream that widened into a pool at the south end.

"You think one kind of energy can cancel another?" persisted Ludwina, following her cousin into the room just before the door slid closed.

"I listened to a scientist speak once," reflected Elisabeth. "He said that energy cannot be created or destroyed, but its form can be changed. Like the heat that powers the steam turbines can be converted to motion. Perhaps magical energy can be converted to more mundane energy in some way."

Back out on the grounds, a nondescript man dressed in grimy overalls picked up an oilcan nearly as big as his head, with a spout longer than his forearm, and boarded the carousel as it coasted to a halt. He strode confidently past multiple rings of horses and beasts while eager carnival-goers scrambled for seats, then slipped inside a hidden door in the great machine's central hub. Presently, the carousel lurched into motion again.

Inside the ride's stationary hub, the man in the overalls glanced at the gears rotating the machine's vast bulk before turning down a short corridor and coming to a halt before a bank of levers and dials. Pivoting to face the hub's center, he delivered two sharp, loud knocks on a plain-looking panel. Almost immediately, the panel slid aside to reveal a cramped chamber, where a dwarfish man sat hunched over a broad dial on which a single slim needle wavered. Flanking the dial were two cylinders of heavy paper, each turning slowly. Hundreds upon hundreds of perforations decorated the paper wound on the right-hand cylinder. On the left one, a quartet of slim pens scratched out rows of squiggles and peaks.

"Welcome back, Colonel," said the technician without enthusiasm, sparing his visitor only the barest glance.

"Have there been any unusual readings today, Herr Prein?" The colonel bent to examine the right-hand cylinder. "Perhaps in the past hour?"

"You're looking at the playlist for the calliope," said Prein, his lips nearly twisting into a smirk. "But as it happens, yes. Perhaps two hours ago there was a definite spike. An hour after that there was a bigger one, definitely from inside the castle."

The colonel's eyes blazed with predatory fire. "That's just the time *she* got here!" he said knowingly.

"She?" asked Prein.

"The so-called Empress of Austria-Hungary, who's come here to visit her batty cousin!" the colonel snapped. "These aristocrats of yours are all related. In the States, we have laws against that much inbreeding."

"So," Prein asked, "you think Empress Elisabeth is some kind of sorceress?"

"Worse. She's some kind of faerie, or faerie-touched creature."

"If you say so, Colonel," replied Prein dryly. "What do you propose to do?"

The colonel stroked his chin. "Do you have one of the professor's whirligigs ready?"

"There's one in the carnival baggage. But it will take more than a day to get it assembled and ready to deploy—and that's if I have a crew to help." The technician pulled out the left-hand cylinder and studied the markings for a moment. "The pattern resembles Greece closely enough, Colonel. There could very well be a portal here, as you suspect. I've no idea where it is, however—somewhere deep in the castle, most likely. We'll have to move the detector a few times to be sure where the source lies, and then carry in the device and get it past whatever protection they have around the portal."

The colonel put both hands on his hips. "You had that speech ready, didn't you?"

"More or less," replied Prein. "What's the big hurry anyway? Who cares if the aristocracy has a little faerie blood, or dabbles in some genuine magic?"

"Because it perpetuates an old, corrupt order, that's why!" the colonel snarled. "How do you think this divine right of kings idea got started anyway? The early rulers really *were* more than human, that's how. That old magical blood still runs in quite a few of the crowned heads of Europe—and they use that power to interfere in the affairs of younger countries such as my own." The colonel turned as if to pace, but the cramped quarters stopped him short. "Hereditary privilege—the bondage of the lower classes—we've stamped that out in the States! Look at that fairy-tale monstrosity out there! What a waste of the people's funds!"

"Well," Prein observed. "It has stopped you in your tracks—for the moment at least."

The colonel waved a hand dismissively. "Bah! It

will fall in time—any fortress does once besieged. It's enough to know for sure that the empress is working some magic. It confirms something our source in Vienna has suggested." The colonel paused to regard the right-hand cylinder and watched it spin for a moment. "Go ahead and move the carnival around the neighborhood for the next couple of weeks and pinpoint that magic source. The empress and her cousin can wait, but I have some business to conclude with that son of hers!"

"It shall be done, Colonel Ames!" responded Prein with more enthusiasm than he felt.

Three weeks later, Elisabeth and Ludwina emerged from the garden chamber.

"So the island was definitely sabotage, and not by rival fey forces," said Ludwina, twisting a lock of hair. "Its energy was captured from outside somehow and turned inward, and it just imploded."

Elisabeth nodded, touching the panel to open the secret passage. "But how did they know it was there? And who was behind it?"

"Did you have any strange visitors?"

"No. No one came through except for the carn...." She looked up suddenly, her eyes flashing. "Ludwina! The carnival! Get rid of it!"

"I could have a fit of temper and ban carnivals in my kingdom, I suppose. But maybe we should pay it a visit."

Elisabeth nodded. The two women turned down a passageway that snaked upward through the castle. After a few minutes of climbing, they emerged onto the rooftop of one of the lower spires. Closing the doorway behind them, they spread their arms, and their forms began to shrink. Feathers sprouted and mouths became beaks. Moments later, an eagle and a dove winged joyfully into the sky, arcing over the countryside until they spied the carnival below.

They glided on the downdrafts into a nearby tree. The

eagle hid among the leaves, while the dove flitted over the various carnival attractions before perching on the dragon carving crowning the carousel. She discovered an opening in its mouth. Darting inside, she hurried into the central core of the machine and heard a voice above the carousel's clanking and music.

"There it is again," came the voice. "Just above—and another source within two hundred yards."

The dove poked her head into the cramped chamber as a short man turned to a telegraph machine.

"Pinpointed the location of gate," he said, tapping on its keys, "plus two smaller mobile sources. Please advise." He crossed to a large dial and examined a paper drum next to it. Presently, the machine signaled an incoming message. "Use Professor's all-around sight-on-bird setting to eliminate mobile sources. Proceed against primary source as planned." The man tapped out a one-word response: Acknowledged. He then crossed the cramped chamber to a small storage box. From it, he took out a rifle with an intricate sight atop it, and a small object that with a touch sprouted a crown of horizontal blades.

Stuffing the odd item into his pocket, he picked up the rifle and made a few adjustments to the sight. "Bird hunting," he mumbled. "What next?" He peered through the sight and let out a squawk, then abruptly swung around to face the dove and fired. The bullet robbed Elisabeth of a few tail feathers as she ducked back into the passage and made her way to the dragon's mouth once more. Emerging onto the top of the carousel, she glanced quickly about and took wing, just as the little man opened the door of the central works and came out with his rifle. Scattering the terrified carousel riders, he took aim once again and fired, this time wounding the dove's left wing. She careened into the tree where the eagle waited as blood dripped from her useless wing.

The eagle extended her own wing and flipped the dove up onto her back, then climbed higher into the tree, cloaked by leaves. Another bullet whizzed past, missing both birds. The eagle glided to an adjacent tree, then another, as more bullets flew. She turned her head around to nuzzle the dove, who gripped her rescuer's back tightly with her claws. Then the burdened eagle leaped into the air, catching a downdraft that carried her over an ornate reflecting pool and into a hedge maze, where she landed on the ground.

The dove clambered off, and both birds changed quickly to human form. "There's a tunnel through the gardener's shed," said Ludwina, grabbing her cousin by her good arm and propelling her through the maze.

Twenty minutes later, the two women were back in Elisabeth's apartment. Ludwina inspected her cousin's shattered arm. "It's already starting to heal from your fey magic, but I'll get my bag and try to hurry the process." She slipped out the door and locked it behind her. Elisabeth busied herself with cleaning the wound and changing out of her bloodstained gown.

Ludwina returned with a black case, from which she extracted two vials of colored liquid—one red and one violet. With a syringe, she injected first one and then the other into the wound, which began to close immediately.

"You're a genius with medicine," remarked the empress. "Who'd have thought a half-fey aristocrat would have a talent for inventing?"

"My madness gives me time to dabble." Ludwina replaced the syringe and vials. "Now tell me what you saw in there."

As Elisabeth related the results of her spy trip, Ludwina frowned. "This whirligig that he put in his pocket— what did it look like?"

"Rather like a child's toy, except made of finely machined metal, with some hidden lever that caused it to unfold."

"If that is the device with which they intend to destroy the gate to faerie, they will try to bring it inside the castle. We must intercept it."

*   *   *

The factory rose from a sea of stumps and moribund crops. The featureless walls stood like the outer works of a vast fortress. Instead of a keep, three squat chimneys belched forth smoke, sparks, and a nasty stench. Concentric loops of streets, neatly paved, ringed the factory's grimy bulk. Rows of neat cottages and a few larger buildings, all made from whitewashed stone, lined the streets. Bits of soot gave the pale stonework a salt-and-pepper look.

As the sun sank beyond the denuded hills to the west, a blast from a steam whistle brought several scores of sweat-stained workers trudging from the factory gate, a wrought-iron affair emblazoned with a pair of entwined salamanders. Some minutes after the gates clanged shut behind the final worker, they swung open again, and a coach and six horses came thundering up. It rocked to a halt inside the courtyard, in front of a door marked simply "Office."

Before the footman could hop down to open it, the carriage door burst open and a tall man dressed in a uniform of midnight blue stepped out. This garb suited him far better than the soiled overalls he had worn outside Neuschwanstein Castle. Waving the footman aside, he adjusted his sword and hat and strode through the door.

Inside, an elderly clerk sprang to his feet. "So good to see you, Colonel Ames! You were not expected."

"A change of plans, Johan," said Ames. "I must see the professor at once."

"He's out on the floor, supervising some retooling."

"I know the way," Ames replied, striding from the office into the factory beyond.

On the cavernous factory floor, gaslights shed an orange glow over rows of benches, presses, and machines. Overhead loomed a web of belts and shafts. Mechanics busied themselves with a few of the devices, not even sparing Ames a glance.

Shortly, Ames spotted a gray-haired man in a long coat, speaking to a team of workers who were busy dismantling a long row of machines. "I must speak to you immediately, Professor," called the colonel.

"Why, Colonel Ames!" exclaimed the professor, turning to face his visitor. "I thought your business had taken you to Bavaria!"

"I've been there long enough to learn what I needed to know," replied Ames. "There are now more urgent matters at hand."

"Splendid, splendid!" said the professor. "And the detector proved useful?"

"Yes! Yes it was vital and continues to perform well. I am now quite certain that the Empress of Austria-Hungary is what scholars call a *Pennatus Patricius*—a kind of fey shapeshifter. Perhaps her cousin is too—they both have the characteristic thin build. And that would mean that the Hapsburg crown prince also has fey blood. I'm on my way to Vienna now to consult with a new contact we have there. We have an opportunity that won't come again. I only stopped here to check on your progress."

"Splendid!" said the professor again. "As you see, we're setting up a new line that will turn out cases and gears for the subharmonic watch. It can be tuned to produce a variety of effects. The human nervous system is quite susceptible to influences that fall outside what the individual can perceive."

"Yes, quite clever I'm sure. Any man might carry a pocket watch, but you might consider how a woman could be induced carry one of your gadgets."

"Oh, quite so!" replied the professor. "A conundrum, I'm sure."

"I trust that you have some prototypes to demonstrate."

"Prototypes? Oh yes, several. Several," the professor managed. "Test subjects, now there's a difficulty—oh yes. Quite."

"Is that so?" Ames skewered the man with a glance. "Well, resolve your difficulties and make your demonstration as soon you are able. I'm planning a mission that might benefit from some of these gadgets. In the meantime, I need to send a telegram ahead to Vienna."

A few hours later, lights burned brightly in a hastily cleared storage area behind the factory. A few wooden shipping crates—each perhaps a meter square and about that high—stood in precise ranks. On three sides of each crate, every second plank had been pried loose, turning the container into a cage of sorts that housed a shaggy, wolfish canine. A few nervous guards carrying sidearms and rifles kept a wary eye on the dogs, as though none too sure that the makeshift cages could hold the beasts. Fortunately, a sizable meal of meat and marrowbones had rendered the creatures docile—at least for the moment. Also in the room stood a half dozen mannequins—faceless, human-sized dummies clad in business clothes or military uniforms.

The professor stood at a bench at one end of the line of cages, laying out at least a dozen very large pocket watches with gleaming brass cases and pale yellow faces. Once he had all the devices arranged in a tidy row, he picked up each one, sometimes opening the case to make some adjustment, sometimes manipulating the crown as if to set the watch, sometimes merely giving the crystal and case a hasty wipe. He was still laboring over his watches when Colonel Ames strode into the chamber, heels clicking on the stone floor.

"All this seems quite puzzling, professor," the colonel declared. "Surely you have not prepared a collection of gadgets fit only for zookeepers and dogcatchers!"

The professor carefully laid down the device he'd been holding. "I am beginning to think, sir," replied the professor coldly, "that I do not care for the term 'gadget.'"

"No offense meant," Ames said affably. "It is merely a

term I find convenient. A figure of speech, so to speak."
Ames paused for a heartbeat, then continued. "Nevertheless, I misspoke. My concern lies more in this direction. You have here a collection of dogs—all part wolf by the looks of things. I conclude that these beasts are to serve as the objects of our exercise. Are these—how did you name them—subharmonic watches—effective only where dogs and wolves are concerned? Or are they more broadly effectual?"

The professor drew a breath and fixed Ames with a hard stare. "You have touched, Colonel, on an important point. But in the interests of avoiding a digression that you would undoubtedly find tiresome, let me assure you that the effects you see here will extend to most things that go forth on two or four legs—saving, possibly, a reptile." The professor picked up a device and caressed it. "Let us proceed, and return to the subject of—ahem—field application, after my little display here has concluded."

"Agreed," replied Ames.

The professor took a device in each hand and gestured to one of the armed guards to place one watch in a mannequin's breast pocket. The man did so then quickly resumed his station, scanning the cages to make sure nothing was amiss.

With a glance toward Ames, the professor raised the hand holding the remaining watch and clicked the crown once. Instantly, a barely audible "ping" sounded from the mannequin, which trembled, swayed, and finally toppled with a dull thud.

"That's it?" asked Ames, puzzled.

"That is not, as you say, 'it,' Colonel Ames," responded the professor with evident amusement. "Examine the mannequin, if you please. Pay special attention to the pocket in which the watch was placed."

Ames bent over the fallen mannequin and tugged at the brass case inside the pocket. To his surprise, he found the watch locked into place. Four claws protruded from its formerly seamless case, penetrating deeply into the mannequin's wooden body. The attachment resisted Ames's attempts to remove the watch with his fingers. With a grimace, Ames produced a knife with a long, heavy blade and used it to pry at the claws. One by one, they came loose with the sounds of splintering wood. When Ames lifted the device free, he saw that, in addition to the claws, a slim needle a few inches long protruded from the watch's back plate. Ames considered the needle's length, which seemed considerably longer than the watch was thick.

The professor watched Ames with some satisfaction. "It looks solid," he said, "but it's hollow and it telescopes. Even so, the needle isn't long enough to deal any serious harm on its own." As Ames studied the needle more carefully, the professor continued. "To envenom the needle would prove simple enough, and a watch could easily carry a lethal dose."

The professor gestured with the hand holding the second watch. "A single device can control many others, but more about that in a moment." He returned the watch to the bench and took up another. "Strictly mechanical applications are essentially limitless," he continued. Taking aim, the professor loosed a pair of spikes from the newest watch. They struck a mannequin with a sound like whips cracking, and the mannequin shuddered and fell. Following that, the professor tossed another watch into the air, whereupon it whirled like a dervish and flew into the room, scattering the guards. Thin chains shot from its case, swiftly entangling two of the remaining mannequins and sending them crashing to the floor, heads and limbs nearly severed.

The professor surveyed the wreckage with satisfaction before calling the guards back to their places. "Now," said the professor, rubbing his newly empty hands, "Let us look into the non-mechanical." He took up two watches and gestured to the guards, who quickly set about clearing away the wreckage of the mannequins. Once that task was done, four men, working in pairs, took up long poles and thrust them though the slats in a cage. The disturbance set the dog inside growling. Taking care to keep well away from the beasts' slavering jaws, the four men pushed and dragged the cage to the center of the floor, then hastily withdrew their poles and took up their weapons again.

The professor picked up a new pair of watches and beamed at Ames. "I believe you will find this demonstration quite satisfactory." The professor paced deliberately up to the cage. He snapped open the cover of one watch and carefully set it on the floor, taking care to aim the open cover toward the cage. Then he took a few steps back and clicked the crown of the second watch. Ames briefly felt as though scores of insects were crawling under his clothes, and he fidgeted in spite of himself. Still, it was the dog's reaction that commanded his attention. Every hair on its body stood on end. The dog yelped and started to chase its tail, but it only managed a quarter turn before collapsing in a heap.

"Dead?" asked Ames, looking from the cage to the professor.

"Oh no," grinned the professor. "But it's unconscious and insensate. It will remain so for several hours." The professor returned the watch he held to the bench. "The effects from this application are extremely potent. Still, it is not necessary to operate the device remotely. With the proper gear, one can keep it in hand and bring down a target several feet away."

"You have such gear?" Ames asked sharply.

"A prototype, Colonel," answered the professor. "Indulge me for a moment, however. I have one more demonstration."

The guards once again rearranged the cages. When the flurry of activity was over, the remaining cages were pushed together in pairs with the adjoining panels removed, so as to create one common space for the two occupants. There were a few whines and growls, but in moments the newly paired canines were quiet once again.

"A living nervous system is subject to disruption, as we have just seen," explained the professor. "It is possible to enliven the senses rather than enervate them." With that, the professor took up a new watch and twisted the crown. Immediately, the dogs stirred, growling and snapping. The first wave of aggression quickly escalated, and in a heartbeat the cages rocked as the dogs threw themselves on each other, snarling and biting. A few animals, wounded, but victorious over their rivals, threw themselves against the cage makeshift bars and broke through in showers of splinters. They stood for a moment, sides heaving and muzzles flecked with blood and foam, before rifle fire from the nervous guards brought them down.

Ames stood transfixed amid the carnage. The smell of blood and gunpowder, and the reports of rifle fire, magnified to earthshaking thunder inside the warehouse, had briefly carried him back to fields where men in blue and in gray strove for mastery. He allowed himself a few moments of reverie before taking the professor by the arm and ushering him back to the factory office.

"These devices," he asked eagerly. "They can disable or enrage anyone?"

"You wonder, I think," replied the professor, "if they can affect the faerie folk. In theory, they can."

"In theory?" Ames snapped. "What good is theory?"

"Theory, my dear Colonel," replied the professor dryly, "made what you just witnessed possible."

"Very well, professor, explain further—if you please," Ames commanded.

"As you know, Colonel, we have had very few faerie subjects for testing. The faerie mind and body are not so different than a human's, but they are, nevertheless, protected against outside influences."

"Yes, I know," Ames said. "They can't take a punch in the jaw, but mentally they're as tough as old leather."

"Quite," responded the professor. "But a careful researcher, or even an enterprising field operative, could take a device and work on one subject, adjusting it until it had the maximum effect."

"I have just such an agent," said Ames with ill-concealed glee. "Pack up a set of these watches. I'll take them with me."

For two days and nights, Elisabeth maintained a discreet watch over all visitors to the castle. On the evening of the third day, her vigilance bore fruit. A purveyor of children's toys was admitted to the castle, where he entertained the courtiers' children with a variety of hand-carved toys. Once he had them enthralled, he slipped away, moving unerringly toward the passage leading to the garden chamber that housed the portal to faerie. In the upper hallway, he tapped on the wall panels until he found one that sounded hollow. But as he felt for the lever that would open it, a blow to the back of his head rendered him unconscious. Stepping out of the shadows, Ludwina searched him carefully until she found the device that Elisabeth had described, then had him locked in the dungeon.

Once in her cousin's apartment, Ludwina threw open the window and assumed her eagle form. Flying low over the courtyard, she sped onward, the device clutched in her talons, until she found the carnival. She landed atop the carousel and dropped the device into the open maw of the carved dragon, then flew away at top speed. A few minutes later, the carnival's patrons witnessed a curious sight. The carousel shimmered and seemed to fold in upon itself. Moments later, it was gone, leaving a large crater in the ground where it had stood.

"As I thought," said Ludwina later, upon returning to her cousin's apartment, "the device had no special tuning. It merely turned whatever energy source was nearby in upon itself."

"At least this gate is safe for now," said Elisabeth,

locking her trunk. "But we must go to Vienna without delay. When I questioned that ugly little man, he said his employer's next target is Rudolf!"

"He plans to kill the archduke?" cried Ludwina. "But why?"

"Evidently this Colonel Ames has discovered Rudolf's fey nature and plans to begin his campaign to expunge nonhuman blood from Europe's crowned heads with him. We have to stop him."

"Very well," said Ludwina. "Mad King Ludwig will become engrossed in another lengthy project. But what about you?"

"Empress Elisabeth will go on to Greece by steamship. As she has taken ill again, she will travel veiled and speak to no one. Teca has posed as me before; she knows what to do."

At a small railway station in the country outside of Vienna, a pair of slim women dressed in royal blue capes over gray traveling suits stepped out with the crowd of passengers from the evening train. A porter pushing a cart loaded with two great trunks walked at their heels. As the trio neared the platform's edge, one woman smiled and pointed at a carriage parked in a long line of similar vehicles. Immediately the women quickened their pace, leaving the porter laboring to keep up.

Both ladies turned when they reached the carriage and smiled broadly as the porter brought the cart to a halt. After pausing to catch his breath, the porter noticed that although handsome, the vehicle was devoid of any markings. Before he could remark on it, a footman with a stern face stepped down from the carriage and laid a hand on a trunk. He gave the porter one level, questioning glance, and soon the two men were hoisting the trunks aboard the carriage.

The moment the task was done, one of the ladies extended a hand to the porter and dropped a coin into his hand. "Merci, monsieur," she said with smile.

"Danke, Herr," added the second lady, also bestowing a coin.

"D-d-danke, Fraulien," stammered the porter, who could not help being pleased with the double tip. He barely noticed as the women boarded the carriage and it thundered off at breakneck speed.

"So good of you to meet us, Eduárd," said Elisabeth as the carriage left the station.

"I'm pleased to assist, Your Highness," replied the man, who looked rather somewhat careworn. "How was your incognito trip across half of Europe?" He turned to Elisabeth's companion and doffed his cap. "I'm Eduárd, servant and *sometime* confidant to Her Highness."

"Forgive me, Eduárd," said Elisabeth. "You may call my companion Félice, from Reims. We're just two schoolteachers on holiday who found each other while sightseeing. We found this charming shop in Munich where we just *had* to buy these matching outfits."

"I see," replied Eduárd.

"It is important that I speak to my son directly, Eduárd," said Elisabeth, assuming a more serious mien.

"He and his baroness have gone to his lodge at Mayerling, Your Highness," Eduárd responded. "The crown prince has had a difficult fortnight. He seems out of temper. There was an incident between the officers of his regiment a few nights ago, and the emperor was livid. The two of them have had some kind of falling out, and the archduke has gone to sulk. Perhaps the baroness can bring him out of it. She seems to have endeared herself to most of the household, even with her odd gifts."

"Gifts?" said Elisabeth.

"She has distributed these watches." Eduárd produced a massive timepiece with a gleaming brass case. "They keep good time, but they're oddly heavy and they have the look of mass production about them. No soul, so to speak."

"Well, tell me about this baroness," said Félice. "I have not had the pleasure."

"My son's newest lady love—she seems to make him happy," said Elisabeth. "They met this fall at a.... By all the muses, Félice! They met at a carnival!"

"Is that bad?" interjected Eduárd.

"Possibly fatal, my friend," croaked Elisabeth. "We must stop somewhere and unpack one of the trunks, then push on with all speed."

"Of course, Highness," replied Eduárd.

They brought the carriage to a halt outside Mayerling's grounds, and Elisabeth ordered Eduárd to take the carriage to the nearest town and see to the exhausted horses. As the clatter of hooves and wheels faded into the distance, Elisabeth drew a pair of heavy pistols from under her cloak and handed them to Ludwina. "I think it is best we fly from here, but I don't think I can carry so much weight aloft. Would you mind?"

"Of course not," replied Ludwina. "The eagle is ever at your service."

Alighting on a balcony at the lodge, eagle and dove returned to their human forms. Elisabeth accepted one pistol from Ludwina and turned to the French doors before them. Drawing the stiletto she kept in her boot, she slipped the slender blade between the twin doors and expertly jimmied the latch. The two women silently crept inside.

After scurrying down several hallways and descending a few flights of stairs, they came to a great hall where a fire crackled in a hearth big enough for three men to stand in. A handsome couple stood silhouetted in the firelight. The man, tall and dashing, looked on bemusedly as his companion, a petite woman with a youthful face, toyed with a big brass watch.

"I wish you'd stop fiddling with that thing, Mary," he said. "You're always playing around with it. It works fine!"

"Oh, but my dear Rudolf!" the young woman replied sweetly. "When it works *properly* it's just full of surprises, and you, my sweet, have yet to enjoy them all."

The metallic click of a pistol cocking broke the mood.

"Step away from him, Baroness—if that's who you really are!" said Elisabeth in a steely tone.

"Mother!" exclaimed the man. "However did you get here? I thought you'd gone to Greece!"

"I'll explain later, Rudolf," Elisabeth replied. "Do us a favor, though, and step away from that woman!"

"That w-w-woman?" stammered Rudolf. "What has gotten into you, Mother? Where did you get that gun, and who is that with you?"

During the conversation, the baroness had quietly slipped the watch into a pocket of her gown, deftly exchanging it for another. Now she stepped forward and offered the second watch to her companion.

"Perhaps it would be best to humor your mother," she cooed. Placing the watch in Rudolf's hand, she glided away to sit on a divan, in front of which stood a low table laden with a bottle of champagne and other delicacies. She calmly helped herself to a canapé.

"Drop that watch, Rudolf!" Elisabeth fairly shrieked.

"What *is* the matter with you, Mother?"

"It would have been best to do as Mommy says!" said the baroness. Her hand slipped into her pocket, and the watch in Rudolf's hand came to life with a sickening snap. The archduke groaned in agony as metallic claws and a slim needle pierced his hand. Clutching at the watch, he sank to his knees.

"Rudolf!" screamed Elisabeth.

In a heartbeat, Baroness Vetsera produced yet another watch. Snapping open the case, she pointed it at the two other women. But before she could thumb the crown, two pistol shots rang out, and her frail body flew back onto the divan, crimson circles blossoming in her chest and torso.

"Quickly, Ludwina!" breathed Elisabeth. "I think that spike is poisoned!"

With practiced hands, Ludwina knelt over the archduke's form.

"Nice shooting, by the way," added Elisabeth. "I fear my aim was a little low."

"You were distracted," replied Ludwina. "Here, bandage his hand while I dig out some supplies."

Once Ludwina had finished treating the injured archduke, and the lodge staff had bundled him off to bed, king and empress met again in the Great Hall, where the baroness's corpse still lay.

"I've explained to the staff that there has been an attempt on the archduke's life," said Elisabeth, as Ludwina bent over the body.

"It should not prove too difficult to invent a story everyone can remember," replied Ludwina. "Wait! What's that? I hear gunfire outside!"

As the latch to a door at the far end of the chamber rattled, Elisabeth assumed her dove form and fluttered into the beams overhead.

Elisabeth had barely hidden herself when the door burst open, revealing Colonel Ames, armed with a Colt revolver. Ludwina sprang away from the divan, upsetting the table and sending the champagne bottle rolling toward the door, its contents foaming and gurgling from the neck.

Feigning terror, Ludwina stammered. "I-I-I heard a shot! I rushed here to find the baroness dead. Where is Archduke Rudolf?"

"So the faerie prince got wise to her, eh?" Ames glanced at the dead woman. "Pity. She was a most useful operative. Good thing I decided to make sure the job was done right." The colonel overstepped the empty bottle. "You play the role of the frightened servant well," Ames hissed. "But you're no servant, and I think you know where the archduke hides. Tell me, is he wounded, or merely cowering?"

"Please, sir, you're hurting me!" Ludwina managed to choke out.

Ames dragged the gasping Ludwina back to the divan and forced her down next to the dead baroness. "You listen to me," he whispered. "No more faeries, vampires, dryads, leprechauns, or other magical creatures will control Europe anymore. It's time to level the playing field here, as we have in the States. Now tell me what I want to know." He brought the barrel of the Colt to her temple.

But he never heard her reply, for at that moment, Elisabeth, back in human form, brought the champagne bottle crashing down on his head, and he dropped like a stone.

"Messy!" observed Ludwina, shaking shards of glass from her hair.

"Colonel Ames!" shouted a voice from the doorway. Four armed men burst into the room, staring at the scene before them.

Ludwina tossed Elisabeth the Colt and retrieved her own pistols from under the divan. Elisabeth dropped the first man with a neat shot through the forehead, while Ludwina blazed away with a pistol in each hand, sending two others reeling back into the doorframe. The last man fired at Ludwina, wounding her in the shoulder.

"Ludwina!" cried Elisabeth. The empress leveled the Colt at the assassin and fired, blasting a hole through his chest.

Falling to her knees beside Ludwina, Elisabeth began to stanch the blood flowing from the wound.

Ludwina opened her eyes. "Duck."

Elisabeth ducked and rolled as Ludwina raised a pistol in her good arm and fired point-blank into the face of Colonel Ames, who had arisen behind her cousin.

Later, the servants quietly cleared away the blood, broken glass, and stained furniture downstairs while Ludwina, ensconced in the archduke's chamber, instructed

Elisabeth and Rudolf on the treatment of her shoulder. "Now dab on some of that green paste and bandage the wound."

"I still don't understand, Mother," said Rudolf, wrapping the bandage around Ludwina's shoulder. "Mary was trying to kill me?"

"That's right. She was a field operative for Colonel Ames, who had a plan to rid Europe of its magic and supernatural bloodlines. Apparently these pocket watches were intended as sophisticated assassination tools."

"My men all have those watches!" cried the archduke. "And so does Father! And most of the senior staff at the Schönbrunn!"

"That could explain the row among your men," said Ludwina, eyeing the array of watches they had taken from Baroness Vetsera and Colonel Ames. "Some of these watches seem to produce irritating subharmonic sounds."

"We'll have to root them all out and destroy them when we return," said Elisabeth. "But for now, we have some corpses to dispose of."

"I do not understand humans," murmured Rudolf, gazing moodily at the body of the baroness. "She said she loved me."

"She lied," said his mother, putting an arm around his shoulder. "Did you love her?"

"I'm not sure. She was delightful."

"He'll have to convalesce for a while in the faerie realm," confided Ludwina in a low voice. "My remedies lack some necessary ingredients."

"Perhaps it is best if he returns permanently," said Elisabeth thoughtfully. "Besides, it wouldn't be right for him to take the Hapsburg throne, since he really bears no blood of that line."

"Yes," said Rudolf. "I believe I've had my fill of humans. Will you take me back to Faerie?"

Ludwina pursed her lips. "He and the Colonel are about the same height, though Rudolf's not quite as beefy. Do you think we could pass Ames off as Rudolf?"

"You mean pretend the assassination attempt was successful?" asked Elisabeth, arching a brow.

"Why not? We could claim that Rudolf and the baroness were so in love that they came here to kill themselves when others insisted they break off their affair."

"A suicide pact?" Rudolf snorted. "Who would believe that?"

"People will believe nearly any lie if it's told well enough," replied his mother. "But her wounds won't hold up as a suicide. We'll have to make it a murder-suicide. You killed her, and then yourself."

"Well, I could have shot my own face off, I suppose," mused the archduke.

A few days later, all of Austria-Hungary mourned the loss of the crown prince. King Ludwig of Bavaria attended the state funeral, along with several other crowned heads of Europe. The wake went much later than expected, as not a single man in the palace could find his pocket watch.

The Transmogrification Ray

Robert E. Vardeman

Robert E Vardeman has written more than eighty science fiction, fantasy and mystery novels. He recently co-authored the novelization of the Sony PlayStation game *God of War*. He has had short stories in the previous Jean Rabe & Martin Greenberg anthologies *Renaissance Faire*, *Terribly Twisted Tales*, and *Timeshares*. Vardeman's collected short stories can be found in *Stories from Desert Bob's Reptile Ranch*, with original stories published in e-format from Kindle and the Apple iTunes App store. He currently lives in Albuquerque, NM, with two cats, Isotope and X-ray. One out of three of them enjoy the high-tech hobby of geocaching. For more info, check out www.CenotaphRoad.com.

The side of the mountain exploded, sending a roiling cloud of dust upward in perfect symmetry with the avalanche tumbling into the canyon beyond.

"Drat," Francis Barstow said. He pursed his lips, pushed up his protective goggles, and began scribbling in his laboratory notebook. As the last of the debris cascaded down on him, he absently brushed it off the shoulders of his white lab coat. Looking into the sky, he saw that brisk mountain winds carried away the dust in a thrice, but he frowned when a single white cloud moved in a direction opposite the ground wind. Air currents were so peculiar in the higher altitudes. He shrugged this off and returned to work, only distracted from entering the tiny, crabbed script when his robotic dog came snuffling over.

"Not now, Fulton," he said, using his booted foot to push away the compressed-air powered dog. The dog whistled and hissed as air escaped past poorly fitted gaskets. "I'll fix your seals later." Francis looked into the dog's glowing ground glass optical lenses and sighed. Over the years he had owned dogs from large Afghan hounds to miniature poodles, but none had been as faithful or attentive as Fulton. He had built the brass gear and gutta-percha-jointed dog before coming to the desolate mountains of Colorado to conduct his alchemical experiments. There had been little else to keep him occupied while his brain masticated the intricate details of his current project. He might be an adequate theoretical scientist, but his hands had to be busy all the time like an engineer.

"Very well, my friend," Francis said, kneeling. He laid aside his lab book and tinkered with Fulton's settings, adjusting the valve controlling the gas release from a pressurized canister until Fulton rocked back on his haunches and opened his mechanical mouth, as if panting. "There. Now let me work." Fulton snapped his mouth shut. This was as close to a delighted bark as Fulton could get. Francis gave the robotic head a quick pat, then looked up to see his chief assistant struggling along the path from the mineshaft toward him.

"Mr. Barstow, there wasn't anything I could do. It just blew up." Lawrence was covered with soot so black he might have been an African native. He took out a rag from his hip pocket and wiped the grime from his eyes, making him look like a raccoon in the negative. More work resulted in the removal of large patches of the soot, revealing a man with a big Roman nose, thin lips, and high cheekbones covered in weathered, swarthy skin. His dark eyes were deep-set and flashed in anger at almost being blown up.

"A miscalculation, I assure you," Francis said. "See?" He held up his lab book, but Fulton clacked his jaws a few times, warning him. If it hadn't been for the robot's constant vigilance, he would have shown his plans to everyone. After the Liverpool theft, he ought to have known better, but working on an experiment always filled him with enthusiasm that overrode common sense. He bit his lip to keep from thanking Fulton. Lawrence and the rest of the crew working here so high in the Rocky Mountains looked askance when he treated the robot better than he would have a real dog, as if a real dog could chew up six-inch-long 5/16"-24 steel bolts.

"You weren't trying for such a tremendous explosion?" Lawrence cocked his head to one side and peered at him. Francis waved off such an absurd idea.

"The vacuum chamber. Did it rupture?"

"It melted before the explosion. So much energy was concentrated at the end of the beam nothing could stop it, not even twenty feet of solid rock," Lawrence said. "Only through the grace of God did we not lose any of the crew."

"Oh, bother, yes, of course. The men. Glad to hear that they are all right, yes, very glad." Francis scribbled a few more notes, did the calculation, and shook his head. "There is a term in this equation that I do not understand. I'll work on it because that might be the cause of so much . . . destruction. Get to work rebuilding the rig."

"The engines were untouched," Lawrence said. He pointed toward the huge engines near the mouth of the lead mine and the tall billowing pillars of condensed steam rising from them. "I'll shut them down."

"Such powerful devices," Francis said absently. He stared at the bank of steam engines but saw something more. The mineshaft bored a hundred feet into the hillside and was lined with rings of Corrigan Rare Earth Magnets, invented by a brilliant one-eyed American only a year before. Francis thought he was the first to make use of the oscillating super-powered magnetic field to accelerate particles created in the modified Crooke's tube down the length of the mineshaft into his target.

"I wasn't able to retrieve the lead target," Lawrence said, shaking Francis from his reverie. "It was vaporized."

"Stop that," he said. "You were reading my mind. That's not good."

Lawrence turned pale under the soot remaining on his face and he sputtered.

"You can read minds?" the man stammered.

"No, you, oh, bother. Never mind. I refuse to believe such psychic nonsense, no matter what Sir Arthur claims." Francis was as distraught as his assistant over a simple case of focused thought. Both of them had considered the lead target—the one he intended to turn to gold—but reading thoughts? Impossible. Unless . . .

Fulton hissed and clacked his jaws, distracting him.

"Yes, yes, you're right. One experiment at a time." He glanced guiltily at Lawrence, who stared at him as if he had gone quite mad. He knew the rest of the crew shared his chief assistant's appraisal, and it did not bother him unduly. A certain cachet went with being considered a mad inventor.

He would show them all madness when he performed the feat of the ages that had eluded the best minds since Albertus Magnus. Their alchemy had been primitive and the techniques entirely chemical. By sending his rays racing along an evacuated glass tube, accelerated by the Corrigan magnets, he would turn lead into gold through electrical means. The fortune that he had spent on buying the mountaintop and the necessary equipment would be a piddling amount compared to what he could produce at will. There was a reason he had chosen a lead mine, after all, beyond the way it so perfectly contained his transmogrification ray—it provided him with raw material and kept curious citizens in the nearby town of Leadville from wondering why he needed slabs of plumbum.

"Are you all right?" Lawrence asked, moving closer. He reached out, but Francis shied from his touch.

"Quite so, thank you. Get to work. Clean up. You and the crew. I need to finish my calculations."

"The explosion was remarkable," Lawrence said. "It came at the end of the . . . ray."

"Not supposed to do that, not at all. But the engines worked well. No trouble with the leather power transfer belts slipping. The vacuum was adequate to permit easy transference of the ray to the target through super-rarefied aether. And the Crooke's tube could not have worked better."

"The ray would have been deadly at a mile or more," Lawrence said.

"Oh, it would extend ever so much farther. That's why I need it backstopped in the mineshaft. Now go, go."

Francis returned to the small line shack where he slept and kept his precision equipment. Meters, glass envelopes and electrodes for the Crooke's tubes and other matériel littered the small interior. He kicked the door shut with his heel after Fulton clanked inside. The robot sat back on its haunches and hissed a little more.

"I'll repressurize you. All right, all right," Francis said. He laid his lab book on the floor. Fulton leaned forward and a bright flash filled the darkened interior. "Stop that. Stop taking pictures of everything."

Fulton looked up, rotated his head to one side and his eyes flashed again. Francis tried to brush away the yellow and blue dots dancing in front of his eyes. The dog was only playing, and he should know this since he had built in the behaviors, all punched into a thin metal ribbon that ran through the creature's innards to give it propulsion control and, it appeared, playfulness.

He fastened the rubber hose onto Fulton's posterior valve, then opened the tank to give a full charge. The needle on the pressure gauge rose slowly until it reached max. Francis turned off the valve and disconnected the hose.

"You're set to ambulate for another week or so. Just don't leak, will you?" Francis smiled. Fulton rocked back on his haunches and clacked his jaws together, as if he understood.

Turning to his workbench, Francis began redoing his calculations. The day faded outside and cold wind whipped through cracks in the walls, but he hardly noticed, lighting a coal oil lamp as he worked. The equations took on a life of their own, and he began to understand what was happening, all except the one recurring term. The goal of the ages fluttered within his grasp if the term would only vanish. He felt it.

When the door to his small shack opened, he jerked around, startled. His lab book fell to the floor where Fulton sat up. His eyes flashed again.

"Stop that," Francis said to the dog.

"I've come for you. There's little time." The unknown woman looked windswept and flustered.

"Who are you, young lady?"

"Who I am isn't important. You must come away immediately."

"Leave when I am so close? Never!" His outrage was directed more toward the notion of quitting before success than at the woman, whoever she was.

She closed the door and stepped closer. He held up his coal oil lamp to better see her. She was thin, but nicely filled out the khaki shirt she wore. Her canvas britches might have belonged to an American miner; the tops were tucked into calf-high, fully laced brown leather boots. She shivered with the cold because she lacked a coat, but she wore a broad web belt with a holster dangling at her right hip.

"Explain yourself," Francis demanded. He motioned for Fulton to remain where he was, but the robot had not budged. He almost bent to examine the mechanism since the dog was geared to rush forward to greet anyone getting too close. For whatever reason, he hadn't budged an inch.

"The king desires your immediate presence, Sir Francis."

"I'm not a knight."

"You will be when we return to England. The king has you on the honors list."

"Whatever for?" Francis mumbled. "I have not completed my experiment here, the one that would entitle me to such an honor."

"You are in great—you must come with me. I have an airship nearby."

"I *did* see an airship! Earlier today, right after my test. The cloud that moved about so anomalously." He held out the lamp and studied her face. She was quite comely, though she had such a serious expression. "Its lower superstructure is painted white to mimic a cloud."

He was pleased to see her amazement.

"You are more observant than most," she said. "That must be another reason the king wishes to honor you."

"King Edward can wait. I need more time, definitely more time. One more test."

"Your weapon is almost complete?" She sounded distraught at this.

"Oh, please, rest easy on that score. This is not a weapon." He bent and picked up his fallen lab book, placing it next to the lamp on his table. "I have completed my equations, though there is a term I cannot explain. It doesn't matter. What does matter is how a new test will prove my theory of transmogrification."

"That's a weapon?"

"Who *are* you, young lady?"

"Nicole, Nicole Larouse."

"You are not English. I detect a most delightful French accent, though your English is quite good."

"I . . . I work for the AFA."

"The Anglo-French Alliance holds no sway over me," he said stiffly. "Politics is beneath me, especially after they stole my work in such an underhanded fashion. Why, they even seized my laboratory equipment, forcing me to deplete my financial resources to buy all this. It took every farthing I had left. And what I did in Liverpool was hardly a weapon, yet they—you!—seized it under the State Secrets Act. Imagine that, a medical device foolishly press-ganged as a weapon!" He waved his arm in an all-encompassing gesture that almost knocked over the lamp.

The woman reached for the pistol at her hip, but Fulton clacked his teeth together and rose onto all fours. She stared at the mechanical dog, then glared at Francis.

"You must come with me. Your life is in danger and a robot bodyguard won't save you."

"Oh, bother. I am in no danger here. Fulton is not my only companion. Lawrence and a half dozen others in my crew are capable of . . ." His voice trailed off when he saw the expression on her face.

"He's not . . . as he seems."

"You are so lovely and yet the lie comes easily to your lips," he said. "Leave now. Get into your airship and leave me be."

"There's war brewing on the Continent, and Lawrence wants your weapon. The test firing this afternoon demonstrated its power."

"It misfired," he said. "And my transmogrification ray is *not* a weapon. I pursue alchemical highways toward—" He bit off his explanation. She did not deserve it. She was more than an interloper on his privacy, she had admitted working for the AFA and that alliance had robbed him of a device capable of saving millions of lives.

"Yes?"

"Go now," he ordered, pointing to the door. "I will have nothing to do with you or your wild accusations."

"You're coming with me," Nicole said, reaching

down to draw her pistol. She had barely unsnapped the leather flap when Fulton launched for her leg, sinking sharpened brass teeth into her boot.

Francis saw that the teeth hadn't penetrated flesh, but it threw the woman off balance. He moved swiftly to enter the fray, grabbing her slender wrist and twisting. With the leverage afforded by the fifty-pound brass dog on her leg, Nicole Larouse fell backward, crashing into the thin wood wall. A plank was knocked loose and let in a gust of cold night air.

It also admitted sounds from the direction of the mineshaft.

"You'd better leave immediately," Francis said sternly. "Lawrence and the rest of my men have been alerted."

"You'll rue this, Mr. Barstow."

"Rue what? Not being kidnapped or passing up the chance to be knighted by King Edward?"

"I'll be nearby if. . . ."

Nicole shook herself free of Fulton's teeth and pushed open the door, then limped into the darkness. He watched her go with a mixture of regret and relief. She was a lovely woman but taken to wild flights of fancy, and he simply did not have time for her at the moment. Not with preparations to be made for the next test. He was sure he had worked out the frequency problem so the transmogrification ray would work its alchemical magic on the lead and form gold.

"Mr. Barstow, are you all right? I heard voices." Lawrence stared at the broken board in the wall, then reached inside his heavy woolen coat as if fumbling for a pocket watch, although his waistcoat would have been a more sensible place to carry it rather than at his hip.

"Oh, it was nothing."

"Your work?" Lawrence pointed to the lab book precariously balanced at the edge of the work table.

"The calculations are completed. I can tune the ray, I am sure of it."

"More power?"

"Oh, it'll be ten times as powerful as today," Francis said, becoming lost in the maze of his own jumbled numbers once more. "But focused. There won't be any unexpected blast. No, no, it'll be contained to the target."

"An order of magnitude more powerful?"

Francis looked sharply at his assistant.

"See that the roughing pump is started to pull the vacuum in the collimating tube. Run it until dawn, then begin the oil diffusion pump for the final evacuation."

"I'll have the magnets powered up, too," Lawrence said. His eyes burned like dark coals. "When will you test the . . . ray?"

"Considering how easy it is to remove the unwanted atmosphere at this lung-straining attitude, the vacuum ought to be hard enough by ten in the morning."

"We'll work all night," Lawrence promised. He looked down at Fulton, who clacked his teeth, then left, shouting to the crew to begin preparations.

Francis felt a surge of excitement not unlike finding a new continent, he believed, or achieving some other landmark in exploration. Tomorrow by this time he would have a ten-pound bar of gold, transmogrified from what had been lead in the morning. Whistling, he turned back to his lab book, frowned at the unexplained term, then drew an X through it.

"Second order term," he muttered. No one bothered with second order terms. Not when there was gold to be made.

Francis Barstow slept poorly on the cot, under the heavy blanket that also had served him well during the Liverpool winter. He finally sat up, aware that sleep was going to elude him because of the thrill of discovery. Today history would be made. By Francis Herschel Barstow.

He stretched, yawned, then smiled.

"Sir Francis. I like the sound of it. I'll be able to supply the Crown with more gold than ever came from the Seven Cities of Cibola."

He looked down at the faithful Fulton, stretched out at his feet. The dog wheezed asthmatically.

"I'll get you the finest rubber joints and connections, I promise," he said. "Why, I could replace your brass parts with gold ones. Yes, I will! What would a half hundredweight of gold matter when all I need do is turn on my fabulous ray?"

He reached down and put his hand on the dog's cold metal head. The glass optics lit.

"Stop it. No photographs." The light died in Fulton's eyes. "Perhaps I can ask your counsel, good and loyal dog." Fulton perked up, as if he understood. "Should I turn this discovery over to the Crown at all? Why, the king—or at least the AFA—sent a woman to kidnap me!"

He shivered in the cold, pulled the heavy blanket up around his shoulders, but did not lie back even as he thought of Nicole Larouse. Such a fine-looking woman with such a mellifluous name. If she had been of a different bent, a different sort of spy or agent provocateur or whatever she was, simply asking him to accompany her on an assignation would have worked. Being alone in the mountains, or alone as far as feminine companionship went, made for nights longer than a mere clock could tick out. She was both comely and had a fiery personality—both traits that appealed to him.

"But she tried to kidnap me," he said with some sorrow. "You prevented that, didn't you, Fulton?" The robotic dog looked up at him and rotated its head to one side, as if listening intently. "I'm not sure if that was for the best, you stopping her as you did. No, what am I saying? Of course it was. My experiment takes precedence over a mere tryst, even with a lovely Frenchwoman named Nicole."

The name tasted sweet on his lips. Would her lips, pressed against his, be as fine?

"What are you doing, Fulton?"

The dog ground gears as he got to his feet, then

plowed straight ahead, head smashing into the door repeatedly until it slipped its latch and popped open. In a
brass flash, the dog darted outside.

"Oh, bother," he said, tossing back the blanket and
going after Fulton. It wasn't as if the dog had to be let
outside. The idea of Fulton leaving behind brass turnings
or spots of lubricant amused him. He followed the dog
up the path of a small hill from where he intended to
view the test. Something moving on the summit slowed
his steps. Fulton clacked his jaws and looked from his
master to the figure lit by the first light of dawn.

Francis motioned the dog to silence and edged
around to get a better view of . . . Lawrence. His assistant hunched over a black box, fiddled with it and then
stood straight. For a moment, Francis couldn't figure out
what he was doing, then saw a brilliant speck from the
hills some miles distant.

"A heliograph," he said softly. He watched Lawrence
diligently send code and receive an answer. Francis almost called to him, then backed away and headed for
the mineshaft to inspect the preparations for the crucial
test to be run in a few hours.

More than once he looked over his shoulder at Lawrence, but by following the curving, rocky path to the
mine, he was quickly lost to sight. Francis scowled as he
considered what his assistant was up to signaling like that,
then forgot about it when he neared the vacuum pump.
It sounded raspy as it pulled out the last atoms from the
aether inside the narrow long glass tube stretching from
the electrodes all the way to the lead target placed in a
bell jar to contain it this time.

"Turn on the oil diffusion pump," he ordered a worker
fiddling with the vacuum system. "There's not going to
be any more air sucked out of the tube using only the
roughing pump."

He spent the next ten minutes inside the mine, a car-
bide miner's lamp hissing on his forehead as he made
final adjustments, more to keep himself occupied than

because it was required. The block of lead was placed directly on the ray's axis. He edged along the shaft and made sure the Corrigan rare-earth magnets were in place. It took only a moment to be certain they were rigged in such a way to oscillate and accelerate the particles produced in the tube. He left the mine and stripped off the miner's lamp, turned off the light, and tossed the unit aside as Lawrence ran up.

"Mr. Barstow, you're here early. I didn't expect you to arrive for another hour."

Francis glanced from Lawrence to the distant peak where the other heliostat had answered whatever message his assistant had sent.

"You look confused, sir," Lawrence said. "Didn't that term fall out properly for you? In your calculations?"

"I . . ." Francis tried to sort out his confused thoughts. Secret signals to who knows where. Did Lawrence contact Nicole Larouse? Francis just didn't know what to think.

Didn't know. . . .

The curious second order term in his equation hinted at something important. He knew that but there was no physical manifestation possible, not if the transmogrification took place.

Fulton's clacking and hissing tore his thoughts away from his calculations.

"What is it, boy?"

"You talk to that damned hunk of brass like it's alive," Lawrence said. He put a hand over his mouth when Francis looked sharply at him.

"Your disrespect is uncalled for, sir," Francis said. "See to the experiment. When the vacuum in the collimating tube is sufficient, we will fire the unit."

"Yes, sir, of course, Mr. Barstow."

Francis watched his assistant closely. His tone was servile, but the set of his shoulders, the way his chin jutted and his eyes—those hot, hot eyes!—told a different story. Lawrence came within a hair of being openly defiant. As he stormed off, Francis started to ask what he carried in his coat pocket that stretched the cloth to the limit—in the shape of a lab book.

Fulton's clacking broke his train of thought, and he looked toward the steam engines that powered the experiment.

"Thank you, Fulton," he said, going to adjust one of the large transfer belts. It slipped and robbed the powerful engine of most of its power. By the time he had tightened it and turned his attention back to the mouth of the mine, he saw Lawrence and two workmen standing close together. His assistant angrily ordered the others around. Francis was taken aback when both men saluted Lawrence before going into the mineshaft.

He trooped over and demanded, "What is going on?"

Lawrence made no effort to hide his contempt as he pulled the lab book from his pocket. Francis grabbed for it but was shoved back.

"You've built the perfect weapon, and all you want to do is blow up tiny blocks of lead," Lawrence said, his tone cold. "I've got your notes. We will get the data from the experiment, so there's no more need for you."

"This is mine! I built the ray!"

"Good King Raoul will use the ray to defend the crown of Portugal," Lawrence said.

"You're a spy!"

"I'm a thief, and the King of Portugal pays me for weapons technology. With this ray, he will have a perfect defense against both the Kaiser's Zeppelins and the AFA battleships cruising along his coast." Lawrence shoved Francis back again and laughed this time. "You could have sold this marvelous weapon, but you were too shallow."

"I am defying the wisdom of the ages. I am seeking the power to transmogrify!"

"Was there any trace of gold? No," Lawrence said. "You blew up solid metal and then disintegrated a hole the size of my fist in the mountainside. The power!"

Francis reached behind him and found the contacts on the Crooke's tube. Wires ran off a safe distance to initiate the test by remote control. He scraped the insulation off one wire using his fingernail and bent the bared copper around so the contacts touched. The tube lit up, its purple glow dazzling to the eye.

Screams came from within the mineshaft as the ray lanced toward the lead target, but also taking the lives of Lawrence's two henchmen.

"Killing them only makes the reward larger for me," Lawrence said, lunging. He tripped and fell over Fulton, who began snapping and tearing at the man's arms. The whine from the engines and pumps ran through his ears like an ice pick, and the tension of high voltage made his hair began to rise on his head, in spite of the sticky pomade he used to hold it in place.

Francis knew grappling with his assistant would never do. The man was stronger, younger, and more vicious. Instead of fighting, he ran for the line shack, not knowing what he would do there since he lacked a weapon. As he stumbled along, he heard the soft whistle of props cutting through the thin mountain air. Above loomed a patch of white. As he stared, it banked slightly, revealing the streamlined frame of a small airship.

"Nicole!" Distance and ambient noise from the steam engines were too great for his voice to carry to her. He veered from the shack, hit the trail leading to the top of the summit where he had spied Lawrence working with the heliostat and skidded to a halt when he found the device. The small black box had been hidden from casual sight between two large rocks. He drew it out and saw the tripod folded beneath it, but there was scant time to set it up properly.

Turning it over and over in his hands, he found the lever that controlled the shutter and the ingress optic that concentrated the sunlight for transmission. He craned his neck until he found the white speck that had to be Nicole's airship, then positioned the heliostat so the shutter pointed directly at it. A few steps and a quick turn admitted the sun into the optical port on the top of the black box. He began opening and closing the lever to send bright flashes to attract her attention. It was wrong to enlist the aid of a woman in such an imbroglio, but she sported a weapon. If Lawrence lacked one, the fray would be over quickly. He flashed his message, such as it was, to attract her attention, but he saw no evidence that she received his impassioned plea.

A terrible screeching noise sounded from the direction of the mineshaft where the experiment ran at full power. The actinic glare from the tube almost blinded him—but the sight of the mountaintop sinking like a fallen soufflé caused him to drop the heliostat and run back down the hill to the mine.

"Fulton!" he cried. The mechanical dog snuffled and hissed, then clacked his teeth as he turned toward the mine. "Is he in there? Lawrence? Is he?"

The dog rotated his head about, then stiffened all four legs in a movement Francis had never seen before. The emphatic nature of the reply told him Lawrence had, indeed, entered the mine in spite of the ray—and in spite of the way the rock above the shaft was curiously sagging as if it melted.

But it never dribbled down as a fluid might. Instead it simply ceased to . . . exist.

"Lawrence, come out! The whole mountain is falling in on your head!" His plea was drowned out by the tearing sound of metal grinding against unlubricated metal as the steam engines started to fail. Then a new sound became preeminent. He glanced over his shoulder to see Nicole's airship swinging about and heading directly for the mouth of the mine, skimming along ten feet above the ground.

"Fulton, go to her. Warn her." He saw more of the mountaintop collapse in on itself but where did the rock go? The mineshaft with the long, evacuated tube containing the transmogrification ray remained intact.

"Mr. Barstow! The entire mountain is vanishing. Come to me. Get into my ship!"

Francis was torn between the safety offered by the woman's airship and examining his experiment before the mountain collapsed.

"My notes. Lawrence has my notes!"

With that, he sidled along the mine's ragged rock wall, the purple beam encased in its glass containment tube just inches away and edged his way deeper. Repeatedly looking up, he saw no hint that the roof was caving in on him, yet there was a sucking sound—or was it the noise of a voracious carnivore devouring its prey?

He moved faster.

The cavity they had excavated for the experiment was lit with the unearthly purple of his transmogrification ray. The block of lead inside the crystal bell jar had vaporized and coated the insides of the bell jar—with a gleaming gold.

"I've done it!" He reached for the jar, only to have his hand batted away. Startled, he looked up at Lawrence, who sneered.

"You've done it. The perfect weapon. It disintegrated the lead the instant it was turned on."

"Give me my notes!" He lunged, knocking the glass collimation tube off target. The purple beam shone brightly against solid rock at the rear of the chamber.

"I'm going to give you what you deserve," Lawrence said.

Something made Francis look up at the roof. His mind refused to comprehend what slipped lower into the chamber. It was a speck so black it denied the very existence of light—and he saw how the rock from the mountain fell into it and simply vanished. He started to warn Lawrence, but only a gasp escaped his lips. The jot of darkness sank lower, and Lawrence appeared to turn to melted butter, flowing into the hole hardly the size of a pinhead. He did not even scream as he was sucked upward. Or did the black eye of God descend?

Francis grabbed the bell jar and held it to his body as he backed away. The blackness continued to sink, devouring solid rock and anything else in its path. When the vacuum in the collimating tube broke, shards of glass flew in all directions before being vacuumed into the nothingness that had somehow been formed during the experiment.

Francis edged back along the mineshaft, then ignored how he was slashed and cut by the tube that had once held a high vacuum and the purple beam he had generated.

"Run, run for your life!" Nicole cried. "The entire mountain is simply disappearing!"

He held onto the bell jar and stumbled toward her airship, which hovered only a few feet above the ground. Then he saw she had anchored it by giving Fulton one end of the tether. The brass dog clamped down firmly with his jaws on the rope, but a breeze was growing. It came from behind Francis and was sucking loose, light debris from the ground into the mineshaft.

Into the tiny hole.

"Here," he said, tossing the bell jar to Nicole. She rolled it away and reached down for him.

"The mountain is half gone. I don't know what is happening, but it will vanish entirely in another minute."

"Lawrence," he gasped out.

"Forget him."

Francis knew that would never be possible. He took Nicole's hands and was dragged up to the floorboard in the airship gondola.

"We've got to get out of here *now*." She dropped into the pilot's chair, trimmed the elevators and gunned the engines.

Francis started to urge her to more speed, then spun about, flopped on his belly and caught hold of the tether, now swaying beneath the rising ship.

"Hang on, Fulton. Hang on. I'll get you to safety." Grunting, straining, his muscles reaching the breaking point, he pulled in the cable until Fulton sat beside him on the airship floor. Several seals had ruptured, and he hissed constantly. "You're safe!" He threw his arms around the brass neck and hugged, then wrenched away when Fulton tried to show affection by clamping his powerful jaws on his neck.

"Don't fall out," Nicole shouted. "We've got a race on our hands."

"Race?" Francis looked out the still open hatch and saw the top half of the mountain where his experiment had been housed simply vanished. Somehow, the collapse caused air to rush downward, pulling powerfully at the airship. And then the ship surged as if they had turned on rocket propulsion. It took Nicole a minute to get the airship into level flight.

"Are you all right, Mr. Barstow?"

"Quite. And so is Fulton." The robot rotated its head to one side in agreement.

"What happened? The entire mountain. I've never seen anything like it. It's all gone."

"The second order term," he said, shaken. "The second order term I couldn't figure out."

"I don't understand."

"That's all right. I don't, either."

"Lawrence is dead?"

"All my crew is gone," Francis said, not sure how to feel about that. "So are my notes. There's no way I can remember what was in them. He had my lab book on him when he was . . . disappeared."

"Then the world has lost a great knowledge," Nicole said, sighing.

"I still have this," Francis said, looking into the bell jar. Every ounce of lead had been transmogrified into gold.

"But you can't duplicate it, Mr. Barstow. You said your notes were destroyed."

Fulton looked up at the woman. His eyes flashed as he recorded her likeness.

"Why don't you call me Sir Francis? And let's make a nice bed for my dog."

She looked at him as if he were quite mad, but he didn't care. He had ten pounds of gold to replace his equipment—and a dog with a photographic eye that had winked at his lab notes the night before.

And there was that second order term to explain. . . .

ABOUT THE EDITORS

Jean Rabe is the author of more than two dozen fantasy and adventures novels and more short stories than she cares to count. She relishes editing anthologies ... this is her 16th ... almost as much as she likes tugging on old socks with her dogs (and she likes that a lot). She resides in Wisconsin, where the winters are too long, the summers are too short, and the football and steampunk are just right.

Martin H. Greenberg is the CEP of Tekno Books and its predecessor companies, now the largest book developer of commercial fiction and non-fiction in the world, with over 2,250 published books that have been translated into 33 languages. He is the recipient of an unprecedented four Lifetime Achievement Awards in the Science Fiction, Mystery, and Supernatural Horror genres—the Milford Award in Science Fiction, the Solstice Award in science fiction, the Bram Stoker Award in Horror, and the Ellery Queen Award in Mystery—the only person in publishing history to have received all four awards.